To Mommy
Your daily kindnesses heal the world. Te amo.

PROLOGUE

Alberto Sousa looked behind him at the colorful waterfront houses growing smaller as the dinghy made its way along the Rio Negro. Only six kilometers to the Meeting of Waters where the striking phenomenon of two converging rivers—one dark, the other pale—appeared to defy the laws of nature.

How did I get so lucky? Alberto thought. He had the job of his dreams, bridging the gap between ancient and modern worlds. He took great pride in the strong bond he'd forged with the indigenous tribes, a deep friendship built over years of mutual respect and trust.

Alberto set the outboard motor to full throttle, maneuvering the boat farther from the riverbank. His pulse quickened with the acceleration. Today he was doing the chief's bidding. Searching the hidden pockets of the planet for flora and fauna possessing medicinal properties the tribes needed to survive. It was the first time an outsider was entrusted with such an important task. With increasing exposure to marauders, neighboring tribes had succumbed to the illnesses foreigners had brought with them to their lands.

Alberto steered into the muddy Solimões River, the lifeblood of the Amazon. The skies were bright, visibility clear. He had sailed these waters before but never alone and he was glad to have his grandfather's compass chained to his safari

1

vest.

Now as he approached the age-old mangroves, the absence of human activity was pronounced. Clear of the dense tangled root system, he cut the engine allowing the boat to glide silently. The only sounds were of exotic macaws shrieking from the rainforest canopy and buzzing insects in search of a juicy bit of blood. Alberto shooed away a giant mosquito and sprayed another layer of DEET before reaching into his sack for his botany kit.

Twenty minutes passed before he found what he was looking for within the forest. They looked exactly as the chief had described them. A colony of miniscule tree crabs hugged the lower portion of the tree trunk nearest him, undulating upward to escape the lapping water. Found only in this region of the Amazon, they were not easily accessible to the Awá, who had settled many kilometers away, sequestered from the relatively populated area. Alberto donned surgical gloves and unzipped the vinyl zipper case, laying out a magnifying glass, forceps, and lab tube. With extreme care, to avoid a mass dispersion, he extended the forceps out to the tree trunk and took hold of a single crustacean, placing it in the tube. Using his magnifying glass, he studied his catch, confirming its genus. Satisfied, he painstakingly began to fill a glass terrarium with the tiny crabs, placing the hood atop. Next would be a far more challenging find.

Paico, an annual herb with reddish stems and tiny yellow flowers producing thousands of tiny black seeds, was used for millennia by the Awá to relieve maladies ranging from stomach upsets to internal hemorrhages. At nearly three feet high, with a strong, distinctive odor, paico ought to be easy to find. Nevertheless, in a massive area, densely packed with foliage of all kinds, it was the proverbial needle in a haystack.

"Follow your nose," is what the chief had said. Alberto pulled out the photo from his pocket. If he could find it, his bond with the tribe would deepen all the more.

A rustling of the trees caught Alberto's attention. He

turned to locate the source of the sound and caught movement on the shoreline. The rainforest was teeming with wildlife. Maybe it was the ubiquitous four-toed sloth or the green anaconda, a boa endemic to the region. As the quiet returned, he laughed to himself. Maybe it was Vanzolini's bald-faced saki. The extremely elusive monkey had been seen only a handful of times over the past century. Alberto was familiar with the native primates though not from a classroom. Rather, in the wild, becoming enamored with the rarest of them. They were remarkable beings. Perhaps someday they would allow him a peek.

Another movement.

He took hold of this rifle. Just in case. The likelihood of a jaguar was slim but best to be on the safe side. He didn't want to leave without the paico, but cooler heads prevailed. There was no point in sticking around. The plant could wait till his next trip. The chief would be happy with the crabs. He revved up the engine and began to reverse course when he felt a sharp sudden pain in his neck. Instinctively he slapped a hand to the spot, shocked to find a dart jutting out.

What the hell?

He looked around, panicked. No one there. His vision began to blur. He grabbed the throttle and pushed it to its limit, jerking the boat while trying to navigate in his increasingly numbed state.

He felt his limbs go stiff as the boat crashed full on into a twisted mangrove, ricocheting off like a pinball. He fell backward into the boat. As he lay still looking up at the foliage above him, he watched as a monkey swung from vine to vine. His last thought was he hoped it was the bald-faced saki.

PART 1

The Past

CHAPTER 1

New York City

The man in the camel-hair winter coat stood at the edge of the playground. He did his best to look friendly, a challenging task at best. His features simply didn't align that way. His hooded eyes and bulbous nose lent him a perpetually severe visage. He knew a middle-aged man loitering near a school in a frigid New York winter could easily attract attention. All he needed was someone calling the cops. *A strange man with slicked-back dark hair is hanging around the playground. He comes by and just watches.*

He took a few steps back from the fence, subconsciously reaching inside his coat pocket. His desire for a cigarette was overwhelming, but having recently gone cold turkey, he hadn't brought his Davidoffs with him. He'd heard chewing gum was a temporary substitute, but he'd rather suffer than engage in the abhorrent habit.

Every few minutes he took a look at the boy. Small in height, slight in build, his anorak swallowed him. At first glance, one would assume him to be the bullied child in the class. The observer would be dead wrong. The boy was a leader—the one deciding who was assigned to which team of stickball, directing where each boy should stand—his confident nature apparent even to the other nine-year-olds. They deferred to him, following his lead.

The man watched as they played. A ball from another game bounced sharply off the fence, ricocheted, and hit the boy hard in the arm, stunning him. He seemed to take a moment to catch his breath, clearly in pain, rubbing the spot. He didn't cry. Another boy, older, came running over, his hand extended, clearly asking for a toss back. From where the man stood, he couldn't hear the exchange. The smaller boy looked up at the other, said something to him, and without as much as a moment's pause, pulled his arm back and threw the ball with all his might, aiming straight for the older boy's head. The ball skimmed his temple, causing him to lose balance and fall hard on the ground. Even from the distance, the man heard the boy yell a profanity no child should know. The teacher rushed over and looked back and forth between the two boys. The younger was now holding himself with deference, his head bowed meekly, his demeanor suddenly doe-eyed. The next thing the man saw was the teacher taking the older boy forcibly by the arm, dragging him toward the building.

The man smiled broadly and walked away.

CHAPTER 2

10 years later
Yankee Stadium
New York City

T he NYU graduation ceremony had turned the iconic stadium into a sea of purple gowns. The sun was just past its midpoint in the cloudless New York sky. A pop singer donning a tan banded Fedora stood mid-field singing into a hand-held mic. He didn't know the singer's name, but the cheerful crowd was following along.

The man with greying slicked-back hair passively watched the performance on the Jumbotron. More than ten colorfully robed university higher-ups were seated on the stage, feigning interest in the proceedings. Seated in the nosebleed section among a smattering of latecomers, the man was content to be in the shade. There was no need for him to sit closer.

He suffered through the boring speeches and tributes, doing his best to remain patient. Finally, the dean of students called upon the most distinguished graduates who shuffled in an orderly line up the stage steps. Handing diplomas to 17,000 people was impossible, and only the most accomplished were given the honor of traversing the stage.

The man felt a palpable sense of anticipation. Years of influencing the boys from afar earned him the status of a benevolent uncle they'd never met. He had bankrolled their upbringings—private school tuitions and niche summer camps, language and chess lessons. Their parents had been most appreciative of his generosity. He fulfilled his part of the bargain and for the most part, they had as well.

The names were announced alphabetically, each graduate handed a leather-bound award document and scrolled diploma, followed by the dean's handshake.

"Spenser Germain."

The man stood, lifted his binoculars to his eyes, fixated on the graduate who was grasping something in his hand. Bespectacled and slim-faced, the purple-clad young man strode with determination, a gait of confidence. Swiftly, he raised a paper sign, holding it high, a steely mien on his face. Simulcast on the overhead screens, the act elicited both good-natured hoots and shouts to move as the next two graduates were now too close together in the timing. The sign read, "We shall overcome."

The man watched as the graduate shook the dean's hand, accepting his diploma. Clearly irritated by the interruption, the dean placed a hand on Germain's back coaxing him along. The boy's smug look remained on his face all the way back to his seat.

The man put down the binoculars, took his graduation program off the empty seat beside his, and made his way down the aisle and out of the stadium. He walked briskly to the 161st Street subway station, and though unaccustomed to the bourgeois of mass transit, he waited for the Manhattan-bound D train. The train pulled into the station, the crowd of every race and creed edging toward the still moving doorways. When the doors opened, a rush of passengers swarmed out, those on the platform shoving past them, intent on scoring a seat. It was the transit system's version of musical chairs.

Crammed among the smelly passengers, he was left to grab hold of the overhead germ-ridden bar. He looked out the filthy window at the bleak Bronx scenery whisking by, obscured at times by another train racing in the opposite direction. As the train carriage shook spastically, he nearly lost his footing, silently ruing what sacrifices his position necessitated at times. Alighting at his stop, he chastised himself. He would not permit benign annoyances to affect his mood today. After all these years, the boys were finally heading into the world on their own.

PART II

The Present

CHAPTER 3

FBI Headquarters
Federal Plaza
New York City

"S teadman, in my office."

Jon recognized his boss's tone. Special Agent Doug Matthews was in overdrive, which meant a new case had come in. The two had entered a truce of sorts. Tolerance bordering on mutual respect. A result of them both facing untold hardship. But all bets were off when Matthews was wound up.

When Jon walked in, Matthews was standing behind his desk tucking his wrinkled button-down into the waistband of his trousers. He shuffled through files, pulling one out. "Have a seat. Remind me what you're working on now."

Jon sat in one of two beat-up pleather chairs. "The identity theft case out of Queens."

"Thieves. Robbing the elderly," Matthews bristled. "Why can't people with enough brains to conjure up such a scheme find a way to make a legitimate buck?" He paused a moment in thought. "Okay, I'm reassigning you. Craig can take the Queens job."

"What's going on?"

Matthews handed over a manila folder. "Here's a printout. The digital version is already in your inbox."

Inside were several high-definition photos of a man

standing on a stage in what appeared to be a school auditorium, a sizeable crowd in the audience.

"Isn't this—?"

"Yes. We need to keep this one quiet."

Matthews gave Jon a few minutes to riffle through the paperwork. "Spenser Germain. NY State Congressman, representing the tenth district including NYU. Up for reelection. Loves the sound of his own voice. He's attracting a lot of attention from his leftie student followers and more recently the national media."

"What's his rhetoric?"

"Changing the status quo. Crap about taking back control of the government by the people."

"That's what college students like to hear. Probably how he got elected in the first place. Sounds like he's just pandering to his base." Jon waved the file.

"He's been accused by some students of inciting violence on campus. Shoving, slurs against those who disagree, things like that. The NYPD has been called a few times to break things up."

"Do his talks qualify as hate speech?"

"Depends who you ask. He's already had four presentations on university grounds, each one followed by several incidents. The university claims they have no legal grounds to ban him, but they keep inviting him back. They seem to be enjoying the notoriety. Each time he's drawn a larger crowd. The last one was nearly a thousand people. He has a strong presence on social media now. Calls himself the twenty-first century Sam Adams after the American revolutionary. His posts are just short of actionable. He's smart. Seems to know what Facebook and Twitter would kick him off for and avoids crossing that line."

"It does sound strange for a politician, but he represents a far-left constituency. If you ask me, it seems like small potatoes. Why's the FBI getting involved in this?"

"The President's campaign manager called my boss,

wants the congressman investigated. He thinks he will damage the President's own reelection efforts. Last thing the republic needs is an army of misinformed twenty-somethings ready to storm Capitol Hill. His words, not mine."

Jon was amazed his boss was only three degrees of separation from the leader of the free world, but the probe sounded more Marxist than the man he was intent on investigating.

"*The* President?" Jon asked, clarifying.

Matthews nodded.

Jon took a moment to absorb that. "What do you want me to do?"

"Get a closer look at Germain. You look about the right age to blend into the NYU crowd. Assess if his rhetoric is socialist hyperbole or treasonous. Get what we need to shut them down."

"We can't just investigate people because we don't like what they have to say. What the hell happened to the First Amendment?"

"This is a national security issue," Matthews said without conviction. "We have enough for a preliminary."

"Not yet, Doug. What about privacy laws? These aren't terrorists. You can't use the same protocols." Jon fell back into calling his superior by his first name, knowing Matthews didn't like it.

"That's enough! I should cite you for insubordination."

Jon's visage matched that of his boss. "What for? My questions are legitimate."

"Goddammit, Steadman. You still have chain of command issues? Or is it trust? Oh right, both. How's it going with the shrink, anyway?"

Jon glared at his boss.

"You want the assignment, or not? You can stay with the Queens case, wait a year or two in hopes of nailing what's likely an overseas scam outfit. I'll put Craig on this." Matthews put his hand out for the file Jon still held.

"What if it's nothing more than typical collegiate passion?"

"Then we keep Germain and the other anarchist-wan-nabes on a watch list. Check up on them every few months."

Jon kept the file in his lap. He hated to admit it, but he wanted the assignment. If it led somewhere, his career would take off. "NYU is close enough. I'll check it out and let you know." He stood to leave. "Anything else?"

"You need to go in this looking like a college student but thinking like a Fed," Matthews emphasized by tapping his temple. "Understand?"

Jon tried to swallow his annoyance at the mini tutorial. He'd suffered through the rigorous training like all the other rookies, passing with flying colors. Unable to suppress his irritation, he saluted his superior, offering "Yessir!" on his way out the door.

***

Jon returned to his desk, Craig eyeing him as he sat down. "Just read the boss's email. Looks like I have a new assignment."

Craig was a good egg. Never complained. He would take on Jon's hand-me-down project with what bordered on a childlike excitement. Some people were born for the jobs they did. Jon wasn't sure yet if he fell into that category. He loved being a cog in the giant FBI machine. It had always been his dream to use his forensics and criminology degrees at this very institution. But he was the first to admit he wasn't good with authority. And that was a big part of the job. Many of his colleagues were post-military, accustomed to the hierarchy, asking no questions. Not him. He would never be one to do things blindly. Either he would rise in the ranks or be kicked out on his butt. Only time would tell.

Jon opened the new file. Congressman Germain was an average-looking man, though too stern an appearance for his years. Balding, with a dark, trimmed beard, pronounced cheekbones, and a wide forehead over intense eyes. He was dressed conservatively, down to the shined loafers. Effort had been made to be taken seriously. His bio listed him as single, only child, reared in a middle-class New York City family, graduate of NYU.

The photo caught Germain mid-speech, the passion burning in his face. No doubt he believed his rhetoric. Several people in the crowd were facing the camera. They appeared enthralled. For a moment Jon flashed back to the case that had led him to his current job with the FBI. He'd seen that mesmerized look before but felt confident these people were not under the influence. They were simply taken in by Germain.

Jon went online, pulled up some media clips on YouTube, and watched the guy in action. Germain knew how to hook an audience. He was amiable, poised, speaking with fervor of the country's deterioration in recent years and the need for a "grassroots changing of the guard." When he was done, the crowd applauded, loudly assenting to his talking points. Twitter announced the next rally. It would be held in a park rather than the school auditorium. The congressman was stepping out into the broader community, bringing his message with him.

Jon put it on his calendar. He would be there.

CHAPTER 4

Eilat, Israel

Gabe Lewis gently exhaled, watching the bubbles rise above him. He didn't know where to look first. The kaleidoscope of corals or the school of angelfish seemingly keeping pace with him. He fluttered his fins and came alongside Terry. She pointed past him. As he turned, a bottlenose dolphin approached within arm's reach. He extended a hand, marveling that its grey hide felt as smooth as years-old leather. He gave Terry a thumbs-up. They had been under water for nearly forty minutes. The instructor who was keeping a close eye on the oxygen meters gave them the signal to head to the surface.

Gabe couldn't help but notice how well Terry's SCUBA suit fit her petite frame when she emerged from the water behind him. He wondered how a headstrong firecracker and brilliant scientist could also be a knockout. Clearly, she'd won the genetic lottery.

He had landed in Tel Aviv only the day before and was already in Israel's southernmost city completing his first-ever dive. It was a magical morning but time alone with Terry was what he'd been most looking forward to. They had stayed in regular contact since parting last spring, and when she invited him to visit, he knew nothing would beat seeing her in person. He was smitten and he could only hope she felt the same.

"So, what did you think?" Terry asked, as she pulled back her sun-kissed hair, squeezing out the excess water, then shaking it out like a supermodel.

"This has been one of the most incredible experiences ever. Almost up there with meeting you."

Terry allowed him to help her remove her oxygen tank and laughed. "I can't compete with those remarkable corals."

"Is it true that we just swam with dolphins in the same sea God split for the Israelites when they escaped Egypt?"

"Very good. You know your biblical history. You did great down there, especially for a newborn," she said in accented English.

"I think you mean *newbie*."

"Eh?"

"Never mind."

Gabe pulled Terry close and gave her a tender kiss. "Thanks for showing me your lovely country."

"There's still one more stop on the tour."

"Oh yeah?"

"My parents' house."

"Excuse me?"

"Tomorrow is Friday. I join my parents every week for Shabbat dinner. If we get the noon flight tomorrow, we'll make it before sundown."

She took in Gabe's expression. "Why are you smiling?"

"I think this means I get to meet the parents."

CHAPTER 5

New York City

Thousands of colorful dried leaves carpeted Washington Square Park. A stone's throw from NYU, the park was a well-known haven for blowhards drawn to the proverbial soapbox, attracting activists of every stripe committed to exercising their first amendment rights. At the entrance, Jon passed a woman wrapped in a rainbow flag, a bible in hand, and three people listening to her preach.

The sun was bright but there was a distinct nip in the air. He was glad he'd grabbed his windbreaker on the way out the door. He liked autumn but not what would come after it. Winter was not his thing. Jon looked at his watch. Ten minutes until Germain was scheduled to start his rant. He took a seat on a chipped wooden bench listening to a young violinist playing a concerto. Despite sounding like a Julliard grad, she was mostly ignored. By noon, a steady stream of millennials sporting NYU swag began to congregate, many kidding around, others plugged into their headsets. Twenty more minutes passed before Germain showed. By then the crowd had doubled, everyone craning a neck to catch a glimpse of him. No one appeared irritated at his tardiness.

Jon stood, and pushed his way through the tight crowd, earning some annoyed looks. Congressman Germain was surprisingly shorter than average at maybe five and a half feet. His trim build was dressed formally in a gray blazer, pleated khakis, and freshly polished shoes. It was the look of a man twenty years his senior.

Perched on a Coke crate, Germain spoke of unaffordable insurance rates, the need for state-paid education, and out-of-control crime rates. He blamed the status quo on the powers that be, both parties, expressing resentment that even his own didn't adequately protect the interests of the people. He vowed to establish a third party, grassroots with the younger generation taking the lead, not the old timers.

Jon noted how well Germain projected his voice without a mic. The guy had a rare charisma, enthralling the masses. To Jon, he was, without question, a modern-day communist. Yet there was no hate speech or violence incitement.

When Jon had heard enough, he shoved his way out of the crowd, standing at the periphery. A young woman, nineteen at most, in a red pompom beanie stood nearby videotaping Germain with her iPhone. She let loose a string of profanities. "Damn, my battery died."

Jon stepped closer. "Hi, wish I could help but I didn't bring my charger."

She looked up, peered at him. "You at NYU?"

"Uh, yeah, grad program. You?"

"Sophomore. I left my psych class early to help Spenser. He has all the right ideas. And the guts to say them out loud."

Spenser?

"So, you agree with his rhetoric?"

The woman jutted her jaw, squinted. "You have a problem with Spenser?"

Others started looking their way. Jon was taken aback by the quick turn in attitude. Belligerent.

He said, "This is my first rally. Not sure what I believe. But I have an open mind."

The girl seemed to soften a bit, considering something. "You should come to his next event. He's planning something big."

"What is it?"

She averted her eyes. "He didn't tell me. But I'm sure it will be revolutionary."

Jon did his best to appear intrigued. "Sounds fascinating. When and where? I'll try to come."

She gave him the details which he put in his phone. "What's your name?"

"Jon Lewis," he replied, using his best friend's surname.

"I'm Gwen. I'll put your name on the list. Maybe we can grab a drink afterward." Someone called out her name. She turned away from Jon and blended into the crowd.

***

Jon took his time heading back to the office. Gwen had a chip on her shoulder. Already disillusioned and not out of college yet. For some reason his thoughts went to Melanie, Gwen's polar opposite—upbeat, open. Beautiful. His now-ex–girlfriend was making big things happen on the West Coast at her new job for a biomedical company. He still loved her, but they simply couldn't make the distance work for them. He had a life in New York, and hers was in NoCal. They decided to move on, agreeing to stay in touch but knowing instinctively that even that would eventually fade with time. The breakup was hard, but therapy and working long hours kept him in check. And of course, Granny Eunice. He spoke with her every Sunday. She was his rock. At eighty years young, she was the main woman in his life, and for now he was content with that.

Two blocks from his office, Jon walked past a flower shop, its door propped open. The scent of lavender hit his nostrils instantly taking him back to Boston. To Ashleigh. It only took a moment before Jon sensed the now-familiar dark cloud beginning to descend. His breathing accelerated, sweat sprouted on his brow. Recognizing the early signs, he pulled out his phone and dialed.

"Doc? It's Jon," he said, his voice shaking. "Can I come by now?"

***

By the time Jon arrived at South Street, the back of his shirt was soaked. He tried to stave off the impending doom by jogging there. Doc said exercise was supposed to help reduce his anxiety, but right now the only effect was his bad leg protesting in pain. He slowed to a stop in front of the nineteenth-century red brick storefront and pulled open the adjacent office door. He took the steps two at a time, saw the waiting room empty, and collapsed on the orange sofa. The therapist must have heard him pounding the stairs and came out to greet him. One look at him and her smile faded. "Jon, are you okay? Shall I call 911?"

"I just ran two miles. I don't need an ambulance."

"You know what I mean."

Jon avoided looking at her. "Can we talk it out?"

"Of course. Just tell me if you feel faint, and we'll get help. Promise?"

He muttered his agreement.

The therapist brought him a glass of water. "Take a seat inside. Catch your breath and when you're ready we'll get started."

***

The next morning Jon worked from his Lower East Side studio apartment. He sent a progress report to Matthews letting him know he would attend Germain's private meeting but so far he detected no reason for alarm. After his therapy session, he'd taken the rest of the day off. He knew Matthews would be notified, as that was the one condition to getting his job. Treat the PTSD. The therapist seemed to think the crowd at the park was the trigger this time. She prescribed a sedative, anti-anxiety meds, and sleeping pills, but he didn't fill any of them. He was going to ride it out. And not as a zombie. He'd seen the destructive effects of opioids and would rather suffer than lose control like that. Instead, he slept in until half past nine, did fifty pushups, and took a freezing shower. It did the trick. *This time.* He was getting good at compartmentalizing even if it wasn't clear that was an effective long-term solution to dealing with his symptoms.

Jon logged into Facebook. He began typing a short message to Melanie, sad for what their relationship had come to, hoping to breathe some life back into it. Something nagged at him to check up on her posts. Her most recent photo was of her smiling with four other people. The man beside her had his arm around her waist. He closed his laptop, the message remaining unsent.

CHAPTER 6

Tel Aviv-Haifa

The flight from Eilat to Tel Aviv took just over an hour. Despite his exhaustion, Gabe couldn't sleep. He looked out the window at the ever-changing landscape, aware he was developing a real affection for the land. They had left the seaside, flown over flowering desert and the ancient Judean hills, and were now—in the span of a few hours—on a bus passing through the fertile central plains. He marveled at this tiny country—so green, a miraculous feat given that when the pioneers arrived, the land was barren, much of it desert.

He turned to Terry who was reading the *Jerusalem Post* she'd purchased at the bus station. Every few minutes she lifted her gaze scanning the other passengers.

Gabe said, "You're still looking over your shoulder. I'm so sorry."

"None of what happened when you were here last time was your fault. But I'm brushing up on krav maga. I won't ever be a victim again."

"You have to admit if I hadn't come to Israel back then—"

Terry stopped him with a kiss. "If you really feel accountable, you'll just have to make it up to me."

He pulled her close. "I would like nothing more."

***

The bus entered Haifa's city limits, a lovely metropolis reminiscent of San Francisco with steep hills leading into the port below. Cruise and cargo ships dotted the sea, a sign of the country's aggressive industry. Gabe and Terry disembarked and found her car parked where she had left it days before.

The sun was low in the sky as they pulled up to a modern looking building, parked the car, and took the elevator up to the thirteenth floor.

Gabe said, "Funny, I don't think I've ever been on the thirteenth floor."

"How is that possible?"

"In the States, thirteen is considered a bad luck number."

She laughed. "Not in Israel. It's good luck here."

The apartment door opened before they could knock. The aroma of fresh baked bread greeted them.

"Ah, you must be Gabriel. Come in, come in. You're just in time," Hannah Lavi said, waving the bemused couple inside.

Terry laughed. "And Shabbat Shalom to you too, Ima."

Terry's light hair and eyes were thanks to her mother. A youthful woman, Hannah overcame her petite build with her boisterous nature.

"He's a handsome young man," Hannah said in Hebrew, then turned to Gabe, switching to fluent English. "We are always happy to meet Terry's friends. She works so hard, we wondered if she had any left."

"Ima!"

Terry looked at Gabe, grinning broadly. *He must find this entertaining. A world-renown scientist embarrassed by her mother. Does he know it's a Jewish thing?*

She led the way to a table decked in white cloth, an ornate silver cup, and bone china. At the far end were silver candlesticks.

"The table is beautiful," he said to Hannah.

"Thank you. Please make yourself comfortable. My husband will be home shortly and then we will sit to eat." To her daughter she said, "Let's go light."

Gabe sat on the sofa and watched as Hannah donned a headscarf, and with Terry beside her, lit the candles. Mother and daughter shielded their eyes, uttering a quiet prayer. When Terry looked over at Gabe he was staring at her with a look of admiration and mild confusion.

Terry felt her heart flutter, something she hadn't experienced for a long time. Years of intense schooling followed by a demanding career had precluded a romantic life. Until now. *But why was life always so complicated?*

The front door opened. A stocky, thick-chested man dressed in a short-sleeved crisp white shirt, black slacks, and sandals walked in. He had a full head of white hair and a broad smile. In a deep throaty voice, he said, "Shabbat shalom!"

"Shabbat shalom, Aba," said Terry who greeted her father with a kiss.

Gabe walked over to Dr. Lavi and shook his hand, "Shabbat shalom, sir. I'm Gabriel Lewis. Thank you for inviting me into your home."

"Ahh! A guest . . . how wonderful! We are pleased to have you join us. Come everyone to the table and let's begin."

***

As the evening progressed, the conversation flowed smoothly on a wide variety of topics—politics, work, the economy. Gabe learned that both of Terry's parents held PhDs, her father as a professor of mechanical engineering and her mother an accomplished genealogist at Haifa University.

Hannah was plating homemade baklava when she said, "Lewis . . . that's of French, Welsh, or English origin. What's your mother's maiden name?"

"Actually, I'm adopted," Gabe said.

"Oh, I see. Do you know anything about your biological parents' backgrounds?"

Terry gave her mother a not-so-subtle look, which her mother chose to ignore.

"My birth mother wanted an open adoption, so I do know her last name. It was Fermi."

"Fermi . . . interesting. An unusual name but one I have come across before." Hannah's pursed her lips. "Let me think where. It will come to me."

Terry was pouring a cup of nana tea when a look of recollection cloaked her mother's face, "Oh! Oh, indeed!"

Her husband looked up from his dessert plate. "What is it, Hannah?"

"I just remembered where I saw that name." She paused, seemingly considering something. It's derived from the Italian town of Fermo in the Marche region."

Gabe dabbed at his mouth with his napkin. "Sounds like I'm Italian. Grazie!"

Terry grinned but Hannah's face was serious. "I would recommend a DNA test and find out for certain."

"Well, it is a fascinating idea, and I certainly know enough people in the genetics field who could do it for me." He winked at Terry.

"As a matter of fact, I have several kits here in my home office. Let me get one for you." Hannah left the table.

Terry whispered, "Sorry about that. My mother can be a bit pushy."

Gabe laughed, then squeezed Terry's hand. "No problem at all. I like outspoken women."

Hannah returned with a colorful box. "Here's the kit. The instructions are inside."

Terry said something in Hebrew to her mother, who shrugged in response.

"You don't need to do this, Gabe," Terry said.

"Actually, it's something I've been thinking of on and off since the technology became available. I'm curious about my medical makeup."

Hannah raised her brows at her daughter in victory. "I'll

check for that as well."

Terry showed Gabe to the washroom, and when he emerged, he handed the kit back to Hannah.

"Excellent!" she exclaimed. "I'll be in touch as soon as I have the results."

"You never know, it could make for a great ice-breaker one day..."

They all laughed. All except Hannah.

Terry and Gabe stayed to help clean up, then said their goodbyes.

"We hope to see you on your next trip to Israel," Hannah said, smiling.

As the door closed behind them, Terry reached up on her tippy toes and pecked Gabe on the cheek. "Thank you."

His face lit up. "For what?"

"For making it up to me."

CHAPTER 7

New York City

J on felt like he'd stepped back in time. To the sixties.
Age of Aquarius. College students sat on pillows on the
floor of the dimly lit Greenwich Village living room.
About fifteen people, snug in a circle. Germain was nowhere in sight. Probably waiting to make a dramatic entrance. The place reeked of cannabis. A joint was making
its rounds, a film of smoke hovering over the human circle.
Gwen had walked in ahead of him, carrying a duffle.

"Hey everyone, this is Jon Lewis. Grad student. He's
new to all this."

"Hey Jon, welcome," said a kid with spotty stubble.

Jon raised a friendly hand and took a seat with the
others.

"You're gonna love this guy."

"Yeah, I heard his speech in the park, then watched his
videos. He's awesome."

"True dat," said Stubble. "He's making waves. Apparently, he has some big news. He's sharing it only with his
closest followers. You're lucky to be here."

Followers?

"Honored," said Jon.

The guy passed him the joint.

"No thanks."

"Come on man, it'll get you in the right frame of

32

mind."

"Nah, I'm good."

The kid was about to say something else when a voice spoke from behind.

"Lay off him, Pete. He's right, that stuff's shit. You need a clear mind for what I have to say. If everyone was high, the world would never get to where we need it to go."

The kid, duly chagrined, put his hand down, letting the roach burn out.

Jon looked at the man behind him, amazed he was a U.S. congressman. Here in the smoky room, Germain looked and sounded no different than the other coeds, despite being fifteen years their senior. A chameleon, he was dressed more casually than before, a rucksack over his shoulder.

Germain had a strong presence, a confidence that oozed off him. And he knew how to play it. He took a seat with the others who scooted over to make room. They looked at him with reverence.

Spenser gestured to Gwen. "Show us what you've brought."

Gwen unzipped her duffle and took out a poster from a cardboard roll. It depicted a man and woman in combat gear, the letters SAU inside the silhouette of a pistol emblazoned on a bright yellow patch on their arms. "Bring the fight home," was the tagline.

"This is our new brand," he said. "I've assembled a team of social media influencers. Our reach will expand across the country."

Gwen pulled out t-shirts with the same insignia and passed them around. Germain said, "Wear these around town. Post selfies. You are my most vital recruiters. If someone asks, tell them who we are. You know the drill. Invite them to our next rally . . . like Gwen did." He offered her a bright smile. Jon watched Gwen blush in response, amazed how Germain charmed the tough woman, now melting like a bashful schoolgirl.

Jon accepted his t-shirt. Everyone began changing into them. When Pete looked at him questioningly, Jon followed suit.

"Looking good, bro. Sorry about the joint. Spenser's right."

"No worries."

Germain spent the next fifteen minutes answering questions and throwing in his socialist talking points, with infectious passion. Jon did his best to appear engaged and pliable. When Germain asked if he wanted to get more involved, he said he would love to and gave his email address. By the time Jon left, he was the newest member of the Sam Adams Underground.

CHAPTER 8

FBI Headquarters
Federal Plaza
New York City

"This looks pretty militant to me," Matthews said, as he studied the poster Jon brought back. Jon was seated in Matthews's office, the door closed.

"They'll soon be hanging all over lower Manhattan. But I think I'm in with the group. He seems to like me . . . but probably gives everyone that feeling."

"The politician's gift," Matthews said.

"Granted, the guy is a snake charmer. He's a congressman who can blend in with both suits and potheads and they all love him. But, still seems borderline to me. He didn't speak of violence. Certainly nothing you could use to shut him down."

"Like I said, the guy seems to stay just clear of the line."

Matthews rounded his desk, leaning against it and looked Jon in the eye. He kept silent as if deliberating something.

"What?" Jon asked.

"It's gotten worse. He handed Jon a file. "This just came in."

"Another one?" Jon said.

"Try another three. Same commie spiel, different cities, quickly building momentum. They're springing up everywhere. It smells of a bigger movement that could be trouble." Matthews pointed at the folder. "Skip to the last page."

Jon did, then looked up in surprise. "Czech Republic?"

"Right, but they're all Americans. That one's a Princeton economics professor on sabbatical abroad. The other ones are an editor for the *Chicago Tribune* and a hotshot lawyer in D.C."

The file included a screenshot of the Chicago editor's Twitter page. The profile photo was of a man reading the Tribune, a cigarette dangling from his lips. He had over fifty thousand followers. Similar numbers for the others. Matthews was right. All three men shared left-wing posts that could have easily been written by the same person.

"How can you be sure they're connected?"

"It's too convenient that they all pop up at the same time with a similar agenda. We now have four of these guys. Three stateside, one overseas. There's strategy here. I've been doing this long enough to know a serious problem is coming. My guess is in a few months, maybe even weeks, they'll join forces. Then, we'll have thousands of people following these loonies, looking to undermine the U.S. government. I won't wait till it gets too big to handle swiftly. But that's what we'll confirm. If and how they're connected."

**

Jon sat at his desk, plugged in his laptop, and accessed the new files Matthews had sent him of the other inciters. He decided to start with the file on Alexander Bilka. Professor of economics from Princeton, using his sabbatical to teach at the Anglo-American University in Prague. Jon opened another screen and logged into YouTube. Typing

Bilka's name in the search bar yielded several videos. One title stood out to him. "Harnessing your anger for world change," he read aloud to himself. Didn't sound like economics to him. The video's location was listed as the Charles Bridge, Prague, Czech Republic. A Google search described it as a pedestrian bridge popular with tourists as a venue for local artisans and ad hoc performers.

He hit play and the camera zoomed in on Bilka. Trim build, clean shaven, on the shorter side. There was something strange, a mental itch he couldn't scratch. Then it came to him. He went back to Germain's dossier, and was struck by the bizarre physical similarities between the two men. They even dressed similarly. If Jon didn't know differently, they could easily be brothers.

Bilka stood beside a younger man playing on a propped-up keyboard, presumably to attract a crowd. It worked. A group formed around the two men. When the musician finished his piece, he introduced Bilka as an American professor and revolutionary. A few people shaved off from the group, others lingering.

He had a throaty voice that carried, strangely similar in tone and projection to Germain's. His speech engaged the crowd, but no one appeared angry or militant. His ramblings, mostly disgust of his native land's capitalism, were unscripted and shorter than Germain's but powerful enough for people to stay and speak with him. When the video ended, a website popped up.

Jon clicked on the site's link. It appeared professionally done with video and social media links, catchy graphics, and regular updates. Hundreds of comments—mostly in favor of his agenda. There was even a donation link. The man was building momentum and clearly had a savvy marketing team behind him.

Jon walked to Matthews's door and knocked.

"Come in."

Jon stood in the doorway. "There's something

strange . . ."

"What is it?"

"The two men—Germain and Bilka—they look incredibly alike."

"Close the door."

After Jon did so, Matthews said, "Let me see those photos again." Matthews went to his computer and accessed the digital file. "Wow, you're right. I'll pull up their DMV records." He zoomed in on the two men's driver's licenses. "Their birthdays are months apart. They can't be brothers."

Jon had a strange thought. "Can you pull up the other two men?"

Matthews glanced at his underling. "I know that look, Jon." He retrieved the other two driver's licenses arranging the four photos beside each other. "What the hell!"

Jon rushed to stand behind Matthews. The four men, each with different facial hair, were near copies of one another. Matthews said, "Something sick is going on. *Now* do you think the Feds should get involved?"

Jon stared at the screen dumbfounded. Without sarcasm, he replied, "Yessir."

CHAPTER 9

Haifa, Israel

D r. Terry Lavi was in her happy place. Walking on the Technion Institute campus, she felt the most in her element, the familiarity of her surroundings offering a sense of tranquility. Lately though, her *happiest* place was with Gabe. Their spectacular week together was the first vacation she'd taken in years.

Things were getting serious. She really loved him and knew the feeling was mutual. Still, they instinctively avoided The Future. He'd left that morning back to the States. Back to his regular life. She already missed him. They planned to see each other again in a few weeks when the school would be closed for winter break. Usually she worked straight through, but this year she would fly to Texas to see him. Though she knew it could only go so far, she would enjoy the relationship as long as possible. She let the thought go for now, aware she would have to face it eventually.

Terry had just left the cafeteria, her salad and coffee in hand, and was heading back to her lab.

"Terry?"

She turned to face Dr. Itai Perlman, head of the cloning lab.

"Itai, hi. It's been a long time."

"Yes, it has. We are both too wrapped up in our own work

to see each other even one building over."

He was right. Despite the proximity of their labs, they rarely crossed paths. Terry walked beside her colleague. He was tall and bony even in his white lab coat. He towered over her slight frame.

"How have you been?" Itai asked.

"Insanely overloaded." She laughed. "You?"

Itai nodded in agreement. "The invitation still stands to come for dinner. Now that the kids are all out on their own, Liat would be happy to have someone else to speak with."

"Even another geneticist?"

He laughed. "Your point is well taken, but even so. You know Liat loves you."

"Thank you for the invitation. I'll be in touch."

"I'll let the noncommittal response slide. Just show up and there will be a seat waiting for you."

She conceded. "All right. L'hitraot, Itai." Behind schedule, she picked up her pace.

"Terry, wait a moment," Itai said, catching up with her. "There's something I've been wanting to discuss with you." He paused, as if considering his words. "It's a breakthrough in my research. Seeing you now . . . well, if you have some time, I'd be honored to hear your impressions."

"Mazal tov! But genetic cloning isn't my area of expertise. Perhaps someone in your field from another university would be a better choice."

"You're being your usual modest self, but regardless, I'm actually looking for a moral point of view."

"Moral?"

Itai looked a bit uncomfortable. "I'd rather not discuss it standing out here. There's much to explain about my work. But suffice it to say, I hold you in high regard. You have a reputation as a sterling medical ethicist. I thought you could help me gain a more objective perspective."

"I have a pretty tight schedule but let me see what I can do to set aside some time. Maybe early next week?"

"Perfect. I'll email you to confirm. Thanks, Terry. Good luck with your projects."

Terry took a sip of her cooling coffee, noting that Itai had deftly managed to whet her curiosity.

CHAPTER 10

Midtown Manhattan
New York City

Jon walked inside The Rusty Nail, a popular bar on the West Side. With a pep in his step, he approached a table near the back. "Bro!"

His best friend Gabe stood grinning from ear to ear. He was wearing a brown leather bomber jacket over his broad shoulders, his face deeply tanned.

"Jon, look at you, all suited up like a regular grownup."

The two men hugged and sat. A middle-aged waitress in dire need of a color touch-up came to take their order. They both asked for light beers. She placed a bowl of nuts on the table and left.

Jon said, "Thanks for extending your New York stopover."

"You kidding? I haven't seen you in ages. We needed to catch up face to face."

"How's Terry?"

"Amazing, as usual." He smiled.

"You're hooked."

"No question about it. I think she's the one, Jon."

Jon was surprised at the speed of his best friend's long-distance relationship, but Gabe's excitement was infectious.

"That's great! How are you going to handle the minor location issue?"

Gabe turned serious. "That's the least of my problems."

"What do you mean?"

"Terry's planning a trip here next month and I was thinking of popping the question."

"Wow! So why the long face? That's terrific news. You guys are great together. You'll find a way around the geography."

"I sure hope so, but the real challenge is that I'm not Jewish."

Jon took that in. "Oh."

"Yeah, oh is right. She's never come out and said it, but I suspect she would never marry a gentile."

"Have you discussed this with her?"

"Not even a little bit. We've been enjoying our time together so much. Neither one of us seems to want to broach that hotwire topic."

"So, what then? Keep things as they are?"

"Honestly, I don't know what to do. I thought about conversion but from what I understand it's quite complicated. Many rabbis frown on conversion for marriage rather than a sincere interest in accepting the faith. And if I'm true to myself, I don't spend much time thinking about religion. Any religion."

"Looks like you have a conundrum."

"That about sums it up." The waitress came with their beers and Gabe took a long pull. "You know what, let's drop that. I didn't come here to gripe about my love life. What's happening with you? Matthews still riding you?"

"Nah, he's all right."

"Whoa. That's quite a change. What happened?"

"Guess you can call it a truce of sorts. We understand each other and know the lines not to cross. Most of the time anyway."

They laughed together.

"And the job itself?" asked Gabe.

"Loving every minute. Never boring. There's always

43

something crazy going on. Let's put it this way, if average Americans knew what was happening out there, they'd never leave their homes."

Gabe raised a brow. "That's not at all terrifying. Are you working on anything big now?"

"Could be. Can't give you too much detail. You don't have clearance."

"I'm impressed. Then, tell me without details."

"Some misguided college kids starting trouble."

"Seems pretty lame."

"Anything but."

"I'll take your word for it." Gabe took a handful of nuts. "How are you doing about Mel?"

"Whole thing sucks. I hope you have better luck with your long-distance relationship than we did."

"You know I love Mel, but you two were great for a season. You were there for each other when you both needed it. Maybe it just ran its course."

"Now you sound like my shrink."

"Glad you're still going. Wasn't therapy Matthews's idea?"

"Yeah. He didn't give me much choice. If I didn't agree he wouldn't have offered me the job."

"I suppose he isn't such a douchebag after all."

They laughed again. And spoke for another hour till Gabe needed to head back to the airport. "I'll be in touch."

"I'd like that." Jon paid the tab and walked his best friend to the waiting Uber, feeling a twinge of sadness as he watched the car drive away.

CHAPTER 11

Rome, Italy

The thieves were small men, bordering on anorexic. Each wore a full black ensemble including knit cap, latex gloves, and rubber-soled shoes. Equipped with state-of-the-art headsets, they could communicate verbally in case they were detected. Otherwise only hand gestures would be used. They had a sign language of their own, bearing no resemblance to that of the hearing-impaired community.

Gaining entrance to the facility was easier than expected, the security decades old. Perhaps no one thought there was anything worth stealing from the national archives. The two men knew differently.

It was 3 a.m. on a moonless night, which was of course a deliberate choice. A lone elderly guard dozed in the lobby, even as the thieves stealthily made their way past him. Despite their significant killing skills, had the guard woken, the thieves would have incapacitated him. Not eliminate. Elimination had not been authorized.

The thieves had memorized the layout of the facility and in fewer than three minutes from entering the building were standing in front of a locked steel door. It was the only one with a fingerprint entry system. The senior of the two slid a small plastic sleeve from his pants pocket. It contained a white shiny card with one black-inked fingerprint. The man placed it against the reader pad pleased to hear the distinct click of the door unlocking. A moment's pause let them know no alarm had been tripped. The fingerprint had allowed them to enter quietly.

The two men made haste entering the records room, where they would face the most challenging part of the caper. They knew exactly what they were looking for but not exactly where to find it. The men split up, each to one end of the room, a rectangular space lined with metal shelving and old beige file cabinets running down the middle. The men were attuned to the baseline sounds, fully alert if any new ones should be introduced.

It took nearly ten minutes till they determined the archival classification method and another ten to find what they were looking for. The file was stamped diagonally across the top in faded red ink. *Classificato*.

One of the thieves removed a tiny camera from his pocket and photographed the thirty pages inside the file folder, then returned it to its place. They retraced their steps. The old sentinel snored peacefully. A total of twenty-six minutes had elapsed. Exactly as planned. No trace left behind.

Thirty minutes later a car dropped off the two thieves —now dressed as successful businessmen—at Leonardo da Vinci–Fiumicino International Airport ready to check in for their flight back home to Israel.

CHAPTER 12

FBI Headquarters
New York City

Jon was at his desk when he saw Craig look up from his computer and let out a low whistle. Jon followed his gaze. A stiletto-heeled slender woman with latte-toned skin walked past them. She wore a black pantsuit and white silk blouse that did little to mask her toned physique.

Jon tsked his co-worker. "The whistle's gone the way of the dinosaur. Any louder and you'll get the whole Bureau sued for harassment. But I have to admit, that is one nice looking Fed."

"What makes you think she's a Fed?"

"No question. For one, she's wearing the female version of the Fed uniform. Also, she's way too confident. Walks like she owns the place. If she weren't so young, I'd say maybe she's Agent Matthews's boss."

"I wouldn't complain if she were my boss. But I'm willing to bet she's not a Fed. I'm going with lawyer."

Jon grinned. "I sense a wager coming."

"Twenty bucks."

"You're on." Jon extended a hand and the two men shook.

As they discussed how to figure out who won the bet, Matthews stepped from his office and called Jon inside.

Craig whispered, "Ask her."

"I will. Get your wallet out."

Craig smiled amiably. "Not so fast, Steadman."

Jon entered Matthews's office, feeling like he'd been spending more time there lately than at his own desk.

Matthews closed the door behind him. "Agent Jon Steadman, I'd like to introduce you to Agent Carrie Santiago."

Yes! It was the easiest twenty bucks he ever made.

"Why are you grinning like that?"

Jon fixed his face. "Sorry just thought of something funny." He turned to Agent Santiago, and shook her extended hand. She was close to his age. And height. Jet-black tresses piled up in a loose bun.

"Pleasure to meet you. Which office do you work out of?" Jon asked.

"Langley."

"I didn't know the FBI had an office there." A pause. "Oh."

Matthews interjected. "Agent Santiago is with the CIA."

"Are you an attorney by any chance?"

"As a matter of fact, I just graduated from Harvard Law. I'm taking the Bar exam as soon as we close the case. How did you know?"

Damn, there goes my twenty. "Just a hunch."

"Hmm. Guess I better bone up on my mysterious vibe. An agent never wants to be read so easily."

Matthews said, "Maybe you two can go get lunch."

Jon turned to his boss. "Huh?"

"You'll need to get to know each other better. You've been matched."

"Matched?"

"Agent Santiago is your new partner."

The woman said, "Please call me Carrie."

Jon said to Matthews, "Not computing. Why am I

being partnered with a spook?" Then to Santiago. "No offense."

The CIA agent smiled. "None taken."

Matthews said, "The case has been given high priority status. An investigation is being opened to determine the presence of a political insurgency. Since it has international elements, the State Department is requiring someone from the Farm to join on this." Jon knew the Farm was another name for CIA headquarters. "They sent Agent Santiago. You can bring her up to speed and she will brief you on the overseas assignment."

"You're sending me abroad?" Jon said.

"That's what overseas means. I have a meeting in five minutes. Go."

Jon was still processing. It happened so fast. He was being assigned to an international case with a spy!

CHAPTER 13

FBI Headquarters
New York City

Agents Steadman and Santiago sat at a linoleum table in the FBI's basement commissary. Jon opened his wrapped chicken sandwich, slathering it with Russian dressing. He took a big bite, the sauce oozing out the side. He accepted a handful of napkins from his new partner and wiped his mouth, then chased the swallow with a gulp of Mountain Dew. "So, tell me your story. What happened before Harvard Law?"

Carrie Santiago put down her plastic salad fork. She'd been eating the vegetables raw, no dressing. Water on the side. She focused her dark brown eyes on Jon. "I'm an army brat. Grew up moving from one European country to the next. It's probably why they chose me for this job."

"And for the CIA in the first place."

"Sure. I was recruited as an undergrad."

"Also Harvard?"

"No. Yale."

"Impressive."

"Thanks. Even so, the CIA interviewed me three times. In the end I signed a contract to work for them for a minimum of six years and they'd pay for law school. I went through the training, but they waited till I graduated to put me in the field."

"Some deal. You pick up any of the local languages as a kid?"

"I speak a few."

"Sounds like you could have done anything you wanted. Why the CIA? No way they can match a big corporate salary."

"As I said, I'm an army brat. Patriotism runs through my veins. When they approached me, I knew it was the right fit. Once we're done with this case, I can start my real job as a lawyer for them."

"Why does the CIA need lawyers?"

"Every agency in the US government has a team of highly skilled lawyers. Experts in constitutional and international law."

"Who knew."

Carrie leaned in slightly. "Your turn. Tell me about yourself. There's something different about you. You're not like the other federal employees I've come across."

She had his attention. "What do you mean?"

"For one, your hair."

"What's wrong with my hair?" He subconsciously ran a hand across the back of his neck, dark locks skimming his shirt collar.

"Nothing at all. Just longer than regulation. And your gait. Not like a New Yorker. You strut."

Jon broke eye contact. "I had a bad injury a while back."

"Sorry to hear it. But if someone told me you'd just been recruited off a dude ranch I'd buy it. So, what's your story? Are you a lawyer as well?"

"Nope."

"Linguist?"

"Only English for me."

She appeared perplexed. "Then why—?" She stopped herself.

"Why am I being assigned to an international case

with a Harvard Law grad CIA agent? Probably because I've proven myself as competent." He debated his next line, then went for it. "Do you recall the UN affair?"

"Of course. It was the story of the year."

Jon closed his eyes, the memory taking over.

Carrie asked, "You okay?"

"Yeah."

"Were you there?"

Jon nodded, wondering what he was thinking bringing up that horrible day. "That's how I met Doug. I mean SA Matthews."

Carrie appeared riveted. "Sounds terrifying. How did you get past that? Emotionally, I mean."

Jon looked away. "Still working on it."

Carrie took out her iPhone, typed something in. She looked back and forth from her screen to Jon. "Wait . . . you're Jon Steadman."

He tore into a chocolate chip muffin. "Right. We covered that already."

"You're the grad student who *broke* the UN case wide open."

Jon smiled uncomfortably. "I don't know that I'd put it that way exactly."

"Maybe you wouldn't but CNN sure did."

"Apparently Matthews sees some potential in me. I'm told he appreciates my raw investigative skills."

Carrie was still reading. "BTI then UNT. Degree in forensics and . . ."

"Right. Okay, I know who I am. Can we talk face to face now?"

"Almost done." She read quietly for another minute then her face turned glum. "Oh, Jon. I'm so sorry."

Jon had been hoping she wouldn't read about his disastrous past. But after the UN his whole life was on display. Anyone with Internet could find it.

"Thanks."

Carrie put her phone face down on the table. "Seems like you got your life in order. Good for you."

Jon needed to take back control of the conversation. "Can we get to the case now?"

"Sure, sorry. I was just trying to learn more about my new partner."

Jon was giving himself a mental pat on the back. Instead of withdrawing when his past was brought up, he acknowledged it. Doc would be proud. "Apology accepted. And if it's any consolation you had me mostly pegged. Grew up in Boston but moved to Texas for my last few years of schooling. I think of myself as a southerner. You have good instincts."

"Thanks."

"Since Matthews wants us to bring each other up to speed, I already looked into Spenser Germain. He thinks I'm his newest acolyte."

"Wild. I read everything there is out there on him, as well as the files you have. He's a smart guy. But honestly, I don't see how he rises to gaining FBI attention, even if there are other people like him elsewhere. It seems premature to go after them at this point."

"I said exactly the same thing!"

"Any theories of what's going on?"

Jon leaned in closer. "This is hot off the presses, and I have no idea what it means yet, but there is something really weird with this case. I haven't had a chance to update the file yet."

"Do tell."

Jon looked around the space. Federal workers were milling about, eating lunch and shooting the breeze with co-workers. "Let's go back upstairs and find a confidential place to speak."

***

Jon had to admit his new partner was impressive. Smart enough to get into Ivy League schools. Two of them! And willing to forego the big bucks for a federal career. He wasn't sure how she would keep a low profile as a spy when she looked the way she did. Too pretty. It was the first time he considered beauty a potential hindrance.

He and Carrie had found an empty conference room where he shared the strange phenomenon of all four men looking so much alike. She too seemed baffled. As much as she had impressed him the truth was, they were both wet behind the ears. Neither had much boots-on-the-ground experience. He certainly had more than she did and that was prior to his job placement. They agreed this was a kind of test administered by their respective bosses, to see if they have what it takes. If they didn't find some link between the four men and a legal way to dismantle their movements, they would be relegated to the mundane for the foreseeable future. Despite the pressure he was glad to have the chance to prove himself.

Matthews made the decision to send them to Prague first, before following up on the D.C. and Chicago guys. Bilka had a disturbingly fast-growing number of social media followers making him next on the list. They were leaving in two days, after they attended Germain's next rally. It was time Carrie met the congressman.

CHAPTER 14

Technion Institute
Haifa

The security leading to the cryo-genetics lab was tight. Each department was restricted to its own staff, meaning Terry couldn't get into the lab unescorted. Dr. Itai Perlman's lab was spotless. Clean white countertops, gleaming beakers. Two scientists wearing light blue hairnets, bibs, and latex gloves sat at their designated stations working quietly with petri dishes, droppers, and microscopes. One ignored them, the other, a young, bespectacled man looked up.

"You can't be in here," he said without malice.

Itai smiled at his subordinate. "It's all right, Amir, this is Dr. Terry Lavi, she works in the lab next door."

The scientist looked dismayed. "Terry Lavi. Child prodigy, youngest genetics professor in Technion, medical ethicist. She doesn't have clearance. The rules require specific clearance."

"Don't worry, she's with me. I'll take full responsibility. How's the analysis coming along?"

"Fine." End of discussion. He fixated on his microscope. They'd been dismissed.

Terry made eye contact with Itai and raised a brow.

After they geared up, she followed Itai into a glass enclosure. Out of earshot from the lab, Itai said, "Don't mind Amir. He's an ornery genius. Came to us straight out of our very own Technion medical school. He's eccentric and likely on the autism spectrum but without a doubt he's one of my best researchers."

"You're a special man, Itai."

"Not really. I just know talent when I see it. Now for why I brought you here." Terry watched as he carefully extracted a labeled tray out of the cryogenic freezer. It was marked *Fragile*. Its label read *Einstein.*

"You're naming your specimens now?" Terry smiled. "No longer happy with the number system?"

Without responding, Itai placed the tray under a micro-scope, focused the lens, and stepped away. "Please have a look."

Terry took a seat on the stool and peered into the scope. It took her several seconds to realize what she was looking at. And another few to fully grasp that the world would never be the same.

CHAPTER 15

New York City

Hundreds of citizens slowly made their way down the center aisle and out of the NYU auditorium. A banner with the new logo hovered above the stage, several twenty-somethings clad in fatigues standing in formation at its base.

During his speech, Germain had used phrases like "rise up," and "fight the good fight." Jon had to admit it was an art form. The man was a skilled orator and influencer. Like a frog in a pot of slowly boiling water, the public was gradually being acclimated to the congressman's militant agenda. By the time they would realize what was happening, they'd be doomed.

Carrie stood beside him, dressed in jeans and a ball cap, her ponytail poking out the back. Without makeup she could pass for a grad student. She was waiting for a chance to meet the man. "Jon, that woman is waving at you," Carrie said.

Jon and Carrie made their way toward her. "Hey, Gwen, this is my girlfriend Carrie. She would love to meet Spenser." He and Carrie had decided it was the easiest way to explain her presence there with him.

Gwen looked at Carrie, a frown on her face. "You never mentioned a girlfriend."

"It never came up. Carrie, this is Gwen. She's the cool girl I was telling you about who introduced me to the congressman."

The compliment had its intended effect. Gwen still looked irritated by Carrie's presence, but it was going to pass.

"Are you also in NYU grad school?" Gwen asked Carrie.

Carrie nodded. "How about you?"

"Still in undergrad. Majoring in psychology. But now I'm reconsidering. Maybe I'll switch to PoliSci. If my parents will pay for the extra semesters."

"Why the change?" Carrie asked.

"Spenser needs more people in the limelight professing his vision. Things need to change pronto. He says I have good raw material to head my own rallies one day."

"Wow. Sounds like he really trusts you. Any chance you could introduce me?"

Gwen beamed. "Sure, come on."

They approached Germain who was now at the bottom of the stage steps speaking with a reporter Jon recognized from the local news channel. The man thanked Germain and cleared out.

Gwen said, "Spenser, you remember Jon Lewis. He heard you speak at the park, and you met him at the Sam Adams Underground meeting last week."

"Sure, the anti-weed guy." He smiled pleasantly. He turned to Carrie. "And who is this lovely young lady?" He spoke as if he were twenty years older than she, when in reality there were only a few years between them.

Carrie put out a hand. "I'm Carrie, Jon's girlfriend. Nice to meet you."

"Did you enjoy yourselves tonight?"

"Very much so," she replied. "You made some thought-provoking arguments for me to mull over."

"Wonderful. That's exactly what I like to hear. Open minds to new ideas. Where are you in school?"

"Yale. Came to see Jon for a few days."

Gwen said, "I thought you said you go to NYU."

"Did I? That's right. I did, for undergrad. I now go to Yale. I must have been distracted with all the activity here."

Gwen looked at Carrie suspiciously. "What are you studying?"

"Law."

Jon sensed the slipup was getting to Carrie. They needed to move on before more questions were thrown their way. Germain wouldn't take kindly to a Fed and a spook infiltrating his events. He would quickly close ranks eliminating any chance of Jon acquiring more intel on the group.

**

Back at Federal Plaza, Carrie looked broken. "I can't believe what a stupid rookie mistake I made." Frowning, she shook her head in disbelief. "I was distracted."

"It wasn't so bad," Jon said.

"It was awful. You saw the look on Gwen's face. She knows something's up. I may have blown our cover."

"She never got your last name. Even if she tries to track you down, she has nothing to go on. But it did teach us something important. We need to get our backstories straight before going into the field."

"Silver lining?" Carrie said.

"Sure."

Carrie paused. Then, "Are you going to mention this to SA Matthews?"

"Not a chance. No reason for him to know. And anyway, you're my partner and we back each other up. Right?"

Carrie seemed to be holding back her emotions. The woman who strode confidently into their offices last week was gone. For now.

"Thanks. It's good to know you've got my back. And I have yours."

Jon liked the sound of that. Other than Granny and Gabe no one had his back.

"What was your take on the meeting?" Jon asked.

"I can see the appeal. It has military and cult vibes. Rebellious but structured with a cool crowd to hang with and an energetic leader. Besides, most kids today know nothing about socialism. They're easily drawn to its concepts, not realizing they've failed miserably time and again."

"That's good analysis."

"Thanks. At least I'm good at something."

"No more beating yourself up. We leave for Prague tomorrow night. Let's work on our backstories and get them down cold. Who knows what Bilka will throw our way."

CHAPTER 16

Technion Institute
Haifa

Forty minutes after leaving the lab, Terry was sitting in Itai's office facing him, her head spinning. "This is more than a breakthrough, Itai. This has global ramifications. Not to mention significant ethical ones."

Itai nodded solemnly. "That's why you're here."

Terry looked at her colleague in disbelief. "This is far beyond the scope of two people. This is for the WHO."

"It's premature to take this to the World Health Organization."

Terry was incredulous. "You've cloned Einstein! No, you've resurrected him. This cannot be kept quiet. The potential applications of this discovery need to be globally monitored. Don't you agree?"

"Yes, I do. But not yet."

"When? Once we have hundreds of Einsteins roaming the Earth?"

Itai appeared dismayed. "Maybe this was a mistake," he said quietly.

"What was? Telling me?"

"I wasn't expecting this reaction. I thought you would be appreciative of our accomplishment and we could objectively discuss the ethical implications in a clinical manner."

Terry took a breath. "I'm sorry. You're right. This is a Nobel Prize–worthy scientific achievement. I am honored that you chose to include me in the small circle of those who know what you've discovered."

Itai looked relieved. "Thank you. What I showed you is DNA in its zygote phase. No embryos have been created."

"But that's the next step, is it not?"

"Yes of course. So far, we've successfully transferred the nucleus of Einstein's skin cell into another whose nucleus has been removed, but they don't survive past the blastocyst stage. The cells cease to reproduce, making them nonviable for implantation."

"How long would it need to survive prior to implantation?"

"Three to five days. Nearly all our work is focused on finding the right materials for keeping them alive long enough."

"And you want me to help?"

"Like all new discoveries it breaks new ground. We have no precedent for offering this emerging knowledge to the world."

"That's why you need an international consensus."

"Absolutely not. Other governments will simply seek to take over and steal our work."

Terry had to concede. "I see your point. The lure of an army of cloned Rambos would be too great for any government. If this became publicly known, your work could be in jeopardy."

Itai said, "Now you're beginning to see the predicament. This technology must remain in the best of hands. People with unquestionable scruples. History has taught us that once ground-breaking technology emerges, it rapidly finds its way everywhere. We won't be able to contain this forever."

"It's just a matter of time before someone else achieves what you have. Without the same ethical concerns." Terry knitted her brow. "The thought is terrifying."

Itai leaned forward, holding Terry's gaze. "Actually, I believe someone already has."

CHAPTER 17

Technion Institute
Haifa

T erry blanched. "What are you saying?" she asked Itai.
"Thirty-five years ago, an Italian scientist ran cloning trials in a private fertility clinic. He harvested many DNA samples, eventually succeeding with two embryos before human rights activists shut him down."

"How is it I've never heard of this?"

"One reason only. The news was overshadowed by what happened the day after it went public."

"What news story could have been bigger than this?"

"The next day was April 26, 1986. The Chernobyl Nuclear Power Station exploded, causing the release of radioactive material across much of Europe. It was the worst ever nuclear disaster. As you can imagine, no one was interested in some scientist playing with DNA in his Milan laboratory. The world was falling apart."

"What happened to the research?"

"It's the stuff conspiracy theorists live for. The Italian authorities refused to discuss the matter. We had no hard proof of any of it. After the accident, serious concern spread throughout Italy about the potential effects of the exposure to radioactivity on fetuses. Induced abortions increased. I've long speculated this fact made it easier for the scientist to find willing carriers."

Terry was floored. "They were implanted? Successfully? How do you know without any documentation?"

Itai took off his glasses, rubbed his eyes. "The scientist's papers were recently found."

"How? Where?"

"I have no idea. Honestly, I don't want to know. Suffice it to say they were given to me by a reliable source. I've studied them carefully."

"And?"

Itai stood up, leaned against the wall, whispering to himself, "In for a penny, in for a pound." He took a deep breath, blew it out. "The results were startling. One child reportedly showed signs of art genius, another of playing classical music by ear. Both at very young ages."

Terry could barely contain her curiosity. "Whose DNA was harvested?"

"Despite our valiant efforts, we never gained access to the genetic profiles they used. That information was not in the papers. My best guess is the carriers were promised their anonymity. Based on the little data we've assessed, our best assumptions are Modigliani, and Verdi, but it's speculative."

Terry's shock was apparent.

"Are you okay?" Itai asked.

"You're telling me two of the greatest artists in history have likely been cloned. That's a lot to take in."

Itai smiled genuinely. "I suppose I've become so entrenched in the details, that I've lost that sense of wonderment. But you are reminding me it is indeed miraculous. These masters may very well be walking the planet again."

Terry was silent for a moment, pensive. "They must bear striking physical resemblances to their predecessors. if that's even the word."

"We refer to them as hosts. Yes, the clones would have the same features, bodies, tendencies. But of course, environment factors in. Their skin tones may vary somewhat, diet may impact their waistlines and such. Comparable to identical twins."

"But in these cases, their twins lived generations ago."

"Indeed." Itai sat back down, lightly rocking in his office chair. He looked drained. "This concept is not new. For several decades governments around the world have sponsored scientists who have been quietly obtaining DNA from their most famous citizens of the past. But there are very few labs advanced enough to do anything meaningful with the samples. Until we discover more sophisticated methods, DNA resurrection requires both know-how and rare resources. Labs simply hold on to their samples for the day when the technology will catch up."

The two professors sat quietly pondering what was discussed. Terry broke the silence. "How is DNA extracted from long-gone hosts?"

"Family members, museums—whomever has a skin or hair sample donates it. It's no longer necessary to exhume the deceased. The challenge—one among many—is finding samples that were well-preserved. Only a tiny percentage of extracted material is viable for resurrection and more recent hosts are better. So Michelangelo would be harder to clone than, say, Fidel Castro. A highly complex chemical compound is applied to the sample, essentially waking it up."

"Castro?" she whispered.

Itai sat, his face solemn. "The potential is there for any viable host DNA to be resurrected. Good or evil."

"Whatever happened to the Italian scientist?"

"His lab was shut down and his research confiscated by the Italian authorities. Local media reported he went into seclusion, defamed. From what I've read, he died a few years ago."

Terry frowned. "What happened to the successful clones?"

"Without access to the research we can't identify or follow them. They would be in their thirties now. Likely showing signs of extraordinary artistic and musical capabilities. I can only assume the unused embryos were destroyed when the lab was closed."

Terry stayed quiet for several minutes, Itai not disrupting her thoughts.

Eventually, she asked, a calmer tone setting in, "How have you managed to keep this out of the news all this time?"

"Several years ago, when I determined what our work here could yield, I contacted the Shin Bet."

Hearing Itai refer to Israel's homeland security agency surprised Terry. "Then there *is* some oversight."

"Absolutely. The Israeli government has known of our project since the early stages. It's only with their financial backing that we've been able to fund the work. We deal with the science and they are in charge of keeping things quiet. They send a team periodically to see how things are going. They will ultimately decide how to use what we've developed."

"I can't fathom how you and even the Shin Bet will be able to successfully contain this information."

"We aren't naïve, Terry. In today's world of hacking, it is just a matter of time till the word gets out. For now, within our lab, we require strict confidentiality. No one speaks of the research even with family. All our staff members sign iron-clad NDAs. Personally, I don't think it's necessary since professional recognition would be jeopardized if the word got out prematurely. These hard-working scientists want to benefit from the acclaim. That won't happen if they share what we are doing before we've finished."

"And yet you're sharing all this with me. I haven't signed anything."

"I was given clearance to speak with you. Our government knows you well, Terry. You are beyond reproach. When I saw you last week, I had just been given the okay. Had we not bumped into each other, I would have contacted you anyway. I understand they are hoping you will lead an ethical council. That's why you're here. I was asked to invite you to Jerusalem for a classified meeting. We agreed it was best for me to be the one to break the news of all this—as a friend."

Terry audibly exhaled. "I see. This is quite overwhelming. Your discovery will change the course of genetic engineering as we know it."

"No question. There is still work to be done before we can go public, and first we need to set an ethical path forward."

Terry sat silently biting her lip. "Yes, the ethical implications..."

"Don't think for a moment that I haven't grappled with these issues from the project's inception. Even before I knew if it would succeed to this extent. But we can't hold back technological advancement. If we don't bring it to the world with respect, someone else is bound to, though as you noted, with little concern for the moral ramifications. At least this way we can control it initially."

Terry appeared skeptical. "Through government regulation? Bureaucracy will always have its own agenda."

"I don't see any other way. Regardless, this is where we are and I hope you can appreciate the magnitude of our work."

Terry wrung her hands, then nodded slowly. "Of course. As a scientist I am in awe of what your team has accomplished. The benefits it can bring to the world are not lost on me."

"Thank you," Itai said. "Does that mean you'll help?"

When Terry didn't immediately respond, Itai said, "Why don't you take a few days to think it over. See if you want to get involved with this. Let me know what you decide, say by Friday?"

Terry shook her head. "I don't need to think it over. As fascinated as I am, I'm sorry but I can't be drawn into this for a variety of reasons. There are aspects here I'm uncomfortable with. Not to mention I simply don't have the hours in the day. My own projects are behind schedule. *And* I have a trip planned to the States." She regretted the abruptness in her voice. Softer, she added, "Surely there are other ethicists far more qualified than I am to assist in such an important endeavor."

"You certainly would not be the only one on the team. But you would be expected to organize the panel of experts, lead them."

"Thank you for considering me. But the answer has to be no."

Itai looked genuinely disappointed. "I understand. I told the Prime Minister that you have a great deal on your own plate."

Terry was taken aback. "You spoke to the PM about me?"

"They spoke to me about you." Seeing her facial reaction, he said, "Don't be so shocked. It's not like they're spying on you. They just know who Israel's future leaders are and clearly you're on their list."

Terry looked away. "I'm not sure that helps."

Itai stood, circled the desk. "Let me walk you out. Thanks for taking the time to hear me out. It goes without saying this was a highly confidential conversation."

"Of course. I won't breathe a word."

"Good luck with your predictive genetics."

Itai escorted her to the building's exit. "And remember, the dinner invitation is still on the table."

Terry smiled and walked out, fully and utterly preoccupied.

CHAPTER 18

Old Town, Prague
Czech Republic

T he black BMW pulled up to the Hotel InterContinental as a light rain fell. Jon and Carrie exited the vehicle, allowing the driver to fetch their bags from the trunk and carry them inside. The lobby was upscale, spacious, and crowded. Jon heard several languages emanating from the sofas and nearby bar. He tipped the driver generously and, along with Carrie, approached the reception desk. A young woman with the nametag Maria smiled at them.

"Welcome to the InterContinental. Are you checking in?"

"Yes. Mr. and Mrs. Jonathan Lewis." He'd decided to stick with Gabe's surname due to its familiarity.

"Passports, please."

"Honey?" he said to Carrie.

Carrie handed the woman two American passports doctored by the CIA. Her wedding band sparkled as she did so.

The receptionist made copies. "Here you are." She handed the documents back along with an information pamphlet about the hotel and local attractions. "I see you are booked with us for two nights."

Carrie said, "That's right. We're celebrating our anniversary." She put her arm around Jon's shoulders. He felt an unwelcome stirring.

"How lovely. We will send up a bottle of champagne as a

small gift. You will be in room 705. Jacob will help with your bags. Breakfast is served from six-thirty to ten a.m."

Jon and Carrie followed the bellhop to the elevators and up to the seventh floor. The room was spacious, decorated in muted colors. Jon tipped the man and he left.

"How did I do?" Carrie asked. "Was I over the top?"

"You did great. Came across as authentic."

"Good. I'm getting my mojo back. Reviewing our back-stories sure helped."

Jon went to the window and pulled open the curtains. The sun was peeking out over a sweeping view of the Vltava River. Boats moseyed along the waterway, medieval turrets poised in the background.

"Come have a look at this view."

Carrie came along beside him, a trail of rosy perfume in her wake. "It's beautiful."

"It sure is," Jon said, avoiding her eye.

Carrie went to her bag, pulled out her laptop, and logged into a secure server. "Here's Bilka's file if you want to review it again. He'll be on the Charles Bridge tomorrow at three."

Jon checked his GPS. "That's a fifteen-minute walk from here. We can check out his university tomorrow morning before heading to the bridge."

"What do we do now? It's only six-thirty," Carrie said, holding back a yawn.

"Let's grab some dinner and get some rest. We're both jetlagged."

They each glanced at the king-size bed. Carrie broached the subject. "What do you want to do about this?"

"Up to you."

"There's no sofa, and we certainly can't ask for a cot when it's our anniversary."

"So…?"

"We'll share. Pillows in the middle. We'll be too tired to care anyway."

Not that tired, Jon thought. He locked their laptops in the closet safe and they left their hotel room together.

As they exited the building, Maria said, "Have a nice anniversary. The champagne will be waiting for you when you get back."

Realizing they were standing a distance apart, Jon reached for Carrie's hand, momentarily startling her. He let go once they were outside. The rain had stopped, the cool air invigorating.

Jon turned to Carrie, lovely in her cream-colored pea coat. "How about we walk a bit, get the lay of the land? It's a nice evening and if we can wait till a normal time to go to sleep, all the better."

"Sure."

They walked the cobblestone streets past an ancient-looking stone building. "There's the Golem synagogue I read about in the pamphlet they gave us," Jon said.

"What's a Golem?"

"A soulless giant made of clay sent from God to protect the Jews from their enemies. Legend has it he still lives in the attic."

Carrie looked at Jon, seemingly assessing if he was serious. "Really now?"

"Yes, Google it. I'm not making this up. If you don't believe me let's check it out."

The streets were dark, the light from the gas lamps reflecting off the puddles pooling between the cobblestones. *Romantic*, Jon thought, quickly pushing the idea away. They approached the building and looked up at the attic window. For a fleeting moment a shadow passed behind the glass.

"Whoa! Did you see that?" Jon asked.

Carrie said, "Stop pulling my leg."

"I saw something. I swear." He took her hand, pulling her to the entrance. "There's only one way to find out."

Seeing his urgency, she cried out. "No, wait. Don't make me go up there."

He stopped and laughed. "You're scared, aren't you?"

"Maybe a little." She giggled.

He put an arm around her amiably. "I'm sorry. But I really didn't make it up."

They both looked up again.

Jon said, "I guess we'll never really know for sure."

They continued on silently, enjoying the unfamiliar atmosphere and camaraderie.

"Do you have a significant other?" Carrie asked.

"Not exactly."

"That's cryptic."

Jon girded himself. Speaking of his personal life was always challenging. Not to mention his chronic trust issues. He tried to use what he'd learned in therapy. "Since Ash, my fiancée, died, I've had one serious relationship. It just ended a few weeks ago."

"I'm sorry."

"It was the best thing for both of us."

"So, it was mutual?"

"Yes. Our post-university lives were taking us in very different directions. But we'll stay in touch. We just want each other to be happy."

"That's sweet."

Jon took her hand, sidestepping a puddle. "How about you?"

Carrie's eyes saddened. "My story is a bit more complicated."

"Couldn't be more than mine. I'm still in my twenties and already lost a fiancée."

"I'm divorced."

"Oh."

"With a child."

"Oh."

"Who has language delays."

Jon refrained from making a third curt response. "That must be challenging."

"It is, but we manage. I'm fortunate to have a great job

that pays the bills and a solid support system. My parents, sister. Everyone pitches in."

"And the father?"

"Comes and goes as he wishes. He's more a big picture kind of guy. Not interested in the details. Like Randy's therapy, schooling, or child support."

"Sounds like an a-hole to me."

Carrie's eyes widened in amusement. "You say exactly what's on your mind."

"No point in sugar coating the obvious."

"I like that."

"Who's with Randy now?"

"My folks. They both work from home. If I'm on assignment they watch him."

"Sounds like you have things under control."

She shook her head with a smile. "I'm twenty-nine with a four-year-old. Not a whole lot of control." She paused. Then, "I miss him terribly."

"It must suck being away from your kid. But if it's any consolation, you seem to have your act together. Most of the time." He smiled.

"Thanks, Jon."

Twenty minutes later they were seated inside a small bistro, heaping plates of goulash and potatoes in front of them, placed beside two tall frothy local beers.

Jon raised his glass. "To Randy. One lucky four-year-old."

Carrie's smile told him he did good.

CHAPTER 19

Prague

T he next morning Jon woke groggily to his buzzing phone. The display said it was Matthews. Six a.m. *A-hole.* He got out of bed as quietly as he could, pulled on his pants, and walked out into the hallway. Carrie didn't stir.

The night before had not been awkward at all. Even when upon returning from dinner they found the bottle of Krug champagne in an ice bucket on the bureau. They ignored it. After showering, they got into bed, pillows piled between them. Turned out Carrie had been right. They had both fallen asleep immediately.

Jon accepted the call. "Doug?"

"It's *sir.*"

Jon paused. "Sir."

"Turn on CNN."

"What's going on?"

"Just turn it on."

Jon quietly snuck back into the room. Carrie sat up.

Seeing the phone in his hand, Carrie asked, "Who called?" Her voice was thick with drowsiness.

Jon reached for the remote control. "Matthews. He wants me to turn on the news."

The room lit up, causing Carrie to shield her eyes. A view of Times Square showed up on the screen. It looked like New Year's Eve, with one major exception. Instead of celebration, it was anarchy. Rioters wearing bandanas over their faces were throwing rocks into store windows, many grabbing merchandise. Police on bullhorns, people shouting back. Jon had never seen anything like it. It was full-on pandemonium.

Carrie was now standing beside him, stunned. Jon turned on the phone's speaker. He asked Matthews, "What the hell is happening in New York?"

Before Matthews could respond, the scene shifted to Seattle with near identical riots and looting. Then Houston and Detroit.

Matthews said, "Someone posted a video of Germain on social media spewing his commie agenda—everything for free and all that crap. He called on the liberal universities around the country to make their voices heard. It went viral stirring up his base. He denies inciting violence. Claims it was never his intention. The video didn't come from his account, but I'm certain his followers were dispatched to these cities to stir things up. There have been numerous injuries, some serious. Hundreds of arrests. The cops are trying to get it under control, but they're outnumbered. The President won't condone force and I tend to agree. Though his decision may be more about getting reelected."

Jon watched as someone set a police car on fire. "You think Germain is behind this?"

"I do. He's clearly building serious momentum, and he has the charisma to pull it off. Unfortunately, so far we don't have anything on him that can stick."

"Do you need me to come back?"

"Not until you've finished your job there. Get anything useful on Bilka?"

"Checking him out today."

"How's it going with Agent Santiago?" Matthews asked.

"So far so good."

"And the cover?"

"Still intact. But no one is interested in us."

"That may change at any point. And even if it doesn't, it's

good training for the future."

"Yessir."

"You patronizing me?"

"No." A beat. "Okay maybe, but this assignment is not dangerous."

"I'll repeat, in the field things can change on a dime. If your cover is not rock solid it could become dangerous fast."

Jon refrained from sharing Carrie's earlier mistake. "Like I said, no problems. We are Mr. and Mrs. Jon Lewis."

"How is *that* going?"

"Managing. She's professional and I'm close enough."

He heard Matthews try to hold back a laugh.

Jon yawned loudly. "I'm going back to sleep. Talk to you after we see Bilka."

***

Two hours later, Jon woke to sun streaming into the room, Carrie standing by the window, dressed casually in black slacks and a pullover. Her hair shone in the light.

"Good morning," he croaked.

"Ready to check out the university?"

"Not unless I can go in my pjs. And after I've had a sizeable dose of caffeine."

She appeared preoccupied.

"You okay?" Jon asked.

"My boss told me if it's necessary I can go to the embassy and be issued a pistol. Maybe we do that first."

"Am I missing something? Both you and Matthews seem to be getting a different vibe about this case. Why would you need a gun?"

Carrie looked out the window again. "Precautionary. Never go into the field unprepared for the worst-case scenario. That's how we're trained at the CIA."

Jon sat up, combed fingers through his hair. "All right, if it will give you peace of mind."

"I mapped it out. We can walk. If we cross the river, we'll hit the Anglo-American University first. Then the embassy is an easy walk from there. If we leave soon we can still make it to the Charles Bridge in time for Bilka's speech."

"Okay, I'll be ready in fifteen."

"I'll meet you downstairs at breakfast."

Jon got out of bed fully aware Carrie hadn't made eye contact once.

CHAPTER 20

Prague

The Anglo-American University was located in the newly restored Thurn-Taxis Palace with its main campus situated beneath the iconic castle just west of the churning, gray Vltava River. According to Bilka's Facebook page he was teaching global economics. Jon thought it curious the professor chose to spend his sabbatical in a former communist country.

Jon and Carrie walked through the ornate doors, crossing the main lobby adorned with crystal chandeliers, remnants of the palace days. Vastly different from the utilitarian architecture of the rest of the republic, Prague's Old Town was a marvel of Gothic, Renaissance, and Baroque buildings frozen in time. As they walked, they heard mostly English laced with a variety of accents.

"Take a look at this." Carrie was standing in front of an old-fashioned bulletin board pointing to a flyer promoting Bilka's pop-up speech titled *The Bright Future of New Age Collectivism*. Fancy words for touting communism.

"Catchy title," Jon said.

"You going?"

Carrie and Jon turned to see a young man wearing a newsboy cap atop a mop of stringy brown hair. Hipster. Eastern European accent.

Jon said, "Thinking about it. You know him?"

"I attended his last lecture. My parents forbade me to go again."

"Why?"

"They said he's lining up to be this generation's Lenin." The kid lowered his voice to a whisper. "Between you and me, I think the professor has a point. It's not like the capitalist model is such a success. I got in here on a scholarship but lots of my American friends are paying full tuition. Who wants to start their life with thousands in school debt? Especially when our degrees will benefit society. It's only fair society pays for our studies."

Carrie said, "Maybe your parents recall the dark side of communism."

"Different time. Our generation is not as materialistic. We are idealistic. Motivated by the greater good. Don't you agree?" He looked back and forth between them, seemingly itching for a debate.

Jon said, "Haven't really thought about it much. Maybe I'll go hear what he has to say."

The kid seemed deflated, shrugged. "Then I'll see you there."

Carrie said, "I thought you said your parents forbade it."

He was already walking away but over his shoulder he said, "They're so out of touch. I stopped listening to them a long time ago."

Carrie looked appalled. When the guy was out of earshot, she said to Jon, "Heaven help me if Randy ever speaks of me that way."

"No chance." Seeing she needed a pick-me-up, he pointed to an umbrella cart stationed outside. "How about a wiener sausage?"

"Nice topic change, Agent Steadman. It's only eleven in the morning but sure, why the hell not?"

CHAPTER 21

Prague

J on followed Carrie into the U.S. embassy. Housed in the grand Schoenborn Palace, the centuries-old manor stood beside Petschek Villa, the ambassador's opulent residence. Jon felt a sense of pride seeing the American flag fly above the entrance.

Carrie had made an appointment with an attaché who, without much dialogue, presented her with a pistol, holster, and two magazines. Jon watched as Carrie expertly secured the holstered weapon under her shirt.

"Have one for me?" Jon asked the attaché.

The man consulted his paperwork. "You're FBI. There's no clearance listed for you. I suggest contacting them."

"Nice to see all the bureaucratic red tape is still ever-present."

A smirk and the guy was gone.

On the way out, they passed a distinguished looking man in shirtsleeves carrying a pile of papers. Well-preserved, mid-sixties. "Agent Santiago, is that you?"

"Ambassador. How are you?"

Jon looked from one to the other, noting the once-over the man gave him.

"It's been a long time. What brings you to Prague?"

"Work."

"Ah. Congratulations. You've been put back in the field."

He eyed Jon. "Who's your partner?"

"Jon Steadman, FBI," Jon said.

The ambassador pursed his lips. "We don't get many of your kind here." Condescension dripped from his voice.

Ignoring the jibe, Jon said, "And you are ... ?"

Carrie flushed a bit. "This is Ambassador Tierney."

The man nodded formally. "Pleasure. Stationed here since 2012. Terrific placement thanks to Obama. Not too much in the way of controversy. Can't say that about most of the world these days."

A moment of awkward silence ensued.

Carrie said, "We need to get going. Nice seeing you."

Jon was glad to get out of there. The atmosphere bordered on toxic.

Out on the street, Jon said, "Tierney has a stick up his ass."

Carrie said, "You have no idea."

"How do you know the man?"

"Previous job."

"I thought this was your first field job."

"It is."

Jon let it go. CIA crap. Everything was on a need-to-know basis and apparently he had no need to know.

"Next stop on the tour, the Charles Bridge."

***

Hundreds of people strolled along the old sandstone pedestrian bridge passing vendors displaying their wares on makeshift tables. Jewelry, t-shirts, magnets.

Prague Castle stood majestic on a hill in the distance, its magnificent gardens surrounding it. As they walked the bridge's expanse, Jon felt like he was meandering through one of Grimm's fairytales.

The sky was threatening, heavy with rain-leaden clouds billowing across a gray sky. *Does the sun ever shine here?* Jon regretted leaving his umbrella behind.

He and Carrie studied the crowd from the bridge's east end.

Several people walked past them. Playing tourist, Carrie took a selfie, a stone head carved into the parapet behind her. She read the plaque below it. "This is Bradáč, the Bearded Man. Seems he watches the level of the water day and night."

"Sounds like a boring job to me."

Carrie pointed to statues mounted to the balustrade on both sides of the bridge. "This says there are thirty statues in total, representing various saints."

With no one in earshot, she asked, "Do you see him?"

"Not yet," Jon replied.

"Why are we lingering here? Let's find him."

"I've been down this road already with Germain. We won't have far to look." He nodded his head past her. "See?"

Carrie turned. A small crowd, many of them students, began to form toward the middle of the bridge, the stringy-haired student from the university among them.

"That's where we'll find him. Let's go."

They approached the growing crowd. Standing beside the railing was a man, same height and facial features as Germain. Scruffy, short beard, neatly dressed in Dockers and a hooded windbreaker.

Carrie stared, mouth agape.

"You see it, right?" Jon asked.

"That's crazy. I never thought ..."

"Never thought what?"

"Nothing. Forget it."

Bilka was testing his headset microphone, tapping it. He cleared his throat, took a drink from his water bottle. "Welcome everyone. Your presence here speaks for itself." Jon looked at his watch. Three o'clock.

"Ladies and gentlemen, I will speak slowly for those non-native English speakers. Some of you remember the days of Soviet Russia and their unwelcome presence here in what was

83

then Czechoslovakia. The oppression, and futile attempts at getting ahead in life. But let me ask this. Was it all bad?"

A murmur ran through the crowd, clearly at odds with the speaker's contention.

Unperturbed, Bilka continued. "Who recalls the economic benefits? Not having to pay for health insurance, schooling?"

A bespectacled, professorial-looking older man pushed forward, bristling. "I remember standing in line for food rations. Lenin said the goal of socialism is communism. He didn't mince words like you are. He also said, 'It is true that liberty is precious; so precious that it must be carefully rationed.' You weren't even born yet. Do you think you know better than those who lived through it?" The man was getting red in the face. Several young people in Bilka's entourage approached him menacingly. One said, "Go away, old man."

"Leave him be. He is bringing up vital points." Bilka spoke like a benevolent ruler. "Sir, with all due respect, this is a different era. Our generation is looking for equality, fairness. Something that was not popular back in those days when divisiveness was the rule of the day. My economic plan would care for everyone. The infirm, mentally disabled, impoverished. The wealth and resources of the world would be spread evenly. No more greedy inducements to lead to class warfare."

The man spoke back boldly. "You are not reinventing the wheel. This has been tried through the generations and failed. Miserably."

Bilka smiled. "All I ask is that you hear my plan with an open mind. See if it looks familiar or new."

The man shook his head and walked away mumbling. "Stupid kids today."

Bilka continued on in the same vein, never once losing his composure. When he finished, his assistant distributed magnets touting his website and signed up bystanders to Bilka's newsletter.

Carrie and Jon waited for the crowd to disperse then

approached Bilka. "Hi," Jon said. We're the Lewises from the States. We found your talk compelling."

Bilka removed his mic and faced them with an open smile on his face. He put his water bottle down on the ground beside him. "Welcome. Which state are you from?"

"The great state of Texas," Jon said.

"I don't hear the drawl."

"I moved around a lot. It got lost in the shuffle."

Carrie said, "You remind me an awful lot of Congressman Spenser Germain."

"You're not the only one to tell me that. Despite his title, he's an imitation. Not the original," Bilka continued. "But the congressman is on the right track. I'm glad other people are getting on board about the benefits of a socialistic society. Especially in the States. The whole system will crash in on itself in the next decade. I'll be ready to help guide them."

Straight-faced, Jon said, "Like the messiah?"

Bilka looked unsure if Jon was mocking him, his smile fading. "I'm not into religion. Thanks for coming. Check out my website." With the dismissal, his assistant handed them magnets and turned to speak with other people.

Quickly, Carrie bent down, picked up Bilka's water bottle, and hid it in her handbag.

Jon looked at her quizzically but said nothing.

A stroke of thunder and the skies opened up. Everyone scattered, running for shelter. Jon grabbed Carrie's hand and together they ran to the nearest overhang, laughing like teenagers.

"I'm drenched, Carrie said, shivering.

"Me too." He caught his breath.

The sky showed no sign of letting up. "We're already sopping wet. What do you say we stroll casually through the rain as if the sun is beaming on us?"

Carrie made a show of thinking it over. "I'm game."

Keeping her hand in his, that's exactly what they did.

***

The man pushed his rain hat lower on his brow, the drops rico-cheting off the brim. *Are spies getting younger or am I just getting old?* Tall and husky, he had learned to blend in with the scenery. It served him well as he followed the two Americans all the way back to their hotel.

CHAPTER 22

Prague

Carrie stepped out of the bathroom in the hotel's mono-grammed terry robe, toweling off her long black hair. "That has to be the best shower I've ever had."

Jon didn't look up from his computer screen. Both their packed bags were by the door. She asked, "Did you check us in for our flight back home?"

Distracted, Jon said, "Hmm? Yeah, did that."

The rain had let up, and the sun peeked out. Carrie looked at her watch. "We have a couple of hours till our flight. Let's check out the clock tower."

Jon looked up, closed his laptop. "I'm in."

It was a short walk. The tower—the tallest building in Old Town Square—loomed above the plaza. Quaint cafes and shops lined the periphery of the cobblestone plaza.

They paid the entrance fee and rode the elevator up to the top of the tower where a waist-high railing allowed for expansive 360-degree open-air views. The rain had kept the tourists away, but now the sky had cleared. There was only one other person taking pictures with his iPhone.

"These views are amazing," Carrie said. Jon was quiet, pensive. "You okay?" she asked.

"Yup, just thinking."

"Want to share?"

"Not yet."

"Gotcha." Carrie stepped away admiring the views from another vantage point, giving Jon his space. When she was out of sight, he took out his phone, connecting to the web. Looking downward, Jon sensed a presence behind him and subtly shielded his phone screen. "Are the views just as good on the other side?" he asked.

Jon felt a strong shove, his body slamming forward against the four-foot railing. Stunned, he grunted, trying to right himself as the assailant wrapped his arms around Jon's torso from behind. Jon felt himself lifted off the ground as the attacker attempted to push him over the edge. Jon yelled out, trying desperately to shake the man off, his body now teetering over the railing.

A piercing shot rang out and the vise grip loosened. As Jon pushed himself backward from the railing, he sensed a heavy thud. Quickly he turned to look down. A giant of a man, Slavic features with a nine-millimeter bullet hole burnt into his right temple. The smoke still emanated from Carrie's pistol.

Carrie rushed to Jon's side, her demeanor controlled, professional. "You okay?"

Breathing rapidly, Jon stepped away from the dead man lying at her feet. "I think so."

"Let's get out of here. Now," she said, authoritatively.

Jon felt light-headed, bile rising in his throat. He gestured to the floor. "What about him?"

"He's dead. That shot could be heard a mile away. The police will be here soon, and we can't be. We need to get on that plane. Move."

Jon absorbed her words. He picked up his fallen iPhone, and the two of them got the hell out of there.

***

"I can't wait to see my son," Carrie said as she calmly undid her buckle. They had reached ten thousand feet.

When Jon didn't reply, she said, "Are you doing better now?" Jon had spent the harrowing ride to the airport in silence holding his breath between deep inhalations she knew was meditative square breathing.

Jon said, "We need to talk."

Carrie flinched at his sharp tone. "About what?"

"I may be new to this, but I'm no idiot." He appeared to be doing his best to restrain himself, keeping his voice to an angry whisper.

"What do you mean?"

"Why did we need to come here? Just to see Bilka's school and hear a twenty-minute talk we could have easily found online? Not to mention getting you a firearm. For what?"

Carrie whispered, "It's a good thing I did given recent circumstances."

He opened his laptop, turned it to face her. Bilka and Germain's photos were side by side.

"The resemblance is uncanny," Carrie said.

Jon looked sad. "I saw you take Bilka's water bottle. That's what we came for, isn't it? I've been researching it. DNA can be extracted from latent prints."

Carrie remained silent.

"There's way more to this case than meets the eye. The growing underground movement, their strange likeness. You knew you might need a firearm. That we would be poking a bear. You said you had my back, like I had yours with Matthews. But that wasn't true, was it?"

No reply. Eye gaze lost. She leaned back in her seat, closing her eyes.

Jon went on. "The only thing I can't really figure out is why I needed to be here. If I'm being kept out of the loop. It can't be for your protection. You already had it in your holster." In the frantic rush back to the hotel, Carrie threw it in the Vlatava.

"Matthews."

"What about him?"

"He insisted on having one of his team along for the ride, even if you couldn't know everything. He felt he was the one to put the case on the radar and deserved to have the FBI involved."

"This isn't your first field job, is it?"

"No. I knew you would pick up on the ambassador's comment of me being back in the field. Bumping into him was bad luck."

Jon asked, "Is that what you think? Otherwise you could have kept the charade going?" A pause. "Do you really have a little boy at home?"

Carrie looked fiercely at him. "Yes, I do. All that was true."

"How the hell . . ." Then he lowered his voice back down. "How can I know which things are true and which aren't?" He laughed bitterly. "That's the question with spooks isn't it?"

Carrie said, "If it's any consolation, I didn't like this arrangement. I told both my boss and Matthews that it wouldn't be fair to you, but he insisted and brought you into his office to meet me. Besides, I'm not accustomed to working with a partner."

"And the slip with Germain?"

"That was legit. I blew it. Big time. I was thinking about Randy. Thanks for keeping it between us."

"You all played me for a stooge. I won't be a party to this any longer."

Jon put away his computer, put in his ear buds, effectively ending the conversation.

He didn't hear Carrie whisper, "I'm sorry."

CHAPTER 23

New York City

"I demand a different supervisor!" Jon yelled at his boss, the door slightly ajar.

Matthews said firmly, "Sit down." He shut the door.

Jon took a moment, then sat.

Matthews followed suit behind his desk. "This was not my idea. Agent Santiago's superior insisted the operation remain on a need-to-know basis. He had backup from ODNI hotshots. I didn't like it, but it was the only way I could have one of my own on the scene." The Office of the Director of National Intelligence oversaw the CIA among other intelligence agencies.

"I'm requesting a transfer."

"You could, but you won't get it. Do I need to remind you of the two non-negotiable conditions of *both* of our positions here in the New York office? You agreed to regular therapy sessions and I agreed to supervise you. Whether we like it or not, we're stuck with each other."

Jon shook his head. "I can't work with people I don't trust."

"That's your problem. You need to follow my orders whether or not you agree with or understand them. It's me or it's find another job outside the FBI. I'll be glad to be rid of the most insubordinate agent I've ever had."

Visibly offended, Jon stood. "No problem. See ya." He

walked out, leaving the door open, making sure Matthews watched as he cleared out his desk.

Craig asked, "What on earth happened?"

"What happened is I quit. Nice knowing you, Craig. Good luck."

As nearby employees watched Jon grab his things and walk to the elevators, Matthews quietly closed the door to his office.

CHAPTER 24

Pompano Beach, Florida

"**M**ore cookies, Jonny?" Granny Eunice smiled down at her grandson seated at her kitchen table, glad he had come for a visit. Eunice Steadman stood a hair below five feet, a full foot shorter than her grandson, a crown of snow-white hair haloing her head. Today she wore her favorite floral housedress. Granny had been Jon's surrogate mother from his early years since he'd lost both parents in a tragic car crash. Their bond was strong and unique. The moment he'd called asking if he could come for a visit, she knew something was wrong. Jon hadn't told her everything because of the nature of his job and she hadn't pressed him. It was one of the rare times she questioned her recent move from up north following her own harrowing ordeal.

"No thanks, Granny. I'm stuffed like a Thanksgiving turkey. I forgot how much I missed your baking."

She cleared his plate. "What would you like to do today? It's another perfect weather day."

"If you don't mind, I'll hang around the condo. I need some R and R before going back to New York and job hunting."

"Maybe your friend Gabe has some leads."

"Not a bad idea."

"Or maybe Melanie could help."

Finding himself with unanticipated time off, Jon had considered a visit to his now-ex–girlfriend but decided against it. The Facebook photos were still on his mind. She had moved on. Their calls had become so infrequent that going out to NoCal would come across as a desperate attempt at reconciliation. His heart nearly healed, he wasn't thinking along those lines. "I doubt it. I'll give Gabe a call. See if he knows of any job openings."

"How's about we go to dinner tonight? Get you out for a few hours. Maybe The Beach House?"

"You mean where all the hipsters and tourists hang out?"

"Yes. Age is a state of mind."

Jon smiled then noted how his grandmother was closing the cookie jar. "How's your hand?"

Granny had lost two fingers in a heinous abduction sparking her relocation to Florida.

"I'm fine, honey. One compensates."

He tried not to dwell on what had happened but felt his pulse quicken. Beads of sweat formed on his forehead.

"Jon?"

"Hmm?"

"I know you want to stay in but I'm getting cabin fever. Could we take a walk?"

He knew what she was doing and loved her for it.

"Sure, Granny." He stood and hugged her. "I'll grab my sneakers."

They walked on the promenade alongside the beach filled with sun worshippers defiant of the dangers from sun exposure. The smell of coconut oil was pervasive. Jon breathed it in, aware that his grandmother's strategy was working.

Granny moved at a slower pace than before, but her stamina remained, and they walked for nearly an hour. With the humidity's effect on Jon's bad leg, they made quite the pair, both glad to finally rest on a beachside bench.

An older man jogged by them and waved. "Hi, Eunice. See you Thursday."

She smiled, waved back.

"Granny?"

She blushed and winked at him.

***

It was just shy of midnight in Dallas when Jon called Gabe. He answered on the first ring. "Hey, Jon. Isn't it crazy late in New York?"

"Couldn't sleep and I'm in Florida." Then, "I quit."

A pause. "You can't be serious."

"Yup."

"Why? You love that job."

Jon told him what had transpired, leaving out details of the case. "I need to find another line of work. Thought you may have some leads."

"Hold on, bro. You and I both know you were made to be a Fed. No better fit. Other than your aversion to authority, of course."

His friend knew him well.

Gabe said, "You need to go back."

"Not a chance."

"Listen, Jon, as your best friend I'm telling you, get out of your own way. This standoff is not going to get you what you want. Eat some humble pie and go back."

Jon nearly raised his voice. "What about his keeping me in the dark?"

"Unless I'm missing something, he trusted you enough to put you out there. Not another agent. You. He didn't want to keep you in the dark. Your partner's boss did. If you want to take it up with someone, rail on him."

"Are you telling me that even though Matthews deceived me about the actual mission, putting me in real danger by the way, I should let that go?"

"Only if you want the job back."

"It's too late. I quit."

"You and Matthews are going to need a way to get along

in the long term because it sounds like your job depends on his and vice versa."

"No way he'd lose his job over me."

"Do you want to be responsible for it if he did?"

Jon didn't answer.

"Jon?"

"No. But I also don't want to—as you put it—eat humble pie when I am the wronged party."

"Was your life really in danger?"

"For a few terrifying moments, yes. Till my partner took care of business."

Gabe didn't ask for clarification. "Sounds then like Matthews didn't put you out there unprotected. Let this go. That's my advice. Whether you're at the FBI or any place with a boss, you're going to have to adhere to their rules. I know it's not your jam but there's no such thing as a freelancing Fed. There's a system."

Jon took a deep breath, trying to absorb his friend's words. "I'll think about it. Thanks. How's Terry?"

"Brilliant as ever."

"You get around to acknowledging the elephant in the room?"

"Not yet. But I don't see how we can ignore it much longer. She's coming next week." A pause. "And I just bought a ring."

"What?"

"Maybe it was impulsive but I'm ready, bro."

Jon could hear the smile in Gabe's voice. "Wow, good luck. Keep me posted."

"You know I will."

Jon hung up. He was glad for the reality check but knew where Matthews was concerned, there was no way he was going to make the first move.

***

The night before his flight back to New York, Jon dreamed of Ashleigh. She was luminescent, twirling happily on the beach in a sheer purple dress. He tried to hold on to her but couldn't gain purchase. They danced without touching. He smelled her lavender perfume even as he woke.

CHAPTER 25

New York City

As soon as Jon returned to his New York apartment, he felt a heavy weight settle inside him. Out the window, a pigeon perched on the fire escape was staring at him with its bulging eyes. It didn't help that with the recent clock change, darkness would soon descend. He pushed away his unfolded laundry and days-old newspapers, falling like a rag doll onto his sofa. He'd hoped the welcome reprieve with Granny would stem the melancholy, but the contrast between the bright Florida condo and his lonely studio apartment was stark. He'd felt lucky when he found the place. It was just barely affordable and within walking distance to work. Now the tiny pad felt sad, in desperate need of a woman's touch. But there was no woman in his life now.

If he didn't find a job soon, he would move. Maybe out of New York altogether. Back to Boston or Dallas? He'd think it over. But not now. He had scarfed down a burger on the plane but was thirsty. Without allowing much thought he opened the bottle of Jim Beam he kept on the bookshelf in the event his buddies showed up. He found a dusty shot glass, poured. The whiskey's heat flowed down his throat. "That's good," he said to himself.

Jon placed the bottle on the coffee table and opened his laptop, ready to begin the job search. The screensaver was a photo of him and Ashleigh at their engagement party. He had uploaded it after things ended with Melanie. Thoughts and dreams of his dead fiancée were becoming more frequent. He took another shot, closed his eyes. A tear squeezed out. He recognized the beginning of the downward spiral but had no strength to stop it. The bottle called to him and he answered.

**

Jon opened an eye. The small movement triggered a piercing headache. He assessed his surroundings, confused. Was he in Florida? No, back in New York. The empty bottle lay on the rug beside him. One leg hung off the side of the sofa. His t-shirt was soaked with a mixture of alcohol and tears. The buzzing from the floor sounded like a drill. He turned on his side, peering at his phone lying beside the empty bottle. *Unknown Caller*. He declined. And fell back asleep.

**

When he awoke, his throat was parched but his headache had gone away. Unsteadily, he peeled himself off the sofa, stripped off his clothes, and took a long hot shower. As he started to feel human again, the guilt settled in. He saw several missed calls from the unknown number. He dialed his therapist.

Hearing his voice, she said, "I missed you last week. You know the rules. Show up or ship out."

"I'm no longer with the FBI."

A silent pause ensued. "When did that happen?"

"A week ago. It was a sudden thing."

"Do you want to tell me about it?"

"I can't pay you."

"I didn't ask for payment."

He told her about his brush with death, the fall-out with Doug, his trip to Florida, and his relapse. She listened patiently without interruption. "I wish you'd called me before your first drink. Maybe we could have found a better way than the bottle."

When he didn't reply, she added, "If you find yourself in that situation again, call me. All right?"

"Yes, ma'am. Thanks."

***

Minutes after she hung up with Jon, the therapist phoned Special Agent Doug Matthews.

"Jon is not your typical guy," she began. "He will give the job his all and has a strong moral grounding. But trust can't be broken if you want an effective agent. You know very well what he's been through. Keeping him in the dark was a poor decision."

"It's not what I wanted."

"You could have sent someone else."

"I wanted him and needed to see how he would handle himself in the field."

"And?"

"He kept his cool. No meltdowns, despite, um, unexpected circumstances. I admit he showed promise to be a highly successful agent. He does well on the fly and his deductive skills are impressive. But let me take a stab in the dark here, he's not doing so great right now."

"That's privileged. Be that as it may, the damage is done. I'd be surprised if you got him back in the fold. Which I know is what you need and maybe even want, if you'll admit it to yourself."

"It's too late."

"You're probably right. But no way to know unless you try. You'll need to win his trust back, Doug."

"He's my subordinate. I'm not going to him."

"You're both the most capable and stubborn men I've

ever worked with."

"I'll take that as a compliment."

"As you wish," she said cryptically.

CHAPTER 26

Andorra–La Seu d'Urgell Airport, Spain

T he man in the camel hair coat brought the Citation CJ4 down smoothly on the landing strip. The Pyrenees loomed above, their peaks already blanketed in glistening snow. With no nearby international airport, the mountain village was a cumbersome destination to access. Unless one had his own plane. Unlike Courchevel, Benasque, and St. Moritz, his village was not overrun with seasonal travelers. Particularly now between seasons, when neither the elite summering crowd nor the ski aficionados would be around. The village was left with only its year-round residents, perfect for the evening's event. He looked forward to bringing the boys here to witness the village's transformation into a winter wonderland. If all went as planned, that day would soon arrive.

He parked the plane beside the hangar, and opened the cabin door, pushing out the stairs. Toting his bag in one hand and Fellini, his Persian Longhair, in the other, he descended to the tarmac where his vintage Alfa Romeo roadster awaited him. He threw the bag in the back and set Fellini beside him in the front seat.

Dusk was settling as he took the winding narrow mountain road, glad the conditions allowed for an on-time departure. He didn't want to navigate the dangerous roads after dark. He slowed through the village and waved at Jean Luc the chocolatier sweeping the shop's stoop. The chef would have ordered a box of truffles for this evening. The road rose once again and ten minutes later the chateau came into view. Perched at the edge of the mountain, the house overlooked the valley, the lights of the village twinkling below. He had several homes, but the chateau was his favorite. Regardless of how many times he made the trip, when he arrived, it took his breath away. He buzzed down the window allowing in the scent from the estate's orange grove. He pulled into his driveway where several cars were already lined up to the side.

He entered the house through the side door, bypassing the guests, and took the stairs up to his private quarters. He thought of the last time they had convened, when he told them two of the three investors were pulling out. He had done his best to dissuade the two powerbrokers, but they had lost patience with the project's snail's-pace progress. Luckily, the remaining investor, a man feared throughout Europe—was willing to acquire their shares. Despite the serendipity, he was not happy to have all the project's eggs in one basket.

With his characteristic efficiency, the man showered, dressed in a pressed white linen shirt and tailored slacks, and eagerly went to greet his guests. He finally had the update they had waited decades to hear.

As promised, the house was ready, waiters in bow ties and tails serving hors d'oeuvres to the intimate group who had made the long flight from points east. Dinner of roast duck was served followed by a raspberry torte garnished with the chocolate truffles he had expected. As was customary, none of the participants discussed the reason they were there. It would wait until after dinner.

At precisely eight p.m., the plates were cleared, and the guests directed to the salon, a French-inspired room of papered walls and Loire fabrics. The man stood, helped himself to a glass of champagne from a passing waiter, took a fork, and clinked, attracting the group's attention.

"Welcome to my humble home." He laughed. The Committee, established in the early part of the last century, was comprised of long-standing active project sympathizers. "I hope you've all enjoyed your day at the chateau. You have waited patiently, and I'm honored to say our work has borne fruit. Our boys are ready. I will meet each of them shortly. Finally, our dream of revered leadership begins."

He spent the next hour fielding questions, the mood celebratory. The committee was pleased with the project's progress and planned to meet back at the chateau again in a few months. The man took a sip of his champagne, knowing by then they'd be living in a completely transformed world.

CHAPTER 27

New York City

J on spent the day searching online job listings, polishing his resume, and creating a LinkedIn account. Famished, he decided on tacos from the new place down the block. He grabbed his jacket and walked out the door nearly plowing into a small boy toting a ragged teddy bear looking up at him, doe-eyed and fearful.

"Whoa!" Jon stopped short to avoid trampling the child.

"Hi," the boy said sheepishly, avoiding Jon's eyes.

"Uh, hi." Jon saw no one else. "Where are your parents?"

"Pawents," he said, attempting to copy Jon.

Jon couldn't see past the corner in the hallway. "Let's find them." Heading to the elevator, he turned the corner and stopped in his tracks. There, bent over tying a shoe was Carrie.

"Randy. Come here," Carrie called out as she stood.

The little boy came running back.

"Say hi to my friend Jon."

"Hi," the boy said again, his voice sweet and shy.

"We've met," Jon said. "What are you doing here?"

"We came to see you."

"Ever hear of a phone call?"

"I tried about ten times."

"That was you?"

"You look like hell. What's going on with you?"

"Listen, Carrie, you and I are not friends. Excuse me." He

tried to get by her. She stood in his way.

"I'm sorry, Jon. I truly am. My hands were tied."

"You lied to me. In my book of life, that's unforgiveable."

"I know. I can't take it back. I realize in your eyes it's not much of a defense, but I was following orders."

"Some things shouldn't be done blindly. You could have told your boss that you wouldn't take the job under those conditions."

"I didn't know you when I agreed to the terms."

This time Jon walked around her. "Cute kid, by the way. See ya around."

***

Ten minutes after he arrived at Taco Ted's, a basket of chicken tacos in front of him, Carrie and Randy walked in. The child was trying to pull his mother toward the counter.

"I'll order. Go sit with Jon." She placed a juice box on the table. The little boy climbed up into the booth next to Jon, detached the straw from the box, taking a full minute to carefully extract it from its plastic sleeve. Jon noticed the boy's frustration but sensed an offer to help would upset him.

After a few sips of his juice, the boy reached for the napkin holder, took one out, and twisted it. The intensity in his face was unsettling. He then used his straw to apply a droplet to the middle of the twisted napkin.

"What are you doing?" Jon asked.

"Doin'" The boy was mimicking again.

Jon watched amused as the napkin unfurled like a slow-moving spider. "That's cool. Let me try." As he did, Jon earned the boy's shy smile.

Carrie came over with a tray of tacos and condiments. "Hey, you two."

Jon put on a serious face. "You tailing me now? How'd you know where I was going?"

"Tricks of the trade. If you'll let me, I'll show you how." She put down the tray and handed a taco to Randy. "Nice octopus."

Jon said, "I gather bringing your boy is part of the strategy."

Carrie shrugged. "Whatever works. You and I had good working chemistry. We need to see the case through. I won't do it without you."

"That's no threat to me."

"But it is for me. I took a leave when I had Randy. When he was diagnosed last year with learning delays, I took another leave. I don't regret it, but I've called in all my chips with Langley. I won't be given any more leniencies. I want to move up in the organization and even today mothers are expected to give 110% to the job. If I blow this, I'll have a stain on my record that will take too long to erase."

"Now the guilt trip?"

"I'm not joking. I already spoke with my supervisor. I told him the deal. I'm with you on this or not at all. He didn't like it. Threatened to cite me for insubordination."

Jon raised a brow. "I can relate."

"But he needs me. I have the skills for this case. He said if I brought you back in you would be told everything, and if I didn't, I should expect to spend the next year behind a desk at Langley. I can't do that. My folks are here in New York. They watch Randy when I'm working. Please Jon."

Randy finished his taco and pointed to a poster of an ice cream pop.

"How about another taco?"

Randy scrunched up his face, shaking his head vehemently.

She laughed. "Only if we all can have." She eyed Jon. "What do you say?"

Jon looked at the excited little boy hanging on his next word.

"Yes!" Jon exclaimed.

Randy scooted over on the seat and leaned his head against Jon's arm, clearly startling Carrie. All Jon could do was melt.

***

"What now?" Jon whispered. He and Carrie were sitting in her car. Randy was asleep in the backseat.

"We go in tomorrow morning for a face-to-face with my boss. Let him meet you, explain the mission. Your boss will be there. If everyone can agree, we'll move forward as a team. If it helps, Agent Matthews didn't want you to be in the dark. It was all CIA red tape."

"I don't know how you can stand it."

"It's not all bad. The job can be exciting."

"We'll see."

***

CIA Regional Office
Downtown Manhattan

The first thing Jon noticed was how new everything seemed compared to the FBI headquarters. The flooring and light fixtures didn't date back to the '70s. He knew the New York headquarters had once been located at 7 World Trade Center. Destroyed on 9/11, it was subsequently relocated to the building he now found himself. He reached for his iPhone, remembering he'd left it in the lobby with the security guards. Seated on one side of the lacquered conference table were Carrie and her boss, Matthews sitting stiffly on the other. No one offered a greeting.

Jon took a seat beside Matthews. If the idea was to intimidate him, they were in for a surprise.

"Is this an interview?" Jon asked. The annoyance in his voice was palpable.

"Something like that," Carrie's boss said.

"Not interested. You need me. That's why I'm here. Make me an offer I can't refuse. And while you're at it, come clean on who the hell tried to kill me in Prague."

Matthews leaned toward him, and softly said, "You're set on doing everything possible to sabotage this, aren't you?"

Jon said aloud. "I'm not into game playing. Put all the cards on the table or I walk. This CIA crap isn't for me."

Matthews stared at Carrie's boss who nodded grimly.

"You appear to appreciate bluntness, so I'll offer you the same. The CIA does not dispense more information than necessary. These types of operations are strictly on an NTK basis. In my estimation a new recruit with no field experience had no need to know. But the attempt on your life changed things. I have spoken with both Agents Matthews and Santiago who have petitioned fiercely on your behalf. They seem to think you are an invaluable asset to this operation. So far I can't imagine why."

Jon was ready to leave when the man took a deep breath then blew it out.

"But I trust Agent Santiago who despite her extended leaves of absence, is one of our most promising operatives. She attests to your superior investigative instincts."

Jon saw Carrie grimace at her boss's back-handed compliment.

The man continued. "I've taken their assessments into consideration and will brief you on all the details. They are highly confidential. If you choose not to move forward, we will cut ties with the FBI on this matter and there will be no further discussion. Understood?"

Jon nodded.

The man clicked a small remote and a large screen descended from the ceiling behind Jon, forcing him to turn his chair around. Four photos were aligned side by side. Each was of a man in different clothing with varying hairstyles. One wore glasses. Jon recognized Spenser Germain, dressed in a suit and tie, seated in the House of Representatives. He identified Alexander Bilka from the Charles Bridge background. The other two were unknown to him yet all four could easily be identical quadruplets.

"Spenser Germain, Alexander Bilka, Felix Salko, and Owen Cantor. We believe they are clones of one another."

Jon swiveled his chair, gaped at Carrie's boss. "I didn't know that was possible."

"Neither did we. For decades there have been rumors of scientists attempting this. Our own government has worked on this for years. Remember Dolly? Scotland's cloned sheep was a success but the ethics of pursuing the science with human subjects would never allow for funding."

"How can you be sure these men are not some freak of nature?"

"That's where the operation comes in. We are procuring DNA samples from each of them."

"So, what if they're clones? Is it the commie stuff that's bothering you?"

Matthews interjected, "That's not the right question, Jon."

The room became strangely silent. "Then what is?"

Matthews said, "Who are they clones of?"

Jon stared at them. He looked back at the photos.

Carrie stepped in. "We have reason to believe these four men are identical clones of Vladimir Ilyich Ulyanov."

"Who?"

"The world knows him today as Vladimir Lenin."

CHAPTER 28

Rome, Italy

"**I** need more money."

Looking out the window at the Colosseum in the distance, Boris listened to his sniveling partner's complaints. The ancient amphitheater was a striking memorial to a more savage time in Roman history. He loved this city, even if it wasn't his own.

Boris addressed his partner, disheveled as usual, his graying hair hippie long. "There will be no more funding, Claudio. Make do with what we have left."

"It's not enough. What about the committee? If they are as excited about my progress as you say, why don't they help finance our venture?"

Boris held his temper. "They provide something much more valuable. Connections. They've cultivated long-standing relationships with some of the world's most powerful influencers. Not to mention they've bankrolled the boys from day one."

Claudio sulked. "It's complicated work. The project needs an influx of cash if the investors want another viable clone."

"You know very well only one benefactor remains. The others waited patiently for years. They believed you were stalling to milk them dry. If I didn't know you as I do, I would have agreed with them. It's too late in the game to court new investors for our confidential work. You're nearly done. I will not risk losing our last backer by pressuring him for more. Besides, you, my old friend, are a scientific genius. You have what you need."

Claudio looked away, spoke just above a whisper. "It's not *my* fault you were only able to get meager amounts of the extract components."

Boris was surprised by his partner's confrontational manner. It was out of character. "You still resent me after all these years?"

"It was only sufficient for three cloning cycles."

"That resuscitation extract is the only reason you are still on the payroll. You should have been able to replicate it by now."

"If Dr. Sousa had lived, I wouldn't have to replicate it. A respected scientist died in vain."

Boris knew his partner wasn't bold enough to directly accuse him of Sousa's murder. "As you know, there was no choice. We had a deal with the tribal chief, but he reneged."

"Only after discovering what you were truly after."

Boris was weary of the circular conversation. When Claudio was under pressure it resurfaced. He indulged him, nonetheless. "The tribe stood to gain valuable resources— medicines and building materials. The chief walked away from a once-in-a-lifetime deal."

"You should have found another way. Dr. Sousa's death was an unnecessary evil. Violence never leads anywhere good."

Boris laughed. "And what you are creating is not violence incarnate? Don't paint yourself as a righteous victim. It's unbecoming and disingenuous."

Claudio took a quieter tone. "My intentions are pure. I want to expand scientific horizons and create a better world."

As Boris walked to the door, he felt his restraint waning. A trace of anger seeped into his voice. "You know what they say about the road to hell, Claudio?"

When his partner didn't respond, Boris added, "Good intentions or not, if you don't produce results soon, we will both be headed down that road."

CHAPTER 29

Chicago

T he upscale bar along the Riverwalk was cordoned off
with decorative planters. Twinkle lights strung along
the awning reflected in the river below. The exclu-
sive event was by invitation only, a fundraiser for the cause—
AFND or Americans For a New Day. Carrie's boss managed to
procure them an invitation.

They had come to a tenuous understanding. Jon would
re-up on the sole condition he was fully briefed with Carrie.
To Matthews's credit, no mention was made of their falling
out or of Jon's unceremonious departure.

Jon presented their names to the well-dressed woman
at the door. In support of their new identities they had purchased appropriate attire, paid for by Carrie's office. Jon loved
his custom-fitted dress shirt with European collar and retro
cuffs. Carrie was radiant in a Dior black sheath number.

Jon accepted a glass of white wine. He recognized the
bottle the waiter held. There were big bucks behind this
event.

Felix Salko was easily identifiable. Though dressed more
fashionably, he was a copy of both Germain and Bilka. Jon
still couldn't get his mind around what these men were. Thus
far, there was no indication they were aware of their clones.
Nevertheless, the mission was clear. They were to obtain
viable DNA from each of the four men to establish beyond

reasonable doubt that they were indeed clones. Given the attack on Jon in Prague, the likelihood was high. Someone was set on impeding their investigation and considered murder an acceptable deterrent. Still, hard physical evidence was required for governmental action to be taken.

If the men were proven clones, more objectives would follow. Determine the existence of a coordinated underground movement and if present, dismantle it. Whoever was responsible would be apprehended.

Jon fondled the wedding ring on his left hand. For some reason it made him think of Randy. The boy was adorable. They'd taken well to one another and he hoped to see him again.

***

There were twenty tables decked in black and gold. A buffet of old Chicago's Polish cuisine was arranged at the back of the room. Kielbasa and pierogi were served by tuxedoed waiters. Jon sat beside Carrie who was sipping her chardonnay.

"Classy," he whispered to Carrie.

"Shh, he's about to start."

Felix Salko took to a small stage, ostensibly intended for the band whose name was headlined at the doorway. He wore a well-fitted suit, skinny tie, and smart glasses.

"It's a pleasure to see such an attractive and intelligent looking crowd here this evening."

The attendees laughed politely. Not all the tables were filled but it was still early.

"Please help yourselves to the buffet and wine bar. We'll get started in a few minutes."

Jon and Carrie walked to the buffet. A middle-aged well-groomed couple standing nearby were discussing their children. "I hope Mr. Salko has ideas for our inevitable college debt," the woman said to her husband.

"He's not a magician."

"Maybe if you hadn't invested in that failed tech company, we wouldn't need a magician." Seeing her husband's reddening face, she lowered her voice. "Sorry, honey. I didn't mean that. Maybe Mr. Salko has real ideas."

"That's why we're here. To listen to what he has to say."

Carrie interrupted. "Excuse me. I'm Carrie Lewis and this is my husband Jon. We couldn't help but overhear you. Don't you think Mr. Salko is a little young? He was just a child when the Cold War ended."

"Perhaps, but we like to keep open minds. Maybe the next generation knows something we don't. Has wider, fresher perspectives."

Jon interjected. "Or naïve, uninformed ones."

The man said, "Then why are you here?"

Carrie gave Jon a firm look. She replied, "I made him come. Open up his thick-headed mind a bit."

The woman laughed. The man didn't. He said, "If you'll excuse me, I'm heading to the chicken." The woman gave an apologetic nod and they walked away.

"What was that about?" Carrie asked.

"What?"

"Bringing attention to yourself?"

"Who cares? Felix isn't around."

"First rule of spycraft, never bring attention to yourself. Your goal should be to make yourself forgettable even after having a conversation. Those people will not forget you."

"Here's what *I've* learned. Guys like Felix Salko want to get close to people like Jon Lewis, the skeptics. To change their minds. It feeds into their God complex. If I'm not mistaken, we want to get close to him, do we not?"

Carrie gave a begrudging nod. They filled their plates and sat back down.

The presentation was more sophisticated than either Bilka's or Germain's. Less grassroots, more glamour. When Salko finished, the middle-aged couple cornered him. Several minutes later, Felix made a beeline for Jon and Carrie.

"See?" Jon said to Carrie with a smug smile.

"Touché."

***

Felix Salko extended a hand, which they each shook, introducing themselves. "I'm delighted to welcome new guests to our events. How did you hear about us?"

Carrie said, "Online. You've been getting a lot of buzz."

"Thanks. I have a terrific social media staff. One of the perks of being on staff at a major paper."

Carrie asked, "Sorry for the ignorance but are you a political journalist?"

"An editor, actually. I started my career at the *Tribune* right out of Northwestern. Been there ever since. At the time they were looking for a token left-wing columnist, as they called it. To balance out the paper's otherwise conservative bent. Thankfully, since then the media industry has become more enlightened overall."

Jon rolled his eyes. "Only to shamelessly *enlighten* the masses with their divisive philosophy. Whatever happened to objective reporting?"

Salko appeared hyped by the debate. "The days of Walter Cronkite and major networks obscuring their political leanings are long gone. Wouldn't you rather know where your news outlets stand than be deceived?"

Jon said, "Point taken. Still, your speech gave me the impression you'd prefer the non-liberal pundits be quieted altogether. As Americans we should be able to choose whatever media outlet we want to get our news from. Wouldn't you agree?"

Salko studied his opponent, leaving the question unanswered. "You have strong views."

Jon felt Carrie's forceful gaze. "I'm simply playing devil's advocate," Jon said. He gestured to the room. "You clearly have impressive financial backing. May I ask how that came about?"

"Mostly my own funds. I was left a generous endowment."

"And you chose to spend it on this?"

Carrie adopted an appalled visage. "I'm terribly sorry for my husband's rudeness."

Felix forced a smile. "It's my passion. I'm sure you can understand that. He looked at Jon. "Some things in life are worth putting everything on the line for. Wouldn't *you* agree?"

Jon hesitated, resulting in a poke in the ribs from Carrie. "Honey?" she said.

"Sure, yes, of course. Though I never felt that strongly about politics."

"This is not merely a political movement, Mr. Lewis. It's a way of life. Capable of positively impacting mankind for generations to come."

"Lofty goals."

"They're the only kind worth fighting for. No point in aiming low. If you'll excuse me." Salko gave a slight bow and walked toward the exit, pulling something from his jacket pocket.

Carrie nudged Jon's elbow. "Look at that."

Jon followed her line of sight. Salko was standing outside the bar's front window tapping a cigarette out of its packet. He lit up and took a deep drag, then lifted back his head as though admiring the clear night sky and slowly let out a stream of white smoke.

Carrie asked, "Did you know Salko was a smoker?"

"Come to think of it, he was holding a cigarette in the first photo I saw of him."

They watched as Salko took a final puff, dropped the butt on the ground and came back inside.

Carrie reached into her bag, pulled out a small plastic evidence pouch and slipped it to Jon.

"Go," Carrie whispered.

"Where?"

"Get the stub. We can get his saliva off of it."

Jon pocketed the bag and headed to the door, passing Salko on his way out.

"Had enough?" Salko asked. The smell of nicotine lingered on his breath.

Jon shrugged. "Just getting some fresh air."

Salko smirked. "I suppose my ideas aren't for everyone. But your wife's one smart lady."

"You don't even know the half of it." Jon stepped outside, watching Felix through the window waiting for him to turn away. Then, he bent down, picked up the cigarette, and placed it in the baggie. Jon was glad the job was done. Now, he could finally get the hell out of there.

CHAPTER 30

Dallas

Terry landed at Dallas-Fort Worth International, utterly exhausted. She'd intended to use the nineteen-hour trip to catch up on much-needed sleep, but only dozed for a short while. Instead, she'd spent the time ruminating over her conversation with Itai. The shock of his achievement hadn't worn off.

She stopped in the ladies' room to touch up her makeup, excited to see her boyfriend. Theirs was an unconventional courtship. Starting with a killing spree and now living thousands of miles away from each other. They'd met the year before when Gabe had flown to Israel seeking her scientific expertise on a matter related to his sister Ashleigh's violent death. In the process, they'd fallen for each other.

As Terry stepped into the arrivals hall with her bags, she felt schoolgirl jitters. The moment she saw Gabe, so handsome, grasping a bouquet of red roses, her heart leapt. He was beaming, just as overjoyed as she was to be reunited. She rushed toward him pulling her bags awkwardly behind her. They embraced, laughing. Gabe kissed her. "I missed you, Dr. Lavi," he whispered in her hair.

Driving by the University of North Texas, Terry felt a jolt of anxiety, recalling the assault she'd once encountered there at the hands of a deranged man. Until that day, she'd been confident she could handle anything.

Gabe instantly picked up on her body language. "Babe, it's all behind us, thankfully."

Terry nodded, trying hard to let it go.

Gabe asked, "How are your parents? How's work? Can you stay longer?"

Terry laughed. "My parents are great. Work just got very interesting. I'm proud for gifting myself this weeklong break. And no, unfortunately one week is as long as I could get away with. Thanks for taking off a few days to spend with me."

"Are you kidding? I've been counting the days."

Terry blew him a kiss. "How's the job?"

"I like my role at the refinery. I'm finally using my hard-earned degree in chemical engineering. Of course, having my uncle as a boss has its perks." He turned, winking at her.

"When are you coming back to Israel?"

"Let's talk about that later. I have a surprise for you."

Terry tried unsuccessfully to restrain a yawn. "Great!"

"Sheesh, what was I thinking? Let's get you to bed."

She smirked at him.

"Not what I meant, doctor. You need to catch up on your z's. I have a lot of fun scheduled for your time here and I'd prefer you to be awake . . . or most of it."

"Deal." She kissed his cheek, put her head back, and fell blissfully asleep.

***

"Good morning, beautiful. How did you sleep?"

"Like a *chayal* on leave."

"I have no idea what that means, but I hope it's good."

"It is," she said. "What is that heavenly smell?"

"Your fresh brewed coffee."

"You're a saint."

"I thought Jews don't have saints."

"You're right. You're a *tzaddik*."

"Ok, I can't pronounce it, but thanks." He leaned in to kiss her. "Ready for a spectacular Dallas day?"

"Sure."

"First have your breakfast in bed and tell me about your exciting work."

Gabe brought in two trays, each with a plate of French toast and steaming coffee. They sat side by side.

Terry ate ravenously. "This is delicious. I had no idea you could cook."

"One of my hidden talents."

She washed down her last bite with coffee. "I was just thinking about my colleague. He's made a tremendous breakthrough and I was fortunate to be one of the few he shared it with."

"Can you tell me about it?"

She shook her head. "It's confidential. But he asked me to meet with government officials to establish a committee related to the work."

"What did you say?"

"I declined. There's too much on my plate already."

Gabe looked at her tray. "Not as far as I can tell." He removed both their trays to the floor, closed the shades, and the two got reacquainted.

***

Terry and Gabe spent the next few days relaxing, taking long walks, and eating the best Tex-Mex Dallas had to offer. On her second to last day, Terry woke early and snuck out of bed to take a solo jog. The time with Gabe had been wonderful and she knew he was holding something back. Maybe he was planning a trip to Israel for an extended stay. She'd love that but didn't want to ask him directly. He would share his thoughts in due time.

Listening to her favorite playlist, Terry made her way to the nearby park, enjoying the quiet early morning. A warm breeze blew the dewy grass into diagonal green waves. She kept to a comfortable stride on the jogging path. After two miles, she decided a sprint would be a fun challenge and darted ahead, the next park bench her intended goal. When she reached it, she slowed, bending over to catch her breath. As she straightened, she was startled to see another jogger standing only feet away. With the music playing she hadn't heard her approach. Terry took out her earbuds. The woman was very fit, in her thirties, her dark corkscrew curls barely contained by a headband. She was moving closer. Instinctively, Terry reached for her pepper spray. Since her last time in Dallas she never left home without it.

"Ze b'seder, Professor." *It's all right.*

Terry was startled by the woman's Hebrew and that she knew who Terry was.

"My name is Shira. I work for . . . Yosef Kahn."

Terry crossed her arms, peered at the woman.

"I've been waiting for days to make contact, but it's been impossible to get you alone."

Terry's adrenaline subsided. "Why are you following me? You simply could have called."

"Israel's secret service doesn't make phone calls, Professor. We observe our assets before approaching in person. Come, let's sit."

Terry knew there was no point in arguing. She would hear what this woman had to say.

"Dr. Perlman informed us that you are unwilling to help your country."

Terry felt her earlier apprehension morph into irritation. "Seriously? That's how you choose to start this conversation?"

Shira considered that. "Okay, I shall rephrase. You are unavailable to oversee the medical ethics committee because you have too much work of your own."

"Correct. Among other reasons."

"And yet here you are on vacation in the United States."

Annoyed, Terry said, "Try again, Shira."

Shira nodded. "I see Jewish guilt doesn't work on you."

"Please just say your piece."

"B'seder. The Prime Minister has personally asked the Mossad to recruit you. He is requesting that your Technion work be temporarily reassigned to a competent colleague while you assist us."

"All this for an ethics committee? Something is not adding up."

Shira's expression remained unchanged. "All will be clear in due time. In addition, you will be amply compensated."

"This isn't about money."

Shira dismissed the comment with a wave of her hand. "Payment will be in the form of one hundred thousand shekel in state-of-the-art equipment for your genetics lab."

Terry's jaw dropped.

"I see I have your attention now."

"Someone knows my weak spot."

"That's our job."

A young couple in matching spandex ran past them.

Terry waited till they were out of earshot. She knew her next question would lead her down an unexpected path. "What exactly would I need to do?"

"Move temporarily to Jerusalem. Ample accommodations will be provided for you. You'll be notified of your instructions in due time."

Could you be more vague? Terry thought. "When would I begin?"

"Immediately. You have one day left here. Enjoy it. But speak nothing of this to your boyfriend. Or to anyone. You will be subject to strict rules of confidentiality for the duration of the project. Several weeks at most. I suggest you create some plausible reason for your absence, one that will discourage unwanted questions." Shira's expression turned grim. "Without exaggeration, this project may prove a quagmire of international security."

Terry understood there was more to this proposal than met the eye, and satisfying answers would come slowly, if at all. She remained silent for a full minute, deliberating. Shira did not interrupt her thoughts. "All right," Terry said. "I'll do it. For my country and my lab."

Shira's lips contorted into the semblance of a smile. "Meuleh." *Awesome.* We will be waiting for you at Ben Gurion when you land. L'hitraot." *See you later.* With that, Shira sprinted away as if the two women had never met.

CHAPTER 31

Chicago

J on fumbled for the buzzing phone, held it between his ear and the pillow.

"Jon?"

"Huh?"

Gabe asked, "You asleep?"

"It's two a.m., bro. Yeah, I'm asleep," Jon croaked, his throat dry.

"Terry said no."

Jon sat upright, turned on the hotel room's bedside lamp.

"You hear me? I'm Facetiming you. Answer it."

Jon accepted the video call. He saw his best friend's heartbroken demeanor.

Gabe said, "You look like a mess. Where are you?"

Jon wiped drool from his chin. "Chicago . . . for work. One sec—she said no?"

Gabe nodded somberly.

"What happened?"

"I planned a romantic picnic. Checkered tablecloth, wine and cheese, the works. Couldn't be more perfect. We toasted to a wonderful week and I did it. I got down on one knee and popped the question, ring box in hand." He paused. "She turned me down flat. Said she couldn't do it. Her life was too hectic. She loves me but needs a break from the pressures of commitment."

Jon watched Gabe put his head in his hands. "I knew I was taking a chance. We haven't been together all that long, but I thought at worst she would ask for more time, suggest an unofficial engagement. You know, keep it only between us till we were ready. Maybe even insist we talk about religion. But she said none of that."

"What *did* she say?"

"That she doesn't want to see me anymore." Gabe's voice caught. "How did I read this so wrong?"

Jon felt terrible for his friend. He knew how much he loved Terry and that the feelings were mutual. "Something sounds off. You've always been a hopeless romantic, but I don't think you misread her. Is it possible something else is going on?"

"Like what? We've been inseparable for a week, every day better than the one before. I even offered to give her time, come see her in a month. She blatantly refused. We're through, Jon."

Jon thought the whole thing bizarre but knew what Gabe needed was a shoulder to cry on. "Hey, how about I come down to Dallas? We'll hang out at The Blue Fox and shoot some pool. Drown our sorrows together. I'm back on the job, but I can ask for the weekend off."

"Thanks buddy but I need to be alone for a while, lick my wounds. Sorry I woke you."

"No worries. Call me anytime. And hang in there. Things will work out one way or another."

By the time the call ended Jon made up his mind to track Terry down and find out why the hell she broke his best friend's heart.

CHAPTER 32

Chicago

"**H**i honey, how was your day in school?" Carrie said into the phone as she ushered Jon into her hotel room. She held up a finger, mouthed, "One minute."

Jon sat on the edge of the bed.

"That's great, sweetheart. Can you put Nana on? Love you."

Jon heard her check in with her mother and was touched by their apparent closeness.

Carrie looked sad when she hung up. "I miss my little boy."

"I know. It has to be hard to be apart so much."

"I hope he forgives me."

"Of course he does. You are an amazing mother."

"Thanks, Jon, that means a lot." She looked out at the view of Lake Michigan, preoccupied. "From here it looks like an ocean." Then, "What do you make of Salko?"

Jon said, "Suave, educated, potentially dangerous if he gets his agenda out there."

"All the more so given his clout at the paper. Do you think he knows about his clones?"

Jon gave it thought. "My gut tells me none of them do. I'm not sure it matters though, practically speaking."

"It does if they collude."

"True. Matthews is convinced there's something bigger at play. A movement. I guess time will tell."

"Any word from the lab on the cigarette sample?"

Jon said, "No, I only dropped it off yesterday at the Chicago office."

"Hopefully they'll give it priority and we'll hear something soon."

Jon stood, pulled out his phone. "I need to take a few minutes for something personal."

"Everything all right?"

"Mostly."

"Go ahead, I just had my personal time. Now's your turn."

Jon stepped into the hallway and dialed Terry's number. He wanted answers not for himself but for Gabe.

The call transferred to voicemail. He left a short message asking Terry to call him back. He put his phone away and walked back inside. Carrie was getting off the phone.

"That was the lab. Salko's DNA matches Bilka's 99.5 percent. It's our first real proof they're genetically identical. We found our first clones."

***

Haifa, Israel

Terry was driven home from the airport in what appeared to be a taxi but was actually an escort by an agent of the Mossad, the country's foreign intelligence agency.

On the drive, she phoned her parents explaining she would be unreachable for an extended period and not to worry. As expected, the declaration had the opposite effect but after her reassurances that all was well, they let it be. They did however want to know about her trip to Dallas, to which she remained decidedly vague. Terry knew her mother would sense something was wrong but was grateful she managed to restrain herself. Perhaps her father was quietly reeling her in.

In truth, Terry was devastated. She'd killed two birds with one stone—kept her clandestine encounter with Shira from Gabe and ended the relationship with her non-Jewish boyfriend. She hadn't intended for things to happen that way, but she knew there never would have been a good time to break up. Given her recruitment by Shira, it became the most opportune one. Though pragmatic by nature, seeing the look on her beloved's face when she declined his proposal would stay with her forever. He was shattered. All she wanted to do was take it all back, apologize. But she couldn't. Regardless of the upcoming assignment, her heritage trumped any love affair including her own. In time they would both move on. *Wouldn't they?*

Terry packed for the next few weeks, while the driver waited in front of her building. When she emerged, she was showered, wearing a fresh change of clothes, towing her wheelie behind her. Her time in mandatory army service had taught her to pack only essentials in record time. Anything more she would need could be procured in Jerusalem. Despite the recent days' upheaval, she looked forward to being in Jerusalem. She loved the city. It was where she met Gabe for the first time. She smiled to herself at the memory. It was mind-boggling how much had transpired since then.

The driver made no attempt at conversation, which suited her just fine. Utterly exhausted, she was lulled to sleep by the cypress-lined landscape racing by. Two hours later she woke when the car stopped in front of a luxury building in the center of town. The driver wheeled Terry's bag to the lobby, providing her with keys to both her new apartment and the on-site gym. He left her in the hands of the security guard who directed her to the elevator, telling her to push the button for the twelfth floor. The apartment was beautifully appointed, purple irises were arranged on the kitchen's marble counter. Recruitment clearly had its perks.

Terry opened the electronic shades and was struck by the view. Large windows faced the old city of Jerusalem, the ancient walls lit up in blue and white. *Gabe would love this*, she thought.

In the fridge, she found two rolls of fresh sushi from Japanika, her favorite chain, and a bottle of Tishbi Riesling. She poured herself a glass and sat on the cream satin couch fiddling with an unfamiliar television remote. She watched ten minutes of Netflix and called it a night.

The next morning, Terry awoke well-rested in her sun-filled bedroom. The bed was perfect with soft white linens, billowy pillows, and a mattress with just the right firmness for her back. She wondered if the Mossad knew even that detail about her. She pushed aside the comforter, dragged herself out of the delightful bed, sniffing the air, alarmed at the aroma of fresh brewed coffee. She reached for her pepper spray on the nightstand fully aware an intruder wasn't likely to be helping himself to a cup. Despite that, she tiptoed into the kitchen, her arm outstretched and at the ready. No one was there. Someone had set the timer on the coffee machine, but how did they know when she would wake? Rather than dwell on the unanswerable, she grabbed milk from the fridge, added a splash to the mug, and downed the coffee.

The moment she drained her cup, she heard an unfamiliar ring. Its source was a screen prominently placed on the glass-topped desk near the window. There, Shira's face greeted her. Terry quickly ran fingers through her hair, then covered the camera lens with her forefinger.

"Good morning," Shira said, her voice devoid of the sentiment.

"If you don't mind, I would appreciate an old-fashioned phone call instead of Facetime at this hour."

"This is the newest tech. Your apartment has been wired

as a smart residence. It will quickly learn your habits and make your life much more efficient."

"That explains the coffee."

"Your floor sensors notified your coffee maker that you were out of bed. Subsequently, I was notified when your cup was filled ten minutes ago. Did I not wait long enough for you to drink it?"

Terry was struck by the absurdity of the question. "If you have a camera in the shower or anywhere else in this apartment our deal is off."

Shira seemed to mull that over. "One moment."

Terry heard tapping on Shira's end. "All right, all cameras are disengaged."

Seriously? Appalled that she had been viewable on camera, Terry said, "By the end of the day, I want to see in writing they will remain that way. And no more morning Facetime without my prior approval."

"Yes ma'am."

"I am going to shower now, and I'll call when I'm ready."

"No need to call back. Your driver will be alerted once you have locked your apartment door. Your first meeting is at 8:30. Please be punctual."

The woman had a penchant for getting under her skin. "Goodbye, Shira." Without waiting for a reply, Terry cut off the communication.

***

The Knesset was located in the center of the city, a modern, flat-roofed edifice fronted by a wide, open courtyard. The seat of parliamentary power, its security was tight but unobtrusive. An aide escorted Terry into the lobby, guiding her past a group of tourists listening to a young female docent explain the significance of the exquisite Chagall tapestries lining the walls. They took the stairs to the lower level where the aide left her outside a sound-proofed meeting room which doubled as a bunker in the event of an aerial attack. Terry entered the room.

Several men and women, some in uniform, others in civilian attire were seated around a rectangular conference table. Terry recognized many of the assembled from television. They represented the upper echelons of Israeli politics and military. The presence of so many high-ranking dignitaries had to be reflective of what would soon be discussed. She took her assigned place beside Itai, aware she was the youngest person in the room.

"Boker tov, Dr. Lavi."

"Good morning, Minister," she replied to the Minister of Defense.

"Thank you for being here. I know it was not an easy decision. We hope you will find it was the right one."

Next to the minister sat the director of the Mossad, Yosef Kahn, a handsome man in his early fifties. He offered her a curt nod. Terry had heard a great deal about him, much of it folklore. Yet consensus deemed Kahn a brilliant, skilled strategist and without question extremely deadly. Taking the lead, Kahn introduced the other members of the classified council, then opened the session. "Several weeks ago, Professor Itai Perlman made a startling breakthrough, one that under other circumstances would undoubtedly result in a Nobel Prize nomination. Given the sensitive nature of this discovery, that is unfortunately impossible at this time." He turned to face Itai. "Nevertheless, we in this room humbly take off our hats to you, Dr. Perlman. What you have achieved is remarkable and will serve the world in wondrous ways."

Itai nodded his appreciation.

Kahn said, "Please give us a summary of your findings."

Itai pressed a small remote. A hologram hovered above the center of the table. Terry had seen the 3-D image technology only once before at a conference in Switzerland. It still gave her goosebumps.

The perspective was of a microscope eyepiece looking down at a skin sample. The image quickly zoomed in to a spiral visible from all sides. Itai explained what they were looking at. "This is a simulation of a host's skin sample DNA string."

The group watched as a yellowish extract was applied from a glass pipette. "Here, the nucleus is being resurrected." The simulation continued. "The revived nucleus from the host sample is transferred to a cell whose nucleus has been removed." It was a highly simplified description of the process but did the trick. The panel was transfixed, watching in awe as the new zygote divided, then multiplied its cells.

Itai said, "We have successfully completed our first clone up to the blastocyst stage."

Terry watched as Itai made eye contact with Kahn who nodded.

Aloud, Itai said, "Of Albert Einstein."

A communal gasp echoed through the room.

"Where did you obtain his DNA?" This from a long-standing Knesset member.

Yosef Kahn interjected. "Following the death of our first president Chaim Weizmann in 1952, Prime Minister David Ben Gurion offered the post to Dr. Einstein. While he declined, he was a strong supporter of our fledgling state and did accept the Technion's request for his skin sample, which he provided three years before his death."

Itai turned off the hologram. "We have not yet achieved embryonic viability. For that, we need to improve the extract. But it's only a matter of time."

Several eager voices spoke simultaneously. One woman called out above the others, "This can easily lead to eugenics of the last century!"

Kahn pounded the table with his fist. "Hold your comments for now. I can already see where some of you will go with this. A task force of medical ethicists will be established to address all your concerns in due time." Once the room quieted, he said, "Thank you, Dr. Perlman. I will now make my presentation."

While Kahn made his way to the front of the room, Terry studied the council members more deliberately than when she'd first arrived, honored to be in such distinguished company. She remained bewildered as to why she was there. Surely, there were others equally qualified for the position of ethics chair. To her estimation, several were seated in the very room.

Kahn pulled down a projector screen. "Please excuse my old-world technology. It's what I'm most comfortable with." He turned off the room lights and flicked on the projector, illuminating a photo of a handsome dark-skinned man. "Dr. Alberto Sousa. A renowned ecologist and pharmacologist. Back in the '80s, he lived in the Brazilian Amazon among the native tribes learning their way of life and becoming familiar with some of the rarest organisms on the planet. His body was found in a motorboat on the Rio Negro, deep inside the rainforest, a poison dart protruding from his neck. His specimen kits were missing. While it was staged to appear like a tribal conflict, we believe he was murdered for what he harvested in the forest.

Someone asked, "What was he working on at that time?"

"Sousa was commissioned by the tribal chief to locate rare indigenous fauna and flora that we have since learned are vital for post-transfer cell longevity, the most complex stage of the cloning process. Obviously, this got our attention. At that time, we dispatched our operatives around the world to identify functioning cloning labs both on and off the radar. Their intel revealed that several countries were investing in startups in the cloning field. This was not shocking. We were doing likewise. The concept has been around since the turn of the last century, so it stood to reason this area of science would be explored. Given the inherent ethical issues, the research was conducted quietly out of the eyes of the media."

Kahn clicked the remote. A dated photo of an unsmiling

young man in a lab coat standing in front of a university building.

"Professor Claudio Giovanni, biotechnologist at the University of Padua. In 1983, Mossad agents gathered unsubstantiated intel asserting that at the behest of the Italian government, he was making significant strides in cloning science. This was thirteen years *before* Dolly the sheep was cloned in Scotland. No records could be found. Truth or legend, we didn't know. Now we do."

The minister appeared transfixed. "What did you discover?"

"He succeeded."

The captivated silence was broken by a collective gasp. Terry heard someone whisper, "Remarkable."

Kahn continued. "His lab was shut down due to its controversial nature. He reportedly abandoned his research when funding dried up. But not before he cloned two famous Italians. They would now be in their thirties."

The minister asked, "Where is the scientist now?"

Another click. A newspaper clipping from *La Repubblica* was projected onto the screen. "This is his obituary from September 2001. If the rumors were true, we suspected his research papers were sent to their national archives, a facility established in the twenties by Benito Mussolini."

Kahn shut off the projector and turned on the lights. He remained standing. "In order to bring you all up to speed I will need to provide a short history lesson. You will soon understand its relevance.

"In 1903, Mussolini, then an Italian revolutionary, and later the country's fascist dictator, was sent into exile in Geneva. At that same time another political refugee thirteen years Mussolini's senior, was living there, also in exile. Vladimir Lenin, the Russian father of Bolshevism. Many have speculated whether the two men actually met. Some suggest Lenin's protégé, a 25-year-old Jewess named Angelica Balabanoff made the introduction between the two future despots.

We contacted Angelica's great-niece who now lives in Tel Aviv. She provided invaluable documentation confirming the two men did indeed meet. One particular rendezvous was referenced which Balabanoff attended. The subject of that meeting was nuclei replication, later to be known as DNA cloning. It was an area of science being vigorously explored since the 1880s. From what we understand, the two men built a lasting rapport. They agreed to allow access to their remains for future harvesting. The objective was to resurrect themselves. According to their notes, they believed in the future, their own memories could be repopulated, and they would live again. While it was fantastical, eugenics was an exciting area of scientific exploration at the time. It was of course later abandoned once the world learned of the Nazi efforts to use eugenics as a means of creating a master race."

Terry was aware of the horrors of eugenics, having studied the topic in graduate school. In reality other first-world countries including the United States enacted immigration legislation based on eugenics, refusing immigrants from Asian countries deemed inferior by unscrupulous scientists. It's what sparked her interest in medical ethics.

The director of the Mossad continued. "Earlier this month I met with our counterparts at the CIA. We agreed to collaborate in this matter and share all relevant information on the subject. They subsequently provided us with a set of fingerprints procured by their agents. They belong to Alexander Bilka, an American professor of economics living in Prague, whom they have been watching."

"What brought Bilka to their attention?" the minister asked.

"He was flagged in their system along with several others."

Terry knew the cryptic response was intentional. She watched the minister type feverishly on his laptop.

Kahn moved about the room as he spoke, past the chairs of the other council members. "Armed with the prints, I sent a team to Rome. Their mission was to obtain Dr. Giovanni's records, if they existed. As we suspected, Bilka's fingerprints unlocked the chamber holding the archived records. It was the first indication of a living clone."

Terry spoke up for the first time. "Why would an American professor's prints open the archive chamber? Is Bilka running the cloning project now?"

"When the archives were established, Mussolini gave Lenin access if he should ever want it. It was a sign of collaboration between the two men. Fingerprint analysis had already begun in the late nineteenth century, primarily to identify suspected criminals and victims of crime. Whoever was the custodian of Lenin's fingerprints, coded them to access the archives once such technology was invented."

Others in the room appeared duly perplexed. With Kahn's presentation seemingly complete, silence returned to the room. He returned to his seat, directing his steely gaze on Terry.

Terry stared back at Kahn. "It can't be."

"It can and is, Dr. Lavi."

The defense minister piped up, irritated. "What are you two talking about?"

Terry cleared her throat, terrified to say the words aloud. "What Director Kahn is saying..."

Kahn projected a head shot photo of Professor Alexander Bilka.

The minister looked at the screen, his face registering a mix of amazement and fear.

"...Alexander Bilka is the living clone of Vladimir Lenin."

CHAPTER 33

New York City

C arrie and Jon were next in line. The SoHo bookstore was too small to accommodate the growing crowd attending Congressman Germain's book signing. Jon thought it was a good problem for a small business to have.

Gwen walked by and gave them a cool hello.

Carrie said quietly, "I'm telling you that girl hates me."

"She must be jealous."

"Or she's picked up on something about me."

"We've been through this. You have nothing to worry about."

Spenser looked up. "Jon Lewis and . . . Carrie." So nice to see you again. He sat behind a folding table laden with a stack of paperback books. He picked one up and signed it, handing it to Jon.

"How much?" Jon asked.

"On the house. I'm promoting it. But if you want to donate to the campaign Gwen will help you out." He flashed a charismatic smile.

"How about I just give it to you now?" Jon put a fifty-dollar bill in an envelope he'd brought, the money nearly falling out.

"Here you go. Oops." He watched as Germain licked the envelope shut and put it in his jacket pocket.

"Thanks, Jon. I hope to see you at our next rally."

Carrie shook Germain's hand and they stepped aside making space for the next person in line. Jon turned the book over. A professional headshot took up the back cover. "Should make for light reading," he whispered to Carrie.

Ten minutes later they were seated in the rental car. Carrie handed him the envelope Jon had given Spenser.

"I have to admit, when you concocted this plan, I was skeptical. But we pulled it off."

"I told you I've been trained in sleight of hand. It's what we spooks do." She grinned.

"You'll have to teach me some day."

"Sorry, tricks of the trade are not shared."

"Fine, then I won't teach you my unique skill."

Carrie raised a brow. "And what skill would that be?"

"Octopus making."

Jon felt a jolt of joy at hearing Carrie laugh aloud.

CHAPTER 34

Jerusalem

The council erupted in a flurry of commotion borne of fear. Kahn allowed a few minutes for the excitement to simmer down. He nodded at the Minister of Defense, whose hand was raised. He was one of few who kept a cool head.

"What did you learn from the Rome operation?"

"A great deal. The information we collected provided Dr. Perlman with the necessary data to expedite his work."

"Einstein," the minister said.

"Correct."

A middle-aged female member of the council interjected. "Just because we think of Einstein as a harmless genius, doesn't make his cloning ethical."

Kahn showed no signs of irritation at the interruption. "These are issues to be discussed. Likely for years to come. A new Knesset panel is being established exclusively for this purpose. It will be staffed by the foremost experts in science, religion, and ethics who will review all related matters. The technology has arrived whether we like it or not. If any country can lead the way effectively, it is Israel."

"Not to mention the benefits to the economy." The critic's tone was nothing short of sarcastic.

"No doubt, but one does not negate the validity of the other."

The woman persisted. "What makes you think there was only one cloning host?"

In the wake of the question, the room's temperature seemed to drastically rise.

"According to the documents, more cloning projects were in a planning phase when the project was shut down. Unfortunately, that line of investigation has gone cold. At this time, we don't know what became of them. However, one thing is indisputable. It is far easier to rid the world of DNA specimens than to eliminate living clones. And, I am certain you would agree, more ethical. If there were others, let's hope they are still in petri dishes."

The minister lifted a hand once again, squinting at his laptop screen. Kahn appeared glad to move on. "Yes, Minister?"

"Going back to the Rome operation, what if the fingerprints hadn't opened the archive's door?" he asked.

"We would have used our usual undetectable methods. Since we did not want to risk drawing attention to ourselves, the operatives photographed all the records rather than taking them." Kahn blew out a long breath, his patience seeming to wane. "Yaalah!" *Onward.* "Dr. Lavi, I need to come clean at this time."

Terry got an uneasy feeling. She knew the man's reputation as a shrewd, scheming spymaster.

"You've been brought here under mildly false pretenses. While I laud your contributions to medical ethics, your presence here is for a more urgent purpose."

Terry felt her face heat up. She despised deception. Which of course was the very nature of an intelligence service. Had it not been Yosef Kahn, she would have left the meeting without regret. Even with everyone's eyes focused on her.

"Given your past association with the American FBI, when we heard Agent Steadman was involved with this case, we knew you were the best candidate for the job."

Terry thought back to the last time she'd seen Jon. In New

York Harbor following an ordeal at the UN. "Jon is involved in this?"

"He is a good friend of yours, is he not?"

Probably not anymore, she thought.

When Terry didn't reply, Yosef said, "We need you to work with him again in the U.S. Learn all he knows."

Terry was livid. *That's why they really coaxed me here. The ethics panel position was simply a lure.* "You want me to spy on my friend? Do you see the irony? You recruit me as an ethicist and then ask me to conduct myself unethically. I won't do it." The council members' heads were bouncing back and forth between Kahn and Terry, like spectators at a tennis match. She didn't regret the outburst. After all, he had chosen to make the conversation public.

Yosef laughed heartily. The other members appeared skittish. "First of all," he said, calmly, "there's nothing unethical about defending your homeland. And secondly, I already said we are working *together* with them, not at odds. You can be as above board as—let's just say—we can allow you to be. And we expect the same in return from our American colleagues."

Terry calmed down. Here was another intelligence officer who got under her skin. More so than Shira. Only this one resided at the top of the totem pole. With all eyes on her, she knew declining the assignment was not an option.

When the meeting ended, Yosef took Terry aside. "Don't be annoyed with us. You are needed here, and we are very appreciative."

"Does this mean I won't be convening an ethics panel?"

He shook his head. "You can be as involved as you like, once you get back."

"Will I still get the funding for my lab?"

"Of course."

Terry let out a long-held breath.

"Tomorrow Shira will meet you at the Ofrit military base to brush you up on basic field skills."

Even as Terry knew with whom she was speaking, the private talk proved helpful. He had appeased her. For now.

***

Terry met Shira at the base at ten the next morning. She was given olive-colored fatigues like those she'd worn during her army service. It was necessary, she was told, to get her in the military mindset. The take-no-prisoners mentality. She was issued a Beretta Model 70 and followed Shira to the shooting range where they spent the next two hours practicing on paper targets and rubber dummies. It had been years since her army service, and she was glad to have the refresher.

Next, Shira reviewed basic hand-to-hand combat. There was a time not long ago when Terry was comfortable with this exercise given her krav maga training. That changed when she had been twice overtaken by assailants on her last assignment. Loath to admit it to herself, let alone aloud, Terry nonetheless swallowed her pride sharing the incidents with Shira.

"I'll demonstrate more advanced techniques, but training exercises cannot compare to the unpredictability of real life. You must learn to shut off your mind, control your breathing, and allow your instinctive reactions to kick in. If not, you're dead."

Nice pep talk, Terry mused.

The two Israeli women spent the next several hours engaging in krav maga maneuvers, and despite Shira's robotic bedside manner, Terry gradually began to respect her skill.

The day went by surprisingly fast. Terry was grateful for the distraction, away from thoughts of Gabe's face in the park after her rejection. When Shira drove Terry home, she handed over a letter confirming the disuse of monitoring devices in Terry's apartment. It was signed by the Mossad chief himself. Membership has its privileges.

***

On her third day waking up in the Jerusalem apartment, Terry had to admit she craved the Italian coffee aroma, the luxurious rainfall shower with four massage jets, and the soft background music that lulled her to sleep. She felt pampered and rested. Once she was dressed, she called Shira.

"What's on my schedule today?"

"Your driver is waiting for you. He will explain your itinerary. Yom tov." *Good day.*

At the curb, Terry saw her driver was none other than Director Kahn. Unaccustomed to being chauffeured by the head of the Mossad, she took a deep breath and got inside. It spoke to the gravity of her role.

"Boker tov."

"Good morning. Today you and I have a special meeting. After that we will discuss your further instructions."

Vague, but she expected nothing less from the man. Ten minutes later, when she saw where they were pulling over, she got butterflies. Two heavily armed guards stood at corner of Azza and Balfour Streets. One remained vigilant, the other greeted the director by name. He looked at Terry and said, "Hello, Dr. Lavi. Are you carrying a weapon?"

Still taken aback by strangers addressing her by name, she replied, "Yes, I am." She turned to Kahn. "Shira gave me one at our training."

"Leave it here. It will be returned to you when we leave."

Once she did so, the car was allowed to pass through the concrete barrier. Inside the complex stood a lovely villa surrounded by a flower garden and mature fruit trees. Terry recognized the citron, the distinctive yellow hue at its peak.

Kahn and Terry were escorted inside and told to wait in the sitting room, a sophisticated, yet unostentatious space. Gleaming white marble floors were topped by colorful, plush rugs, the furnishings a Mediterranean take on mid-century design. Terry imagined residences of this nature in other countries would be far more ornate. She was oddly proud of the restraint. She took a seat on a white leather sofa. Kahn remained standing as if on alert.

Their host entered, a warm smile on his handsome face, his hand extended. Terry stood, saying, "Prime Minister, it's an honor to meet you." She meant it. The man was a legend, both politically and militarily. His family had served the country admirably, his older brother giving his life to save his fellow Israelis in one of the boldest intelligence missions in the state's history.

When they were all seated, the Prime Minister asked Terry if she was on board with the assignment. She said she was. He explained that given the fluidity of the situation, the mission could take her away from her lab for several weeks. Was she still willing to move forward? She said she was.

Kahn sat silently throughout, giving Terry the sense she was being tested, with Kahn both her judge and jury. After several more minutes and an offer of sachlav, a warm vanilla-scented porridge—which they declined—the Prime Minister stood and excused himself. The guard showed them out and returned her firearm. From there Kahn drove her to the Knesset. This time it was only the two of them in an office overlooking the courtyard. Terry had no idea where the Mossad was headquartered and expected she never would.

"You are oddly calm, Dr. Lavi."

She laughed. "Not always. I've been called hot-tempered more times than I can count. But when faced with challenges I am at my best."

"I've noticed. It's a skill you will certainly need for this assignment."

Terry found herself pleased by the compliment, certain it didn't come easy to the man.

"Was the meeting with the Prime Minister a test?"

He laughed again. "You do say what you're thinking. A true sabra," referring to the cactus fruit-based moniker given to Israelis. Prickly on the outside, sweet on the inside.

"Here is the file. Please review it here in my office and ask any questions. From here forward your point of contact will be Shira. Her number is in the packet." He left her to read, closing the door behind him.

Terry noted he'd dodged her question. She spent the next hour reading every word of the file. When she was done, she made a list of follow-up questions and called Shira. To his credit, Kahn sanctioned answers without any measure of duplicity. She thanked Shira, left the file behind as instructed, and was driven to her apartment. She needed to pack again.

CHAPTER 35

Rome, Italy

Boris sat on the roof lounge of the Hotel Campo del Fiori overlooking the square's flower market. It was in this architectural delight that he kept a pied-à-terre for the occasions requiring an extended stay in the Eternal City.

As per his request, the roof was closed to other hotel guests whenever he needed some outdoor thinking time. He paid steeply for the privilege, but his most inspired ideas were born in such environments. Others found epiphanies in the shower, he in lofty outdoor spaces. He nursed his Negroni and allowed his mind to focus on recent events.

The early autumn sun was setting, casting a golden glow over the ancient city. From this vantage point he indulged in an inner sense of omnipotence, a connection to his revered great-granduncle. Power was coded in his genes.

In retrospect, enlisting the thug to intimidate the U.S. agents in Prague proved foolhardy. But when the Slav reported the two American spies appeared young and inexperienced, he made a rash, less thought-out decision. He didn't so much regret the thug's death as he did the result of his actions. Boris's sources informed him the agents were ramping up the investigation.

As the great-grandnephew of Vladimir Lenin, Boris was awarded the task of fulfilling his ancestor's wish. Boris's father left Lenin's letter in his will explaining his son's inherited responsibility—one that had been passed down from his father, and his father before him.

Along with Lenin's letter, the will provided a substantial endowment for whoever would oversee the project. Boris was fortunate to be the first to live in a time when Lenin's resurrection could be realized. But his penchant for expensive cars, his beloved Citation jet, and several homes had significantly diminished those funds. He was pleased he'd had the foresight to skim off the top of the investor's contributions, allowing him to maintain his comfortable lifestyle.

Boris took a sip of his cocktail, now watered down, and considered Claudio's words about evil. He never questioned that violence lived in his DNA. He'd come by it honestly. He'd read studies theorizing that prior generations' life choices became genetically coded, passing down to future generations. Any evils he would need to perpetrate were not his fault. He was wired that way.

Had it been over three decades since he met Claudio? They'd both been so young. Younger than the clones were now. Boris still believed it was kismet that he'd spotted the small article in the paper. A Milan laboratory experimenting with genetic cloning had been shut down. With the committee's approval, Boris reached out to the head scientist, Dr. Claudio Giovanni, vowing to help him complete his work, this time with private funding. If the scientist had any reservations about cloning Comrade Lenin, he never voiced them. All he wanted was to continue his work. And get his hands on the extract ingredients.

In the weeks that followed, Boris set up the secret lab, employing his connections to make Claudio disappear from the public eye. Eventually, he submitted the scientist's obituary to the local paper. No one questioned it. Once the extract was acquired, they agreed to test it first on Modigliani and Verdi. If those went well, they would proceed with Lenin. Boris couldn't risk creating a Frankensteinian version of his ancestor.

Finding carriers for the Lenin embryos posed no challenge. Following the Chernobyl disaster, infertile couples became increasingly desperate for a safe way to conceive. What was safer than embryos kept in a vault far from any radioactive pathogens?

Boris and Claudio were highly selective, seeking only the healthiest of women, who espoused a left-leaning political orientation. Once the best candidates were chosen, Boris explained the terms. He would provide for the children and be solely responsible for their education, checking up on them periodically from afar. He never told the couples of their children's clone status. Even now, he believed it was unnecessary. They were overjoyed to be parents and would consent to anything to fulfill that wish.

Boris and Claudio had worked together ever since. Given their respective natures, Boris took on the investors, wining and dining them while Claudio worked diligently in his lab. He recalled the euphoria when they discovered the cloning had worked and Lenin would rise again. They'd been following the clones closely ever since.

He would never admit it to Claudio, but he was right. Eliminating Dr. Sousa nearly upended the project. When the tribal chief backed out of their deal, Boris had no choice. He couldn't risk Sousa learning about their work. A message the scientist believed was sent by the chief requested he forage for the extract's necessary ingredients. In reality, the dispatch had not come from the chief, but from a rival tribesman Boris had bribed with a shipment of antibiotics. In return, the Amazonian followed Sousa, appropriated the organisms . . . and killed him.

At the time, the hit seemed prudent. Boris had considered taking out the chief as well but decided that was ill-advised. Poking the bear in that part of the world would unleash unpredictable results. Boris, if nothing else, was a practical man. He'd weighed his options with the assumption he would soon find someone to retrace Dr. Sousa's steps, and harvest more of the ingredients.

That didn't happen. In the wake of Sousa's death, the local authorities closed off the area, completely banning access to that part of the rainforest, leaving Claudio with precious few components. Those had been used long ago on the early clones. In the years to follow, hundreds of thousands of dollars had been spent on developing a synthetic extract.

Eventually, all but one of the benefactors backed out. Boris never regretted eliminating governments from the investor pool. Maintaining control of the project was only possible with private funding. With the exception of his undeclared service fee, what remained, covered Claudio's salary and hefty lab expenses.

Boris left his empty glass on the roof's ledge and returned to his room. Given the short flight from Rome, Boris decided to begin with Alexander Bilka. He booked a flight to Prague for the next morning, ecstatic he would finally meet his great-granduncle in person.

CHAPTER 36

Jerusalem, Israel

Terry wiped the tears from her face as she placed her written prayer between the ancient stones of the Western Wall. She stepped back, careful not to interrupt the murmured supplications of the pious women dressed in long skirts and head scarves seated nearby. Worshippers of all faiths had been unburdening themselves at the holy site for nearly three thousand years. The steady hum of prayers bolstered her spirits.

Terry returned the sarong she'd been given to cover her slacks to the elderly custodian and crossed the wide plaza. It was early, the sun's rays would soon peek over the wall, the chill in the air burning off. She ascended the stairs to the Jewish Quarter, navigating through a throng of black-hatted men, their eyes gazing downward, hurrying past her on their way to morning services.

With her flight back to the States scheduled for the afternoon, it was a rare chance to wander the Old City. The upcoming trip would be different from the last. She wouldn't see Gabe. He wouldn't even know she was back in his country. The thought forced a tear from her eye.

Terry weaved her way through the ancient streets, finding herself in the Arab Quarter. The fading echo of the musaharati's drum reached her ears, a wakeup call to devout Muslims to eat before the Ramadan fast.

The narrow alleyways of the souk were deserted, the market's plastic awnings absorbing any natural light. Stalls normally showcasing colorful tapestries and painted olive wood trinkets were shuttered in reverence to the holy month. A dove cooed from its nest atop one of the stalls, the sound of Terry's clacking heels the only other disturbance. The solitude was just what she needed.

A sign written in Arabic directed her to Damascus Gate, one of few arched pass-throughs built into the Old City walls. As she rounded the corner, the gate came into view, its façade brightened by daybreak. A hunger pang brought on a craving for a butter croissant and latte from Café Rimon. As she checked the time on her phone, Terry was swiftly pulled backward into the shadows, an arm snaked around her neck. Her throat closed, no sound could escape.

With lightning speed, Terry slid her hands down the back of her head, hooking them hard on the attacker's wrists, creating a gap. She tucked her chin to her shoulder and struggled to get her head out. Unrestrained, she turned, and like a charging bull forced her head into the attacker's stomach, grabbed at the waist, and flipped the assailant onto the ground, grazing the tip of her unsheathed Swiss army knife along the carotid artery.

"Metzuyan!" *Excellent!*

Breathing hard, Terry stared at the immobilized assailant. "Shira!"

"Well done, Doctor Lavi. I couldn't have reacted better myself. Mind giving me a hand?"

Terry employed every ounce of restraint not to kick the woman. "You scared the life out of me! Are you insane?" After a moment, she helped up her trainer.

Shira brushed the dust off her camo pants. "I needed to know you were ready for the mission. Actually, *you* needed to know. Your confidence was shaky. I will be your handler, and a handler is only as good as her asset. Understand?"

Terry leaned against the alley wall, closed her knife,

pocketing it. "I could have killed you," she whispered.

Shira didn't appear disturbed by the pronouncement. "This is how we prepare our new recruits for the real world. You passed with flying colors. You allowed your instincts and training to take over. You're ready."

Terry felt her fear, anger, and adrenaline subside. "I need a coffee. Now."

Shira's lips twitched into the semblance of a smile. "It's on me. You've earned it."

The newly minted Mossad agent and her handler stepped silently through Damascus Gate and into the New City.

CHAPTER 37

CIA Headquarters
Washington, D.C.

J on watched his best friend's ex walk into the meeting room. "Hello, Terry."

It was surreal to see her here in the CIA headquarters. She was even thinner than when he last saw her. Along with her small stature, she looked immensely vulnerable. He knew she prided herself on self-sufficiency, but her appearance concerned him.

He was glad there were other agents in the room. It kept him from deciding whether to hug her. As his best friend's ex, the rules were unclear. But with Matthews, Carrie, and her CIA boss present, a hug wasn't appropriate.

Terry offered a cautious smile. "How are you? I haven't seen you since ...?"

"The UN debacle."

"Right."

An awkward silence ensued. Thankfully, Carrie came to the rescue. She looked the consummate professional. More corporate than spy. "Dr. Lavi, I'm Agent Santiago. Carrie. Glad to meet you." She gestured to a file in her hand. "I read your profile. You have quite an impressive dossier."

Terry smiled her appreciation. "I've seen yours as well. Your skillset is admirable."

Carrie's boss invited them all to sit around the conference table. It was large enough for twenty but with only five attendees they clustered together toward the middle. A male receptionist rolled in a cart with coffee and pastries, placed the items on the table, and left. Each of the participants opened their respective laptops.

"This meeting is for the express purpose of sharing information. The mission has been placed under the auspices of the CIA's Directorate of Science and Technology. You've all been briefed on the details so far, so let's keep this meeting to new intel only.

"To date we have made contact with three of the four known clones of Vladimir Lenin. They are Congressman Spenser Germain in New York; professor of economics, Alexander Bilka in Prague; and Felix Salko, newspaper editor in Chicago. The fourth is Judge Owen Cantor located here in D.C. His DNA has not been acquired, but given his appearance, we've decided it won't be necessary. He remains on the list. You will find his picture in your files. All four men are heavily involved in left-wing politics, with one—the congressman—suspected of being at the helm of a virulent organization. So far, there's no evidence of a collaborative movement among the clones. That's what you will look for."

Jon asked, "Do you suspect there are more Lenin clones we haven't found yet?"

Terry jumped in. "Scientifically, the likelihood of more than four viable clones from one host is statistically miniscule."

The CIA man nodded. "Our Israeli friends have confirmed the DNA match of Professor Bilka and we have done the same with Salko. We should have results soon from the congressman. The Mossad has shared valuable intel on the origin of Lenin's host sample and how these four men have come to be the clones we are investigating today. You'll find it in your dossiers.

"Each of you will infiltrate one of the clone's inner circles. Agent Steadman will stay with the congressman. Santiago, I'm assigning you to Salko, and Dr. Lavi, you're with Owen Cantor. Stay close to your marks. Your mission will be to learn everything you can, determine their true objectives, who they confide in. You must track down those responsible for their existence. We suspect we're only seeing the tip of a dangerous iceberg.

"What about Professor Bilka?" Jon asked.

"Given your recent altercation in Prague, we will try to avoid offending the Czech Republic with our presence unless it becomes absolutely necessary. Unfortunately, they got wind of your recent visit."

Carrie's boss paused, waiting to see if more questions would come. When they didn't, he said, "We'll reconvene next week." He looked at his watch and stood. They'd been dismissed.

***

Terry assembled her papers and laptop. She had already reviewed her assigned clone, Judge Owen Cantor, and would do so again before going into the field. She observed Carrie Santiago from across the room speaking with her boss. Dressed in a tailored pants suit and heels, the woman was stunning. Tall, built like an Olympic swimmer, enviable complexion. She wondered if Jon was taken with her. It would be easy to imagine. But she knew he'd recently broken up with Melanie and doubted he could transfer his feelings so easily. *Could a man move on so fast?* she wondered. She hoped not. The thought of Gabe with another woman made her sick to her stomach.

As the group dispersed, polite small talk was exchanged. To Terry, the difference between American and Israeli business etiquette was stark. Things were substantially more formal in the U.S. Having lived in Boston as an adolescent, Terry was familiar with the culture, but felt more comfortable with a more relaxed work environment.

Jon approached Terry. "Have a minute?"

"Sure."

"Glad you're on the case."

"Seems I was assigned partly because I know you. I am not sure that will be a benefit given the circumstances." She walked toward the door. Jon followed.

"That's sort of what I wanted to talk to you about. Did you get my voice message?"

"No, when I accepted the assignment my phone became off limits. Let me guess. You called to defend your best friend's honor." She said it without malice. More so with respect. Loyalty was a rare commodity these days, she mused, aware that she herself was a transgressor.

"He's devastated," Jon said. "Now that you're on the job, I'm wondering if you were asked to dump him."

"I don't like that word."

"I don't sugarcoat. I'm a lot like you that way. Let's call a spade a spade. That's what you did, so I'll stick with dump."

She grimaced but didn't argue further. Carrie came out into the hall and looked at them. She waited a beat, then walked away.

"She's lovely," Terry said.

Jon replied, "She and I have had some issues, but she's smart."

"Sure, if you call Mensa smart."

"What?"

"Didn't you read her file?"

"No. It was never offered to me."

"Hmm, interesting," Terry said.

Jon looked irritated. "That's not what I wanted to talk to you about. It occurs to me you ended things with Gabe because of this operation. You'll be back together when this is all done. Right?"

Terry looked solemn. "You're a great friend to Gabe but this is really none of your business."

"Gabe's a brother to me. He deserves an explanation."

She waited a beat. "I admit I handled things very poorly. It kills me that I hurt him. But while this assignment expedited the breakup, it was not the cause."

"Religion?" Jon whispered.

Terry glared at him. "How do you know that?"

"Gabe's not stupid. He knows how important your heritage is to you. But he says you never even discussed it with him."

"What would be the point? A coerced conversion is the same as no conversion."

"Love isn't coercion."

Her cheeks turned crimson. She lowered her voice. "This isn't something I'm comfortable talking about. Whether or not you agree with my decision, it remains mine to make." She took a deep breath. "I hope we will be able to work effectively together."

Jon shook his head. "I don't understand any of this."

He stomped away, and ran after Carrie, leaving Terry on the verge of tears.

***

"Is there something personal between you?" Carrie asked, as Jon walked her to the parking lot.

"Terry and I worked together in the past." He paused. "Actually, it's way more complicated than that."

"I won't ask. But it's an odd coincidence that you'd be working together again, given you represent different countries. Particularly since she's not a trained intelligence officer."

"No coincidence. They brought her in *because* she knows me. The powers that be seem to think we'll work well together."

Carrie got into her silver SUV, started the ignition, and buzzed down the window. "From the little I saw, you two have some unresolved issues. Let's make sure they don't get in the way." Jon watched her pull out of the lot and drive away.

CHAPTER 38

Prague, Czech Republic

Professor Alexander Bilka exited his girlfriend's building. He enjoyed spending time with her but she was no intellectual. Her interests lay in makeup, weight loss, and fashion. Any efforts on his part to discuss political economics resulted in a blank stare and confusion as to what he was jabbering about. In all fairness, her attention to the aesthetic certainly paid off. She was a Czech beauty. Stunning on the outside. Empty on the inside.

The autumn chill was a welcome surprise and he was glad to have his travel coffee mug in hand. He'd gotten off to a slow start this morning. It was already ten o'clock and he had a great deal to prepare before his upcoming lecture. He made a mental note to call his mother. While her prognosis was good, the chemo had taken his toll.

The traffic was heavy this morning. He looked both ways and was crossing the thoroughfare when a man in his sixties approached him. He was dressed in Italian couture, his graying hair precisely cut as if he'd just left the barbershop. Though Bilka was certain they'd never met, he looked oddly familiar.

"Alexander Bilka," the man said. Not asking. Affirming.

"Yes, sir. Have we met?"

"Not formally, but in a manner of speaking, yes, we have. Needless to say, you are famous in my book."

Weirdo. "Perplexing. If you'll excuse me, I need to catch

my tram."

"May I join you?"

Alexander frowned. He'd hoped to get some work done on the commute. "I suppose there's nothing to prevent us from taking the same tram."

The tram arrived as they reached the curb. The men paid their fares and took seats beside each other.

Boris said, "Allow me to introduce myself. My name is Boris. I am American, living part time in Italy."

"What brought you to Prague, vacation?"

"No. You."

Slightly alarmed, Bilka asked, "Are you a proponent of my writings?"

"You could say that. But as it turns out we are actually related."

This caught Bilka's attention. He did not have much family. He was an only child. His parents had been infertile for years before he came along via artificial insemination. They had always been open with him about it, making him feel like a blessing his entire childhood. They showered him with affection.

"I thought I knew all my extended family. Did you find me on one of those genealogy websites?"

Boris didn't answer directly. "We share much of the same genetics. We are both members of the Lenin family."

"John Lennon? That's amusing. I'm not musical in the slightest."

Boris smiled patronizingly. "Vladimir Lenin."

"Oh."

"It's no coincidence you have your particular communist leanings. They are in your genes."

"I'd like to think I've come to my own thought-out conclusions."

Boris waved a dismissive hand. "Nonsense. You were brought up in the quintessential American family. Public schools, Princeton graduate, a short stint in corporate finance, followed by a PhD. Not the typical path to communism. It's in your blood."

Bilka looked around at the other passengers. "I'm somewhat disturbed that you know so much about me."

"All these things are readily available online. But I know far more."

Bilka's curiosity morphed into unease. "This is my stop. I need to go."

He got off the tram, tightened his neck scarf. Boris walked beside him.

"I can help you, Alexander," Boris said.

Bilka walked fast, hoping to shake off the old man. "With what?"

"Building the movement you are so desperate to spearhead. I know your aspirations. I want to help you achieve them."

He gave the man a sidelong glance. "Why? What do you gain from that?"

"Fulfilling my great-granduncle's deathbed wish."

"Lenin? What did he wish for?"

"To come back to life."

Unsettled by the strange man, Bilka stopped walking, made eye contact. "I don't understand."

"He did it, you know. He came back to life."

An overwhelming sense of dread came over the professor.

Boris placed a hand on Bilka's arm. "You, Alexander, are him. You are Vladimir Lenin."

***

Bilka's coffee had turned cold and his body shivered. The strange man had convinced him to sit a while in the school library. They found a quiet corner in the biography section.

Boris took an envelope out of his jacket pocket. "This document will confirm what I have told you. It is for you to keep. The original is in a safe place in Rome."

Bilka warily opened the envelope, took out a single piece of paper. It was a well-done reproduction of a hand-written letter. It was written in Russian. "I'm a bit rusty in Cyrillic."

"There's an official translation on the other side. You can easily verify its accuracy on any app."

Bilka read aloud, his hand tremoring as he did so. "I am Vladimir Lenin, Chairman of the Council of People's Commissars of the Soviet Union. I submit my mortal remains for safekeeping. In the future when science has unleashed the power of resurrection, I wish for my body and memories to be restored. I will once again humbly lead the masses to equality, strength, and imperialism. Signed V. Lenin, January, 1924."

He put the paper down on the table. "How do I know this hasn't been forged?"

"This letter was attached to his will and testament. It was given to his niece, and eventually passed down to me. As far as its authenticity, you can compare it to other documents written in Lenin's hand. Could it be forged? Certainly. But it wasn't. Your existence is proof that the letter is true."

Bilka stared at the letter, dumbstruck.

"Prior to being embalmed, Lenin's skin samples were harvested. One day you may choose to visit his mausoleum in Red Square. His remains are on public display there."

Boris placed another sheet of paper on the table. "This is your genetic mapping, as well as of others whose DNA matches yours precisely."

Bilka blanched. "What are you saying? I have twins?"

"No, Alexander. You have duplicates. You are all identical clones of Lenin."

Bilka shook his head in denial. "There are two different handwritings here."

"Excellent observation. Yes, the other was written by his collaborator for this venture."

"It looks like Italian."

"It is. The author was Benito Mussolini."

Appalled, Bilka said, "The dictator."

"The revolutionary. Like Lenin. Like you."

CHAPTER 39

Georgetown University
Washington, D.C.

Healy Hall seemed to go on forever. Terry walked briskly by the magnificent Gothic edifice, its towering parapets the iconic image of Georgetown University. The regal building exuded old money and privilege. Turning the corner, she passed sweater-clad students seated on the leaf-strewn grass, their book bags scattered about. Some were studying, others blissfully laughing with friends, oblivious to the world's ills.

While researching Cantor, Terry learned he was scheduled to speak at today's symposium, *The Ten Most Influential People Under 40.* This is where she'd make contact.

The hall was filled with students and faculty. Recognizable in many academic circles, Terry wore a lanyard displaying her name and credentials. She sat in the front row, directly across from Owen Cantor. There was no confusing him. Slim, intense, Slavic.

The afternoon went smoothly. As a lecturer at Technion, she'd forgotten how much she enjoyed sitting on the other side of the lectern. During the Q & A session, she made a point of drawing attention to herself, asking probing questions, genuinely interested in the answers. When the program concluded, everyone gathered their things and dispersed. Following her plan, she did not approach Cantor. She would wait for him and only initiate if necessary. It wasn't.

On the way out the door, she heard from behind, "Professor Lavi?"

Terry kept her face flat. "Yes?"

Cantor fell in step beside her. "It's an honor to meet you."

She offered a tight smile. "Judge Cantor. I enjoyed your presentation."

"I'm honored you attended. Your reputation as a premier geneticist is widely known. Perhaps we could grab coffee, chat one-on-one?"

"I don't think that would be possible. I have another engagement shortly. She looked at her wristwatch. "Feel free to email me."

To his credit, Cantor didn't give up. "Email is so impersonal. How about after your appointment?"

Terry nearly laughed aloud.

"Not even for one of the youngest judges appointed to the federal bench?"

She smiled more broadly. "You have a bright future. I will be able to say I knew you when."

He seemed to like that. "Is that a yes?"

"All right. Coffee. I saw a place on the main road near the bookstore. I'll meet you there at five."

"Terrific. Thanks, Doc."

***

Over the next several days Terry met Judge Cantor for coffee two more times. She feigned deep interest in his philosophy. No mention was made of his connection to the other clones or to a more widespread movement. Unsure how to proceed, she called Jon. She needed to get things back on track with him anyway. The longer the friction lingered, the worse things would get. He picked up on the first ring.

"Terry." No hello.

"Still mad?" she asked.

"I'm not mad."

She moved on. "I need some guidance. I'm getting nowhere with Owen Cantor. Are you having any luck with the congressman?"

"He doesn't publicize it, but he started the SAU and they're building serious steam."

"What is that?"

"The Sam Adams Underground. It's essentially a group of unarmed student communists dressed in fatigues demanding a change of the guard. They're growing rapidly across campuses."

"Sounds more like a coup. But Judge Cantor is not like that. He has a more subtle, clinical approach. I can't see him connected to that sort of movement. I'm fairly certain he has no awareness of his clones. But if Germain will be on the news, that can't last very long considering how similar they look. People are bound to notice."

"I hadn't thought of that," Jon said. "Maybe that's not a bad thing. Let's see how it plays out."

"Any suggestions on what I do with Cantor at this point?"

"You're doing what you're supposed to. Just keep gathering intel and store it away."

"There *is* one thing I need to look into."

"What?"

"He mentioned a virtual guru he's had for years. Someone he asks questions to online."

"That could be something."

"I'll try to find out more. Thanks for the ear."

"You're welcome. Maybe you can call Gabe, check how he's doing."

"That wouldn't be wise."

"Are you scared you'll fall back in?"

She paused, deciding if she should answer. "Yes."

Jon's voice turned softer. "Then perhaps there's nothing wiser."

CHAPTER 40

New York City

The chat with Terry did little to allay Jon's confusion. He couldn't share with Gabe anything about the case or that Terry was working with him. It felt like lying, something he despised most. He'd figure something out.

With all the recent travel he was glad to be home. He took a step toward the cabinet where he kept the whiskey, wondering if there was any left. Then stopped. He went instead to his kitchen, grabbing a soda from the fridge, then sat at his desk, and powered up the desktop.

The investigation was moving slowly. Publicly, Germain gave no hint of being anything other than what he purported to be—a visionary with no hidden agenda. Despite Germain's suave manner, his presentations had taken on a more militant vibe. Unless he espoused a treasonous stance, his role in the SAU was not actionable. Jon thought it ironic that the rights of free speech and assembly were his protectors.

It wouldn't be long before Germain expected his full commitment to the cause. Gwen seemed calmer now that Carrie wasn't around but remained aloof. If nothing else, the girl had good instincts.

It occurred to him that Germain never brought up the misplaced fifty. Which made Jon think of Carrie's unexpected pickpocketing skills. Which made him think of what Terry said about Carrie's bio. He really didn't know anything about his new partner's background other than the little she'd told him. He decided to do something about that. He emailed Matthews and twenty minutes later was reading her file on his computer. It read like a gripping novel. Immigrant grandparents. Army brat. Fluent in five languages, skilled in sleight of hand, black belt in karate, two years in the Air Force. Then Harvard and Yale. Married, kid, divorced.

Jon closed the tab. His partner was the quintessential overachiever. Almost like she had something huge to prove.

***

Chicago

Carrie was disappointed when she'd been assigned back to Chicago. She was hoping to stay in New York with Randy. His selective mutism had recently picked up again. His therapist had increased treatment to three times a week. She was worried but didn't consider requesting a swap with Jon. Gwen was onto her and besides, this was the job she'd signed up for. They had already made many accommodations for her, and now she had to prove herself. Again.

Sticking with her previous backstory, she had emailed Felix Salko directly using the address he'd given out at his last fundraiser. He responded five minutes later, inviting her to the evening's event—a sunset boat ride on the Chicago River. The ticket price was outrageous, but her boss had given her a generous expense account. If she could get close to Salko, it would be worth it. Carrie took her place on the queue, her mind reverting to her son. Maybe she'd bring him here when he got older.

The evening was unseasonably warm for late autumn. Thirty or so people were lined up on the dock for the architectural tour, one of the Windy City's most popular attractions. Ahead of her in the queue was a young woman wearing a press pass standing alongside a short man carrying an expensive-looking camera around his neck.

Once on board she avoided posing for press release photos and went below deck where she found Felix Salko standing by the bar reviewing his notes. He looked up. "Hello, Mrs. Lewis."

"Hi, Felix."

He looked behind her. "Is your husband here?"

She shook her head. "He couldn't make it today."

He nodded. "He doesn't care for my politics."

Carrie shrugged. "I'm sorry."

"There's nothing to apologize for. You're here."

Felix's phone buzzed. He looked at the screen, excused himself, and stepped away, typing furiously.

Carrie took the stairs up to the viewing deck, delighted by the sweeping panorama. The tour guide was explaining the design of the Wrigley Building, a marvel in its day and still a beautiful mainstay of the city's skyline. It was obvious Felix Salko knew how to throw a fundraiser. It was classy but not stuffy, attracting an intimate, monied crowd. Word was spreading in the right circles.

When the boat reached Lake Michigan, the guide handed the mic to Felix. Carrie listened as he introduced his team. All educated and well dressed. He announced a museum benefit scheduled for next month. Proceeds would be evenly divided between his think tank and a local special needs program. He spoke eloquently, projecting an easy confidence.

Ten minutes into his speech, Carrie went downstairs and found what she was looking for. Felix's satchel. The bartender eyed her. "Can I get you something?"

"A gin and tonic would be great."

When he turned away, Carrie deftly swiped Felix's phone and slipped it into her sleeve. The barman handed her the drink fully unaware. She left a ten on the bar, sipped her drink, placed it on a table, and walked to the ladies' room.

Inside, she was pleased to see there was no password

needed. Millennials had no sense of privacy, she thought. She had been prepared to steal the device and crack it later, but this was better. She quickly scrolled through his texts and calls. The most recent correspondence was from thirty minutes ago when he'd abruptly left their conversation. The text stream was with someone unnamed. Using her phone, she took photos of the texts and the phone number. The whole process took less than five minutes. When she came out Felix was standing there looking disappointed. Her stomach flipped.

"Sorry you missed my talk," he said.

"Not at all. I heard everything except the last few minutes. I needed the restroom."

"What did you think of my presentation?"

"Very impressive. You are exceptionally well-organized. And I couldn't agree more with your proposal for universal healthcare."

He seemed pleased with her assessment. "I wrote an article in last week's op-ed. Let me show you." Felix made a move toward his bag.

Carrie took hold of his arm. "You deserve a drink." She turned to the barman and said, "Please make something for Mr. Salko, on my tab."

Felix smiled. "Thank you. I'll have a rum and Coke."

Carrie used the distraction to stealthily return the phone to his bag, then went back for her drink. She raised her glass, waiting for Felix to do the same. "To fair winds and a following sea!"

Pleased with herself, Carrie watched her mark readily drink to her toast.

***

New York City

Boris learned from his mistake with Bilka. He would approach the other clones with kid gloves. Appeal to them with affection, not fear. Logging in to the congressman's website, Boris located the page he was looking for and clicked donate.

***

"Fifty thousand dollars?" Spenser asked. Seated at his desk, he put down his pen and looked up at Gwen. While his two staff members had left for their lunch break, she remained behind.

"Take a look." Gwen turned the laptop to face Spenser. Leaning over his shoulder, his cologne nearly got the better of her. If only he saw her as a woman rather than a mere disciple. *Doesn't he notice how much I care?*

After years of unrequited affection, she had given Jon Lewis more than a passing thought, until Carrie showed up. Something was up with his girlfriend, and she was determined to figure out what it was.

Gwen got her head together, took her laptop back. "The donor signed in as anonymous but wrote a comment." She read to herself. "He's requesting to meet you in person. He left a phone number."

"Any idea who he is?"

Gwen shook her head. "If he can just drop fifty grand . . ."

"That's how it works in politics. People pony up the cash."

"Something's off," Gwen said, taking a seat on the sofa, a safer distance from the intoxicating musky scent.

Spenser said, "I appreciate your protective nature, but may I enjoy the moment?"

Gwen recognized the patronizing tone he'd become so

adept at.

"If you're set on meeting him, I'll go with you. It would be best before things get crazy with the congressional primaries. Your reelection campaign is the priority."

"I'll go alone."

Gwen was offended but said nothing.

He stood, took his suit jacket from the back of his chair, and put it on. "I have a meeting. I'll walk you out." Pausing, he looked her directly in the eyes, softened his tone. "I'll find another way to make you happy."

Gwen's jaw dropped. As she passed him out the door, she never saw Spenser's infamous patronizing smile.

***

A multitude of holiday lights lit up the barren trees surrounding Central Park's Boathouse, bathing the restaurant in a magical aura. Spenser walked inside and stood at the entrance to the bustling dining room, scanning the inviting space. Panoramic windows overlooked the placid pond. The room buzzed with the sounds of parallel conversations and clinking flatware. He could almost taste the power in the room.

The maître d' approached, took Spenser's name, showing no sign of recognition. He studied his roster, then waved to a passing waiter, who, after taking Spenser's coat to the check room, escorted him to his table.

Waiters rushed by, trays overhead. While Spenser had no idea what the man he was meeting looked like, he didn't have to wonder for long.

"Spenser Germain. At long last."

Alongside a table covered in a white linen cloth, stood a man in his sixties, impeccably dressed, his paunch well obscured by the fine cut of his suit. A retro, striped silk square peeked out from his breast pocket.

Spenser shook the man's hand. "It's a pleasure. Thank you

for the generous donation. I never got your name."

The older man gestured for Spenser to sit, and with a near-imperceptible hesitation, he told him.

***

Spenser felt like he met a soul mate. Boris was himself thirty years into the future. Successful, influential. They spoke at length about politics and the upcoming primaries.

A waiter approached the table with a dessert menu. Boris waved him away. "There is something I need to tell you."

Spenser moved his chair back. So, there were strings attached to the money. "What is it about?"

"You've inherited extraordinary leadership skills."

Relieved, Spenser dabbed at his mouth with his cloth napkin. "I don't see how. My parents were both introverted engineers."

As though he hadn't heard him, Boris said, "It will be a shock at first, but it's all true."

Spenser noted the man's change in demeanor. Intense, calculated.

Boris leaned in, lowering his voice. "Before you were born, an Italian scientist made a monumental breakthrough in genetic engineering. He found a way to successfully revive DNA."

Spenser found the turn in conversation peculiar. "Whose DNA?"

"A great leader of his generation."

"Who?"

Boris held up a finger. He clearly needed to ease his way into whatever he had to say. "This leader made arrangements to be resurrected, as it were. I was tasked with overseeing the fulfillment of that wish."

Spenser couldn't hide his skeptical expression. Boris's fifty grand was already in his account. He would listen and then leave.

Boris said, "You find this hard to believe."

Spenser shrugged.

Boris pulled an envelope from his suit breast pocket, handing it to Spenser. "Please read this. It's been authenticated."

He waited while the younger man read.

"Lenin?" Spenser whispered, stunned.

Boris nodded.

"And you say this scientist was successful?"

"That's right."

Spenser turned silent. He felt sweat beading on his brow.

Boris took out his smartphone, clicked on something. "Have you ever seen photos of Lenin at your age?"

When Spenser didn't reply, he turned the device to face him. The resemblance was undeniable.

"Are you suggesting that I am the resurrection of Lenin?" He laughed weakly.

"We prefer the term clone. You have his DNA but not his physical body or memories. Those advances have not yet been made."

Spenser looked at Boris's face for any sign of comedy. There was none.

"How do you explain my parents?"

"Artificial insemination. Surely, you observed you look nothing like them. They were thrilled to have you, especially at your mother's age."

Spenser couldn't speak for a minute. His stomach was in knots.

"Tell me when you're ready to hear more."

"There's more?"

Boris nodded. "I want you to be able to process this."

Spenser looked around, reassuring himself no one was eavesdropping. He kept his voice low. "That will take way longer than one dinner."

"I understand." He put a hand on the young man's shoulder. "I'm here for you. We're family, actually. I am Comrade Lenin's great-grandnephew."

Spenser was astonished. "How on earth did you land your position with that lineage?"

"My ancestry is not common knowledge. My grandparents changed their names when they came to this country. Records were not what they are today. Stalin's granddaughter did the same."

Spenser stared at the man in awe. "Incredible. Is there anything else you want to share? May as well rip off the bandage."

Boris tapped his device again. This time he showed Spenser the photos of Felix Salko, Alexander Bilka, and Owen Cantor. "These are your clones."

"Oh shit."

Boris ignored the vulgarity. "Each of you is an individual despite having identical genes. You've all accomplished a great deal in different ways. But you, Spenser, are the star. You have come far in a short time. I've been quietly supporting you behind the scenes for many years."

"You have?"

"How else did you earn a full scholarship at NYU?"

"I was a good student."

Boris raised a brow. "And your teenage run-ins with the law? Who made those disappear?" When Spenser looked away, Boris went on. "The wrestling classes? High school debate team? Russian-speaking summer camp?"

Spenser was flabbergasted, unsure if he felt appreciative or exploited.

"More recently, how did you gain so much support in Washington at this stage in your career? Who pulled the strings to get the major campaign donations that helped you win your place in the House?"

"You did all that?"

Boris grinned. It looked out of place on his face. "Happily. I believe in you, Spenser."

Hearing Boris, it now seemed ludicrous to think he could have achieved all of it alone. He was embarrassed he'd ever thought otherwise.

Spenser spoke as if to himself, "So, it's no accident that I've always been drawn to Lenin's philosophies? My parents never gave socialism a second thought."

Boris nodded. "In time you will understand the great benefits of who you are. You and your clones are wired to lead, to take the world to new places. You've been groomed for it. Whatever you've worked hard to achieve, can happen on a much grander scale."

Spenser's head was spinning, the entire interaction surreal. Yet, this odd man had his full attention. While inconceivable, his gut told him the extraordinary account rang true.

"How?"

Boris waved over the passing waiter pushing the dessert trolley. "Now, that's the fun part."

***

Boris strolled alone through Central Park's Sheep Meadow, awarded with an expansive view of the surrounding buildings. It was a lovely, crisp evening for a walk back to his hotel. He made his way through the ubiquitous crowd at Strawberry Fields, offering his mental salute to another Lennon. He exited the park at 72nd Street. Passing the Dakota, he turned right onto Central Park West, then left on 75th. He walked by one of his favorite eateries, regretting he was full from his meal with Spenser.

The meeting with the congressman could not have gone better. What a difference from Bilka. Despite their identical genetic makeup, Bilka was scared and skittish, while Germain, though apprehensive, quickly appreciated the possibilities. It was true what they said about nurture. It played a strong role even in these extreme circumstances. Yet, Boris was putting a great deal of money on Germain's nature prevailing.

Boris's thoughts turned to Claudio back in Rome. He was on the verge of completing the DNA resurrection of the next host. When they spoke, Boris recognized the frenetic energy in his partner's voice, heard the push to get off the phone and back to his work. On their last video call, a messy cot was visible in the room. It meant Claudio was sleeping there. The only other time he'd done that was prior to the Lenin breakthrough. Boris didn't understand how the man could work alone in a dreary lab for weeks on end without getting outside, but was glad for it. From the beginning, the isolation had been Claudio's preference. After the government shut him down, the scientist became paranoid, fearful others would inform on him. Back then, Boris conceded that secrecy trumped speed.

Though it seemed an outrageously long time to wait for another success, it was nothing in the grander scheme of history. They always knew they'd be playing a long game.

Boris arrived at his hotel, his feet aching from the long walk. He sat on the edge of his bed, took off his shoes. A side trip to Chicago was unavoidable. He needed to meet Felix Salko. Perhaps he was getting too old for all this travel. Good thing the Windy City's culinary scene had improved since his last trip. Even as he massaged his stocking feet, his mouth watered for the eighteen-course tasting menu at Alinea.

Still, he had one more meeting scheduled while in New York. And it promised to be the most memorable of all.

CHAPTER 41

New York City

T he Russian ambassador to Italy exited the Consulate General on 91st Street. The weather had turned colder overnight, making him long for his homeland. He was a compact man, short and rotund, his round features leaving no doubt of his long lineage of Slavic ancestry. He turned left on Fifth Avenue, walking south past the Guggenheim Museum. The cylindrical building was designed by the Russian's favorite American architect, Frank Lloyd Wright.

Turning into the park, the reservoir shimmered in the morning light. A smattering of diehard joggers clad in cold weather running gear swerved around him. In the near distance, he saw the two men. Boris stood beside Spenser Germain. He felt a jolt of excitement. He had come far for this meeting, waited so long. He pulled his ushanka lower on his brow, the rabbit fur soft as silk, and raised a hand in greeting. He stepped past Boris, and smiled at the younger man.

"I have waited a very long time to meet you, Congressman Germain. It is an honor and a privilege."

Spenser looked at Boris for guidance. In turn, Boris said something to the ambassador in fluent Russian.

The Russian's eyes widened a bit and then he nodded. To Spenser, he said, "So, you've been told who you are."

"Yes, sir. Apparently, I am Vladimir Lenin reborn." Spenser said this with a note of humor.

The Russian ambassador chuckled. "Correct, and with some tweaks you will be him in toto."

Spenser's face sobered.

"The physical similarities are striking. You even have his passionate nature. All that remains is for you to acquire his memories. Those you will need to relearn, as it were. The vital nuances of how he achieved greatness."

"Not to be rude, but would someone please explain the purpose of this meeting?"

"Yes, of course. Come let us enjoy the view while we speak," the Russian said, strolling leisurely, his hands clasped behind him. "Lenin, our most effective and esteemed leader had a vision, one that exceeded his time on this earth."

Spenser said, "And you would like for me to continue his work in the United States?"

"It is *your* work. Don't be mistaken, you are he."

Spenser shrugged. "My work, then."

"You will lead the world in communism."

Germain stared at the man, speechless.

"Your clones will have critical supporting roles for spreading your ideology to the corners of the globe."

"Pardon my skepticism, but I don't see how a junior congressman can reach such heights."

The Russian stopped walking, drawing Spenser's attention, then holding the younger man's gaze with the intensity of his own. "You will enter the U.S. presidential race."

Spenser paled. "President? You must be joking."

The ambassador's expression left no doubt as to the gravity of his words.

Spenser found his voice, shaky as it was. "I don't think I'm ready for that."

The Russian looked pleased. "Spoken like a true leader. Wasn't it Moses who asked, 'Who am I to be their savior?' You, Spenser, have demonstrated a charisma that will be necessary. The rest is commentary."

Boris saw the look of panic in Spenser's eyes. He didn't like how bluntly the ambassador was speaking, fearing he would undo all his hard work to win over Germain. But the man was his superior, chair of the Committee. "Why don't we take a break from all the details?" Boris said this while looking at the ambassador, who nodded.

Spenser turned to Boris. "Can we speak privately?"

"Certainly."

The Russian ambassador said, "I will excuse myself."

When they were alone, Boris said, "You appear overwhelmed."

"Wouldn't you be? You invite me for a chat in the park, and the next thing I know, I'm primed to be the future president of the United States. Yes, I'm overwhelmed."

Boris solemnly nodded. "I know it's a great deal to absorb and I wish there was more time for you to adjust, but your arrival has been long awaited and plans are well underway. We must make arrangements for your new campaign before the deadline to declare your candidacy."

Spenser began pacing nervously. "Do *I* have any say in all of this?"

"Certainly. That is why there are other clones. If after full consideration, you decide not to take on this responsibility, we will approach the next in line."

Spenser stopped, looked at his mentor. "Oh, I see."

"I'm sure you understand the circumstances require backup. If you can't or won't fill the position, we would require another clone to lead."

Spenser appeared ambivalent. "Yes, of course."

Boris put an avuncular hand on Spenser's shoulder. "I have an idea. Why don't we find somewhere warm to sit, enjoy a stiff drink, then mull over the details? Jacques, perhaps?"

Spenser perked up. The Lowell Hotel's famed bar was a

favorite watering hole of New York's elite. He paused. Then, "If you choose to be a second in command we'll discuss *that* course of action."

Spenser grimaced at the suggestion of a less substantial role, but with the pressure off him, the young man exhaled. He looked around at the splendid grounds. "All right."

Boris smiled. His work today was nearly done.

CHAPTER 42

New York City

J on hadn't been officially invited to the live broadcast of
Spenser Germain's interview. He simply followed Gwen
and Pete into the studio. No one stopped him. The stage
was smaller than expected, sleek, with blue-lit walls. The
New York skyline was the backdrop. There were two camera-
men, and a few people milling about with clipboards, one of
whom he assumed was the director. Others worked behind a
glass partition.

A relaxed Spenser sat behind a wide desk, across from
the interviewer, a nipped-and-tucked woman wearing a fitted
red dress, perusing the notes in front of her. Someone dabbed
makeup on Spenser's forehead. Moments later, Jon heard
someone yell out, "Action!"

The interviewer welcomed Spenser, introducing him.

"Congressman Germain, the primaries are coming up.
How are your reelection efforts going?" She crossed her toned
legs, smiled engagingly.

Jon watched as a camera focused on Germain, his face filling the screen. "We're in great shape. The polls are giving us
a significant lead. Which is a terrific segue for my important
announcement."

The interviewer leaned in closer, practically salivating.
"Announcement?"

"This morning,"—he paused a beat for effect—"I officially

declared my candidacy for president of the United States."

The interviewer appeared genuinely surprised. "Congratulations. I'm honored you chose my show for this special occasion."

Spenser smiled, seemingly gratified. "I'm making overtures to *all* Americans, not only to those who already agree with my policies."

She skillfully put her notes aside. "Isn't it late in the game? Your opponents have been campaigning for months."

"But none of them are viable or desirable candidates. I've listened to the people of this land. They want change but all they see are blowhards with the same old ideas. My opponents simply don't have the same record as I."

"Quite a bold statement given that several of them have at least twenty years more experience in public service than you do."

Spenser smiled, seemingly glad for the opening. "That's the problem, is it not? It's why my platform is so successful. I've brought positive change to my district that will catch on across the city, the state, and soon, the entire country."

Jon thought his words were pompous and self-aggrandizing. Apparently so did the interviewer who appeared to be holding back an eye roll. "Let's go to the clip."

Jon saw it come up on the screen to his right. It was taken at Spenser's NYU speech. A group protesting outside the building. The video made it appear to be a big crowd, but Jon knew it was only a handful of people. The image then switched to students marching on stage. Jon recalled the reporter and cameraman.

"As the founder of the Sam Adams Underground, how would you describe your platform?"

A shadow of surprise registered on his face. "I plan to upgrade the capitalistic foundations of this country. The citizens are angry, and justifiably so. Parents are unable to send their kids to college due to insurmountable tuition fees. The elderly can't afford the medications they need to stay alive.

We will give them a government to be proud of, which will take care of them." Jon was impressed that instead of denying his involvement with the militant organization, he defanged her taunt and went on the offensive. *Well played.*

Remaining poised, the interviewer said, "Isn't what you're describing another word for communism?"

Spenser lifted a hand like a school crossing guard. "Communism is the antithesis of capitalism. My plan is an enhancement."

"I've read your writings, Congressman. I can't see any noticeable difference."

"I'd be happy to point them out in greater detail."

"That won't be necessary," she said, her tone firm. "Give me *one* definable difference between communism and your movement."

Spenser's smile faded. "Unlike communism, we want to see all Americans live freely, not under dictatorship. We are not looking to create a revolution like in Russia. We want to educate the masses, not overtake them."

"That's hard to believe, given that your members are wearing fatigues."

Match point, Jon thought.

"They're not armed," Germain said, his voice gruff.

"Because that would be illegal."

For a moment, Spenser appeared flustered. "It's good marketing. I'm sure you understand."

"Actually, I don't. This movement of yours is the same as communism. Your end goal no doubt the establishment of a police state. You just can't call it that because it would be deemed treasonous under the Constitution. You're fooling no one."

The studio turned momentarily still. Jon saw Spenser's jaw tighten, then quickly rebound, remaining outwardly calm, and even managing to espouse some of his policies. If elected, he promised socialized medicine, welfare expansion, and salary caps. He would meet regularly with his counterparts in China and Russia to exchange ideas and build bridges, as he put it. "Many of my policies are no different than those of previous presidential candidates. The difference is I have the guts to implement them."

When the interview ended, the host took off her mic and walked away, Jon and everyone else noting her obvious disgust.

Spenser stomped past Gwen, hissing, "Get me out of here. Now!"

***

Washington, D.C.

Owen Cantor got out of the shower and turned on the television. The run in Volta Park did him good. He loved his townhome in trendy Georgetown. It was a vibrant neighborhood in the heart of the city. The rent was astronomical, but he had few other expenses. No car, kids, school tuition. And at thirty-five, he was one of the youngest judges on the District's bench.

In the shower, he'd thought of Terry again. She was something else. Beautiful, brilliant, and that sexy accent. But she seemed to have no interest in him other than his politics.

Maybe he'd find something distracting to watch before heading to bed. He was toweling off his hair with one hand and channel surfing with the other, when he froze. He blinked, moved closer to the screen. He fumbled with the remote, turning up the volume.

What the hell? Owen was looking into the dark eyes of a young man with Slavic features being interviewed on MSNBC.

Owen was looking at himself.

***

New York City

Spenser paced his Greenwich Village apartment, fuming. After the interview, he insisted on being alone. He despised that newswoman. *How dare she publicly ridicule him!*

He poured himself a glass of Merlot, swirled and sniffed the bouquet before sipping, his thoughts turning to Gwen. She was just as angry as he was. She was a devoted soldier. If he liked the passive-aggressive type, they would have been an item by now. In the early days, Gwen, an incoming freshman, along with several of his other followers, had canvassed the left-wing corners of his district, soliciting the necessary signatures for him to run for Congress. He was elected by a wide margin, the city's residents ripe for change. He knew she was in love with him but while he was careful not to encourage her, he used her commitment to his advantage.

He turned on his tablet. Hundreds of emails had come in since the interview aired.

Perhaps the old adage was true after all. There's no such thing as bad publicity. He took another sip of wine, the liquid turning him contemplative. He never would have attempted such a bold move as a presidential run only three years after his congressional win. It was still early in his career. But hearing of Boris's vision convinced him the time was ripe. He had a substantial following, one that would take him much farther than the House.

He walked to the bedroom, studying himself in the full-length mirror. He straightened his tie, then pulled back his shoulders. Aloud, he said, "I, Spenser Alan Germain, am the next president of the United States of America." He looked strong, felt strong, knowing he'd be the first to alter the country's way of being governed.

As much as he resented the interviewer, one thing was certain. She understood his agenda just fine.

***

The next morning, Boris waited patiently for the chamber-maid to finish cleaning his room before watching a recap of the interview. Seated on the room's sofa, he finished the espresso the maid had brought him. He powered on his tablet, patting the cushion, inviting Fellini to join him, glad the cat was taking well to the extensive travel.

He watched with deep interest as Germain remained poised even as he was challenged. Well-spoken, but no match for the interviewer who had seen it all before. Still, the interview would make Spenser Germain a household name.

This is what Boris had been waiting for. With the Committee's extensive network of powerful friends, Boris would ramp up the congressman's base support, acting as a campaign manager from behind the scenes.

Despite the caffeine intake, he let out a hearty yawn. Fellini took note and curled up into a ball, closing his eyes. Boris had risen early, arranging plans for the next leg of his trip. Perhaps a short nap would prove beneficial before his flight to Chicago. This was the calm before the storm. He turned down the lights, got into bed, enjoying the feel of fresh sheets against his skin. As Boris nodded off, he realized the ultimate goal was suddenly just around the corner.

CHAPTER 43

Chicago

Boris's flight arrived at O'Hare fifteen minutes late. The strong winds off Lake Michigan created unsettling turbulence, delaying the plane's landing. Though he loved piloting his Citation, he was glad it wasn't him in the jet's cockpit.

As he walked off the jetway and into the terminal, he considered his strategy. He'd planned to introduce himself to Felix Salko in the same manner as with Germain, contributing to the editor's fundraiser and sending a request to meet. It had seemed to be the best course of action. Salko was quickly rising at the newspaper. With a circulation of nearly half a million, he had Chicago's ear. Far-left-leaning editorials, once considered a weak attempt at fair reporting, now held a regular spot in the daily paper. It was a slow indoctrination of the masses, and with Salko at the helm, it would surely speed up.

Boris got in a cab, and leaned back against the headrest, closing his eyes. Now he would wait.

***

Felix Salko had received the donation notification while on the boat ride. He had typed a quick thank-you and received a request to meet, indicating he should expect a follow-up in coming days. Ten thou was nice but should get the man entry to his next event, not a private dinner. In time he would turn down these chump-change donors. Nevertheless, it was an opportunity to build his pool of supporters. Days later, when he received a follow-up message from a new number, Felix agreed to dinner, scheduled for tomorrow evening. He'd always wanted to try Alinea anyway.

***

CIA Headquarters
Washington, D.C.

Jon, Carrie, and Terry reassembled at CIA headquarters to compare notes. Matthews and Carrie's boss were not present, making the conference room seem too spacious for only three participants.

Carrie said, "There was no name in Salko's phone, only an overseas number." She shared the text stream she'd pilfered, confirming the meeting between Salko and an anonymous donor. "My office is working on finding out who this person is."

Terry said, "It shouldn't be that difficult."

"Actually, it could be," Carrie replied. "We're not dealing with amateurs. The phone was a burner. Whoever it is, will have worked hard to cover his or her tracks."

Jon said, "I agree. Let's see what The Farm comes back with. If necessary, we'll need to find another angle."

Terry said, "Where do we go from here? I think I learned as much as I can from Cantor. Continuing to meet with him will send a message I don't want to deliver."

Jon looked at his clasped hands resting on the table. "We go back to Prague."

Both women looked at him. Carrie said, "Our bosses said they want to avoid creating another incident on Czech territory. We can't just ignore that."

"It's the obvious next step. We need to follow up on Bilka, especially knowing now that we've found a possible overseas player. There could be a connection. Frankly, it's the only lead we've got."

Terry said, "I would need clearance from my boss. I don't know the policy on sending field agents over there."

Jon busied himself with a paperclip. "I don't think you should come."

Terry frowned. "Why not?"

"You aren't trained. It's one thing to attend a university lecture and meet someone for coffee. It's something else to put yourself in harm's way, particularly in a place where I've already been assaulted. Whoever is pulling the strings knows us. They may try to stop us again. We can't spend our time protecting you."

Terry looked angry. "I didn't realize you had decision power over who participates in the mission."

"I don't, but I can and will make recommendations."

"Is this about Gabe?" Terry asked, bluntly.

Carrie looked back and forth between the two.

Jon said, "Of course not. I just said what it was about."

"I don't believe you. I *have* been trained. Maybe not to the same extent as you both have. But I know my way around a firearm and have improved my combat skills since the last time we met."

Jon looked away. "I still don't think it's a good idea."

Carrie spoke up. "That's enough! You two aren't capable of working together effectively. I don't know who thought this was a good idea, but partners need to be on the same page, or all of our lives will be in danger."

Terry stood up and stalked out.

Carrie glared at Jon. All he did was shrug.

***

"Is Terry right?" Carrie asked. She and Jon were alone now in the conference room, the tension having dissipated with

Terry's departure. "Are you going to recommend excluding her because she broke up with your friend?"

"No, Terry is a genetics professor, not an intelligence officer. Do you want to be responsible for her getting hurt? Because that could happen."

Carrie waited a beat. "No, of course not. But it's not our decision."

"Maybe not, but in the meantime, we first need to get the go-ahead to return to Prague. See if Bilka has any connection to the person messaging Salko."

"And if he does?"

"It's another path toward finding the cloners."

"All right. I agree it is the next logical step, but my boss has a valid point. We don't want to create an international incident by leaving more dead bodies behind."

"As long as those bodies aren't ours, we'll do what we need to."

"You're as sensitive as ever, Jon."

He smiled. "Thank you."

***

"Why am I not surprised you screwed this up?" Matthews said into the phone, his voice at the edge of restraint.

"I didn't screw anything up," Jon said.

"You can't bring your personal life into the job."

"Why don't you believe me? She's not good for this part of the mission, Doug."

"After all my concerted efforts, you still have no understanding of how authority works. This is not your decision and you certainly shouldn't have said anything to Dr. Lavi." A deep sigh, then, "The CIA and I have given the okay for you to go back to Prague."

"That's good news."

"I don't like getting angry calls from the Mossad, Jon." He

paused. "But this time you win. Dr. Lavi will sit this one out. But, from now on, be nice to her and no more playing director. Got it?"

Jon stayed silent.

"Got it?" Matthews yelled.

"Fine."

Matthews hung up before Jon had a chance to beat him to it.

***

At the very same time, in an outrageously expensive eatery in downtown Chicago, Boris met Felix Salko in person. He felt the same exhilaration as when he'd laid eyes on his other two clones, regretting there was only one left to meet.

CHAPTER 44

Chicago

Felix Salko was as floored by Boris's revelation as the others had been, but didn't dwell on the experimental way he came into the world. He soon shifted into business mode, tapping into his pragmatic nature. He requested proof of the man's assertions and was rewarded with the Lenin letter and photos of the dictator, as well as his clones. When Boris presented a photo of himself with a pre-pubescent Felix posing outside his childhood Chicago home, it triggered a flicker of a memory.

"That was you?" he asked, incredulous.

Over a decadent dinner, the two men bonded, Felix quickly understanding that to advance his agenda, it would be prudent to avail himself of Boris's contributions.

***

As much as he'd enjoyed his time in Chicago, Boris needed to get back to his day job before his absence was questioned. He'd make an appearance there, then return for one more U.S. stop. To meet the final clone—Judge Owen Cantor.

***

Prague

Jon and Carrie waited for Professor Alexander Bilka in the hallway of the Anglo-American University, staying out of the way of students rushing to and from their classes. They had done their homework and knew Bilka would soon be finishing his lecture, the last one before winter break.

When Bilka walked out, Jon thought he'd aged years since they saw him last.

Jon approached him. "Hey, Professor. Remember me?"

Bilka looked at Jon and then Carrie. "No, who are you?" The man looked scared.

"We heard your talk on the bridge a few weeks ago. Maybe you remember my wife?"

Bilka took a moment and then said with relief in his voice, "Oh yes, that's right. What can I do for you?"

"We were hoping you could make some time to chat. Exchange ideas. Maybe dinner?"

A look of puzzlement crossed Bilka's face. "That's very kind, but maybe another time. Please excuse me." He tried to walk past them.

"We know about the cloning," Jon said, blocking the man's way.

Carrie stared at Jon, dumbstruck.

Bilka looked like he was about to faint. "I don't know what you're talking about."

"Jon?" Carrie whispered. "What are you doing?"

"We need to shake things up." To Bilka, he said, "I think you do."

Bilka's eyes darted around the hallway. "I need to go."

"This isn't going away, Professor."

The man looked like he was on the verge of tears. "I didn't do anything wrong."

"Not yet. But whomever you're conspiring with, is. They

have illicit intentions. You get caught up with them and you'll be put away for a very long time. What would your doting parents think of you then?"

Hearing this, Bilka swiped away a wayward tear. "We can't talk here. Let's go somewhere more private."

"Lead the way."

***

Per Bilka's request, Jon and Carrie would follow him home at a distance. They weren't concerned they would lose him. He was not skilled in spy craft and they knew where he lived regardless.

Bilka sat at the front of the tram, back slumped. Defeated.

"If you ever pull something like that again, I'll walk," Carrie said, seated next to Jon in back of the tram.

Jon said, "You saw how it played out. It was the right call."

"We had operational plans. You threw them out the window without a word to me," she hissed.

"Sometimes plans change in the moment when an opportunity presents itself."

"Yes, in dire circumstances. Not in a college hallway! What were you thinking? Forget it, you *weren't* thinking. You fly by the seat of your pants. You're a loose cannon. I can't handle that."

"Calm down. No one got hurt. Bilka was scared. You saw it too. He's ready to talk, just needed a push. If we'd waited, we would have lost him. Now we're on our way to getting answers."

The tram stopped and Bilka got off the front. Jon and Carrie alighted from the back. They watched as he crossed in the middle of the road, making a beeline to his apartment building directly across the street.

The screech of accelerating tires drew their attention. Before they could react, a black BMW with darkened windows slammed into Bilka propelling him ten feet in the air. His body tumbled to the ground. Cars honked trying to avoid him. A Peugeot ran over him as another car swerved into a line of parked bicycles, toppling them like dominoes. The two agents darted to Bilka, crouching alongside his splayed body. Drivers yelled out their windows, sirens blaring in the distance. Carrie took Bilka's head in her hands. His eyes were frozen open in silent shock. She took his pulse, looked at Jon, shook her head.

Jon stood, did a one-eighty. The BMW was nowhere to be found.

***

Jon knocked on Carrie's hotel room door. Carrie stepped aside, letting him in. "Still think your idea was a good one?" she asked as she threw the last of her items into her bag. They'd left the crash scene as soon as the ambulances showed up and were leaving town fast. And empty-handed.

"He was killed because someone was watching us."

Carrie stared at him hard. "He was killed because he was going to talk. Which was your doing."

Jon was subdued even as he was irritated with her assessment. "Isn't that what we wanted—for him to talk?"

"Yes, but in a measured, careful way that didn't end with our asset being murdered before he could talk to us."

Jon's phone rang. He looked at the screen, tapped the green circle. "What, Doug?"

"Good morning to you, too. Another dead body in Prague?"

"Couldn't be helped."

Carrie glared at him.

"Let me talk to Agent Santiago."

Jon hesitated, then turned on the speaker, and passed the phone to Carrie.

"Hello, sir," Carrie said.

"I need you to tell me exactly what happened."

Carrie recounted the events. Jon noted she deliberately left out his confrontation with Bilka.

After a few minutes, Carrie handed the phone to Jon, avoiding eye contact.

"Sir?"

"Sounds like you did everything by the book. But too bad about Professor Bilka. It could have led somewhere. Get back home."

Jon hung up, looked sheepishly at Carrie. "Thanks."

All she said was, "Now we're even."

***

Boris was devastated. He didn't want to kill Alexander. He was family. All his hopes for the young Lenin were shattered the moment he plowed into him with his car. But there was no other way. He couldn't allow him to tell his story. Boris had spent days agonizing over how he'd approached Alexander. Rethinking his earlier bluntness, he'd sought out the professor at the university, intending to discuss things in a more tactful way, present the limitless possibilities of his existence. Alexander had seen him sitting in the back of the lecture hall. Upon recognition, his eyes registered what Boris lamented as abject terror.

When Boris saw the Americans cornering Alexander, he cursed to himself. Something had led them back to Prague. Witnessing Alexander board the same tram as the American agents, he understood the clone would talk. The moment of impact would remain with him forever. The years of work, watching, cultivating, waiting. All to end so suddenly.

The cloning benefactor would be irate, ask for Boris to step down. But he wouldn't, of course. There was no one else to do his job, and they all knew it.

Later that evening, when he told Claudio what happened,

the scientist cried unabashedly, whimpering into the phone like a boy who'd lost his puppy.

Though repulsed by the man's weakness, Boris felt a weightier emotion. Vengeance. He would make the Americans pay. With their lives.

CHAPTER 45

Washington D.C.

T erry had just ended the call with Shira, spending most of it railing about Jon. She was second-guessing her decision to get involved in the mission. All the work she'd left behind at home was now being done by her subordinates. And for what? She'd been sidelined by her team. Alone in a Washington D.C. hotel, she missed her job, her family. Gabe.

To Shira's credit, while Terry wondered aloud if it was too late to back out, her handler didn't try to sway her. She simply listened. The truth was, Terry knew she wouldn't bail. That wasn't her style. Once she committed to something, she saw it through, regardless of how tiresome. Jon was still harboring resentment, as if the offense had been perpetrated against him instead of Gabe. That level of devotion was admirable, but a persistent problem given their current circumstances. Even so, she recalled his advice, deciding to dig deeper into Judge Cantor's virtual mentor and see where that led.

Terry knew she was taking a chance. Cantor was clearly enamored with her and she didn't want to give the wrong impression by asking *him* out. But if she was going to learn who was behind the cloning, there was no choice. She texted him, asking if they could meet. He responded immediately suggesting the Watergate Steps. Terry had never heard of the place.

She quickly checked it out online before agreeing to meet him there in an hour. She dressed in jeans and a down jacket, ordered an Uber, and arrived at the location with ten minutes to spare.

"We're here?" she asked the driver, looking around.

"Yep, that's it right there." The driver pointed to a series of wide granite steps facing the Potomac River. As she exited the car, a chilly wind blew off the water, her hair billowing behind her. Snuggling couples were seated on the steps watching the sunset over the Rosslyn skyline across the river. Terry guessed the timing was not happenstance.

She saw Owen Cantor descend the stairs and approach her, a bottle of champagne in one hand, two glass flutes in the other. "Isn't it beautiful?" he asked.

"Yes, it is."

He sat down, began twisting the bottle's cork. Terry remained standing, tempted to tell him to dial down the romance, but didn't. She needed to gather more intel. Once that happened, she would make a hasty retreat, hopefully never to see Judge Cantor again. She sat.

Owen popped the cork, held the bottle at arm's length, the silver liquid spilling over. The sudden burst drew the attention of several people nearby.

"These steps were intended for visiting dignitaries who docked along the river. The idea was that they would ascend the grand staircase to the Lincoln Memorial as they entered the capital, but it was never used for that. It's one of my favorite D.C. hidey-holes." He handed her a glass and poured. "L'chaim! Isn't that what you say?"

She offered a smile, nodded, and took a tentative sip.

Cantor stared off in the distance for a few moments.

Terry said, "You seem distracted."

"A really strange thing happened."

"Oh?"

"You know how people say everyone has a double?"

Terry felt a surge of excitement. "Sure."

"I saw mine on television."

Terry nearly dropped her glass. "Really?"

"I was watching an interview of a man who looked just like me."

Terry inwardly kicked herself. She'd completely forgotten to watch Germain's interview. "That must have felt strange."

"It sort of freaked me out. Afterward, I thought maybe it was the lighting, or the makeup they put on these people."

Terry did her best to keep her voice even. "Makes sense. What was he talking about?"

"I don't even know. By the time I turned up the volume, the interview was nearly over. Honestly, I was so stunned I wasn't focused on what he was saying. I suppose I could look online, find his name, and check him out, but what would be the point?"

Terry nodded. "I agree. No point." Fixing to change the subject, she said, "Last time we spoke, you told me you were waiting to hear from your virtual mentor. Has he contacted you?"

Cantor looked at her strangely.

Seeing his expression, Terry asked, "What?"

"That's really weird. I hadn't heard from him in a couple of weeks and he just emailed me today."

"What a coincidence. You should know I have a degree of ESP. These things happen to me all the time. I think of someone I haven't seen in years and then they show up out of nowhere."

Owen appeared to be tuning out again. "Right."

"What's the man's name?"

"Believe it or not, I don't know. He goes by the name Richard Krasny, but I know it's an alias. I couldn't find anyone of significance with that name."

Terry was genuinely bewildered. "Don't you think it's odd not knowing this person's identity? Why the mystery?"

"I've always assumed he was important somehow. He

seems highly informed about the D.C. legal world. Perhaps he's a retired federal judge himself, looking to give a leg up to someone like me, without the fanfare. Honestly, I never pushed the issue. All he's done is help me. Why look a gift horse in the mouth?"

The sun had fully set, and the wind picked up. Terry shivered. Several people were preparing to leave. Owen moved closer, put an arm around her. "How much longer will you be in the States?"

"I have a few more lectures in D.C. and then I'll go back home."

"I've never been to Israel. I'd love to get there sometime. Maybe you could show me around."

Terry broke eye contact. "That would be fun." Despite her best efforts, her tone suggested otherwise.

Owen drained his glass and was readying to pour another when his phone buzzed. Terry could tell he was tempted to look at it.

"I don't mind if you check your phone. You're a very busy man."

He seemed to like that.

"Oh," he said as he read.

"Everything all right?"

"It's another email from Richard. He says he doesn't want to correspond by email anymore."

Oh no, now we'll never find him, Terry thought. "I'm sorry. I know how much you value his opinion."

"You don't understand. He wants to answer my questions in person. Next week."

Terry smiled seemingly happy for him, but her true satisfaction came from knowing that the evening had just paid off in spades.

***

Carrie sat beside Terry in the CIA conference room, dark circles under her eyes. Her stomach growled. The sun had set and all she'd eaten was a bag of airplane pretzels and a granola bar. They'd left Prague early. While Jon went straight on to D.C., she stopped in New York to see Randy, and then rode right back to the airport. Her son was making less eye contact and appeared to be retreating into his own world. Her parents reassured her everything possible was being done for him, but she was terribly concerned. She promised to be back with them for the holidays. With all that was going on in her personal life, Carrie was in a very bad mood.

The team wasn't meant to meet for another few days, but Terry reconvened them, excited to share something she'd learned about Owen Cantor's mystery advisor, and time was of the essence.

As Terry debriefed them, Carrie noticed she avoided looking at Jon. The situation was untenable. She had never worked with two partners before, and Terry seemed to bring out the worst in Jon. He was petty and downright mean at times. Carrie felt like a referee sending each fighter to their corner of the ring. It took much of her self-control not to call them out.

The meeting was productive given Terry's new intel on Judge Cantor's upcoming rendezvous. They suspected this could be the same person Salko was texting with. It was a major break in the investigation. Carrie congratulated Terry, pleased when Jon nodded his agreement.

The decision was made that Jon and Carrie would tail Cantor. As the judge's new friend, Terry couldn't risk being spotted following him. She reluctantly agreed to stand back again and allow the other two agents to take the reins.

***

The high Terry felt from sharing the intel was almost worth the loneliness. She saw the appeal of spying. It was exciting and adventurous. Still, she was trying hard to suppress the resentment for being sidelined. So far, she wasn't doing such a great job.

**

Jon stepped out of the room. He had to admit he was wrong —at least to a degree. Terry had come through with valuable intel. He felt a twinge of guilt for how he'd treated her, but couldn't get past her ironclad decision to end things with Gabe. He hadn't spoken with his best friend in a while. The guy must be a mess. He took out his phone and dialed.

"Hey, Gabe, how are you doing today?"

"One sec," Gabe whispered.

When he came back on the line he spoke in a regular volume.

"Did I catch you in a library or something?" Jon asked.

"Not exactly."

"Lecture?"

"Synagogue." Gabe chuckled.

Jon was taken aback by Gabe's upbeat tone. He wasn't sure he heard his friend accurately. "Come again?"

"I know you'll think I'm nuts, but I've been meeting with a rabbi every week."

"You're the least nuts guy I know. What's this about?"

Jon heard Gabe take a deep breath. "I spent countless hours agonizing over what happened. Spoke to my folks too. I know Terry loves me. If she was willing to forfeit a future together for her faith—and I'm convinced that's what it was— then I want to know what's so compelling about it."

Jon was relieved that Gabe sounded logical. "Did you figure it out?"

"Despite visiting Israel twice, I admit I knew close to nothing about Judaism. There's so much depth. Many life questions I had put on the back burner are getting answered."

Jon was silent for a while.

"I knew you'd think I'm crazy."

"I don't think that. It just seems kind of extreme. You've never been the religious sort. Even after Ash died."

"I know. I can't really explain it more than I have. And truthfully, I have no idea where this will lead, but the rabbi has been very accommodating. He invited me to a Shabbat dinner."

Jon was tempted to tell him about working with Terry, but he couldn't. He was in enough trouble already. "Have a good time."

"What do you think I should bring? Flowers?"

"Wine. They drink wine at Shabbat dinner."

"That's right. How do you know that?"

"I read."

Gabe took a serious tone. "Thanks for not going off on me."

"No prob, bro. If this brings you peace of mind, it will be a good thing."

"I have to get back to the rabbi. Talk soon."

CHAPTER 46

Washington, D.C.

C arrie sat shotgun beside Jon in a black Ford rental, the most inconspicuous vehicle they could find. They were parked down the block from Cantor's George-town apartment, waiting. Dusk had fallen, and Cantor's curtains remained drawn, the lights on. The drive-by allowed a peek inside the front window. He was there. Made things easy.

"How's Randy?" Jon asked.

Carrie yawned loudly. "Sorry. I'm wiped." Then, "He's not doing so well."

Carrie was touched by Jon's look of alarm. "Other than to me and my parents, he doesn't speak."

She wasn't used to talking about Randy's condition. Most people avoided the topic of her son's awkwardness. Made believe he was a "normal" kid. Jon's approach was refreshing. "Researchers are learning more about selective mutism but much of it is still a mystery. He's fortunate to have a team of therapists working with him at school and at home. He had been making real progress. But now . . ." Carrie teared up. "Maybe if I was there more, he wouldn't be regressing. But if I give up my job, I won't have a way to afford his care. It's the worst kind of catch-22."

Jon drew her to him. She put her head on his shoulder.

He said, "You're a wonderful mother, Carrie. Randy knows you love him. He's lucky to have a mom who made sure he's well cared for even when she can't be there. He's with doting grandparents. I can offer firsthand insight about the nurturing power of grandparents."

As Carrie wiped away a tear, something caught her eye. She pointed out the window. "Cantor's on the move." She sat up, pulled herself together, and buckled her seatbelt. "Let's go," she said, switching instantly from mom to spy in the blink of an eye.

***

They followed Cantor for three miles, most of it along Constitution Avenue, passing the Smithsonian museums abutting the long grassy lawns of the National Mall. The Capitol rose ghostlike in Carrie's side mirror.

They overshot Cantor's car as he parked near the Vietnam Veterans Memorial. It was late enough that parking spots were readily available. All the government buildings and museums were closed. Jon and Carrie watched as Cantor exited his car, a bounce in his step.

It was nearly nine p.m. and few people were about. They watched Cantor walk along the Mall, the reflecting pool shimmering in the street lamps' ambient light.

Wordlessly, Carrie got out of the car and followed Cantor at a distance. The evening was blustery, tree branches trembling in the wind. The Mall was vast, allowing excellent sightlines. Jon pulled binoculars from the glove compartment, focused them on the two men. An older man in a wool overcoat strolled alongside Cantor, leaving a six-foot gap between them. Slowly, the gap closed, and the two men began talking. *This must be him.* Their body language suggested a lack of familiarity. He turned his head slightly, noting they were a good distance ahead of Carrie.

Jon watched his partner take out her phone pretending to snap photos of the Washington Monument at the far end of the Mall, the men prominent in the foreground ahead of her. As she returned the phone to her coat pocket, she stumbled back, dropping to the ground.

Jon didn't hesitate. He dashed from the car, sprinting toward Carrie, his bad leg protesting. Twenty feet from Carrie, he felt something whiz by his ear. Someone was shooting at them.

Finding Jon beside her, Carrie shouted, "Get down!"

Heeding his partner's command, Jon dropped down on all fours. There was nowhere to take cover. He grabbed Carrie by the hand and bolted. Their training kicking in, they ran in a zigzag motion making themselves harder targets. Heart pounding, Jon's bad leg dragged slightly behind its mate.

The shooting stopped. Jon knew whoever it was wouldn't risk coming out in the open, meaning they were likely out of range. They made it to the car, breathless. He turned on the ignition, slammed the accelerator, and beat it out of there, eventually pulling over, eyeing his partner. "Are you all right?" he asked.

Carrie leaned back against the seat, closing her eyes. "Yeah, you?"

"Your coat is ripped."

She looked down at her sleeve. No blood. "That was close."

Jon's adrenaline had hit its peak and quickly began to plummet. He started laughing so hard he couldn't catch his breath.

Carrie looked over at him. The laugh was contagious, and she soon followed suit. Their hysteria lasted for several minutes, stopping and starting in spurts, tears rolling down their cheeks.

Carrie finally caught her breath. "What the hell are we laughing about?"

Jon managed to say, "Haven't a clue, but I think we found Clone Man."

"Clone Man?" Carrie couldn't hold it in. The laughing

started anew, lasting the rest of the drive back to HQ.

Terry was waiting for them when they arrived, eying their disheveled appearances. "What happened?"

Carrie filled her in, then called her boss, and Jon did the same with Matthews.

"Good thing you weren't there," Jon said to Terry.

She ignored the comment. "Did Owen see you?"

Carrie said, "I don't think so. Neither did the other guy. They were walking ahead of me, and the gun had a silencer, so they didn't hear the commotion behind them." She pulled out her phone, checked her photos. "I got a few pictures before the shooting started." A burst of pictures were taken of Owen Cantor walking alongside a large, well-dressed man.

"Oh no," Carrie said.

"What?" Terry and Jon asked, simultaneously.

Jon took the phone from Carrie whose expression he couldn't decipher. "That's . . ."

Carrie nodded. "Boris Tierney. The United States ambassador to the Czech Republic."

***

New York City

Matthews had a strange relationship with his counterparts at the CIA and Mossad. The agencies knew their teams must work together but were naturally skeptical of the collaboration, each pursuing its own agenda.

Following the report of Ambassador Tierney's involvement, the FBI initiated an investigation into the man. The President insisted the matter be deemed classified. Matthews suspected the request was more a matter of the leader's embarrassment and reelection efforts than anything else.

He arranged for a conference call of the three agencies' representatives. They determined the next steps would be to track down the ambassador, trace the source of the cloning project, and cut it off—before Germain made it to the primaries. Without any legal means to discredit the congressman, their hands were tied.

What they needed was irrefutable evidence of treason, or they would surely spark another series of nationwide protests. With the primaries and national conventions mere months away, they were running out of time. If they failed, the next leader of the free world could very well be President Vladimir Lenin.

***

Jerusalem

Yosef Kahn was confident he'd made the right choice with Terry. He was tired of defending his position with his U.S. counterparts. Her team members were sidelining her, and Yosef took personal offense. If it weren't for her, they'd never have found Tierney.

He needed Terry close to the scene gathering vital scientific intel that would be a critical boon for Dr. Perlman's cloning work. The USA would not be the only country benefitting from what was discovered. One thing was certain—when it was commandeered, Kahn's agent would be right there on the frontlines.

***

Washington, D.C.

Boris knew his cover was blown. The Feds would already be alerted, checking into his private affairs at that very moment.

He'd been notified by text moments after the agents got away. They'd followed Owen straight to him. Always prepared, Boris had brought his bodyguard along. Still, they got away. He would use the situation to his advantage and allow the agents to continue to follow, catching them in his net.

The unfortunate incident cut short the meeting with the judge. Despite the resulting complications, the conversation with Cantor had gone better than expected. Upon learning of Boris's pedigree, the young man was attentive, even reverential. When he was informed of his own genetics, he asked numerous technical questions, which Boris indulged.

Owen appeared relieved to hear that Congressman Germain, his television doppelganger, was in reality his clone. Lenin's letter and photos were accepted without question. He engaged Boris in what he already knew of the Premier, fixating on their common choice of legal career. Boris understood the judge was experiencing a form of shock. Inevitably, the reality would hit him hard.

Boris couldn't stay in the United States or return to Prague, his primary home city for the last several years. He'd enjoyed his appointment as ambassador for the last four years, a role that fit him perfectly. One of glad-handing and hosting extravagant galas in his home, paid for by the U.S. government. Not to mention the incredible culinary pursuits the diplomatic placement afforded him. Now the job was behind him.

Boris knew this day would come and had prepared well for it. His financial holdings remained virtually untraceable in offshore accounts. A recent call to a Geneva bank confirmed an impressive balance.

He allowed himself a moment's sentimental reflection, then let it pass, choosing to focus on the future instead. After all these years, it was finally time to convene the boys.

CHAPTER 47

Rome, Italy

Claudio put down the phone, his hand shaking uncontrollably. *What have I done?* Weeks ago, he'd made a deal with the devil. Desperate for a cash infusion, when Boris hadn't come through, he'd looked elsewhere, receiving what he needed from the project's long-time investor. In return, he'd agreed to something unimaginable.

Today was the third time this month the investor had called inquiring about his progress. But Claudio needed no further incentive to get the job done. He worked around the clock. No harder than before, just longer, sleeping in the lab to save time on the commute.

The investor had delivered on his promise. Willing his hand to stop trembling, Claudio agonized over how he would keep his. And stay alive.

***

Rome Fiumicino Airport

The former ambassador to the Czech Republic stroked his soft, trimmed beard, still unaccustomed to the facial hair. His eyeglasses were now exchanged for colored contact lenses.

He wore tailored slacks and a Brooks Brothers sweater draped over his shoulders. In time, he would adjust to the casual attire.

Waiting in the long line at passport control, Boris missed his diplomatic credentials. For years, they had whisked him through the tedious process. He regretted waiting to upgrade his personal jet to allow for longer-haul flights. With a range of 800 miles, the Citation couldn't make it across the Atlantic. Standing behind a woman carrying a screaming infant, he made a mental note to remedy that.

Boris passed through uneventfully, bearing forged documents with photos reflecting his new look. They were prepared long ago, supporting an identity he had developed over the years. He retrieved his bags, and along with Fellini in his pet carrier, made his way outside, taking in the mellifluent sounds of Italian dialects. Relieved to be back on the Continent, he was filled with renewed energy. There was much to prepare for his disciple's arrival in Rome.

***

Once settled in his pied-à-terre, Boris arranged for a groomer to collect Fellini. He drew a warm bath and dressed in the hotel's robe, dined on chateaubriand delivered to his room from Bella Carne. He ate slowly, enjoying each bite, the steak cooked to perfection.

When the bellman returned Fellini to his room, Boris reaffixed the cat's sparkling collar. He poured a bowl of milk for the pet and a glass of Prosecco for himself.

After placing the empty plates outside his door, he phoned Claudio to inform him of his return to Rome. Clearly distracted, the scientist cut the conversation short, saying he needed to get back to his work. *Fine with me*, Boris thought. The sooner the next host was ready for cloning, the better. The two men had never spoken of the specifics of what the clones were destined for. There was no point. Claudio had no interest in these things. His sole focus was the science. What became of it once it left his lab didn't concern him.

Boris brushed and flossed his teeth, changed into his silk pajamas. He needed rest. Tomorrow was a big day. Spenser Germain had a great deal to learn before taking his place as the future czar of America.

***

Boris waited for Germain in the back of a sleek powder blue Bentley Mulsanne. Other than Fellini, it was his most prized possession. He would show the presidential candidate the royal treatment. Have him become accustomed to the finer things. It was an addiction worth coaxing that could one day prove a valuable motivator.

When he saw the congressman exit the terminal, he buzzed down the window, offered a regal wave, attracting his attention. A slight raise of the brows was all Boris needed to know he was on the right track with the car. Spenser got in and the two men shook hands, waiting while the driver stowed the luggage and got behind the wheel. Boris instructed him to take the long way to the hotel, then raised the glass partition. He and Spenser discussed the latest polls, and the recent flare-ups in cities across America. They drove by ancient ruins, baroque fountains, and magnificent architecture. Boris pointed out the Piazza Venezia anchored by the grand Il Vittoriano monument, mildly disappointed the congressman had never heard of *Roman Holiday*, the iconic motion picture filmed there.

They pulled up to Boris's hotel where he'd arranged for the presidential suite. The room was ornate with Italian paintings and furnishings, and a balcony overlooking the Piazza Navona. A king-size bed laden with French linens. A water closet likely larger than the congressman's Manhattan apartment. Boris was pleased Spenser hadn't commented on the opulence. Class could not be taught, it was inborn. And he had all the right genes.

After freshening up, the two men went for a stroll, the strong Mediterranean sun compensating for the cool December air.

Boris led the way through the Ghetto, Rome's centuries old Jewish quarter. Its cobblestone streets seeming wider now that the tables had been brought inside for the season. They stopped for gelato, then continued their walk. Boris spoke of family history and shared tales of his ambassadorship. The conversation turned to their respective upbringings and the pride Boris had felt at Spenser's college graduation.

"You were there?" the younger man asked, stunned.

Boris wiped a bit of chocolate from his mouth, threw out his used napkins. "Of course. Both your parents were gone by then. And you were always my pride and joy." He told him of the times he'd checked on him. "You had a few skirmishes early on."

Spenser seemed surprised by the knowledge.

"Your parents were concerned. I knew once you learned to channel that aggression, it would help you lead more effectively."

"They put me in therapy."

"And who do you think paid for it?"

His eyes widened. "I still struggle."

"Aggression is not always a bad thing."

Spenser appeared to consider the notion.

By the time they arrived back at the hotel, an easy rapport was developing between them. "Go rest. Tomorrow will be a long day. We'll get down to business."

***

The next morning, the two men met in the lobby. This time

it was a silver Maserati with its trademark grille, sleek headlights, and elongated hood cradling over 400 horsepower. As
the valet pulled up to the curb, Spenser nearly drooled, realizing the car was there for them. The driver got out, handing
Boris the key fob, who in turn dangled it in front of Spenser.
"You may take the wheel, if you wish."

Germain scurried to the driver's side, barely waiting for
the older man to take a seat before revving the engine and
pulling onto the road. Boris navigated them to Via Noment-
ana, a lovely tree-lined street a short distance from the famed
Galleria Borghese. As the road curved, he directed Spenser to
approach a wrought-iron gate fronting a well-manicured estate, a small screen attached to its side. An Italian Renaissance
villa was visible between the gaps of the manicured ever-
greens surrounding the property. Inconspicuous surveillance
cameras were positioned along the periphery.

"Where are we?" Spenser asked. It was the first thing he'd
said since entering the vehicle.

"The Russian consulate."

"I don't understand."

"Everything will become clear very soon."

Boris told Spenser to tap the screen.

"Shto?" said a deep, accented voice.

"It's me," Boris said.

The gate opened automatically. Spenser drove inside.

CHAPTER 48

Rome

Ambassador Boris Tierney and Congressman Spenser Germain were welcomed warmly. Like the dignitaries they were. The Russian ambassador to Italy embraced Boris as an old friend. He ushered his guests inside the building which doubled as the Russian's private residence. Turning to Spenser, he said, "We meet again, congressman."

He led them into a dimly lit salon adorned with Italian crystal chandeliers, crimson Bukhara rugs, and furnishings decked in thick rich fabrics. A yolka, the tinsel-laden fir, a distinctly Soviet tradition, stood in the corner, a red star at its apex.

There were three other suited men in the room, each sporting a visible bulge at his hip. This, along with their watchful gaze, easily pegged them as bodyguards rather than diplomats.

The Russian poured each of his guests a drink from the polished oak bar. "You are doing exceptionally well in the polls."

Spenser took a seat on a royal blue velvet chair and nodded. "I'm pleased. We're working hard."

"As are we."

Boris explained. "The ambassador is the chair of a special committee. They have been quietly supporting your efforts."

Brow furrowed, Spenser said, "I wasn't aware of that."

"To function effectively, the Committee must maintain a low profile."

Spenser took a sip of his drink. "Is it a legal entity?"

"It's comprised of a group of highly successful men and women whose sole purpose is to help you and your clones."

Despite the evasive response, Spenser didn't push further.

The Russian said, "The others arrive tomorrow. We've taken the liberty of preparing accommodations here for all of you. You will find it quite comfortable. We have an Olympic size pool as well as a spa and gym. All meals are prepared by our master chef."

Spenser said, "I like my room at the hotel."

Boris chimed in. "You're only here for a few days. It will be like a family reunion. Why don't we stay here, get a sense of how things operate?"

Spenser appeared conflicted. "I can't stay long," he reinforced. "I need to prepare for the primaries, and Congress will be back in session after the new year."

"Of course. I'll send for our bags. Perhaps you would enjoy a swim?"

"Actually," Spenser said, a smile spreading across his face. "I was hoping I could take the Maserati for another spin."

CHAPTER 49

CIA Headquarters
Washington, D.C.

The team had spent all week trying to locate Ambassador Boris Tierney. The man was a ghost. He had abandoned his post at the U.S. embassy in Prague and no one had heard from him in days. At this point it was fair to assume he had managed to get out of the country undetected. The CIA and FBI were working on tracking down his finances. They located an account in Geneva linked to a company Tierney had started twenty-odd years ago, but they couldn't obtain any information. The Swiss officials were more protective than Fort Knox.

Jon and Terry had remained in D.C., webcamming Carrie who was back in New York appearing bleary-eyed.

Terry said, "Maybe we're going about this the wrong way. We need to look at it from the clones' side. They all had contact with him."

Jon replied, "The number Carrie got off Salko's phone led nowhere. It was a burner."

Irritated, she replied, "Thanks, I remember, but what if Tierney wants to meet Salko or Germain in person like he did with Cantor? They would need to go to *him*, a location Tierney would choose."

Carrie said, "Excellent thinking. You have the makings of a top-notch investigator."

Jon and Terry watched as Carrie took out her phone and tapped away.

Terry smiled at the praise. "Do you think he's in Europe?"

Jon said, "That would be most logical, but there's no guarantee. He could be anywhere at this point."

Carrie said, "Let's play the odds for the time being and assume he's in Europe where he has political connections." Her phone dinged. "I texted Felix Salko with a random question, and he wrote back immediately. It's the middle of the night in Europe. He's obviously in or near our time zone. If he's planning a meeting with Tierney, it hasn't happened yet."

Jon said, "We have a guy watching Cantor. We know he's in D.C."

Terry said, "Good, let's keep tabs on both. If either of them makes travel plans, we'll be right there."

"I like it," Carrie said.

"Me too," Jon said, a begrudging note in his tone. "What about Germain?"

When no one replied, he took out his phone and dialed. "Hi Gwen, it's Jon. How're you doing?" A pause. "Listen, I have a few friends who like what I told them about the SAU. They really want to meet Spenser this weekend—" Another pause. "Oh, okay. Thanks." He hung up. "That woman does not like me."

"What's not to like?" Terry asked, her face straight.

"What did Gwen say?" Carrie asked.

"She claims Germain is under the weather."

"I'll check with the field agent assigned to him," Carrie said, making the call.

As she listened, her face turned angry. "What? How's that possible?" A minute later she ended the call, Jon and Terry staring at her.

Carrie said, "Germain had a well-advertised speaking gig planned at Columbia University this weekend. He canceled it last minute. The agent is heading to Germain's place now."

Forty minutes later, they were informed that the congressman had not picked up his mail in two days. No lights were on in his apartment. His neighbors hadn't seen him.

Terry said, "He's gone to Tierney."

Jon said, "Damn. Now what? Confront Gwen?"

Carrie said, "No chance. She'll alert Germain and Tierney. Our only option is to take over from the field agents and stick to the other two clones like glue. I'll stay with Salko."

Terry said, "I'm with Cantor."

"What about me?" Jon asked.

Terry tried to hold back a smirk. Unsuccessfully.

CHAPTER 50

Chicago

The weather was unseasonably mild, nearly breaking the day's record, luring young Chicagoans outdoors to enjoy the welcome effects of global warming. Felix Salko was running along the Riverwalk, the State Street bridge rising up ahead. Carrie was ten paces behind him, wearing a U Chicago sweatshirt, dark glasses, and a ball cap with her pony-tail sticking out the back. Unless Salko was looking at her head on, he wouldn't recognize her.

Carrie decided it was best if Jon didn't join her again in Chicago as her pretend husband. Since no events had been scheduled for Salko this week, she spent her time conducting basic reconnaissance. She looked at her watch. Her practice was to speak to Randy twice a day and take a stab at Facetime. He hadn't gotten the hang of it yet, leaving the phone while lining up his cars on his bedroom floor. Her maternal guilt was ever-present. She promised she'd see him over the weekend and today was Thursday.

Ten minutes into the run, Salko stopped short, looked at his phone, reading for a moment and quickly reversed course. Carrie turned away allowing him to pass her. He picked up speed. Something was up and she was going to find out what it was.

***

An hour later Carrie was sitting in her rental car outside Salko's apartment, logged into the man's Wi-Fi and reading his email. Among her diverse skillset were rudimentary hacking abilities, something she hoped to develop further. She pulled up his search history.

Jackpot! Salko had just booked a flight to Rome departing tonight. She felt the glimmer of a growing tension headache. Randy was in New York and her job was taking her to Rome. There were no second thoughts this time. She was going home to see her kid for the holiday. If she got fired, so be it.

***

Washington D.C.

Owen Cantor turned down the thermostat, grabbed his duffle, and locked his apartment door behind him. He was running late and didn't want to keep Terry waiting. Seemingly overnight, his future looked brighter than ever. The meeting with the ambassador was life altering. Today he'd been notified that Virginia's senior senator threw his name in the pool for the recently opened court of appeals judgeship. He suspected this was Ambassador Tierney keeping his word. He would need to be nominated by the president, and if confirmed by the Senate, he would be the youngest federal appellate court judge in history.

If by some miracle, Congressman Germain made it to the White House, his confirmation would glide through effortlessly. His numbers were good, but pundits thought them temporary. He was new and shiny but inexperienced. The fascination would soon pass.

As grateful as Owen was, he understood politics and knew favors never came for free. He now owed the ambassador. When Boris summoned him to Rome to discuss his future, he willingly accepted. Even when Boris suggested altering his appearance to distinguish himself from Germain. He rubbed his growing mustache, mentally preparing himself for a hair color change once it was fully grown. Though he had no need for prescription glasses, he purchased a clear-glass pair. Having spent much of the past week studying Lenin, he knew while inconvenient, Boris's advice was prudent. They needed to tone down the stark resemblance among them.

Then Terry surprised him with a call. He wasn't expecting to see her again after their date at the Watergate Steps. She didn't seem into him. Obviously, he'd misread the signals. She was pursuing him and he liked it. Maybe it was his new mojo since finding out who he really was. She was drawn to the power in his genes.

Owen entered the coffee shop and saw her sitting at their table, her blond hair held back in a clip. He would love to see it down brushing her shoulders but would have to wait until he got back from Italy. Let them both have something to look forward to. Seeing Terry made him wish he could share the revelation with her. But of course that was impossible.

***

Terry waited for Owen at what he referred to as *their* table. He was fifteen minutes late. She already ordered two peppermint lattes that were getting cold. She hadn't heard from him since their champagne-fueled evening and was strangely worried he wouldn't show. He was an awful flirt and borderline sleaze, but she needed him to show up.

When he walked in, she breathed a sigh of relief.

She almost didn't recognize him. Owen was dressed in casual clothes, a canvas duffle weighing down his right shoulder, a growing mustache. Glasses. He dropped the bag at his feet, bent down to peck her cheek, then sat across from her. He offered no apology for his lateness.

Terry resisted the urge to wipe her face. "You look like you're heading somewhere."

He nodded. "I have a flight in a few hours. I figured I'd meet you, then head straight to the airport."

"Where are you off to?"

Owen paused. "My college buddy is getting married in LA I must have mentioned it to you."

She was both disappointed and impressed with his lying skills, looking her straight in the eye as he fibbed. "Sorry, I must have forgotten. Sounds fun."

"Wish you could come."

"Maybe I can." She nearly choked on her flirtatious words.

His eyes panicked at his slip. He coughed. "Oh, it's not really an option. There was no plus-one on the invitation."

"That's too bad." She feigned a disappointed tone.

Owen changed the subject to the judgeship opportunity. Terry listened, grateful he didn't ask any probing questions about *her* life. After a few minutes of empty chatter, they drank their lattes in silence, both deep in their thoughts. When their mugs were drained, he rose, planted another peck, and said he'd call when he got back, hopefully before she had to leave herself.

Terry watched as he exited the shop and turned out of sight. She called Shira with an update and then messaged Carrie and Jon. She ordered an Uber and asked the driver to wait outside her hotel while she packed a bag.

Twenty minutes later, she placed her bag beside her in the back seat. "Dulles?"

"Yes."

"Where are you headed?"

"I have absolutely no idea."

***

Ten minutes from the airport Terry received a message from Carrie with her destination. She was going to Rome.

***

Chicago

Carrie put down her phone, Terry and Jon would make it to Rome days before she would. She sat on the edge of the hotel room's bed and let out a long-held breath, then dialed Jon in D.C. on Facetime.

When he saw her, he said, "Is that relief I see on your face?"

"Thanks for having my back again."

"I told you I would, and I mean what I say."

"I'm learning that."

With both clones on the move, Jon had told Matthews he and Terry would go ahead to Rome, but that Carrie would follow in a few days. Neither boss liked it but Jon was clear it wasn't up for debate. She was a mother and that came first. Let them try and fire her. They'd be in court for the rest of the century.

"Meet us when you can. Say hi to the little guy from me."

"Grazie," Carrie said with a perfect accent.

Jon flashed a broad smile. "Prego."

CHAPTER 51

Washington, D.C.–Rome

J on heard the last call announcement for the flight to Rome, arriving at the gate moments before they closed the boarding door. The last few days had been both exhausting and overwhelming, with little time to process the latest attempt on his life. He expected the anxiety would catch up with him sooner or later. Hopefully not at an inopportune time. He wanted to prove himself as worthy of the mission.

My life isn't normal, he thought, oddly uncertain how he felt about that fact. He found his seat and placed his carry-on in the overhead bin. He nodded at Terry seated across the aisle, getting a like response.

He collapsed in his seat, glad for the nine-hour flight time. Once off the ground, he allowed himself two small Smirnoffs to help him sleep. They didn't. Now, an hour from landing, he was irritable, and having Terry along on the mission was not helping.

Seeing her sleep soundly, he thought of Gabe dealing with a broken heart, trying anything to win back his lover. There was only one person to blame.

Jon felt his ears clog as the plane made its descent. They were due to land a half hour before Salko. Carrie's boss notified the local CIA agents and Jon would contact them for support once on the ground.

He lifted the window shade. The sun was mid-sky, the

outskirts of the Eternal City beginning to take shape. It seemed like another lifetime when he and Ashleigh planned to honeymoon in Rome. When she died, he'd sworn never to visit without her, and here he was. He pulled down the shade.

Focus on the here and now. Not the past, Jon thought. It was a tactic his therapist professed. If he wasn't vigilant, his fatigue could bring about an onslaught of melancholy.

Jon allowed his mind to turn to the mission. He and Terry would need to take extra precaution to avoid crossing paths with Cantor. If he laid eyes on Terry, the whole operation would quickly disintegrate.

One hour later, bags in hand, Jon and Terry exited the terminal. A middle-aged man sporting a Cubs cap approached them. "Steadman?" His accent was distinctly New England.

"Yup."

"Buon pomeriggio." *Good afternoon.* He handed Jon a black briefcase. "Your protection."

Jon snapped it open, peeked inside. Three pistols, gun clips, and twenty-round boxes of ammo.

The man double clicked a key fob. They all turned to the sound. "Your wheels."

Jon eyed the tiny Fiat. "No frills transportation, huh?"

"It was all we had on short notice." The man handed the keys to Jon. "There's an update. Cantor's delayed. He's stuck in Paris. Flights are grounded due to a strike so it's unclear when he'll get here. We'll keep you posted."

Jon asked, "Do you have an ETA on Felix Salko's flight from Chicago."

"He lands in a few hours. I've got a guy keeping a close eye for other unexpected flight changes. I'll be in touch." He walked into the terminal.

Terry said to Jon, "I guess I don't have to worry anymore about bumping into Owen."

"True. Sounds like we have a new mark."

Terry got in the passenger side of the Fiat. Jon placed the briefcase and their bags in the back seat and got behind the wheel.

"What's our game plan?" Terry asked. They were the first words she'd spoken to him since leaving D.C.

"We have two CIA guys inside the terminal keeping an eye out for Salko. They'll let us know where to pick up his tail."

"So, we just wait here?"

"Yup."

The vibe in the car made it clear neither one of them was very happy about that.

Jon asked, "Mind if I close my eyes for a minute?"

"Fine."

Relieved that slumber would release him from the car's toxic environment, Jon put his head back and was asleep in seconds, spared from hearing Terry's muttered grievances.

***

Paris, France

Whatever good fortune Owen Cantor had enjoyed before getting on his flight to Rome was quickly offset by a series of unfortunate events. His two-hour layover in Paris turned into a nightmare with the sudden strike of air traffic controllers. Until their needs were met—protecting their pensions from government reform—all flights would be grounded. He couldn't even get a private plane out. He'd contacted Boris, who after checking with his connections, informed him the strike would last for no more than three days. The French government would capitulate by then. He would still make it in time for the reunion.

Though he'd hoped to tour Rome, now he was in Paris. *First world problems*, he told himself. He had brought work along with him, but would make time to stroll the Champs-Elysées. If only he'd been able to invite Terry along. They could have been together in the City of Love.

CHAPTER 52

Rome

F elix Salko strolled along the Via del Corso as if in a dream. A towering spruce draped in string lights and colorful ornaments stood at the center of the piazza. Was it only hours ago he was in Chicago jogging along the Riverwalk?

Rome's main shopping area was footsteps from the Spanish Steps. He climbed them to get a better view, passing a group of carolers dressed in traditional costume. The city was vibrant and intoxicating, as were her women. At the top of the steps, he turned right and stopped to look in a shop window displaying leather jackets. They were impeccably designed, made of the most supple hides. He was about to enter the shop when he saw Jon Lewis, Carrie's husband. With another woman. They were at the end of the street arguing, the woman gesticulating with her hands. Felix momentarily considered greeting them but thought better of it. He pretended not to see the arguing couple and entered the store thinking, *What a strange coincidence.*

***

Jon noticed the moment Felix Salko made them. He and Terry had exchanged a few heated words and dropped their guard.

He'd once again allowed his personal life to affect his assignment. Unfortunately, this time Carrie wasn't here to bail him out. Terry's face was still flush with anger.

He said, "He's seen us."

Arms crossed, Terry said, "He doesn't know me."

Jon assumed a calmer disposition. "He knows *me* as Carrie's husband, and is probably wondering what I'm doing in Rome with another woman."

"Could this cause problems?"

"I hope not, or I'll be looking for another job."

Terry's shoulders relaxed.

Jon said, "There's nothing we can do about it now. If we see him again, I'll approach him, play it as a coincidence, and introduce you as my work colleague."

"Fine. Now what do we do?"

"We'll let the CIA guys stay on him." Jon sent a text to the field agents stating his intention to leave the scene. Without explanation. "Let's go," he said, leading the way.

They descended the iconic steps along with a myriad of tourists oblivious to the surreptitious happenings around them.

***

Felix held his phone in one hand and his newly purchased leather jacket in the other as he exited the store. Ambassador Tierney was on the line. "My driver will pick you up from your hotel at four p.m."

"I'll be ready," he told Boris.

"Did you enjoy your afternoon in Rome?"

"Very much so. I don't know that I'll want to go home." He turned toward the steps. Jon Lewis and that woman were gone. "I just had the strangest coincidence."

"Do tell."

"I saw one of my donors. Her husband, actually. He was arguing with a woman, not his wife."

"Perhaps their marriage is in trouble."

"I suppose. Too bad. I like Carrie."

"Carrie?"

"His wife."

Silence on the line.

"Are you still there?"

Boris replied, his voice tense. "I'm going to send you photos of two people. Tell me if you recognize them."

A moment later Salko's phone buzzed. He opened the pictures. A handsome couple. The cowboy and the Latina. "That's Jon and Carrie Lewis. The donors I mentioned. How do you know them?"

Boris cursed aloud. "They're not only donors, Felix. They're intelligence officers. And they are following you."

***

"I lost him," the local spook said into the phone. He didn't sound particularly disturbed about losing his mark.

"How's that possible?" Jon was furious, but he took it down a notch. It was his own fault to begin with.

"I tailed him from the Piazza di Spagna to the metro station, watched him buy a ticket and wait for the orange line. But he wasn't on the train when it left the station. He shook me off. I thought you said this was a regular guy."

Damn! Someone tipped him off, told him what to do. Jon knew he had messed up royally.

He opened the shutters looking down on the Ghetto. He was glad Terry was in her own room and didn't hear the conversation. He would need to tell her Salko was off the radar. If she chose to notify Matthews, he would face the music, but there was nothing to gain by offering the info himself. With Salko gone, their only remaining recourse was to follow Cantor, the last locatable clone. And there was no way Jon would mess this one up.

***

Boris was on full alert. He needed to find out who the "other woman" was traipsing the streets of Rome with Agent Jon Steadman. Another agent? He had no photo to go on, only a weak description from Salko. Blonde, petite, fiery. So far two attempts to rid himself of these menaces were botched beyond belief. They knew about Felix Salko, which meant they would be waiting for Owen Cantor. Cat chases mouse. Dog chases cat. He would take care of things once and for all in the best way possible. By himself.

CHAPTER 53

New York City

Carrie wasn't much of a crier but lately it was waterworks. The difference in her son was apparent the moment she entered her parents' apartment. Ricky Martin was singing in the background. Randy had his eyes closed, his head held back, and was twirling, clearly enjoying the music. He looked content. He'd smiled when he saw her, tolerating a hug and kiss.

Still, it was obvious her son was turning inside himself, using less of his hard-earned speech, becoming more easily agitated as if he spoke a language no one else understood. His psychologist had not diagnosed him with autism, but Carrie knew it was a possibility and dreaded the thought of ever hearing that word used to describe her son. Despite the psychologist's optimistic disposition, Carrie read her face—a skill she was well-trained at—and it told a less rosy story.

The therapist gently suggested starting him on meds, but Carrie would get a second opinion before going that route. She wanted Randy, not a drugged version of him.

Carrie's mother was bringing dinner to the table, while her dad sat in his recliner reading the paper. Photos of family members in uniforms representing various branches of the U.S. military, were neatly arranged on the living room's side tables. Carrie gave her mother a hand, then told her parents she would stay, take another leave of absence from her job.

They were emphatic. She needed to go to work, find fulfillment, and make a living, they said. When he was older, she could arrange a more balanced schedule. But for now, they were thrilled to have the time with their only grandson. "We'll be here when you get home."

Her parents knew very little of her profession. Yet they understood it was a government post requiring a great deal of travel. They never asked questions about her work, which suggested they suspected it was in the intelligence field. Carrie wondered if they understood the dangers inherent to her job. Maybe they just took that for granted. After all, she was a veteran, from a military family. They were a patriotic bunch and if she was serving her country in any capacity, they were proud. She would go back into the field. It was her duty. She'd sworn to protect and defend. That oath protected her son as well.

Carrie ate pot roast and yams with her family, hugged her parents, and kissed Randy till he pushed her away. Back in her car, as she glanced up at her parents' window, she began to sob all over again.

***

Rome

Owen Cantor passed through customs, retrieved his bags, and stood in the taxi line. He had been to Rome once after college, traversing the continent hostel to hostel with a backpack and long-gone girlfriend. He heard she was now living in Detroit with a right-wing conservative.

Rome wasn't his favorite European city. That would be Barcelona. The music, food, women. His thoughts went to Terry. He hoped she'd still be in D.C. when he returned. He was excited to meet Boris and plan his future on the appellate court, though he suspected there was much more to be discussed at this evening's meeting.

The air was chilly, gray clouds gathering above. Owen felt a drop land on his forehead. He was happy to be on the ground if a storm was coming.

***

Déjà vu all over again. Jon tapped the steering wheel, waiting in the Fiat outside the arrivals hall when Judge Owen Cantor exited the terminal. This time Carrie sat beside him. She had arrived an hour earlier, and he was glad of it. He told her about his mistake, appreciative to have a partner who was well-trained and level-headed. She didn't rail on him. If anything, she was subdued, but when he'd asked, she attributed it to the long flight. He assumed her mood was related to Randy.

The local CIA guy had found Cantor on the flight register, saving Jon many hours of reconnoitering. Neither Jon nor Carrie had ever met Cantor which made things a lot easier than with Salko. It was why Terry was back at the hotel waiting for an update.

Jon and Carrie watched as Cantor entered a taxi. Jon pulled in behind it. There was no reason to stay back. With so many cars on the road, theirs wouldn't stand out. Thirty-three minutes later they slowed near the end of a narrow tree-lined street. The taxi had been allowed entry into a gated estate.

"What is this place?" Jon said.

Carrie Googled their location and turned her phone to show Jon. One hundred feet behind them was a location pin. Ambasciata di Russia. *The Russian embassy.*

***

Boris watched the security cameras as the taxi pulled up to the circular drive. He moved the cursor panning the area surrounding the embassy. The cameras had been positioned high enough to offer a full view of the street as well as halfway into the adjacent one. An unfamiliar car was parked on the road. Street parking was designated for diplomats and residents only. The simple Fiat didn't belong. He couldn't see inside the vehicle but had a good idea who its occupants were.

***

Carrie said, "We should move. Tierney knows we're onto him. I'm sure the building has cameras."

Jon pulled out of the spot. A traffic barricade had been set up at the far end of the narrow, curved road requiring him to turn around. He made a three-point turn. An elderly man was crossing the road, a paper bag held in the crook of his arm. Jon stopped the car to allow him to pass. They watched as the bag tore open, apples falling to the ground, several rolling under his car.

"Merda!" the old man cursed loudly.

Carrie buzzed down her window and said something in fluent Italian.

The old man replied.

"I'll go help him," she said. "Stay in the car."

Carrie got out. Out of the corner of his eye Jon saw something pressing against his window. There stood a uniformed man, his bulk twice the size of Jon's, an assault rifle in his hand.

"Get out," the man said in a distinctly Russian accent.

Jon shifted his eyes to see where Carrie was. Another guard had a machine gun at her back. The abduction took no more than seconds. The old man looked terrified. The guard beside Carrie said something to him firmly, handed him a wad of bills. The old man scurried away, leaving his apples sprawled across the road.

Jon got out of the car and he and Carrie were escorted inside the Russian compound.

***

Boris smiled at what he was witnessing on the screen. Things were improving nicely. He didn't understand why Felix Salko said Steadman was with another woman when Agent Santiago was with him. He would solve the mystery later this evening. Right now, he had another matter to attend to.

***

The reunion that took place in the consulate's salon was nothing short of historic. It was the first time since Claudio had resurrected the premier's DNA that the clones had come together. Filmed discreetly, the three men assessed each other, stared, and laughed awkwardly. Boris encouraged them to spend the rest of the day bonding. A camaraderie was quickly forming. After dinner, Boris arranged for a private screening. Spenser led them to the media room, as if he was already in charge. It made Boris proud.

The featured film was a dramatization of Lenin's life and philosophy, and his meteoric rise to power. When the lights came on, Boris asked the men to take out their copies of Lenin's will addendum.

"The letter each of you holds is of monumental importance. You three are special, chosen men, each on a specific path to success. You will define history. Children will learn about you in grade school. Not solely for how you came to be, but for the contributions you will make to the world."

Spenser stood, leaning against the wall. Felix and Owen sat riveted.

Boris continued, "The Committee, a long-standing federation of powerbrokers, was established prior to Lenin's death. It is a multi-generational secret society dedicated to the propagation of his ideals. Think of them as the communist version of the Freemasons. It is with their significant influence in media and government that you three have succeeded so quickly, Spenser's run for the presidency at the forefront."

Owen shifted nervously in his chair. "What you're describing sounds like a revolution."

"Yes, though a more subtle approach than the last Russian revolution. The next generation of Americans is already drawn to our principles."

"Then, why not allow it to play out naturally?"

"Our objective does not stop at the United States. Like the previous incarnation of capitalism, the rest of the world will follow their example. We will soon begin the next round of clones to succeed you."

Felix shook his head in apparent disbelief. "Lenins across the world?" He took a pack of Marlboros from his pocket. Boris looked at him, shook his head. Felix hesitated, then put back the cigarettes.

Boris grinned. "In every corner of the globe. As any revolutionary faction, the Committee will continue to exist as an underground offensive. Their considerable resources will continue to buy the support of politicians and industry moguls, be it through lobbies, bribes, or blackmail."

Owen said, "I've dedicated my career to law and order..."

Irritated with his irreverence, Boris said, "As I recall, you were involved in—shall we say—a sensational test-taking scheme during your junior year in college? Your expulsion was imminent."

Spenser and Felix looked at Owen, his face reddening. "That was..."

Boris held up a hand. "I am not judging you. It was I who had those charges dismissed. Had they gone through, you would never have been accepted to law school or be in the upwardly mobile position you are today—well on your way to obtaining a nomination for a federal appellate judgeship. From there, you will be groomed for the Supreme Court of the United States."

Cantor laughed. "That's impossible!" The words seemed to tumble out. He quickly quieted.

Unruffled and smiling amicably, Boris said, "Please speak your mind."

Owen paused. "All right. My appointment would necessitate nomination by the President of the United States. With all due respect, as powerful a man as you are, I don't think you have that kind of clout to ensure Spenser's victory."

Boris held his temper. The man was brazen. He reminded himself Cantor was his great-granduncle and calmed. "It's one of the reasons you needed to alter your appearance. Your nomination will bring you a great deal of attention and widespread exposure. Your face will be seen across news outlets. We can't risk people noticing the resemblance to Spenser." He studied Owen's face. "There is still more we can do in that regard."

Owen appeared to hold back saying anything in return.

Boris gestured to Spenser. "I preferred to avoid burdening you with the details but..."

Spenser lifted a quizzical brow.

"There's no sense in keeping it a secret from the family. A series of well-orchestrated protests will erupt once again across the country. They will be timed for maximum effect."

Spenser asked, "It was you behind those protests? The right-wing conspiracy theorists were pinning it on me."

"The less you knew the better. I made sure the instigating social media posts originated from outside the U.S. so you wouldn't be liable. You will soon learn those who oppose you will sling whatever they can your way, hoping something will stick. It comes with the territory. The videos were a success, quickly going viral. The next series of riots will be more widespread and militant than before. They will boost your campaign. Spenser, your SAU members will be trained and militarized, as will other student groups around the country."

Cantor's jaw dropped.

Boris allowed the news to sink in, then turned to Felix

Salko. "If you accept your role, you will be installed at the helm of ComTech."

Felix stared at the man as if he were unhinged. "But that's —"

"The largest media conglomerate in the world."

Felix was speechless.

"The Committee will enable your appointment. You'll reign over a network of online, television, and radio outlets, invaluable for the purposes of disseminating our agenda."

An uneasiness settled in the room. Boris knew Salko and Cantor were overwhelmed, perhaps even envious of Germain.

"You will find comprehensive files about your respective roles in your rooms. Please review them thoroughly. I require your decisions by the end of your stay here in Rome."

The men were subdued, pensive. All small talk had ceased. Once Felix and Owen were shown their rooms, Spenser said to Boris, "Neither of them is capable of leading as president. I've made the right decision to accept the role."

Boris detected a distinct note of superiority. "They will prove worthy allies. You must support each other as brothers. Now, come, let's enjoy a nightcap and discuss your future as President of the United States, the *New* Soviet Union."

CHAPTER 54

Rome

"I'm done," Claudio whispered into the phone. He had waited nearly four decades to utter those two words. "Congratulazioni, Dr. Giovanni!"

The investor had kept his side of the bargain. Claudio had found twenty thousand euro in a private account far from Boris's view.

"Grazie."

"Do you have the female carriers?"

"Yes. I will contact them."

"Excellent."

"Can I tell Boris?"

"Soon. But not yet."

Claudio didn't like it. He was a dreadful liar. Boris knew him so well it felt at times like he was reading his mind.

***

Jon rubbed his shoulder. The guard had pushed him the whole way down into the underbelly of the villa with the butt of his rifle. Carrie, to her credit, was keeping it together. They had been relieved of their weapons and phones, told they would soon be met by their employer and "to make themselves comfortable." This was said with a malevolent smirk.

Of course, there was no place to get comfortable. Two

metal folding chairs in a cavernous room with three of the walls made of stone, the fourth a mirror. A leak from somewhere yielded a powerful smell of mildew. Jon didn't like closed dark spaces. Despite the chill in the air he felt sweat bead on his forehead. He took a moment to calm his heart rate, mentally going through the exercises he learned from his shrink.

He guessed the building was several hundred years old. Built to last. Its formidable structure would not easily allow them to escape. Not that Jon planned to. Despite his unfortunate circumstances, he wanted to meet former Ambassador Boris Tierney again. He would have preferred being detained in a room with a window, but told himself if this was how they would learn about the resurrection project, so be it. He'd figure out a way to get free afterward.

Carrie and he knew better than to speak openly. There was no question the room was wired. She mouthed asking if he was okay. He nodded in response. She did a few jumping jacks and push-ups to get her blood flowing. Jon followed suit. If anyone was watching them, they would find the scene peculiar. Carrie moved close to Jon, put her lips to his ear. "What's the plan?"

"We wait," he whispered back.

"Does Terry know where we are?"

"Only if the CIA told her. The car's GPS is linked to them."

Carrie looked satisfied and inched away.

***

Carrie was mentally going through all her SERE training. *Survival, Evasion, Resistance, and Escape.* What to do when captured by the enemy. Avoiding panic was the top of the list. She kept her mind from veering to Randy. She needed to stay strong—physically and mentally. The exercise helped but Jon was still a rookie, and right now, she needed an experienced partner to feed off of. She couldn't worry about him and the bigger picture at the same time.

Carrie watched Jon take timed deep breaths as if it were a regular exercise and was relieved to see them calm him. She hoped he would stay that way when things got dicey. As she knew they would, very soon.

*****

In Boris's estimation, the evening's clone meeting couldn't have gone better if he had scripted it. The men had gotten along famously, spending time comparing notes about their lives, though to Boris, the loss of Alexander Bilka was palpable. The Lenins, as he now thought of them, were more curious than apprehensive about the establishment of the movement. Spenser was the clear leader with neither Salko nor Cantor questioning it. Any earlier envy seemed to have shifted to relief from knowing they'd acquire notoriety without the burden of Germain's responsibility.

Before long, Spenser would establish the ultimate foothold in American politics while the two other surviving clones would be optimally positioned to provide the most vital support from the highest echelons of the judiciary and media.

Boris left the salon, making a mental note to speak with Claudio. The man was becoming more of a hermit—eccentric and insular. Cloning results were needed soon. Their main investor was restless, though Boris hadn't heard from him in weeks. He wasn't complaining, but the change was of mild concern.

Jetlagged, the clones retired early. All the better. Boris couldn't afford to be interrupted for the late evening's events. Boris approached the cellar door, clearing his mind so he could properly tend to his unexpected visitors.

CHAPTER 55

Rome

J on stood as soon as he heard the lock being manipulated. Carrie remained seated. They hadn't exchanged any more words. They intuitively understood much of their plan would depend on two things—what Boris would do next and how quickly the CIA would find them.

***

Washington, D.C.

The CIA guys couldn't get a read on Agents Steadman and Santiago. The GPS signal had stopped in front of the Russian embassy. Neither agent had reported in. They contacted their boss in D.C. who cursed at the worst possible location. Russian territory in a foreign land. How on Earth would they get the agents out safely if they were not there of their own accord? Given the identity of the clone's host, that needed to be assumed. Carrie's boss had no choice but to call Matthews and Kahn. The consensus was to wait. See if they emerged in the next two hours. If not, the U.S. ambassador to Italy would contact the Russian ambassador and find out what the hell was going on.

***

Jerusalem

Yosef Kahn was not a patient man. He learned long ago that when a handler loses track of his field officer sitting on matters could go very badly and fast. He didn't intend to engage in a dispute with his counterparts in the States but there was no way he was letting the operation flounder. He picked up the phone and called the one person who could help immediately.

***

Rome

Terry grabbed the phone on the first ring. It was Shira.

"We have reason to believe your team members are being detained against their will at the Russian Embassy."

"Dear Lord," Terry cried. "I've been worried sick waiting hours for an update from them. Can we get them out?"

"The Americans are concerned about ruffling the feathers of their Italian allies, not to mention going head-to-head with the Russians."

Terry processed that. "And we're not?"

"Thankfully, Israel has excellent relations with those two countries, but they won't take well to knowing one of our assets—you—has been operating under their noses unannounced."

"We need to help them."

"Correct, but we also need to find out what they're learning inside the embassy. We know our American friends. If their agents come out of this alive, they will keep what they learned about the resurrection project close to the vest leaving us out in the cold."

Terry sensed what was coming. She struggled to keep her voice from trembling. "What do you want me to do?"

"I have devised a plan. To succeed, it will require cunning, fortitude, and use of all I've taught you."

Terry thought of Jon, Gabe's closest friend. *Her* friend, despite all their squabbles. "Tell me."

And she did.

***

Boris entered the villa's subterranean room. More like a modern-day dungeon, he thought. He considered the two people imprisoned there. A cocky American FBI agent pacing the space as if ready to dictate a speech. He walked with a distinct limp, his hair beyond regulation length. Seated was the Hispanic female CIA agent whom he'd met several years prior, shortly after her recruitment. They had crossed paths when he came to New York and stopped at the CIA field office for the annual powwow. She'd impressed him with how much a person of her race and gender could achieve these days.

"Agent Santiago, when we met in Prague I said I was glad you were back in the field. I didn't expect it would put us at odds."

Carrie remained seated, her face a mask of neutrality. "Neither did I. I'm disappointed you're involved in this."

"And I for you. Agent Steadman, I read a lot about you. I must apologize. This room must make you quite uncomfortable. But I really had nowhere else to put you. The other guests are having a grand time getting to know one another. I didn't think it wise to have you bump into them."

Jon stopped pacing, glared at his captor. "No apology for trying twice to kill me?"

"We've been working on this project for many years. Greater people than you have had to pay the ultimate price for getting in the way of its progress. It's nothing personal."

Angry at the dispassionate response, Jon said, "Lenin, huh? You couldn't clone Gandhi or Mother Theresa?"

"Vladimir Lenin was my esteemed great-granduncle. His contributions far surpassed those of senseless do-gooders."

The two agents were noticeably shocked by his pedigree. It gave him a sense of pride. They must be confused how that significant detail escaped all their background checks. Of course, he had gone to great pains to conceal his lineage.

Carrie said, "Your scientific achievement is laudable."

"Thank you. It's too bad the scientist who made these wondrous clones cannot be given due acknowledgement, but secrecy is a small price to pay for full proprietorship."

Jon said, "What do you want from us?"

"First of all, I want you to tell me how much you know about our project."

"What's second of all?" Jon asked.

"To get you and your organizations out of the way. My gut tells me a polite request won't suffice."

Jon said, "Do you actually think you can abduct two Americans inside an official embassy without devastating repercussions?"

"It would not be the first time. Turkey? Russia? Agents disappear. A few years of sanctions and all goes back to normal. There will be no war over you."

"Maybe not a public one, but the retribution will be fierce. An eye for an eye."

"I don't concern myself with Russian intelligence officers. If the Americans want to take them out, they can be my guest. My work continues."

"Why are you doing this, Ambassador?" Carrie asked, using his now defunct title.

Boris much preferred speaking with Agent Santiago. "It was the comrade's dying wish. He was never able to fulfill his ultimate dream. To expand his ideals across the globe. He was taken at fifty-four. Had he lived, the world in its entirety would be under Soviet rule."

When neither agent offered a comment, Boris said, "Tell me what you already know."

Carrie said, "We know about the clones and where they reside. And that they are here to convene."

Jon looked at her sharply. Boris took note.

"Thank you for your candid response. It saves us a great deal of unpleasantness."

Jon asked, "Is there anything you'd like to share with *us*?"

"Fair question. But as they say, once I tell you I'll have to kill you." Boris laughed at his own cliché.

Carrie looked uncomfortable but kept quiet.

Boris shrugged. "Very well. Our movement will spearhead the rebirth of the Soviet ideal."

He was pleased with their horrified countenances.

Jon asked, "You're planning to resuscitate the U.S.S.R.? It was a resounding failure."

"The New Soviet Union is not in Russia."

"Then where the hell is it?"

"Haven't you put the pieces together? It's right where we've all come from. The late, great U.S. of A."

Carrie and Jon were speechless.

"Congratulations, you have just become the first prisoners of war."

***

Though they knew this was the likely plan for the congressman, Jon maintained his stunned appearance. He needed Boris to keep talking, confirm the agencies' as yet unsubstantiated suspicions.

"You intend to place Lenin at the helm?" Jon asked.

"Yes. Of course."

"Which one?"

"I think you know," Boris said.

"The congressman."

Boris nodded.

"Do you have any idea what you've embroiled him in?"

"It's what he was created for. He's an outstanding orator, persuasive, charming. He's the most accurate clone of the three."

"You mean four, don't you?"

Boris couldn't hold back his ire. "If you hadn't gone to Prague, Alexander would still be here. That interference is unforgivable."

"You had him killed, not me."

Boris took a determined step in Jon's direction, the guard shadowing him. "He was worth billions—" Jon held his stance. Boris stopped himself. "No, I will not dirty my hands with you. This has been a wondrous day and shall remain such. Now, Agent Steadman, I must insist you sit and tell me the purpose of your mission. Who was the woman with you at the Spanish Steps?"

Jon remained standing, his face a mask of disgust. Boris made a near imperceptible hand gesture. Swiftly, the guard jabbed the butt of his gun into Jon's gut. He doubled over, expelling a lungful of air, falling to his knees. His eyes watered. Ignoring the guard, Carrie went to him, helped him to sit. "Take it easy," she whispered. "I'll handle this."

***

"I need to speak with Ambassador Tierney," Terry said, her voice firm.

"Miss, this is the Russian embassy. There is no ambassador by that name."

"I know he's there and unless he agrees to speak with me, I'll have a television crew outside your building in time for the evening news."

The man on the other end of the line told her to hold.

Another man with a heavy Russian accent came on the

line.

"Who is this?"

"I'll tell you what I said already. I want to speak to Tierney."

"What makes you think he is here? He is an American."

"I don't have time for this. The next time you hear my voice will be on the news."

"Wait."

Terry held her breath.

The man said, "Give me your number and I'll have him call you."

"No chance. Get him on the phone now. I'll hold."

**

Jon was still groaning from the blow when a second guard entered, causing Jon to flinch. The brute said something to Boris in Russian, who despite the seconds-before violence, politely excused himself. They heard the door lock behind him.

Carrie whispered, "An unknown woman is on the line for him."

"You speak Russian as well?"

She shrugged.

He came over, whispered in her ear. "Terry?"

She nodded. "I sure as hell hope so."

**

"My name is Dr. Terry Lavi. I am a geneticist at the Technion in Haifa, Israel."

Boris thought the name was vaguely familiar. "How did you know I was here?"

"I followed Owen Cantor."

Boris needed to process the confession. Perhaps she was

the woman Felix saw with Steadman. *The other woman.*

"Would you be so kind as to hold while I confirm your credentials?"

"Please do."

Boris put the phone down, went to his laptop and typed in her name. She was legit. The name was familiar for good reason. She was a trailblazer in the intimate world of genetics.

He came back on. "What do you want?"

"To help you."

"Assuming I know what you're speaking of, why would you want to help?"

"There's no time for game playing. I only have a few minutes left to call in a television crew for the six o'clock news. To be blunt, there is nothing altruistic about my offer. It will help me as much as you."

"Hmm, go on."

"Following a significant discovery, I lobbied for years to earn a Nobel prize in genetic sciences, only to have another scientist outshine me. Not for her skill but her connections. Call it sour grapes, but that's what motivates me now. In exchange for learning about your advances, I will freely offer my expertise to speed up the next...experiment."

"Were you with Jon Steadman yesterday?"

She didn't hesitate. "Yes. He was one of my ways to you. I knew Owen was involved but I couldn't follow him on my own. I used Jon for that. I knew him from a job I helped him with last year. It's through him that I heard about you. I don't like the man, but he led me here to Rome. When I caught up with him, I was surprised to see he had Felix Salko in his sights, not Owen. Seems Owen's plane was delayed. But I was excited to see Salko. He is an impressive clone. I pressed Jon to back off. This isn't a government affair. The science world needs to explore this freely without crippling regulation."

While she spoke, Boris sent a message to the Russian ambassador, chair of the Committee, requesting a deeper dive into the woman's background. Within mere minutes Dr. Theresa Lavi's name was mined for any affiliation with the intelligence world. There was none.

Boris read the ambassador's reply. "Dr. Lavi, do you know who Owen is?"

"Yes. And I am pleased with your selection. A visionary. Let's cut to the chase. I have a great deal of experience. And if I were you, the goal must be to work on the next clone immediately. I have the know-how and skills to do that. It's a win-win. I share the accolades once things are made public, which is only a matter of time. You, in turn acquire a scientist who will speed up the project. Regarding that, I'd be pleased to make some suggestions for future viable hosts."

Boris heard enough. The Committee had entrusted him with securing outside funding, but there had been no word from the project's investor for weeks. If his cash cow bailed, the consequences would be dire. The only way to avoid that would be by finishing the next clone. Fast. Claudio would hate him for being forced to share the credit. But it was his own fault.

"No need, Dr. Lavi. We already selected one." Boris paused a moment, then said, "I think we may have a deal."

CHAPTER 56

Rome

T erry got off the phone, depleted. She couldn't believe what she had just done. Her body began to shake uncontrollably. She sat down, closed her eyes. Once she could, she went to the room's minibar and poured herself a glass of red wine.

Shira had come through for her, enlisting a Mossad techie to plant bits of personal data across the internet, supporting Terry's affinity for a revival of communist policies in Israel, such as an expansion of the once-popular kibbutz movement. Her social media posts from recent years would read like a card-carrying member of the hammer-and-sickle club.

She'd convinced Boris Tierney he needed her. He was a man who had no compunction to kidnap two intelligence officers. He killed at least one person she knew of and likely many more. He had admitted to cloning one of the most devious madmen of the last century. And she was meeting him tomorrow.

***

Jon and Carrie huddled together on the floor. The guard had brought them a blanket, a pot for urinating, and two bowls of kasha. They huddled for warmth and to converse more easily.

They kept their voices low.

Jon asked, "Where the hell's the cavalry?"

"My guess is they're waiting to see if we emerge on our own rather than spark a multi-national incident."

"*We* didn't spark it," he hissed.

She put her finger to her lips. "Be that as it may, it's procedure. They'll come for us tomorrow."

"We could be dead by then. You told him everything we know. He has no reason to keep us alive."

"No point in suffering *and* dying, right?"

Jon quieted.

"We'll be okay, Jon. We're employed by two of the best intelligence agencies in the world." Then, "Are you also thinking of family?"

The question seemed to subdue him. "I don't have any. It's just me and my grandmother."

"Parents? Siblings?"

"I'm an only child. My parents died when I was very young."

Carrie frowned. "I'm so sorry. I had no idea."

"It wasn't in my file?"

"No, I would remember that."

Maybe Matthews redacted it, he thought. He had a few redeeming qualities after all. Jon smiled at the thought of Matthews blocking out parts of his file with a Sharpie.

"What are you smiling about?"

"Just thinking of my boss."

Carrie made a funny face. "And that makes you happy?"

"He can be a real hard-ass but he's also sort of a weird father figure."

"Hmmm. Can't say the same of my boss."

"How's Randy?" Jon asked.

At mention of her son's name, Carrie's face contorted. She looked like she was trying not to cry.

"I didn't mean to upset you," Jon said.

"I'll be fine. It's Randy I'm worried about. He's come so far in the last year and now he's taken a turn for the worse. Instead of being with him, I'm trapped in a makeshift prison half a world away. What kind of mother am I, Jon?"

He held her close, whispered. "You're Randy's mom. That's what kind of mom. And there's no one better for that job than you."

Carrie's eyes watered, a sole tear sliding down her cheek. He wiped it away with the pad of his thumb. The urge to kiss her was strong but he resisted. She put her head on his shoulder.

They stayed that way till morning.

***

New York City

"We've waited long enough, dammit!" Matthews yelled into the phone. The CIA boss was pushing to keep waiting. He didn't want the morning papers filled with headlines of two American spies being extracted from a Russian embassy. They left the Mossad man out of the conversation. His agent was safe. The decision on how to act would need to come from the two of them and they were at odds.

Matthews brought his voice down. "They were abducted."

"We don't know that."

"It's been hours without contact. Heaven knows what those two are enduring."

"They're trained for this, Matthews. What matters now is the spin. And the fact that we didn't inform our Italian friends of their presence."

Disgusted by the CIA man's callousness, he said, "How long are you willing to wait?"

"Till after the morning news has been reported. Print and

television. Nine a.m. local time. Unfortunately, nothing can be done about online reports."

"That's not for several more hours! Are you insane? If something happens to them I will hold you personally responsible."

Ice in his voice, the man said, "And if you can't keep your personal feelings out of the mission then you need to retire."

Matthews slammed down the phone. He would wait till the morning as much as it killed him. For no other reason than realizing the CIA guy was right. Somewhere along the line it had become personal.

CHAPTER 57

Rome

T erry had an awful night. She couldn't sleep, mentally rehashing the phone conversation she'd had with Boris Tierney. It was six a.m. now. She mouthed a silent prayer it wasn't too late to get Jon and Carrie safely out of the embassy. She wouldn't allow herself to think what was happening to them. Shira told her to await instructions, which is what she'd been doing since speaking with her about the plan hours earlier.

Her phone buzzed, making her jump and bang her head against the headboard. She rubbed the spot, thinking if she didn't calm down before meeting Tierney, she'd put herself and the others in jeopardy. Looking at her phone, relief ran through her. "Shira?"

"How are you holding up?" the Mossad handler asked, her voice laced with concern.

Terry was surprised by the question from the typically stoic woman. "Jittery, scared."

"All acceptable emotions."

Thanks.

The two women reviewed details of the plan once more. Shira assured her that a team would be nearby at all times. She was not to mention any of this to Carrie or Jon's bosses. This was an exclusively Israeli operation and would remain classified. Terry wondered aloud how anyone could keep all their secret allegiances in order at any given time.

"The less you talk, the less likely you'll mess up."

The simple advice sounded wise enough.

"You will find the necessary tools for the job in a package at the front desk. If you have questions, ask them now. We will need to limit communication once the operation begins. After that, only contact me if you require urgent assistance."

Terry asked a few follow-up questions and was satisfied enough with the answers.

"Are you ready?" Shira asked.

"As I'll ever be."

Terry showered and got dressed, went downstairs. She helped herself to an apple and instant coffee in the lobby, then walked to the front desk. "I'm expecting a delivery." She offered her name and room number and was handed a large box of significant weight.

Back in her room, she opened the package. Inside was an Israeli handgun. She still had the gun the CIA guy brought for her at the airport, but preferred this one, identical to the pistol she'd practiced on. Beside it were three gun clips. *Three!* Also, a set of car keys, a recording device, SIM card, and two GPS sensors.

She activated one of the sensors and stuck it in her jean's pocket along with the keys. She'd attach another to the chassis of the new rental car she was told would be waiting for her. When she'd asked Shira why she needed her own car rather than rideshare, the answer was disturbing. "In case you need to make a speedy retreat."

The Fiat Jon and Carrie were driving had last been seen outside the Russian embassy and would remain there. The CIA wouldn't venture to get it.

She swapped the new SIM card for her old one and grasped the gun. She took a few moments to acclimate to the feel of the cold metal in her hands. She wouldn't want the first time holding it to be when she needed it.

Even she knew that.

***

Boris stood in the hallway near the bougainvillea-laden veranda. It was a spectacular Roman morning. The men were finishing their breakfast. An elaborate spread of fruit, breads, and cheese had been devoured. Floral-motif porcelain teacups sat empty on the wrought iron table. A brotherly rapport was developing, delighting him. They would be leaving soon for the airport, returning to their respective cities, far more enlightened than when they'd left them.

Boris watched Felix and Owen laugh heartily at something Spenser said. Observing the threesome, it was clear the congressman was the most natural leader. Boris debated whether to show Spenser the room downstairs. While he had notified the Russian ambassador of their unexpected guests, Germain was a different story. The congressman had been reared in typical American culture, oblivious to much of the real world. He was still soft, unaware of the difficulties his leadership role would eventually entail. Till now Boris had allowed him the perks of what would be his role, while shielding him from the harsh realities. Recalling Alexander Bilka, Boris worried that Spenser was not ready for a crash course. Still, he mused, *Was there ever a good time to teach the finer points of illegal imprisonment?*

Boris stepped onto the veranda and caught Spenser's eye. "May I have a word?"

The young man approached, leaving the other two in deep conversation.

"Please come with me." Boris led him to a locked doorway at the end of the hallway. "This door leads to a subterranean room, part of the foundation of the villa dating back to the late 1700s. We rarely make use of it, but as of last night we have."

Spenser raised his brow in curiosity. "What for? Cloning?"

"No, that is done in a more secure location, far from the embassy. Are you familiar with the vaults of the Tower of London?"

"Like in Dungeons and Dragons?"

"This is no game."

"Are you saying you're holding prisoners down there?"

"Spies." Boris said this with a humorless face. Spenser's eyes widened. Boris let this sink in, then continued. "While few know of our project, what we have accomplished with you, Judge Cantor, and Mr. Salko has attracted unwanted attention. There have been bold attempts at impeding our progress."

Spenser's eyes darted to the basement door. "And they showed up here?"

"They followed Owen here. Each one of you has been under their surveillance for some time."

"No one has been spying on me. I would know."

Boris didn't say any more. He took a key out of his pocket and unlocked the door. Spenser hesitated a moment and then followed his mentor down the stone stairway and into the abyss.

***

Boris led Spenser into a small, dark room, the main wall made of two-way glass. He flicked a switch illuminating the other side. Two people woke, a blanket swaddled around them. The woman straightened her hair, allowing the man to help her up.

Realization settled on Spenser who stared dumbfounded at the prisoners. "Jon? Carrie?" He turned to Boris. "*They* were spying on me?"

"For many weeks."

Spenser's face grew red with embarrassment. "I welcomed them into my fold and they played me for a fool." Eyeing Carrie, her makeup smeared, her hair still mussed, he said, "Gwen, one of my SAU associates, warned me about her.

I chalked it up to paranoia but obviously I should have taken her concerns more seriously."

"They are employees of the FBI and CIA."

Spenser exploded. "The bastards! I've done nothing illegal."

"They will claim you've been recruited by an enemy of the state determined to build a communist regime in America."

"They will undermine my campaign!" Spenser shook his head, then regained control. "I won't allow that to happen. His face contorted in hatred. Eyes burning, he faced Boris, stood up straighter, and turned to the door. With sarcasm dripping from his voice, he said, "They are now the enemies of *my* state."

Boris raised a questioning brow. The schoolyard Spenser was back.

***

Spenser paced the salon. "I regret losing my temper."

Boris watched him closely. "Their betrayal was a shock, no doubt."

Distracted, Spenser said, "If I'm to be president, I cannot tolerate spying within my ranks. Their actions can't be ignored."

"I agree. How would you like to handle it?"

Spenser appeared stumped by the question, confused at the power being bestowed on him. "What would you advise?"

Boris was pleased the congressman was seeking his advice. It was precisely as he intended it. Spenser as president while he guided his hand. "It's my opinion they need to be made examples of."

The young man nodded without conviction, seemingly unsure what Boris meant.

"If you agree, I will see to it that they don't interfere with our progress ever again."

This time Germain nodded more vigorously. "I'd like to pack up my things now."

"As you wish."

CHAPTER 58

Rome

Terry looked at the time on her phone. Tierney was late.
She checked the address he'd sent her. Looked at the
building. She was in the right place. It was an old
four-story stone building with ten-foot-high double wooden
doors. The day was chilly and overcast. She had come dressed
in jeans but added a touch of professionalism with a fitted
blazer and soft leather briefcase. She'd been lucky and found
a parking spot across from the small corner café. A single un-
occupied table sat on the cobblestones in front. She hoped
she'd understood the parking signs and the car would still be
there when she got back. *If* she got back.

Ten minutes past the meeting time, Terry wasn't sure
what to do. Call Tierney? Contact Shira? No. She'd specifically
been told not to do that. She would wait another ten minutes,
then call the embassy from the car. Have them pass along a
message. Threaten again to bring in the news reporters. She
shuffled in place against the cold. A black Mercedes pulled up
alongside her. A large man of about sixty wearing a superbly
cut camel-hair coat exited the vehicle. He was holding a long-
haired cat. The car drove away.

"Dr. Lavi, it is a distinct pleasure. I'm terribly sorry for
my tardiness. It couldn't be avoided." He offered no further
explanation. "Let's go inside." He unlocked the large wooden
doors and clicked on a hallway light. They passed a series of

mail slots. A wide spiral staircase was ahead to the left. No lift. They took the stairs up one flight and Boris rang the doorbell of the only apartment on the floor. She heard a click and they stepped inside.

The apartment was a spacious duplex, open concept with a small galley kitchen that led to an expansive living room. Two sofas, a television, and various knickknacks. A set of narrow metal stairs open to the room lined the wall. They led to a loft. Terry followed Tierney to the top where they had a birds-eye view of where they just were. The floor-to-ceiling windows offered a lovely scene of the street below. A light rain had begun to fall, creating puddles among the cobblestones.

They arrived at a narrow hallway. There was a washroom to the left and a low-hanging doorway straight ahead. Boris ducked his head to enter. Petite as she was, Terry had no difficulty. The building was from another era, the room likely once belonging to small children. Inside, the lighting was harsh and uninviting, the interior incongruous with the rest of the flat. It had been completely retrofitted. A man around Boris's age with long gray hair held back in a ponytail sat at a counter facing his laptop. He was surrounded by laboratory equipment. Petri dishes, microscope, freezer, pincers. An unmade cot rested in the corner.

Boris settled the cat on the floor. It began pacing, its tail raised as if on high alert. "Claudio."

The man turned, took the glasses off his face, allowing them to fall to his chest on the lanyard. He'd been pulled from his state of concentration. "Boris! Welcome back. I was surprised to see you on the intercom screen." He stood and hugged his friend but as he looked at Terry, his face turned unfriendly.

Boris said, "I have brought with me a new acquaintance."

"You never bring anyone here. Not even investors."

"True, but this is a very special exception."

Claudio eyed the blond intruder. "What about our confidentiality?"

Boris gestured to Terry. "Our guest is highly incentivized to keep our secret. Do you recognize her?"

Claudio approached within a foot of Terry's face and put his glasses back on his nose. His eyes grew wide. "Dr. Theresa Lavi? Is that you?"

She smiled broadly, extended a hand. "And you must be Dr. Giovanni. I heard you died years ago."

He took her hand in his, kissed it. "Don't believe everything you read in the papers." He gestured for them to sit before realizing there was no adequate seating, then moved some papers off the chair next to his own and offered it to Terry. Boris remained standing. "To what do I owe this honor?"

"The honor is mine, doctor. I have been privy to the successful cloning of Comrade Lenin. Now that I see it is you behind the scenes, it makes complete sense. You were always ahead of your time. Now your work can change the world. For the better."

Claudio was clearly pleased with the comment. "Coming from you that is high praise."

"Much deserved. I would love to learn from you and help you complete your cloning project."

Claudio paled.

"I understand you've been working for many years on the next clone. Clearly you've faced some challenges."

"I had trouble obtaining necessary, um, supplies." He looked meekly at Boris while saying this.

Boris said, "Don't you think it's a splendid offer? A world-renowned geneticist offering to assist you? You've been overworked, stressed. I know you've always preferred your solitude, but it's a great burden to do all this work alone."

"Why now? I'm so close."

"I haven't heard from our backer in quite some time. I fear he will pull funding before you can complete your work. The risk of bringing in outside help is overshadowed by the investor's needs. I thought you'd be overjoyed with the help."

Claudio didn't initially respond. He looked at Boris beseechingly, then stammered, "Y-yes, of course."

Glancing around, Terry said, "I gather you're not accustomed to having someone share your workspace. Once you explain your methods, you can give me my job and I will do my best to stay out of your way."

Boris looked pleased. "When do you want to start?"

"Right now." Terry pulled out a small sandwich she'd brought with her and a bottle of water. Claudio looked panicked.

"Splendid, I'll leave you to it then." Boris turned to leave. "Will you mind if Fellini stays with you? I have some business to attend to for the next few days."

Claudio said, "Boris?" his eyes imploring his partner.

Boris offered only a stern look in return. "I'll expect progress in short order." He turned and left.

Terry smiled at her new work mate, pointed to the counter nearest her. "Is this space okay?"

Claudio looked like he would faint. It took Terry only a half hour to realize why. He didn't need her help at all. He was already done.

CHAPTER 59

Rome

"Mussolini?" Terry couldn't keep the horror from her voice. She was floored.

The scientist nodded, looked anywhere but at her.

She needed to tread lightly. The scientist appeared to be barely holding it together.

"May I call you Claudio?" Terry asked.

The scientist's face was drained of color. "Yes," he mumbled, putting his head in his hands. "I don't know what to do."

Terry had reviewed his scientific findings. They were indeed remarkable. The cloning results were a combination of many years of one man's labor, and serendipity in acquiring Dr. Sousa's herbal extract. It was something Dr. Itai Perlman would kill for—figuratively. Boris *had* in the literal sense. Terry understood the horrifying murder of Dr. Sousa had forced Claudio to spend years creating a synthetic version necessitating countless cycles of trial and error. The process was slowed considerably by his refusal of assistance.

Terry moved her chair close to his. "I know we've just met, but you are familiar with my credentials. You can trust me." She felt a punch of guilt knowing if required, she would betray him the first chance she had. But life and death always took precedence, and she would do what was necessary. "I'm terribly disappointed to have missed the final stages of your

270

work. I don't understand why you haven't told Ambassador Tierney. He and your investors have been waiting years for this clone."

He shook his head. "I'm sorry. I can't talk to you about this. I need to think."

"All right." She stood. "Since there's nothing here for me to do, I'll be going." She zipped her briefcase.

Claudio looked up. "Wait."

She stopped, looked at him, a question in her eyes.

"What will you tell Boris?" he asked.

"I don't know. I haven't thought about it. But he will ask me how the day went."

"You can't tell him."

"He'll know something is wrong when I don't come back tomorrow. I won't be comfortable lying to him."

Claudio accepted the chastising. "Maybe we can help each other."

Terry sat back down, put her bag on the floor. "What do you mean?"

"I'll tell you my dilemma and perhaps you can help me figure out what to do. Tell me what you want in return."

Terry didn't hesitate. "The formula for the synthetic extract. I don't see it in any of your paperwork."

"Absolutely not. That's my ticket."

"Then just tell the investor you won't lie anymore to your partner."

"Impossible. He is too powerful. Besides, he bankrolled all my work for the last several years even when the other investors backed out. It was he who chose Mussolini. He claimed he was his hero since childhood. After so many delays, the other investors were sure I would fail. He stayed with me. I can't betray him."

Terry had a moment's pity despite the man's evil doings. He looked miserable. "Sounds like you either betray him or your partner."

"That's why I need your help."

"Who is the investor?"

"He never said his name, but I know. His voice is distinct."

"Who is he?" she repeated.

He took out a piece of paper, seemingly fearful to utter the name aloud. Terry watched as he wrote, stunned. Claudio had written the name of Italy's most infamous mafioso.

***

Claudio unburdened himself. He explained the investor, a third-generation don, wanted to employ Claudio, steal him away from Boris. Actually, he insisted. There was no discussion or negotiation expected. He offered a significant increase in salary and assured Claudio the notoriety he sought would be his. He would continue to bankroll the lab. Claudio was torn between his loyalty to Boris and the investor whom he couldn't refuse even if he wanted to. He feared for his life.

Terry listened intently, the cat now burrowed into her lap. Eventually, the two geneticists came to an understanding. Terry would help him any way she could without explicitly lying to Boris. As Shira instructed her, she told him she knew people who could help, but needed a few days to work things out. And in return, if he walked away unscathed, Claudio would give her the formula for the synthetic DNA resuscitating extract. As part of the deal he would always be known as the inventor of human cloning.

Together, they called Boris, saying they were making quick progress and should have results in a few days. Both were true.

***

Back at the hotel, Terry called Shira. As far as she was concerned, it was an emergency. If she were to continue the dangerous charade with Claudio and Boris, she wanted the Mossad to help Jon and Carrie.

Shira spoke firmly. "Your one and only priority is to secure the extract."

"I won't leave here without them," Terry said, her voice steely.

"You are a stubborn sabra, Dr. Lavi," Shira said. "But you are right."

Terry wasn't sure she heard correctly.

"I may not be an emotional person," Shira added, "but I am a moral one. Your assignment is the extract, but I will speak to Yosef. Maybe he can help the Americans."

Terry was deeply touched. "Thank you."

"As soon as you get the formula you must bring it to us. In person. Once you have it, contact me by the method we discussed. The sooner we have it, the sooner we can all get out of Italy. The Americans as well."

Terry had engaged in more negotiations in the last few days than in her entire life prior. She didn't count her childhood haggling for five more minutes before bedtime. She sincerely hoped today's bargaining would prove immeasurably more successful.

***

Jon was feeling the effects of the windowless room. He tried not to focus on who was watching them from behind the mirror. Carrie's presence was a huge help, but with each passing hour the walls seemed to be closing in on them. Both their phones and watches had been confiscated, the absence of natural light making it impossible to keep track of time.

Jon whispered, "I don't understand why no one's come for us yet."

"They will."

"We can't simply wait. We need a plan to get out of here. If they don't kill us, they'll leave us here to die."

"What do you suggest we do?" Carrie asked.

"We bargain for our freedom."

"With what?"

"Let's brainstorm what we can offer."

Carrie said, "Their interests lie with communism and cloning."

"I can't imagine how we could help with those."

"Money?"

"Doesn't seem to be an issue for them."

The door opened and the guard walked in, pointing his semiautomatic their way. In a gruff Russian timbre, he said, "Time to go."

CHAPTER 60

New York City

Matthews stared at the clock. It was the middle of the night on the East Coast and a quarter past nine in Rome. He had dozed off a few hours ago but at midnight, his wife Erica came to bed, waking him. Stress kept him awake since.

He'd kept his part of the bargain. The media had reported nothing about an international incident involving American spies on Italian soil. There was still no sign of Steadman and Santiago. Seated in his home office, he picked up the phone and called the American ambassador in Rome and told him what to do.

***

Forty minutes later he heard back. The Russian ambassador denied knowledge of American assets inside his facility. A request to send over a delegation was denied. And, were they accusing them of holding Americans against their will? A disgrace!

***

Matthews understood there was only one other option. Force. For that he needed clearance from someone far above his pay grade. Unwilling to jump through lengthy bureaucratic hoops, he instead paid homage to Jon by bucking the system. His next call was directly to the White House.

***

Rome

A SWAT team of ten surrounded the villa in what was now broad daylight. Each man was armed to the teeth. The hope was the show of firepower would be enough to avoid even a single discharged bullet. But these were Russians, and no one could predict how they would react. Particularly after the team bypassed the property's high-tech security perimeter.

The Russian ambassador came to the door appearing genuinely terrified. He stood aside as the American soldiers invaded. No other occupants were found on the first floor. The second-floor bedrooms were vacant. It appeared they had been recently evacuated.

On the main level, was a door at the end of a long hallway and beyond it, a steep flight of stone stairs leading to a subterranean room. It was empty. The smell of urine was still prevalent. Adjacent was a smaller space, a two-way mirror along the common wall. They cleared the house and the perimeter. The Americans were gone.

***

Boris had a lot on his mind. He wasn't in the embassy when the Americans broke in looking for their agents, but it was too close a call. More importantly, he hadn't anticipated the reaction, having assumed they would first resort to several attempts at diplomacy, not one mere phone call to the Russian ambassador. Perhaps the imprisoned agents were more valuable than he thought. He had been on his way back from the airport when the irate ambassador called to warn him. Thankfully, the clones were already on their way to the States. They couldn't get caught up in this. Before being dropped off, Felix and Owen had consented to their destinies, Spenser appearing glad to have it all finalized. It was meant to be a joyous day. Steadman and Santiago had once again thrown a wrench in his good fortune. The first challenge was what to do with them. He had his guards whisk them to a secure location while he went to the lab.

When he arrived, he found Claudio alone in the lab, hovering over his computer. No sign of Dr. Lavi.

Claudio turned to face him. He seemed skittish. "I wasn't expecting you today."

Boris said, "Fellini?" Upon hearing his name, the cat came out from under Claudio's desk.

Boris lifted the cat, petting him gently. "I had an unexpected change in plans. Is there a problem?"

Claudio's face flushed. "No, no. Of course not."

"Where's Dr. Lavi?" Boris asked.

"She wasn't feeling well. Something she ate, apparently. She should be back tomorrow."

Boris thought it curious that someone who had gone to such great lengths to meet the scientist would allow a stomach bug to keep her down.

Claudio said, "I intended to call you later."

"What about?"

Claudio asked his partner to take a seat.

Boris placed the cat on the floor, looked at his partner, his body tense. "What's on your mind, friend?"

Claudio fidgeted, averted his eyes. "I've been keeping something from you."

Boris kept very still. "What?"

Claudio's speech sped up. "I wanted to tell you but didn't know how."

"Tell me."

"Our investor contacted me."

Boris frowned. "Why would he do that? He always speaks with me directly."

Claudio appeared to brace himself. "He wants me to come work for him."

Boris jumped to his feet. "The devil! How dare he! Owning forty-nine percent of the project isn't enough? He wants it all. I'll drop him. Now that you're so close to completing Mussolini, we don't need him anymore."

Claudio shook his head. "You can't do that."

Boris peered at the cowardly man. "Why ever not?"

"We have a deal with him."

"His attempt at stealing you away forfeits any agreement."

Claudio whispered as if the walls were listening. "Do you know who he is?"

Of course he knew. Boris's eyes narrowed. "Do you?"

Claudio nodded. "I figured it out. The man on the phone had the same voice as one I've heard many times before on the news. All of *them* speak in the same dialect." He whispered the name.

Damn! Boris thought. "What did you tell him?"

Claudio was shaking now. "He didn't give me any other choice."

"You accepted." It was not a question.

"I had no choice," he repeated.

Boris sat down again. "After all our years together, how could you? I've sacrificed everything. My position as ambassador. I've done questionable things for this project. For you."

"I don't *want* to work for him. I'm happy with our partnership. Was I wrong to tell you?"

Boris feigned a calm demeanor. "Of course not. You did the right and only thing. I know he can be persuasive, but he wouldn't risk harming you even if you refused his offer. He needs you."

"What should I do?"

Boris turned cold. "I will handle it."

"How?"

"I haven't involved you in my methods before. This wouldn't be the time to start."

Claudio looked frightened but remained silent.

Boris stood. "Get back to work, Claudio. That's all you need to worry about." He closed the door softly, his cat remaining behind. Only when he stepped into the washroom did he punch his fist into the wall.

CHAPTER 61

Rome

After nearly an hour spent on two phone calls, Terry checked the GPS signal on the tracker she'd dropped in Claudio's work bag. He'd agreed to carrying the device as a security measure. He hadn't left the duplex the whole day. She had hoped he would seek out Boris the first chance he got as they had discussed. Which would in turn lead her to Jon and Carrie. They agreed not to speak by phone in case someone was listening. Better paranoid than dead.

Matthews had phoned her with an update. The villa had been evacuated. While he was certain the clones would soon resurface on American soil, the agents were gone. Despite the awful news, she was appreciative he contacted her directly. Informing Yosef Kahn would have been enough to meet his obligations of the alliance. But he understood she was hungry for news of her partners. *Her friends.*

He told her the Americans were under fire for storming the Russian embassy. Once again, the U.S. was seen acting on allegedly ironclad intel only to find nothing. Just like Saddam. The president was being lambasted, made all the worse so close to the election. Matthews was sure Jon and Carrie had been moved only a short time before the SWAT team showed up. Now they were off everyone's radar. She heard the frustration in Matthews's voice. She was terrified for Jon and Carrie. Her thoughts turned to Gabe. How would he cope with losing his best friend? She needed to do *something*.

Terry looked at her phone for the umpteenth time. She couldn't figure out why Claudio wasn't with Boris. They had discussed what he needed to do. Find Boris, tell him he was coerced into signing on with the mafioso, and she would help him dislodge from both of them. If all went according to plan, Claudio would be rid of both Boris and the mafia. And she would earn the synthetic extract formula. But, he still hadn't left the duplex. Perhaps he changed his mind. If Claudio didn't lead her to Boris, she'd never find her friends.

***

Claudio had a perfect view from his perch above the street. He watched as Boris left the building. He quickly put on his jacket and raced down the stairs. He followed Boris as he turned the corner, unsure what he would do if Boris drove off. For now, he was on foot. Terrified of being caught, Claudio stayed back. But Dr. Lavi's instructions were to follow Boris, and that's what he would do.

***

Terry's mind was heading in many paranoid directions, debating whether to phone Claudio, when she saw the tracker pin shift. The scientist left the lab and was on the move.

***

Claudio watched as Boris crossed the Piazza Navona, passing Bernini's Fountain of the Four Rivers, its obelisk towering above. Weaving through the narrow streets, Boris passed the Campo d' Fiori flower market, then entered a lovely boutique hotel, its window boxes overflowing with resplendent crimson geraniums. Claudio saw the doorman greet him as if they knew each other. He'd always assumed Boris had a pied-à-terre in Rome. Perhaps this was it. If as Boris's long-standing partner he had never known where it was, no one would.

Claudio was unsure what to do. He couldn't risk walking inside. He was ready to return to the lab when Boris exited the hotel. He'd changed out of his camel hair coat into a dark anorak and leather gloves. His dress shoes had been switched for work boots. He never looked Claudio's way.

***

Boris stomped past the flower carts still reeling from Claudio's confession. To think the don would be so brazen as to steal his scientist! He would handle the mafia boss, but knew it would be tricky given the man's reputation. As the boss of the Banda della Magliana, Rome's most notorious criminal organization, he was feared throughout all of Italy, grown men trembling at his name. Boris would need to pin the revenge on someone else. No better stooge than the people who had caused him the most trouble. The American spies.

Boris stopped outside a small church and looked in the window, relieved to see the man he sought inside. It was a favored hotspot for devout mafia kingpins and their lieutenants to confess their sins. The man worshipped here like clockwork every Wednesday night, when there were few if any parishioners. First the local trattoria then the church. It was a routine Boris had learned of and filed away in the event it would one day be of use.

Boris entered the chapel, took a pew in the back. He bowed his head just enough to see the man make a beeline for the confessional. Twenty minutes elapsed before the man emerged. He was mid-forties and large—horizontally, the bulge at his hip prominent under his suit jacket. His earlier drinks at the trattoria kept him from walking a straight line.

The man kissed the priest's right hand and exited through the door to the left of the altar. Boris followed, his rubber soles treading quietly on the stone floor. The door led to a narrow alley, the only light emanating from a waning moon. Stray cats leapt from one trash bin to another, foraging for their next meal. The man's back was to him, his gait unsteady. Boris screwed the silencer on to the barrel of his Glock 19 and shot him in the back of the head. He stepped around the body and kept going.

***

Claudio lurked in the shadows, watching Boris emerge from the alley at a heightened pace, heading away from him. He glanced down the alley, a cat bolting past, startling him. And then he saw it. A large bulky shape on the ground. It took his brain a millisecond to register it was a human body, a man. And that Boris had murdered him. He tasted the bile rise in his throat. The urge to run home and hide under the covers was overwhelming. Should he call the police? No. No one could know he was here. No one knew he was alive.

Claudio looked where Boris had gone. He was now far ahead, walking more casually, as if nothing had happened. If Claudio didn't move, he'd lose him. He turned off his mind, and battling every fiber of his timid being, he followed.

***

This makes no sense, Terry thought, pacing her hotel room. The tracking pin was all over the place, finally stopping at a church in the city's Monti district. Jon and Carrie couldn't possibly be held in a church. Without further deliberation, she called Claudio.

He answered on the first ring, his whispered voice panicky, terror-filled. "He killed him!"

Terry instantly felt light-headed. "Jon?"

"No, no. The mafia guy. Boris killed him in the alley behind the church. I knew he was angry at the don's betrayal, but I never thought he'd do this. He will kill me too for my own betrayal!"

Terry was so overwhelmingly relieved the dead man wasn't Jon, she closed her eyes, willing her hands to stop shaking.

"Are you still there?" Claudio asked.

"He needs you," she said, her voice firmer.

"That's what everyone is saying. I'm needed. I don't know anymore. Boris will come back to the lab. When he doesn't see me, he'll know something is wrong. I haven't left the lab in weeks." Terry heard Claudio take several shallow in-and-out breaths. He was hyperventilating.

"Please calm down. You need to think clearly. If you want to be free of Boris we need to stick to our plan."

Claudio let out a long breath. "I did as you asked. I followed him."

"Okay, good. What do you see?"

"It's an industrial area of small factories and warehouses. Everything is closed for the evening. No one is around. Hold on. Boris is slowing down in front of an old building."

"What building?"

"I can't get any closer, but I can make out some of the words. Ah, *macchine da cucire.*"

"What does it mean?"

"It was a sewing machine factory." A pause. "Boris knocked on the door and was let inside."

"Thank you, you did great."

Claudio whispered into the phone. "I'm going home now. I can't do this anymore." He hung up.

***

Terry noted the exact location when Claudio hung up on her. According to the map application, it was an industrial section of the city, just as he said. If Boris was imprisoning Jon and Carrie, this would be the place.

*

Back at the loft, Claudio went to the bathroom and hurled his last meal. Only then did he notice a fist-size hole in the wall that hadn't been there before.

CHAPTER 62

Rome

Word of the Banda della Magliana sottocapo's murder spread like wildfire, as was the case in the underworld circles. The don was notified his top lieutenant had been shot execution style with a weapon particular to CIA operatives. *But why?*

The papers were flush with the story of two missing American agents. Clearly, they were hiding. He would find them and kill them. In the most painful way possible.

***

Boris Tierney prided himself on his stratagem. He'd wielded his revenge. Stealing Claudio away would be tantamount to crippling his lifelong project. He would have preferred taking out the don, but finding him without a bevy of bodyguards would be impossible. Now he hoped the don would be too preoccupied with a dead underboss to concern himself with Claudio.

Boris had made the don's acquaintance all those years ago when quietly looking for someone to deal with Dr. Sousa. When the tribal chief reneged on the deal to trade the extract components, the scientist was doomed to die. The poison arrow was an inspired red herring, sending the authorities on a wild goose chase. The alliance ultimately led to a business agreement, the don becoming the project's main financier. The Lenin success was a valuable incentive to make a substantial investment in the cloning of the infamous Italian dictator, Benito Mussolini.

He sat on his room's sofa and checked his phone. Online news reports broke of a long-suspected mafioso's murder in the alley beside the mobster's oft-frequented church. *That was fast.* The sottocapo's body was not yet cold.

Boris smiled inwardly as he read how the polizia anticipated fierce retribution. It had been the mafia's way for centuries. One sorry pundit suggested a preposterous conspiracy theory—a connection between the murder and the disappearing American spies. Speculation was they were now the mafia's targets. The don denied it all, denouncing the press's suggestion of violence in their ranks.

Things were going as planned. All that remained was to offer up the American agents to the don on a silver platter. Boris took a piece of paper from his desk and penned a short note to the don, signing his name. He sealed it in an unmarked envelope and wrote urgent on the top. He called for a bellman and explained where it was to be hand-delivered. The man appeared frightened by the request. Boris tipped him generously and he left. He was glad not to have to get his hands dirty again today. That job was now given to the godfather.

***

Jon's mouth was parched. They hadn't been given anything to eat or drink in many hours and the cavernous room they now inhabited was stifling. Despite his discomfort, his mind was sharp, calmer now than before. He and Carrie kept their speaking to a minimum in case someone was listening. The factory was no longer functional, all the machinery long gone. Only a few bolted-in metal tables remained, draped in cobwebs. The ceiling's flickering fluorescent light fixtures emitted a low hum that seemed to echo louder in the space.

They were tied to their chairs and to each other. Jon conjured up an image of Indiana Jones, wondering what he would do in his shoes. He couldn't hope for a fake wall leading him to freedom, but perhaps a distraction. He looked around the space again with a more discerning eye. Nothing loud to tip over, no candle to start a fire. The guard was outside the door, his shoulder visible each time he paced by the small glass window. Jon worried for himself but more so for Carrie. If he was gone, the impact would be minimal. Granny, Gabe, maybe Mel. But if Carrie didn't make it out of here, Randy would be an orphan. Like himself. That tragedy would never be forgotten by an already-challenged four-year-old left to grow up without his mother.

"How are you holding up?' Jon asked.

"Hanging in there."

Ever the professional, Jon thought. He knew she must be as terrified as he was, yet she hadn't complained once.

"Can you think of a way out?" he asked, his voice low.

Carrie shook her head.

Outside, they heard a car screeching to a halt. Its headlights filtered through the filthy street-facing window, bouncing against the wall behind them. Two doors slammed shut. The outer factory door opened. Loud Italian from one side, softer speech from the other.

The guard walked toward them, a fearful look on his face as he ushered in a stout, well-dressed older man in a gray pinstripe suit. At the sight of him, Carrie's body stiffened. Jon had no idea who the man was, but clearly she did..

The suited man spoke in heavily accented English. "You are the American spies."

They didn't answer.

In one leap the guard was at Jon's chair, holding a gun to his temple. Jon closed his eyes, whispered something no one could hear.

"You pray? I thought all Americans were atheists."

Jon opened his eyes, didn't reply.

The older man gestured for the guard to stand down. He took a gold lighter from his pocket, then a narrow wooden box. He proceeded to snip and light a cigar, taking a deep puff. The pungent odor quickly filled the room. "You come to my country, my turf, and yesterday, kill my underboss. My cousin. Why?"

Jon was stunned at the allegation, but held his tongue. If the man noticed the shock in their faces, he didn't let on.

"Don, I am Carrie Santiago. I give you my word we had nothing to do with your family. We came to Italy for a specific purpose."

"To kill my man."

"With all due respect, we have been incarcerated for over twenty-four hours. We couldn't have done that."

The man shook his head. "I have it on good authority that it was you two."

Jon wondered what that meant. Who would pin this on them? "Ask the guard, do the math. It wasn't us."

He seemed not to hear. "You will die, but first confession is necessary to purify your souls."

Jon said, "Our assignment had nothing to do with your underboss."

"Enlighten me, then. What was your assignment?"

Despite knowing the reply would be unwelcome, he said, "We can't tell you that."

"Agent Santiago, can *you* tell me that?"

She shook her head.

The man turned to the guard and said something in Italian. The guard moved toward them. Carrie flinched. He removed the binds to the chair but kept her hands bound together and did the same to Jon. "Face the wall."

Jon walked toward the wall, Carrie slowly behind him. He'd always teased death. But now as he faced his last moments on Earth he had a morbidly late epiphany. *He didn't want to die.* This time he'd lost the game of chicken.

His thoughts went to Ashleigh. He'd be with her again.

Reaching the wall, Jon tried a Hail Mary. "I did it. I killed your man. I did it alone. Just as you said. For revenge. Agent Santiago was working a completely different assignment. She didn't even know."

The man took a puff of his cigar, deliberating. "Then you will be the first to die. She will not be spared."

Jon saw Carrie's eyes filled with tears. She mouthed a thank you and then did something more courageous than anything Jon had ever witnessed. She turned, faced her executioner, eyes wide open, defiant.

The man nodded in respect. "As you wish." The Italian uttered a few words at the guard who racked the slide. Jon closed his eyes and whispered, "Ash, I'm coming."

CHAPTER 63

Rome

T he firepower was louder than Jon would have imagined. Actually, he didn't think he'd hear it at all. A split second and he realized it was not a single gunshot but a barrage.

He felt his body being pulled down. Carrie had an iron grip on his arm, dragging him under a metal sewing table. The rapid-fire flashes of gunpowder in the dim room were blinding, but he knew the guard was not shooting at them. He was defending himself from an onslaught. The mobster had his own weapon, getting off a shot at the window, shattering the glass, and made for it. He was going to run. A heavy thud was heard from near the door where the guard had been standing seconds ago. The only shouts came from the mobster, half of his body now out the window. He let loose a loud string of obscenities as he was apprehended. A scuffle and the room turned silent.

***

Boris looked at his gold Rolex. The Americans would be dead by now. Daybreak was mere hours away. He only had to wait till then to anonymously tip off the polizia to the don's murder of two American intelligence officers.

***

"It's safe to come out now."

Huddled below the iron table, Jon could barely hear the words, his ears still ringing from the shootout.

A young woman with a Mediterranean complexion and strong accent donning full body gear helped him and Carrie out from under the table. She cut the bindings and escorted them to the exit.

"Who are you?" Carrie asked, her face dripping with sweat and tears.

"You can call me Shira." The r was throaty, glottal.

"Your accent sounds like Terry's."

"Very good, Agent Santiago."

Jon was shocked. "You're Israeli? Mossad?"

No smile. "We don't say that out loud. And we were never here, Agent Steadman."

They emerged onto the street where they saw three other soldiers dressed as Shira was, standing outside a dark van. Not one said a word. Jon realized the entire rescue operation had been absent of all speech.

Jon glanced around. "Where are our people? How did you find us? Matthews?"

"Some, not all, of your questions will be answered. But one thing I can tell you. The next time you see Dr. Lavi, you must thank her. You both owe her your lives."

***

Jerusalem

Yosef put down the phone. The mission had been successful on every front. Now the Americans owed them a huge debt. He already knew what the payment would be.

***

Rome

In the van, Shira explained that Terry tracked them down, omitting mention of Claudio's help. In return for saving their lives, she requested they hold off on informing their superiors they'd been freed. Another few hours wouldn't matter in the larger scheme of things. Jon knew this was a device of sorts, but he was infuriated that Matthews and the CIA had left them to die. He got Carrie on board and agreed to wait.

***

The Mossad agents treated the don with infinitely greater humanity than he deserved. He sat in the safe house's starkly lit room, his hands free to hold the espresso in front of him. His Cubans had been denied. His feet were shackled to the floor. Still, he held himself like a king.

The clock on the wall read four-thirty a.m.

Shira sat across from him.

"You want me to believe that Ambassador Tierney, a man I've known for decades, killed my underboss in cold blood?"

"He's aware of your deception."

The man laughed. "You need to be more specific."

"Your intent to recruit Claudio Giovanni without his knowledge," Shira said bluntly.

The Italian godfather took a dainty sip. "Your sources are mistaken."

"He arranged it so you would do his dirty work, killing two birds with one stone. He gets his revenge on you, and you get rid of the Americans for him."

"It is a brilliant strategy, but if he wanted me out of the

cloning game, he would have taken me out, not my lieutenant. I could still get Claudio."

"Not if you're in prison. He knew you would personally handle those who allegedly murdered your underboss. He kills him, then puts you on death row for two other murders." Shira let that sink in.

She noted the don's slight eye shift. He was weakening his resolve.

She continued. "Ask yourself how you found out they were in the sewing factory."

"The ambassador was expressing his thanks for years of funding."

"Why didn't he meet you there in person?"

The don's face reddened, something seemingly breaking inside him. He banged the table so hard his empty demitasse jumped, landing on its side. "He set me up!"

"We want your help to bring Tierney and his operation down."

This caught his attention. "What do I get in return?"

"As this isn't my country, my bargaining power is limited. But we can recommend life instead of capital punishment."

"Not good enough. I want immunity."

Shira didn't mince words. "That will never happen. You were seconds from murdering two American nationals. There's no chance of immunity." She looked him dead in the eye. "You and I know how many other unprosecuted hits you've sanctioned."

The don was smug. "And yet you seek my help."

"Immunity is not in our power to give. And don't be mistaken. If you don't help us, we will find another way to achieve our objective. This is your chance to retaliate against the man who killed your underboss and made a fool of you." She said this so straightforwardly there was no room for retort.

An hour later they arrived at an agreement.

***

Carrie quietly entered the small kitchen at the other end of the safehouse. She had showered. Her face was clean, her hair damp. She filled the electric kettle and turned it on. When it boiled, she made herself a cup of green tea, carrying it to the kitchen table, and sat on the old vinyl banquette next to Jon. He declined her offer to make one for him as well.

"Just called home. It's late in New York but I needed to hear Randy's sleepy voice, you know? My mom sounded scared for me but didn't ask questions."

"How is he?"

"Same. He's speaking less often. His therapist is still pushing for medication."

"I'm sorry. That has to be a hard decision." Jon saw her face fall. He put his hand on hers. "How are *you*?"

"Happy to be alive. That's all I can focus on now. Thanks for trying to save my butt at the factory. It was beyond chivalrous."

"I told you I'd always have your back. You have too many people counting on you being around."

"As do you."

"Not really."

"Short list, huh?"

He nodded. "Yeah, it is."

"Then you can add one more to it. Me."

He drew her in for a hug. He liked the sound of that a lot.

***

New York City

Matthews had just ended the conversation with the Mossad chief. The call was unexpected and awfully embarrassing. But a blessing, nonetheless. Jon was found alive. He was dehydrated and bruised but would be all right. Carrie was physically fine. Both were undoubtedly traumatized. The raid was a disaster, mostly for the president. Matthews felt no compassion. The decision to wait was a direct result of his political avarice. He deserved whatever he got.

Now he had Jon on the line, hoping the young agent wouldn't detect what he felt in his voice. "Glad you are both okay."

"What the hell happened? Where were our guys?"

Matthews recognized the sound of hurt masking as anger.

"I did what I could to get you out." While he couldn't share the details of his battle with Carrie's boss, one thing was certain. He would find a way to get the asshole fired.

"We were seconds from death, Doug. He had us against a wall, gun cocked."

Matthews cleared his throat, trying not to pull up that mental image. "I'm sorry." He knew the apology was of little consolation.

If Jon was surprised to hear his boss's voice catch, he didn't let on.

Matthews added, "We're bringing you home."

"Not a chance. We're not done here. Tierney is still out there. He set this whole thing up to frame us."

"We still have the CIA guys on the ground. They'll handle it from here."

"Are you referring to the same ones who couldn't find us, left us to die?"

Matthews had no answer to that. He had little fight left in him. "You want to stay on this?"

"Absolutely. No one is going to take this man down other than me and Carrie."

"Your covers are blown. The Italians won't allow you to walk a block."

"I'll let *you* fix that, Doug. Speak to whomever you need to, and make sure we don't get sidelined by the local authorities."

Matthews began to argue he didn't have that sort of clout overseas. But he stopped. Maybe this was a way for the CIA to atone for its many misdeeds.

"I'll see what I can do."

"Good."

Before Jon could hang up, Matthews softly said, "Take good care, son."

***

Rome

Terry's lack of sleep was overshadowed by the overwhelming relief at Jon and Carrie's rescue. She badly wanted to see them in the flesh, but Shira instructed her to keep away from the others until her assignment was complete.

***

When Boris entered the lab to check on the progress, Claudio looked up from his computer, his face pale. He excused himself. *Perhaps Dr. Lavi really did have a bug?*

He heard Fellini meowing. Bending down to get him from under the desk, he saw Claudio's work bag. He never went anywhere without it. Hearing groans emanating from the washroom, Boris shuffled through it, and was shocked to see a tiny flicker of light at the bottom. At first, he thought it was a phone battery. It wasn't. It was a GPS tracker no bigger than a cough drop. Someone was following his scientist. Best to leave it in place. Let the spy think no one was onto them. If it belonged to the Americans, there was nothing more to worry about. But Boris was a cautious man. He was going to find out for certain.

CHAPTER 64

Rome

Terry had a tight grip on the phone, her voice a mix of frustration and confusion. In contrast, Shira's voice sounded steady, her face filling the screen.

Terry asked. "Why hasn't Tierney been arrested?"

"The Italians don't have enough on him for the under-boss's murder. Even if they look for him *and* find him, there's a strong chance he won't be charged. The Americans will want to bring Tierney back to the States to try him there. But given the strained relationship between them and the Italians, it's unlikely he'll be extradited."

Terry was incredulous. "He kidnapped my friends!"

Shira said, "Who will verify that? Claudio and the Russian ambassador won't testify against him and the don is not exactly a reliable witness. Jon and Carrie's testimony is the only thing that can bring him down. For now, it's in the Americans' best interest to deal with Boris themselves, and leave the polizia out of it for as long as possible."

Terry asked, "What about the clones?"

"I've heard the CIA and FBI are facing a similar problem stateside. They can't arrest the clones. They've committed no crimes."

Terry hated feeling helpless.

Shira said, "Right now, your sole priority is acquiring the extract formula from Claudio."

Terry said, "I arranged the rendezvous. But I do
if he'll show. He saw Tierney's victim and wasn't thi.
clearly. I fear that with my sudden absence, Tierney w
quickly add things up. Claudio may be in terrible danger."

Shira's face took on a schoolmaster's stern expression.
"Let's hope he recalls the deal you made and why he needs you.
His predicament hasn't changed. He remains trapped between
two dangerous men. He doesn't know we have the don. You're
still tracking Claudio. We can keep an eye on him."

"And Tierney?"

Shira smirked, a twinkle in her eye. It was the most emo-
tive Terry had seen her. "Ah, the ambassador," the Mossad spy
said. Terry expected her to rub hands together in devilish anticipation. "Him, we bait."

***

Claudio walked hurriedly past the Pantheon, his briefcase
firmly in hand. The imposing granite Corinthian columns of
the ancient Roman temple filled him with a sense of guilt for
what he was about to do. It was not part of Dr. Lavi's plan,
but he no longer knew who to trust, and the don was the
one person who had actually come through for him. He'd seen
Boris's murder victim, and knew what his partner was capable
of. Claudio would beseech the don for protection from Boris.
Once reassured, he would inform the women carriers of their
imminent implantation.

He crossed the Ponte Umberto, oblivious to the ubiquitous tourists along the bridge photographing St. Peter's
Basilica in the background. Fifteen minutes later, he passed
through a black iron fence fronting a sprawling Mediterranean home. Marble statues spanned the expansive lawn, stone
cherubs spewing water from a gauche, oversized fountain. He
paused a moment, and then rang the bell.

***

rage. Watching his partner from a distance, control to refrain from pouncing on the traitor. He couldn't believe Claudio was actually going to betray him, taking his work to the mobster. He had always thought of Claudio as weak. Perhaps he'd misread him. It took guts to do what he was doing. At that moment, Boris decided he would kill him. How Dr. Lavi played into the deception he still didn't know. But he would find out. Soon. If she proved innocent, he would allow her to take over the project from Claudio, and run with it. If at any point he sensed betrayal he would get rid of her as well.

***

Hours later, Boris sat on the velvet loveseat in his pied-à-terre perusing the day's news on his tablet, Fellini asleep by his side. A cocktail sat on the coffee table before him. There were no reports of dead American spies. He wasn't surprised. He understood the CIA would labor to keep it out of the papers.

He heard a light tap on his door, watched as an envelope was slipped under it. He rose quietly to avoid disturbing the feline. Inside the envelope was a hand-written note. The don was summoning him, fully unaware Boris had earlier been outside his home stalking Claudio and taking precautionary measures. *How is he not in jail?* Boris had left an anonymous tip about the don with the polizia. The mafioso obviously had powerful connections throughout Italy, including in law enforcement. Yet, even he was not untouchable. It was only a matter of time till he took the fall for the deaths of two American intelligence officers.

Boris finished the last of his Bellini. The unexplained summons was not unexpected, particularly after the don's meeting with Claudio. Perhaps the don wanted to offer thanks for tipping him off to the Americans who'd murdered his underboss. Or maybe he wanted to suggest a deal for Claudio. Boris had no intention of negotiating with the don. He would cut him out of the investment completely, leaving him to the CIA wolves.

***

A mute, expressionless bodyguard stationed at the villa's front door took Boris's camel-hair coat. He hung it by the front door beside several others, then frisked Boris before allowing him to enter. In all these years, Boris had never been invited inside the inner sanctum. All prior business transactions with the don had been conducted remotely to protect them both and maintain the secrecy of their association.

Boris entered the ornate room, more a museum than home office, the guard following behind. Impressionist paintings adorned the lime-green papered walls, marble busts of ancient warriors were perched on stands around the room. The villa's gaudy, white-veined marble flooring and dark heavy fabrics were an assault to Boris's high-brow tastes.

He was astonished to see Claudio sitting sheepishly in the corner, like a disciplined child dreading his father's arrival back home. He had been here all these hours. Boris thought he heard the chattering of the pathetic man's teeth.

Boris offered his colleague of many years no more than a deadly stare before facing the don. The godfather was seated in a high-back, tufted leather chair behind a monstrosity of a carved wooden desk.

The don, dressed in a pretentious neck scarf and burgundy smoking jacket, gestured to a chair across from him. One bodyguard flanked the desk, the other stood beside Claudio. Boris sat.

"How are things with the congressman?" the mob boss

asked.

"He is everything I hoped for. He will make a great statesman."

The don nodded, his face unreadable. "The sun will never set on communism, giusto?" *Right?*

Boris forced a tight smile.

"Your great-granduncle would be proud. And the Mussolini clones?"

"We are close."

"I've heard that from you for months. I've been exceedingly patient. It's time for me to see the return on my investment."

Boris had anticipated this. "I can't make my scientist work any faster." He said this as if Claudio was not in the room.

The don nodded knowingly. "There are other ways to make a show of good will."

"What do you have in mind?"

"You will remain on the payroll as a show of good faith. But Claudio will continue his work here at my home. I've built a state-of-the-art lab for him and assigned qualified assistants. It's a marvel he's been working alone all this time."

Boris leered at the man. "We couldn't risk others acquiring his formula. While your offer is a generous one, there is no need. I recently recruited a world-renown geneticist to help him speed up the process."

"Si, la Dottoressa Lavi. She can work here as well."

Boris was disgusted with how much Claudio had told the don. "Claudio has a fine arrangement where he is. He won't want to move."

"Let me worry about that."

Boris bristled at the don's blasé attitude. "He's my partner, not an employee to be reassigned."

The don leaned back in his chair, clasping his hands on his protruding belly. "Are you refusing my offer?"

Boris felt Claudio's judging eyes boring into him. His ire rising, he was fully aware this time, he wouldn't be able to control it. "I gave you the investment of a lifetime and you repay me by stealing my scientist!"

A guard took a step closer to Boris, stopping at the don's gesture. "Don't kid yourself, Ambassador. I bought Claudio long ago. While your other investors jumped ship, I funded all his cloning work which took many years longer than you promised. I've gone as far as to tolerate your skimming off my investment. Did you think I didn't know? Where is the appreciation? Your air of superiority has always irritated me. You're merely a middleman who no one needs anymore."

Boris stood, livid. "You will not push me aside on the verge of Mussolini."

The guards moved in, and once again, the don stopped them.

"You see how unessential you are, Boris? You don't even know the clone has been completed."

Boris couldn't hide his shock. He turned to his partner. "Claudio?"

Claudio appeared to shrink into himself like a turtle into its shell. Boris wanted to put his hands around the scientist's neck and squeeze the life out of him.

"This is not over." Boris turned to leave.

"No, it's not. Do you think I would allow the man who murdered my underboss to walk out of my house a free man?"

Boris stopped cold, his face blanched. He felt a tingle of something unfamiliar. *Fear.* "The American spies killed him."

The door beside the don's desk opened. Jon and Carrie entered the room.

Boris stared at them in shock.

Jon said, "Hello, Boris."

"You're alive."

"Good observation. By no fault of your own."

The don said to Boris, "You double crossed me and for that you'll pay." The don took a pistol from his drawer, pointed it at Boris.

Jon yelled, "No!"

In the next moment several things happened. A piercing gunshot was immediately followed by an earsplitting explosion echoing off the walls. Jon tackled Carrie, hitting the ground, his body shielding hers.

When the eruption died down, Carrie cautiously moved out from under him, crawled beside the don who sat crouched partway under his desk, and put her pistol to his temple. The don didn't flinch. Without a word, he took his hand off the smoking gun. Carrie took it away. She reached into his pocket and took out the recorder.

***

Jon looked around the don's salon. There was no bomb, no wreckage. Earlier at the Mossad safehouse, he and Carrie had prepared the ruse with Shira, the Israelis graciously willing to loan the don to them for the day, before releasing custody to the Italian authorities.

When he and Carrie had arrived at the don's house, they entered through the kitchen door, set up the audio, and listened in, surprised to hear another man's voice projected from the don's salon. It was clear they were completing a transaction of sorts. When the don spoke the other man's name, he and Carrie were shocked. The infamous Dr. Claudio Giovanni was alive and well. And had successfully cloned Benito Mussolini!

The pieces were beginning to fall into place. Boris had the clones' creator in his corner. What Claudio was doing at the don's home was something Jon would need to investigate once the current situation was dealt with.

Jon had emptied the guards' handguns. Nevertheless, the baffled guard posted beside the desk was lying prone, his pistol outstretched, still seeking a target. A moan rose from the far end of the room. The second guard lay there, clutching his chest. Before Jon or Carrie could react, he grunted and went

limp. Jon felt for a pulse. There was none. Somehow the mafioso had accessed a hidden loaded gun. He could have killed
them all. In the melee, he had missed Boris, killing his own
man. Their failure to check his desk drawer proved a fatal
error.

"You okay?" he asked Carrie.

"Yeah, I'm fine. You?"

"Nothing broken except my eardrums. What the hell was
that?"

Carrie looked out the window. "Well-placed fireworks.
Best guess is a diversion. Boris's escape hatch."

"It worked. He hightailed it." Awareness dawned on him.
"Where's Claudio?"

CHAPTER 65

Rome

T erry was waiting at the Villa Borghese gardens on
Pietro Raimondi Street, speculating why Claudio was
twenty minutes late. Had he meant what he said, and
changed his mind? She had done her best to convince him that
she could offer refuge from the two dangerous men he was
caught between. But conning his partner and his investor was
surely causing him great stress.

They'd agreed then to the rendezvous, the gardens a
short walk from her hotel. She'd decided against driving. Finding a parking spot could take too long.

Shira had selected the wide-open, uncrowded space to
keep the meeting private. But the longer she waited, Terry
felt increasingly vulnerable. She reminded herself that until
now Claudio had heeded her instructions and followed Boris.
Anxious to get what he needed out of the deal, Claudio hadn't
asked why that was a necessary part of the agreement. But
without him, she'd never have found Jon and Carrie alive.

Now, all that was left was to complete their deal. Claudio
would bring the formula and she would disclose the details of
how to keep him safe.

She checked the GPS tracker she'd dropped in his bag. He
was nowhere nearby. The man was skittish, uneasy even in his
normal state. Given Jon and Carrie's recent abduction, all sorts
of horrific possibilities entered her mind. She calmed herself.

She called Shira. "I know I'm not supposed to call, but the scientist never showed up."

"Understood," Shira said in a clipped tone. "One moment."

Terry heard Shira put down the phone. She heard the tapping of computer keys. When Shira came back on the line, she said, "He's at the don's house."

"What? I don't understand what he's doing."

"Maybe the don made Claudio a better offer. If that's true, he could bail on us."

Terry felt unsettled with all the unknowns. She couldn't call Claudio while he was at the don's estate. Nor could she wait indefinitely for him to show. He was now nearly an hour late and still a distance away.

"Should I keep waiting?"

"Negative. He may have told the don about you. Take no chances. Find a safe place. I will contact you with an update."

Terry knew a "safe place" meant a crowded place. She picked up her pace, anxious, her eyes scanning for threats, and headed straight for the closest and busiest place she could think of.

***

Seeing the murderous look in Boris's eyes as he realized Claudio had betrayed him had chilled the scientist to the bone. Yet it paled in comparison to witnessing the don aim and shoot at Boris, the bullet whizzing inches from his own head, lodging in the guard's chest. The gunshot had the effect of an Olympic race start. He bolted out of the house. Pausing briefly at the coat rack, he noted the guards running toward the smokey area outside the office window, completely unaware of him.

Claudio clutched his work bag tightly to his chest. He would never be able to work with Boris or the don. One was going to jail and the other bent on revenge. Boris would hunt him down. Of that he was certain.

He was out in the open and needed to find a safe place. Till now, the only thing keeping him alive was currently in his bag. He had kept the developing synthetic cloning formula in an encrypted file on his computer. When he'd arranged the rendezvous with Dr. Lavi, he printed a hard copy, placed it in his work bag, then deleted the file.

Dazed, Claudio ran for as long as his legs would allow, sweat dripping from his forehead. He'd arrived at the banks of the Tiber River. Exhausted, he leaned against the white brick wall, looking out at his beloved city. Small boats glided along the waterway, the sky streaked in purples and oranges in the wake of the setting sun. The world's deceptive beauty saddened him like a cheating lover.

How did things get to this point? The don nearly killed Boris right before his eyes and the Americans were working with him. The alliance made no sense to him. He needed to think, find a place to catch his breath, and calm down. Where would he go? He missed the rendezvous with Dr. Lavi. She would be gone by now. He couldn't return to the lab. Someone could be hunting him still.

He looked around. No one was paying him any mind. He took out his phone, ready to call Dr. Lavi and paused. It seemed everyone had a hidden agenda. Maybe Dr. Lavi did as well. She showed up out of nowhere. He was glad, despite the horror of the moment, to have had the presence of mind to drop the tracker in Boris's coat pocket which had been hanging beside the front door. Until that point, the GPS tracker at the bottom of his bag was the formula's only means of security. But now, he didn't know who, if anyone, to trust.

He returned his phone to his pocket.

Claudio took in his surroundings once again. He'd arrived at a quiet street lined with black iron lampposts, their gaslights flickering on with the onset of dusk. A quaint pub occupied the ground level of a three-story building directly across the street. Drained and afraid, he noted the street name. Via Santa Louisa. It was his mother's name. *Mamma, you had such high hopes for me.* What would she think of her son now? Claudio choked back a sob. A few moments passed till he pulled himself together. He crossed the road and walked into the pub.

***

Two hours later, the grasp on his bag had loosened, but only slightly. Claudio knew he was drunk, but it would take much more than three whiskey sours and a local stout to separate him from his precious work. He was calmer now, less paranoid, thankful his spontaneous decision to get a drink had also served to throw off any pursuers. Over the years, his impulsivity had brought him more grief than respite, especially his decision to conspire with Boris all those years ago. But coming here this evening had proven a sound idea.

There were only a few other patrons. A couple flirting at the far end of the bar and two men shooting pool. The music took him back to his youth when things were simpler. Both his parents had been scientists making it natural for their only child to follow suit. His love of biology was coded in his genes. What he once thought of as serendipity that led him to Boris, he now viewed as a curse.

A lone tear trailed down his cheek. "Un altro per favore," he said, lifting a finger.

The barkeep eyed him in the way only a seasoned barkeep can, seemingly assessing the man's threshold. "One more and you're done."

Claudio watched the man fill a new glass from the tap, the golden liquid nearly running over. He would nurse this one as long as he could. After all, there was nowhere else for him to go.

CHAPTER 66

Rome

J on couldn't help himself from looking down at the bulky form of the guard's body, now covered with Boris's signature camel-hair coat which Carrie had found hanging on the front door rack. The ambassador took off without it. Jon had seen more than his fair share of death, and he knew the look in the guard's eyes as his life slipped away would remain with him. Jon felt his pulse race, his brow sweaty. He'd been through this enough times to recognize the symptoms.

The mobster remained sitting quietly at his desk, seemingly pensive, no indication he'd just shot a man to death. Of those in the room, he appeared the most relaxed. If not for his now-bound arms, he could easily pass for a preoccupied businessman. Jon needed to get out of the don's house—as far away as possible.

Eyeing Jon, Carrie covered the mouthpiece of her cell with her hand. "You okay?" she asked.

"What is taking them so long?" Jon asked.

"Hold on," she said into the phone, tapped the mute button, and walked over to where he stood. She kept her voice low. "This has to be handled delicately. We can't just call the police. Matthews pulled some serious strings allowing us to remain in the country and use the don for our purposes. He assured the Italian authorities we would be operating peacefully." She gestured to the dead man. "The CIA will try to contain what gets out and spin the rest, hopefully with minimal damage. A team is on the way. They'll handle everything. Why don't you step outside, get some fresh air?"

"I'm not leaving you till they get here."

"Then at least sit down. You look like you're about to tip over."

Jon took a seat as far away from the mafioso and dead body as possible, taking several timed breaths, hoping the technique he'd learned in therapy would be enough to calm him.

Carrie got off the phone, looked past him out the window, and ran to the door. "They're here."

A team of four men entered the room, carrying bagged gear, the shape of their guns discernable beneath their jackets. The room quickly felt crowded. One of the men took photos, and two others got the don to his feet, leading him away between them.

The apparent leader, a muscled, baldheaded man with intelligent eyes said, "You Agent Santiago?"

"Yes."

"Well done."

"Thanks. This is Agent Steadman of the FBI. We worked the case together."

The man looked at Jon. "You're a Fed?"

Jon nodded.

"Wouldn't have guessed." With that, the team leader gestured to his remaining man who helped him lift the corpse along with the coat, swiftly bag it, and haul it over his shoulder like a pair of skis. Jon watched through the window as they placed the remains in the back of a black van, slamming the door shut. The leader pounded the side of the vehicle, signaling the driver to leave. He then came back inside.

Jon was struck by the team's efficiency. With the guard and don gone, he felt the color return to his face, his insides no longer clenched in knots.

Facing Carrie, the team leader said, "No need for you to

stick around. Call in your report and get your orders."

"On it." To Jon, she said, "I need to call my boss. I'll catch up with you in a minute."

With the house clear, Jon made for the door. He couldn't get out of there fast enough.

***

Terry blended in with a bevy of Spanish tourists taking pictures of the purple-streaked sky behind the Palazzo Poli, the magnificent palace backdrop to the Trevi Fountain. She sat along the travertine ledge and looked around. Everyone was on their phones, obliviously snapping away, scrolling, posting. The crowd had thinned some since she arrived, likely heading to their dinner reservations.

Checking her phone's app, she saw the red tracking circle that had pulsated over the don's home, had moved. Claudio was heading away from their planned meeting spot.

"What is wrong with me?" she yelled aloud in Hebrew to no one in particular, as she jumped to her feet. Several people turned to her, some stepping away, the suspicion of these times allowing her wide berth. She pushed her way through the crowd garnering irritated looks. "Mi scusi," she mumbled.

She was an ethicist, chosen to educate her country's leadership on morality, and yet she was leaving a defenseless man to his own devices, after encouraging his deception. She was aware of her tendency to be hard on herself but this time it was justified. She had met the man, spent time with him. Despite the treachery of his work, Claudio was not a conniver. Rather, he was guileless, almost childlike. If he was being ambiguous, it must be for an extreme purpose.

Terry sensed she'd hit her limit of requests with Jon and Carrie's rescue, and wouldn't dare ask Shira to get involved with what she needed to do now. For all she knew Claudio was totally fine. But Terry's gut was screaming.

She hurried to the street corner. Several cabs were lined up nearby anticipating the dinner crowd. She hopped in the back of one, gave the driver the name of the street. "Pronto!"

CHAPTER 67

Rome

W hen the cab pulled up, Terry threw a wad of bills into the front seat and bolted out. She looked around at the magnificent homes.

"Terry?

She spun around. There was Jon, his face ashen, his clothes disheveled.

She ran to him, bringing him into a tight embrace. "Oh, thank heavens! I was so worried about you."

Jon hugged her back. "We're okay now. Thanks to you."

Terry was about to ask a question when Carrie came out of a house fronted by an ostentatious stone fountain, its cherubs spewing water.

Terry said, "I'm so glad to see you."

"Same here. Things got shaky for a while."

Terry looked toward the door, then down the block. "Where's Claudio?"

Jon said, "He took off. Must've been spooked. The don tried to kill Boris but shot his guard instead."

"I'm sure he's terrified. I've been tracking him." She pointed to her phone. This was his last location. Now he's moving all over."

"You knew about Claudio?" Carrie asked.

When Terry didn't reply, Jon started to say something, then stopped himself. Instead, he looked at her app. "That's moving too fast. It has to be a vehicle."

"Let me see," Carrie said. "It's moving southeast. Wait. That's not Claudio."

"What do you mean?" Terry said.

"The tracker just stopped in front of the American embassy. It's where the cleanup team took the guard's body. It must be in the coat pocket."

Terry asked, "Then, where is Claudio?"

Carrie said, "He left a while ago. At this point he could be anywhere. If I'm not mistaken, I think the good scientist just outsmarted us all."

***

CIA New York Office

Two hours after Dr. Claudio Giovanni was last seen, Carrie's boss reported no leads on his whereabouts. While they were still trying to locate his lab, with some digging, they had found his home address, the same one he'd lived in before his untimely death. He wasn't there. He had no living family. His credit card hadn't been used and no flights had been purchased in his name. He had dropped off the radar, probably running scared. Now the only choice was to wait for him to resurface on his own time.

***

Rome

Shira ended the call with Yosef. Advanced satellite detection had located Claudio. She had heard of the famed Ofir 48, its technology a generation beyond that of first-world countries. She didn't ask for details, not that Yosef would have provided them anyway. The man never failed to impress her. He had the mind of a master chess player, always strategizing, seeing what lay several steps ahead. She could only hope to rise to his level someday. Satellite images found Claudio entering a pub on the outskirts of the city, along the Tiber River. Yosef was clear. He wanted Terry to bring him in. While Shira had the skills to abduct him, she didn't have the finesse to *lure* him with the soft touch like Terry could. She dutifully took her boss's order. Either way, one thing was certain. They would not lose Claudio again.

CHAPTER 68

Rome

As luck would have it, a new bartender took over the stingy one's shift. She was much more generous, replenishing Claudio's glass several more times. He used the bathroom, then moved to a table, and dozed for a few minutes till he was startled awake by the sound of a glass shattering on the floor. His head spun with fear and alcohol. With a deep well of hatred, he looked at his bag sitting in his lap, the fabric straps now wrapped around his wrist. *My life's work in a bag. How utterly pathetic.* He stumbled to a stand, brushing off the bartender's words of concern. She asked if he wanted her to call a taxi.

"No." *I have nowhere left to go.* He needed fresh air. He recalled a door beside the men's room. He would take it out the back, in case someone was waiting for him in front. When he opened the door, instead of an exit, it was a staircase. Disoriented, he looked up. He grabbed the railing, and with the bag knocking against his leg, Claudio pulled himself up one step at a time.

***

Terry entered the pub moments after Claudio found the staircase. She looked around, distraught that he was no longer there. Mixed with the guilt of not sharing Claudio's where-abouts with her partners, she was in a sorry state. She approached a pretty, dark-skinned bartender, wiping down the bar.

"Buonasera, did you happen to see an older man with a ponytail?"

The woman looked around. "He must have just left. I offered to call a taxi for him, but he declined. I hope he didn't drive. He was in no shape for that."

Terry walked to the back of the bar, knocked on the bathroom door. "Hello?" When there was no answer, she looked inside, finding it empty. There was no backdoor exit, only stairs to the roof. With no other obvious alternative, she started to climb.

***

Terry reached the roof door, panting, realizing it was slightly ajar. She pushed it open. Claudio stood feet from the roof's edge, teetering unstably, a lighter in his hand. He lit it with a flick, holding it under his briefcase, the flame seemingly teasing the fabric. He looked at Terry as though he was expecting her. "This project has brought nothing but death and destruction. All I wanted was to perfect my work, help the world. The opposite has happened." His words were slurred.

She moved closer. "I know how you feel, Claudio. But a scientific breakthrough can be used for good *or* bad. We just need to find a way to use it for good. I can help you do that." Feeling genuinely remorseful, she said, "I lied to you about my motives. I'm terribly sorry for that. I'm actually working on behalf of my country." Then, "Please put down the lighter."

Claudio bowed his head, his shoulders shaking as he sobbed. He placed the bag beside him on the rooftop, stumbling as he did so, the lighter slipping from his hand. Terry watched in horror as Claudio's pant leg caught a spark, flames suddenly licking at the cloth. Seeing Terry's face, he looked down, first curious then panicked. He stomped, desperate to extinguish the flames. Like a trapped, wounded animal, he howled. His bag caught fire, burning through the fabric. Balancing unsteadily on the beams, he removed his jacket and pounded the flames, the bottom half of his trousers scorched, patches of red skin now visible.

When the flames finally subsided, Claudio stared, his mouth agape, at the bag's scorched remains. Terry took a careful step forward, extending a supportive hand. Instead of moving toward her, Claudio neared the edge of the roof, pure despondence in his eyes.

Terry said, "Let me help you."

Moaning in pain, Claudio gave her a side glance.

"You are a brilliant scientist. Yes, you've done wrong. We all have. But you had pure intentions. And right now you have something so precious. You have life. And life allows you to make amends, turn a corner, right the wrongs of your past. You'll get a second chance."

"Not if I'm in prison."

Terry said, "We will work something out. Please come down. Let's talk and find a way to turn this thing around."

Claudio appeared torn, peering down at the street three stories below. Wincing in pain, he slowly nodded. Stepping toward Terry, his shoe caught on the charred handles of his work bag. He stumbled and fell, emitting a loud grunt, and rolled downward, his hands flailing, seeking purchase, groping for something to hold on to.

Terry leapt from where she stood, like a baseball player sliding home, head first, landing prone. She grabbed hold of his wrist, his body now dangling over the edge.

"Hold on!" she shouted, digging the tips of her shoes into the shingles behind her, trying desperately not to go over the side with him. Claudio looked up at her, desperate. "Aiutami!"

With every ounce of her strength, she pulled. But it was no use. He outweighed her by nearly a hundred pounds. His hand slipped from hers. Helplessly, Terry saw the terror in Claudio's eyes as he fell.

CHAPTER 69

Rome

Armed with the lab's address provided by Shira, Carrie called in her CIA colleagues, who were now swarming the place. So far, no formula was found. Jon wandered around the duplex, thinking of the scientist who remained unaccounted for. He tried reaching Terry to tell her to join them, but she wasn't answering her phone. Even though she hadn't immediately shared her intel of Claudio's existence, he felt bad to leave her out. She'd saved his life. And yet, he needed to be here when the spooks were poking around.

While Carrie was checking in with the other agents, he entered the messy lab. A freezer stood in the corner, empty, the Mussolini embryos gone. Someone had got here before them.

A small movement from above caught his attention. There, on the hutch atop the desk, was a cat, nearly starved. The tag read, *Fellini*. Jon found a can of cat food and snapped it open. The cat jumped down and ate ravenously.

Carrie found Jon in the lab, eyed the cat. She picked it up, stroking his fur. "Poor baby. I'll bring him to the hotel. We can figure out what to do with him later."

Jon's phone buzzed in his jacket pocket. *Matthews.*

"They found nothing?" his boss asked, his tone anxious.

"Nothing, sir." The title was not said sarcastically. "The spooks tore the place apart."

"There's no way research of that magnitude wasn't backed up somewhere."

"Agreed, but if it was, no one seems to be able to find it. The CIA guys are confiscating his computer."

"Those bastards at Langley will never share what they find with us. Stay close to Carrie and her CIA companions. Understood?"

"Yessir." He smiled. Carrie was holding his hand. She was as close as she could be without it being deemed intimate. Which it wasn't. The relationship seemed to naturally gel into a deepening friendship, the seed of romance no longer there. The near-death experience and confidences they shared were bringing them closer than many long-term friendships could. He muted his phone, said to Carrie, "I need a minute." He let go of her hand and left the room.

Into the phone he said, "I'm assuming you pulled some strings with local authorities. I haven't seen them."

"The President had to call in a boatload of favors to make that happen. He's not happy."

"Where's the Mossad team? I thought they would want to be here."

"They're keeping a low profile. They've agreed to wait for us to share our findings."

"I'm surprised they're so trusting," Jon said.

"Don't be. We paid steeply for that trust in the form of collateral—defense weaponry."

Trust but verify. "If we find the research documents, will we share all of it with them?" This he asked in a whisper.

Matthews said, "That's above my paygrade and I'd strongly recommend you never pose that particular question again. Israel is our ally. Actually, our only democratic one in that part of the world. We wouldn't want to jeopardize that."

Jon knew diplomatic BS when he heard it. "Should I get on the next plane home?"

"Not yet. I need you to stick around there, document every piece of intel the CIA does. Be a nuisance if need be. I'm sure that will come naturally."

Jon glimpsed Carrie speaking with an agent in the next room. "Very funny."

***

Back at the hotel, Carrie invited Jon to her room and shut the door. The cat was sleeping on the sofa, an empty bowl of milk beside it. Carrie rinsed out the dish in the bathroom sink. Above the sound of the water, she asked, "Other than his cherished clones, what was most dear to Boris?"

Jon shrugged. "I don't know."

Carrie came back into the room, gestured to the cat curled up in a ball. "Fellini."

Jon walked to the cat, sat beside it. Fellini didn't stir, his wide silver collar gleaming in a ray of sunlight pushing its way through the narrow space between the curtains.

It took Jon a moment. Then, "The collar."

Carrie nodded. "The collar."

Five minutes later, surviving a battle with the feline, Carrie held a small SIM card in her hand, the collar left on the room's nightstand.

Jon took it from her. "This should fit in my phone." He switched the chip with his and powered back up.

"Go to the files app."

Looking over his shoulder, she pointed to the screen. "Click here." And with that, the two agents hit the mother lode.

***

"It's all here. The formula. I can't believe it," Carrie said.

"But Fellini is Boris's cat."

Carrie went to the nightstand, turned the collar around

323

in her hand. "Wow."

He came to stand beside her. "What is it?"

"A mini transceiver. A transmitter and a receiver combined in one unit. I think this collar was collecting data from Claudio's computer via Airdrop. Once he inserts the SIM card in his phone, he can send the data anywhere."

Jon was flabbergasted. "Incredible. But the formula wasn't on Claudio's computer."

"They must have been deleted at some point."

Jon carefully removed the SIM card. "This can't possibly be the only copy."

Carrie said, "It very likely is. Remember, at the don's house, Boris didn't know the Mussolini clones were completed. He never had a chance to download it. If he had, he would've known."

Jon stared at the device cradled in the palm of his hand, amazed that because of something so tiny, the world would never be the same.

CHAPTER 70

Three months later
New York City

Congressman Germain drained his coffee and set the *Times* down on the seat beside him, then buckled in. He would be on the ground in twenty minutes. Recent weeks had been a whirlwind of travel from state to state, eating flapjacks in a roadside coffee shop in Iowa, kissing babies in New Hampshire, and gladhanding casino owners in Nevada. Victories in those early primaries led to a landslide win on Super Tuesday.

He appointed Gwen his executive assistant. She kept tabs on his campaign headquarters popping up around the country, recruiting the most ardent students among them into the SAU. She was made for the role. Organized, passionate and loyal, she kept the same long hours as he did.

As Boris had promised, the Committee came through, filling the campaign coffers with more funds than any of his opponents could solicit. The money had not only been allocated to the congressman's campaign. The SAU was on the payroll as well. Spenser had long ago learned the power of youth, its unbridled idealism. He was determined to harness it and maintain his lead in the polls. With Boris's guidance, anti-establishment protests—several turning to looting frenzies—erupted in cities across the country. Most, if not all, were instigated by members of the SAU, a grassroots student group he publicly denounced, but privately took pride in. The police were quickly becoming a despised entity. Once he took office, the SAU would replace them, becoming an army that answered only to him.

Since returning from Rome, Spenser had remained in loose touch with Felix and Owen. They were keeping low profiles in their respective cities, surely anxious to ascend to their new roles—titans of media and jurisprudence. Their appointments would take place days after the presidential inauguration. Once in office, he would welcome his clones into his inner circle.

The episode with Agents Steadman and Santiago weighed heavily on him. On his request, Gwen had made inquiries, discovering the two agents were back in the States. He had never asked Boris what became of them, but clearly he had let them go free, though Spenser imagined not before teaching them a painful lesson.

Still, he couldn't let go of their deception. If things stayed the course, he would soon be named the undisputed party candidate. With so much at stake, he couldn't risk another interference. If necessary, he would teach them what Boris failed to—no one betrayed Lenin and lived.

***

Gwen waited on the curb outside LaGuardia's Delta terminal. She was dressed in a form-fitting red dress, lipstick on her mouth, holding a bottle of champagne. Following the primary sweeps, she received an unexpected call from a man named Boris, a self-described long-time supporter of Spenser's, confirming he was the one who had made the generous donation to the congressional reelection campaign. As someone who wanted to see Spenser win this election, he was of the belief that a powerful man needed an equally strong woman by his side. Was she willing to be that woman? The subsequent proposal offered her the sense of importance she knew she'd already earned.

Gwen's heart leapt as she caught sight of Spenser's compact, muscular frame. He walked confidently out of the terminal. Spotting her, he smiled broadly, causing her to regret her passing attraction to Jon Steadman. No one matched Spenser's charisma and bravado. With time, he would acknowledge her devotion and his feelings would surely grow.

A pristine black Town Car idled at the curb in front of them. Spenser glanced at Gwen, his eyes lingering on her mouth. He lifted a brow.

Challenged to keep the pride from her tone, she said, "Boris called." As if that alone would explain her presence and feminine attire. "Congratulations. On the primaries."

A chauffeur came around, opening the door for them. Once inside, Gwen popped the cork, pouring two glasses. As the driver pulled into traffic, Gwen carefully handed a glass to Spenser. "To the next President of the United States."

Spenser laughed, stunning her with a kiss brushed across her lips. "Gwen, my dear, I'll drink to that."

***

Jon did as Matthews had asked, staying on top of the spooks in Rome. But after a week of no progress, he and Carrie went home. It was a frustration like no other. Claudio was in a coma and Boris had vanished. He was getting away with murder and treason, and possibly even the Mussolini embryos, which remained unaccounted for. Until they turned up a lead, the case would remain in a holding pattern. *Is this what it's like to be a federal agent—putting my life on the line, and the bad guys get away?*

He and Matthews were getting along unusually well. He assumed it was a response to the close call in the Rome sewing factory. Something had shifted between them and both were respecting the change.

For now, the focus was on the clones. Felix Salko and Judge Cantor were under constant surveillance. Neither showed any indication of trouble. If anything, they had become less active in their political lives.

That left Spenser Germain. With the nationwide riots, the anger at the current administration sent his star rising at a meteoric pace. He was closing in on the presidency. Yet, there was no way to stop the Lenin clone. He had done nothing illegal, at least nothing provable. Being a genetic clone was not a crime. The more his popularity grew, the greater the need for actionable evidence to impede his progress. They needed a break in the case, or come November, America as a capitalist society would be a thing of the past.

***

Jerusalem

Terry strolled through Sacher Park, Shira silent by her side. The Knesset stood high on the hill behind them, riotous colors of spring wildflowers surrounding them. She breathed in the scent of gardenias, the aroma taking her back to the last time she smelled the distinct fragrance. In Eilat. With Gabe. How she longed for that time. For him. Her mind turned to the recent trauma in Rome. So much sadness.

Shira said, "Stop thinking about it."

Terry blinked away her thoughts.

"You did everything possible to help Dr. Giovanni."

Terry said, "He's been in a coma for months. I should have told him who I was from the beginning."

"Then *your* life would have been in danger."

Terry shook her head. She'd played the scene over in her head countless times. It always ended the same way. Claudio falling off the roof, her hand grasping at air.

Shira said, "I've been checking on him regularly. He suffered a broken leg, fractured wrist bones, and a cracked pelvis. His doctors will soon attempt to wake him from an induced coma and check for brain damage."

"I pray for him every day."

The two women returned to an amiable silence. They walked past children on swings, couples picnicking on the grassy expanse. *Life goes on.*

Terry asked, "Do the Americans know about Claudio?"

"They do now. We told them we found him, that he had a bad accident and is unresponsive. All true, of course. We simply left out the part about you following him onto the pub's roof."

"Any word on Tierney?"

"The Americans found nothing at the lab. But they have located his pied-à-terre in Rome. They plan to go there to investigate."

"Shall I meet them there?"

Shira shook her head. "Our countries' respective agendas have become clear. While they seek to apprehend Boris, our focus remains on Claudio. Go back to Haifa, to your regular job. If and when Claudio wakes, your orders will resume."

"What about Jon and Carrie?"

Shira said, "You will go to Claudio alone."

"And if our agenda should clash with theirs?"

Shira stopped walking, faced Terry. "Dr. Lavi, you already know the answer to that."

Terry paused, then nodded. For better or worse, she did.

PART III

CHAPTER 71

New York City

C arrie fiddled with her sparkly bracelet. Randy liked it also, staring at her arm for minutes at a time as the gemstones danced in the caught light. His behavior was erratic. Some days tuned in to her, others in his own world. His speech was limited to a few sentences he mimicked from cartoons he watched. Carrie sat in on the therapy sessions, glad to see he seemed to enjoy them, but with a new school year on the horizon, she had an important decision to make. Maintain the status quo or enroll him in a special needs school?

Carrie ran a finger across the bracelet's rough edges. The only time she took it off was to shower and even then she kept it in sight.

Before leaving Rome, she left Fellini with one of the CIA field officers. He was a cat person, glad to have a non-needy companion waiting for him when he got home from work each night. After a long conversation with Jon, they agreed to wait before telling either of their bosses about the SIM card. The ramifications of prematurely handing over the device were clear to them both. Instead, they decided to brainstorm ways to use it to lure Boris from his hidey hole. Fellini's collar became Carrie's bracelet, its contents still intact.

***

Spenser locked the door behind Gwen, surprised at what had

just taken place. Perhaps it was the champagne. Or her deep red lipstick. Either way, it led to a fierce passion, the heat coming fast, before he could stop it. If she'd been getting mixed signals before, it had just become much worse.

He put his shirt back on, buttoned it. He recalled seeing a package outside his door and brought it inside, placing it on his desk. *Par Avion.* No return address. He opened it. Inside, was a small white envelope lying atop folded fabric.

A simple card. *Congratulations. We are almost there. Wear this well. It will take you to great heights. -B*

Spenser pulled out the heather gray garment. *Comrade Lenin's uniform!* Once again, he disrobed, then changed into the Soviet military garb. Looking at himself in the mirror he was the spitting image of Vladimir Lenin. He admired how well the uniform fit him, the gold buttons, red piping, and taupe belt enhancing his physique. Once in office, he'd consider having his barber style his hair exactly as Lenin's. Studying his reflection, Spenser sensed an intense emotion. Stronger and more intoxicating than lust or passion. He smiled as he realized what the feeling was.

Power.

***

FBI Headquarters
New York City

Few people knew of the clones' existence. The President was of course on the shortlist. With only a few months until Election Day, and the tide swiftly turning on him, the Commander-in-Chief dialed up the pressure. It didn't take long for it to trickle down to Matthews. The President wanted Spenser out of the race, claiming that even if he lost, it couldn't be to a commie. The country would never recover. While it may have been his typical rhetoric, Matthews believed the man actually cared.

The result was, after months of monitoring, Salko and Cantor were finally being brought in for questioning. The message was clear—spill what you know about Boris and his machinations, or your careers would be deep-sixed before they could blink a cloned eye.

The two men agreed to speak without their lawyers in return for the signed immunity now on the table before them. Everyone involved wanted the matter to remain quiet. The day they arrived at FBI headquarters, they were shown into a small office, rather than an interrogation room. Matthews knew there were at least ten people in the next room waiting to act on whatever intel he would get out of them.

Matthews studied the men. In person, their likeness to each other and to Lenin was truly remarkable. The initial disagreement among the powers that be to offer blanket immunity was quickly put to rest when the two men offered to do their utmost to bring down the country's leading presidential challenger. They claimed to have been seduced by the charismatic Ambassador Tierney and were now remorseful. True or not, it didn't matter to Matthews. He needed information. He did his best to put them at ease, telling them they were small fish. In reality, the two men—more than anyone—had the power to do what they promised.

Matthews turned on the recorder. "Please state your names."

The men did so. After several minutes of preliminary Q & A, Matthews asked, "Where's Professor Claudio Giovanni's research?" The scientist apparently had suffered a serious accident and sustained significant injuries. He was being kept in an induced coma until his brain swelling subsided.

The men looked at each other, seemingly distraught that neither knew the answer to the first real question.

Salko said, "No idea. We never met him."

Matthews crossed his arms, looked at them sternly. "Really?"

Salko said, "I swear. We had no contact with him whatsoever."

Matthews leaned closer to the recorder. "The suspects claim never to have met Dr. Giovanni, their cloner." He hoped the use of "suspects" would get their attention.

"What can you tell me about Spenser Germain?"

The men looked at each other, confusion on their faces. "He's preparing for the convention."

Matthews knew that was old news. The congressman had been AWOL for the last 24 hours. The men had better pony up some useful information or he'd be raked over the coals for pushing through their immunity deal.

"You need to think really hard about the next question."

Seemingly anxious to help, Cantor replied, "Shoot."

"Where's Tierney?"

The two men fidgeted in their seats. "The last time we saw him, he'd dropped us off at the Rome airport."

"And you haven't heard from him since?"

Cantor broke eye contact. Matthews turned to Salko who suddenly seemed to find his hands fascinating.

Matthews had had enough. "If you think you're walking out of here with a sweet deal for nothing, think again! Whatever semblance of a life you've had before all this will vanish in a puff of smoke." He snapped his fingers to make his point.

Salko remained silent. But Cantor spoke up. "I think he has a place somewhere in Rome. Spenser stayed there before moving to the embassy."

"Do you know where?"

Cantor shook his head. "Spenser said it was an upscale hotel." He closed his eyes in concentration. "I think he said something about it being near a flower market."

Matthews knew the intel was spurring a flurry of activity in the room next door.

"Tell me about the SAU."

The men seemed on firmer ground now. They spoke freely, sharing their information on a group known as The

Committee. Matthews listened intently.

When Matthews completed the questioning, he said, "You'll need to stay in New York for the time being. In case we have more questions."

The men seemed perturbed by the pronouncement. "For how long? We have our work to get back to."

Your lives will never be the same. "A few days, assuming your info leads us where we need to go."

Cantor said, "You won't get him, you know. Claudio. The Committee has reach beyond your imagination. They'll take care of him before you get ahold of his work."

Matthews shut off the recorder and opened the door. A suited young man escorted the two men away.

He walked to the next room and opened the door. "Get me that hotel address. Now."

***

Rome

Jon and Carrie had mixed feelings about being back in Rome. The memories of their near-death were fresh. But they finally had a solid lead. Though they knew the odds were the ambassador was long gone, the CIA field officers kept a round-the-clock watch on the Hotel Campo del Fiori. Tierney had kept a place there for years, under an assumed name.

The boutique hotel was a beautiful pre-war structure. Jon and Carrie found the manager waiting for them in the lobby, a lovely space designed in rich fabrics and dark wood, a Murano chandelier glowing above. The manager explained he had not seen Boris in months, the timing corresponding to his theatrical disappearance from the don's home. Jon and Carrie followed him up to Boris's apartment.

The rooms were luxurious, a stark difference from his partner's accommodations at the loft. While Claudio slept on a cot in the lab, Boris was dreaming atop a thousand-count linen.

The room had been cleaned, awaiting its resident. The closet was replete with custom shirts and suits, pairs of polished wingtips lined the floor.

The manager watched as Jon and Carrie took their time looking through pockets, moving things around. Though he appeared uncomfortable, he said nothing. His tolerance had been paid for.

"Jon, over here."

Carrie had moved the sofa away from the wall. Behind it were dark fur balls. Clearly, the chambermaid had not made the extra effort. Jon helped Carrie tilt the sofa forward. Attached to the underside by what he assumed was Fellini's fur, was a slip of paper, most of its print faded. He could make out, *EuroFPL* and *LEU*.

Carrie picked it up, pocketing it.

They thanked the brooding manager, and minutes later were outside the building, Jon tapping on his phone. "Got it! EuroFPL is a flight plan."

"And LEU?"

Jon turned the phone to face his partner.

Carrie read aloud. "La Seu d'Urgell Airport. Where on earth is that?"

Jon took a moment to read. "It's in Andorra."

"Andorra. It's one of the smallest countries in the world. It's in the Pyrenees. Bordered by Spain and France."

Jon raised an arm, inviting Carrie's high-five. "Partner, I think we just took a huge step closer to the ambassador."

CHAPTER 72

Rome

I t was early evening when Terry entered Claudio's hospital room. She was surprised to find no one posted outside the door. Claudio was sitting up, his computer propped before him. His hands were splinted, only allowing him to awkwardly peck at the keyboard. His left shin was wrapped in gauze. It was a drastic improvement from where he'd been months before at death's door. When Shira told her he'd been revived without evident brain damage, she let out a months-long breath.

Terry took a seat beside the bed. "Hello, doctor. You look so much better. How are you feeling?"

Claudio looked up from his computer. His face was pale, somber. "I have second-degree burns, but it could have been much worse. My leg has healed well since they removed the cast. The physical therapy and Vicodin help." He regarded his visitor with a glimmer of a smile. Are you an attending here now?"

Terry was glad he was making jokes. "Only a visitor."

He took a moment. Then, "I was drunk, you know. I never would have done what I did had I been in my right mind."

"Don't think about that now. Are you up for a chat?"

He turned to face her, emitting a groan. "About our earlier conversation?

"That's right."

"What would be the point?" He gestured to the closed door. "The police have been keeping an eye on me. Ironically, they're calling me the resurrected man. They thought I was dead."

"There's no guard outside."

"He only comes during the day. I guess I'm not much of a flight risk in this condition."

"Have you been charged?"

"Not yet. My guess is they're building a case, figuring out what to charge me with that will stick. It's just a matter of time. And even if by some miracle I won't be arrested, why would you help me now without the data?"

"You worked out the cloning formula once, you can do it again."

"It took me decades. I won't live that long."

Terry leaned back in the chair. "You aren't reinventing the wheel. You already know much of what has to be done."

He shook his head. "I don't know how long it will take."

"I have a colleague who can help."

Claudio appeared doubtful.

She took the older man's hand. "You've been through a great deal. Don't you want that second chance?"

When he didn't respond, she went on. "I have not always been completely forthcoming, but I believe you know that I'm honorable and seek to do right by you. Can you possibly trust me?"

Claudio wearily closed his eyes. He seemed to have aged ten years in only a few months. "I don't know who to trust anymore. How will the Italians ever let me leave?"

"You've disappeared once, you can do it again."

Claudio opened one eye, "What are you saying?"

Terry noticed a nurse peeking through the glass, then step away. She lowered her voice. "The offer to help you still stands. But I need an answer now."

When he didn't reply, Terry patted his hand and stood to leave. As she reached the door, she heard one softly whispered word. "Wait."

***

While Claudio changed out of his hospital gown, Terry looked at her phone, reading a message Shira had sent. When he emerged, she said, "My colleague will meet us in an hour at the Great Synagogue. She will guide us from there."

A clap of thunder rocked the window.

"A storm is coming," Claudio said. He donned the wide-brimmed hat and a belted jacket he'd been admitted with. Together they exited, no one giving them a second look.

Terry pulled out her phone. "I'll order a car."

"Don't bother. It will be quicker to walk."

A strong wind picked up as they made their way across the piazza. "Are you sure you are up for this?"

He looked up at the sky. "We should arrive at the synagogue before the storm hits. Anyway, I've been in bed for months. I need to get used to walking again."

Terry would have liked to pick up the pace, but Claudio was shuffling. Under normal conditions the walk should take no more than twenty minutes. She reminded herself he was thirty years her senior, just left the hospital, and she slowed. It was dark now and a steady rain began to fall. She pulled up her hood.

"The synagogue is this way," Claudio said.

The man was a lifelong Roman and Terry followed his lead as he turned west, the iconic Colosseum lit up in the distance.

***

Jerusalem

Yosef Kahn reached Shira minutes after speaking with Matthews. "Where's Dr. Lavi?"

Shira checked Terry's GPS signal. "She's fine. They're heading in the right direction."

***

Rome

"Are you sure this is the right way?" Terry's coat was soaked.

"Of course I'm sure. It's a shortcut."

Directly across from them stood the Colosseum. The ancient amphitheater, a cavernous behemoth, appeared threatening in the gathering storm. The street was deserted. No gypsies or tourists. Even the locals were nowhere to be found. The inclement weather had kept them all indoors.

Terry slipped on the slick pavement. As Claudio put out a hand to help her, she felt something buzz by her ear, followed immediately by another, a few feet away. Still holding Claudio's hand, Terry forcibly pulled him to the ground, causing him to fall beside her.

"What—?"

"Someone's shooting at us!"

Claudio momentarily froze. Despite his painful protests, Terry ran, firmly tugging the scientist behind her.

***

Shira was prepared—as always. She had made all the logistical arrangements, though she'd left the web of diplomatic challenges to Yosef. The mission was in its final hours, a time she knew to be the most precarious, when all moving parts needed to line up perfectly. She waited in the beautifully ornate sanctuary of Rome's Great Synagogue, admiring the intricate art nouveau design, soaring ceilings, and velvet-bedecked holy ark. The rabbi, a dear friend of the prime minister, had arranged for access to the sanctuary if and when needed.

Listening to the angry rain pounding on the synagogue's dome, Shira took a moment to consider Dr. Lavi. She wondered if in retrospect Yosef Kahn was regretting his decision to recruit her, aware of the extent of danger involved in this case. Though her years of mandatory army service gave her a leg up, the doctor's field training had been basic at best. And yet, the petite professor had exceeded expectations. The next step of the mission could prove treacherous, and as her handler, Shira didn't want to be responsible for her demise. Dr. Lavi had slowly grown on her.

Yosef had sounded concerned on the phone. Which made her concerned. She checked the GPS yet again, stunned to see where the professors were located. She closed her eyes and whispered a silent prayer. Then she made a call.

**

Jon was standing under a flower cart's awning, checking flights to Andorra, when his phone rang.

It was Shira, the Mossad agent. He put the call on speaker. "Have you heard from Dr. Lavi?" The Israeli's voice sounded uncharacteristically strained.

"No. What happened?"

"Her phone signal isn't working. I'm using other technology to pinpoint her location. They should have arrived by now," Shira said.

Carrie exchanged a look. "They?" Jon asked.

"That's not relevant. Where are you?"

Jon understood something important was going on, but

if Terry was in danger, it would need to wait. Near the flower market in the Campo d'Fiori. Where is she?"

Shira said, "At the Colosseum. They must be evading someone."

The Colosseum? "Maybe they took shelter from the rain."

"She would have called. There's something wrong. It will take me too long to get to them. You are closer, only a few minutes away from there."

Carrie nodded to Jon. He said, "We're on our way."

Jon saw Carrie check for something in her bag. He felt for his pistol, glad they were both carrying. The rain was picking up and they sprinted to their rental car, Carrie taking the driver's seat. As soon as they closed the doors, blustery winds began spewing horizontal rains, scattering tree limbs across the pavement. She started the car, ran the wipers. They didn't do much.

Jon took out his phone. "I'll read up on the Colosseum's layout."

The one benefit of the vicious storm was theirs was the only car on the road. Carrie floored it.

***

There was nowhere to hide. Other than the towering Colosseum, the rain-drenched Via Sacra offered no shelter from the bullets.

"There!" Claudio pointed to one of the amphitheater's story-high iron gates. "The local kids used to break this lock. I played in here when I was a child." He pushed hard on the black metal. The gate opened with a loud grinding groan. Terry rushed in behind him. Floodlights illuminated the entrance and a bullet ricocheted off the metal bars.

"This way!" Claudio seemed to be in control now, familiar with his surroundings. "This path leads to the underground tunnels."

Terry didn't like the sound of that, but with the lights shining down on them, she had no choice but to follow.

***

Claudio and Terry leaned back in the shadows, catching their breath. Drenched in a mix of rain and sweat, they had descended a series of stone stairs, taking several turns as they went.

Claudio's body was shaking, his eyes rapidly scanning the stairs.

"Are you all right?" Terry asked.

"I-I don't think they'll find us here." He hadn't answered the question.

She felt for her gun. "Let's rest a moment." She tried to make out the space in the dim lighting, noting several areas on the periphery were cordoned off with scaffolding. "What is this place?"

"It's where the gladiators prepared for battle—and where they kept the caged beasts. Tigers, lions."

Terry was horrified. She could almost smell the terror of those unwilling warriors. She took out her phone, careful to veil its emitting light. No signal. "I need to message my contact for help. I'll have to get back outside."

Footsteps. Someone was headed straight to their hiding place. It occurred to Terry the ground was soft. *They must be following our shoeprints.*

She put a finger to her lips and gestured forward. Breathing heavily, Claudio led the way.

***

Jon and Carrie arrived at the main entrance to the Colosseum.

They left the car parked illegally and approached the gate, pulling the hoods up on their coats, doing what they could to keep the rain out of their eyes. Jon now saw Carrie was holding a lock pick set in her gloved hand.

Jon said, "There's a series of subterranean passages. They can be accessed from all sides. I'll approach from the north, you go east." He pointed as he spoke.

She put a hand on his arm. "Do we trust Shira?

"We have to find Terry," he said, aware he wasn't directly answering her question.

Carrie got the gate open. "We need to proceed carefully, and only do what's in the best interest of our country, Jon. It's obvious they have ulterior motives. Understand?"

Jon said, "No, Carrie, I don't. Terry saved us from the don. If I have the chance, I'll happily return the favor. Do *you* understand?"

Carrie hesitated only a moment. Then nodded. "Sorry, you're right. See you inside. Be careful."

Jon gave a thumbs-up and the two took off in opposite directions.

***

The storm raged, creating a deafening echo in the cavernous space. It prevented Terry from hearing any pursuers but also helped mask Claudio's heavy breathing. He was clearly spent, looking both terrified and disoriented.

Terry asked, "Do you know where we are?"

He squinted in the darkened room. "I'm not sure."

The scaffolding was everywhere now, open toolboxes and bags of cement lined the barred cages. Water dripped from the gaps in the stone ceiling, pooling into puddles on the floor. They had stumbled into a reconstruction site. Lights strung up haphazardly began to flicker. Terry noted several exposed electrical wires, careful to avoid them. They'd reached a dead end. The only way out was the way they had come. She took Claudio's hand and turned back, stopping in her tracks. Standing ten feet away, blocking the exit, was Spenser Germain.

"You're a hard man to find," Spenser said, though he was looking at Terry. "Why are you running from me? Am I not your creation, your brainchild?"

Claudio seemed unable to speak. He was staring at the gun in Germain's hand.

"We will leave now, together."

"No," Claudio said. Terry was amazed at his sudden gumption.

Spenser got off a shot, spitting up the gravel at Claudio's feet, making the scientist dance like a marionette. The sound was overpowering in the enclosed space.

"I've been primed for this. You and Boris made me. I will be the leader of the New Soviet Union. Your research will keep Lenin…me…going for countless more generations."

"It's gone, destroyed."

Spenser sneered, let out a snort of disgust. "For a genius, you know so little. Suffice it to say, your work continues." He waved the pistol.

Claudio backed away, shaking his head. "I won't help you. Never."

"So be it." Spenser aimed. The next bullet was as deafening as the first. This one came from Terry's pistol. Germain fell to his knees, his gun falling from his hand. He glanced down at the red bloom in the middle of his chest. A look of shock plastered his features as his lips emitted a distorted *oh*. He fell face first into the gravel.

Terry looked at her smoking gun, wanting desperately to throw it aside. She went to Claudio, his eyes closed, mumbling to himself.

"No!"

Terry spun around. A young woman she'd never seen before ran into the room, rushing to Spenser's side. She held his head in her lap, her tears falling onto his face. "You killed him!"

she shrieked. "We were going to be together. He loved me!" The woman stood, took something from her pocket, a look of dire menace contorting her face.

Just then, Carrie ran in behind her, Jon a moment later.

"Gwen?" Carrie said.

"You! I knew you were a spy!" She looked from one agent to the next, her eyes finally settling on Claudio, the scaffolding at his back. He appeared catatonic.

Gwen moved toward him, pulling a switchblade from her pocket, flicking it open.

***

In a split second, Jon sized up the room. Everyone was too close for him to get off a clean shot.

Gwen glared at Claudio. "All he wanted was your stupid research." She choked back a sob. "He died for it." As swift as a tiger, Gwen lunged for Claudio, the knife aimed at his throat.

Before Jon could react, Carrie leapt at Gwen, shoving her aside. The knife spun from Gwen's hand, its metal handle knocking against an electric cable lying on the floor, thrusting it like a writhing snake into the puddle beside it.

"No!" Jon shouted.

Carrie landed in the puddle. Her body shuddered violently as electrons flowed through her, her limbs spasming like a rag doll. Desperate, Jon grabbed a rubber mallet off the floor, forcing the cable from the pooled water. He kneeled beside his partner, her eyes closed, her hair and fingertips singed. She wasn't breathing.

Jon leaned over her, held her head back, and squeezing her nostrils, blew into her mouth. He placed the heels of his hands on the center of her chest, and pressed down hard, pumping, counting in his head.

...28, 29, 30...Blow...

After what seemed like forever, Jon felt a hand on his

shoulder. He heard a faraway voice, laced with agony. "She's gone, Jon."

It was the last thing he remembered.

CHAPTER 73

Rome

Panicked, Gwen ran from the tunnel, following the muddy footprints up the stairs back to ground level. Rainwater poured down the ancient gutters, the sound of a million heavy drops angrily ricocheting off the ground. She couldn't process all that had just happened. It was only due to the grotesque scene that she'd managed to get away. The dark-haired female agent had been electrocuted, her colleagues trying to resuscitate her. The old scientist was catatonic, oblivious to what was happening around him. No one paid attention to her hasty exit.

Gwen caught her breath. Tears, mixed with rivulets of rainwater, streamed down her face. Her hair was a drippy mess, her clothes soaked. She leaned against a stone wall, slid to the wet ground. *Spenser! The next president. My love. Dead.*

When he'd told her he was going to Rome, she was stunned he would leave so close to the election, even for a few days. But when he'd asked her to join him, she was overjoyed. Their lovemaking was still fresh in her mind, she could feel his hands on her still. He'd said he wanted her to meet Boris, the man she'd spoken with after the primaries. Gwen dropped her head in her hands, sobbing. "Spenser, tell me what to do!" she yelled.

Call Boris. She heard Spenser's voice in her head, aware she was in a state of shock.

She still had Boris number in her phone. One last time, she heeded her lover's advice.

***

Casa de Las Naranjas, Andorra

The girl's sobs were racked with heartbreak. It took Boris several minutes to decipher what had happened. Spenser was dead. By the hand of a woman. Gwen described her as blond, petite, with a strange accent. *Dr. Terry Lavi.*

Grief-stricken, there was no time to fit all the pieces together. Or to mourn his beloved clone. The national convention was imminent. As always, he was prepared. It was time to activate the congressman's replacement.

Even if the agents attempted to expose Spenser's death, the reports would be deemed nothing more than an outlandish scheme. After all, who would ever believe a crazy conspiracy suggesting the existence of the congressman's exact replicas?

***

Jerusalem

Of those not present in the Colosseum, Yosef Kahn was the third to hear of the congressman's demise. The first was the former U.S. ambassador to the Czech Republic, the second, Terry's handler. With Agent Steadman's impaired condition, and the apprehension of the congressman's young female cohort, the intel was especially valuable. He took some time to determine how best to leverage it. In the end, simple was best. He picked up his phone and called his new best friend in the White House.

***

Washington, D.C.

Since taking office, the President thought he'd seen and heard it all. He was wrong. He was eating dinner with his family in the West Wing's private dining room when a call came through from the head of Israel's Mossad. After excusing himself, he took the call in his study. He listened to what Kahn had to say, thanked him, and hung up.

He flipped on the television, quickly finding election coverage. His political opponent stood on a stage waving to the crowd. The President froze the image and stared at the man. He saw no discernable difference in his appearance from recent months of footage.

And yet, Yosef Kahn had just informed him this was not Congressman Spenser Germain. It was one of his two living clones.

***

New York City

Several hours later, Matthews was notified of the situation. The President had convened an emergency meeting of his most trusted advisors. The consequence of his administration making such an outlandish allegation as a cloning conspiracy would surely backfire, and the President would be accused of running a smear campaign like no other.

The decision was made. Until they got their hands on admissible evidence, the congressman's death would remain quiet. Since the incident at the Colosseum, U.S. diplomatic relations with Italy were further strained. Getting the Italian government to admit to the existence of the cloning documents hidden in Rome's archives, let alone release them, was unlikely. And with Claudio Giovanni back in the hospital, and his physician denying him visitors, there was little they could do. The Israeli offered the photos, but photos would never be enough. With the election weeks away, the FBI and CIA were charged with finding hard evidence. Fast.

CHAPTER 74

New York

Two days in the Rome American Hospital were followed by a transfer to New York's Mount Sinai Hospital for a psychiatric evaluation. This time Jon had no choice but to take the offered meds. They made him loopy, his waking hours spent in a fog, his memory spotty. His grief made an unwanted appearance in his sleep. Twice he'd been shaken awake by the night nurse, her soothing voice a short-lived cure. After a week, he was deemed stable. Now discharged, but on temporary work leave, he was glad to be back on his therapist's familiar sofa.

"Jon, are you listening?"

"What?"

"I suppose that answers my question. What are you thinking about?"

"My dream last night."

"Do you want to tell me about it?"

Jon lay his head back on the cushion, closed his eyes. "Ashleigh and Carrie were together, speaking in a strange language. But I knew instinctively they were talking about me. They were getting along great."

"How did the dream make you feel?"

Jon paused, thinking. "Relieved they had each other. Sad I couldn't understand them."

The therapist remained silent for a minute. Then, "Do

you see a connection between the two women?"

"Other than both are women I couldn't save?"

"I read Agent Santiago's report."

Jon opened his eyes, abruptly sitting up. "What report?"

"After your confrontation with"—she looked at a file, lifted a brow—"the don, Carrie submitted an incident report. Much of it was redacted but I read the parts about you."

"And your conclusions?"

"It's no accident you've chosen this line of work."

"How so?"

"Tempting fate. Taking unnecessary risks. Only now you have another reason to feel guilty for surviving when others did not."

"I've earned the guilt."

"No, Jon. You haven't. If all you've been through has suggested anything, it's that we have no control. Not really." The doctor took a page out of the file. "May I?"

Jon shrugged.

She began to read. "Facing the wall and a gun pointed at his head, Agent Steadman whispered, 'I'm coming, Ash,' as though he couldn't wait. He's the bravest agent I've known."

"She wrote that?"

"Seems to me you're committed to recreating the original sin of Ashleigh's death, so you can do things differently."

Jon broke eye contact.

She said, "Perhaps it's working. You've already saved many lives in your short career with the FBI."

"Not Carrie's." Jon put his head in his hands.

"Can you talk about your feelings now?"

Driven to live up to Carrie's description of him, Jon said, "I'll try."

And he did.

PART IV

CHAPTER 75

Ordino, Andorra
Five Months Later

The drive north to Ordino took Jon close to an hour, some of that time spent slowing down to admire the mountain scenery. It was a small village, seemingly ripped from the pages of a fairy tale. Stone buildings with slate roofs and wooden balconies overflowed with pink flowers. An alpine stream ran through the village, bubbling across smooth dark rocks.

Jon got out of the rental and stretched his legs, the cool air a respite from New York's oppressive heat. With few inhabitants, it shouldn't be difficult to find Boris. The question was if one of the locals would warn the ambassador that someone was asking questions about him.

Since his discharge from the psych ward, Jon hadn't told Matthews about the flight plan Carrie found at the Rome hotel that led him here. He knew his boss would never allow him to pursue Boris once the case became personal. Unfortunately, that meant he was now on his own.

Hungry, he stepped into a small café. Skis were bolted to the wood-paneled walls as decoration. The smell of fresh brewed coffee beans permeated the room. His stomach growled. He eyed the delicate pastries, glad to have his appetite back, aware he'd lost too much weight since Carrie's death. He ordered a cold coffee and croissant and took a seat, considering his next move.

Jon took a pill bottle from his pack, swallowing two capsules with his drink. The drugs he'd refused for so long now ran through his veins. He'd agreed to take the meds until he could function without them. Among the side effects was episodic memory loss. While he felt the associated emotions, he couldn't picture himself in the Colosseum. Or Carrie. That, along with other snippets of his last trip to Rome, was gone. The doctors told him the memories would return when his brain was ready.

A young woman wearing a blousy white top and shorts accentuating her light brown skin, approached him. "You are a tourist?" She spoke in a thick Catalan accent.

He nodded.

"We have chocolates." She pointed across the street. "Please come."

"Thank you, perhaps later. Why don't you join me while I finish my croissant?"

The young woman smiled, took a seat, played with a stray curl. "You are American, no?"

"Yes."

"I like American boys. Very fun." She moved her chair closer.

Jon said, "Are you from here?"

"Yes, of course. I live in Ordino all my life."

"Lucky. It's a beautiful place."

She put her hand on his. "Yes, many things here are beautiful."

Jon left his hand under hers, smiled. "Maybe you know a friend of mine."

"You have friends in Ordino?"

"He is an important man. Keeps to himself."

"What is his name?"

"Boris. Boris Tierney. Do you know him?"

The woman scrunched her brow. "No. It is—how do you say—strange. I know everyone in Ordino. Maybe he is a tourist like you. Comes, goes."

"He is about sixty years old, big guy. Well-dressed."

She thought a moment. "Ahh. You mean Benito!"

Benito? Jon thought Boris had a sick sense of humor naming himself after the cloned Italian dictator. "Yes, that's him. I guess that's his Spanish name."

The woman seemed pleased to have solved the puzzle. "Now you finished your food. Come, I will show you the chocolate shop."

Jon stood. "Thank you, but I must be going. I have an appointment."

"Appointment? What is appointment?"

"Meeting, you know?"

"With Benito?"

"Yes."

"I will go with you. When you finish, I show you Ordino." She took his hand.

Jon assumed her tour would entail more than he was up for at the moment. But he needed to find Boris and this woman knew how. "All right. I'm Jon, what's your name?"

"Sophia."

"Sophia," he repeated, then kissed her hand. "Let's go explore."

***

Casa de Las Naranjas, Andorra

Boris leaned back in his leather Barcalounger, the 4K projector delivering a crisp image of the party's convention on to the media room's 120-inch screen. Observing the states' cheering delegates holding their banners high, he felt the devastation of not being in attendance.

After all I've done to see this day, I'm relegated to watching from afar, Boris thought.

Observing his clone appear on the stage, he chided himself for allowing anything to diminish his elation. Even Spenser's death. He raised the volume, amplifying the crowd's applause. Following the widespread riots, Spenser had won the majority of delegates. But, with tonight's historic vote, it was Felix who became the party candidate.

Following a lengthy introduction and benediction, Felix—now answering to Spenser's name—was called on to speak to the American people. Dressed in a navy-blue suit and pinstriped tie, the clone approached the podium. He spoke clearly into the mic calling for unity, and reiterated his clone's promise of free healthcare, schooling, and welfare. The cheers from the crowd rose to greet him. Felix had done a fine job studying Spenser's positions on various political matters, seamlessly slipping into his new role.

All Boris's hard work was culminating in this, his proudest moment. Decades of toil, deception, and bloodshed. It had all been worth it to witness the fulfillment of his great-granduncle's dying wish. To live again, rise back to power. Boris studied the crowd. Thousands of supporters filled the stadium cheering for his mentee. Young and old, every race represented. Boris beamed with pride knowing in a few short months, Comrade Vladimir Lenin would be the next President of the United States.

***

Ordino, Andorra

Jon was amazed that there were still places in the world where a woman would enter a stranger's car. But Sophia did so without a second thought. She guided him up a winding road, then pointed.

"This is the house." It was a stately home surrounded by an orange grove.

Jon slowed to look, then kept going.

Sophia asked, "Where are you going?"

"I just remembered Benito said he would only be home later this evening. Sorry for the trouble."

"No trouble. We will have time to see my village."

Jon knew there would be no discouraging this woman. But he got what he needed for now. Best to return after dark, anyway. "Lead the way."

***

The next few hours were spent touring the Casa d'Areny, the town's historical museum housed in a seventeenth-century mansion, followed by a stop at the chocolatier, Sophia's father's shop. The truffles were like nothing Jon had tasted before. The complex flavors burst on his tongue, reminding him why the confections were long considered an aphrodisiac. He found Sophia to be quite affectionate. Perhaps it was the region's Spanish and French influence. He wasn't complaining. But when she said she was needed back at home, he was relieved. He had come here for a purpose far more alluring than chocolates and flirting. He'd come to Ordino for revenge.

***

By the time evening fell, the air was chilly, particularly near the top of the mountain where Jon was kneeling out of sight. He lifted his binoculars to his eyes. The chalet was dark with the exception of two windows at the far end, a flickering light suggesting a fireplace. He readjusted his sightlines, noting a steady stream of smoke rising from the stone chimney. Boris was in for the evening.

Jon scanned the home's exterior. The only security appeared to be expensive-looking locks on the doors and windows. He assumed Boris was confident no one knew of the secluded chalet. He was about to pay for that arrogance.

Jon felt a prickle of fear as he mentally prepared for what he was about to do. If only Carrie could be here, they would back each other up. But Jon was here *because* Carrie wasn't. There was truth to what his shrink helped him see. The death wish he once harbored had morphed into something else. He didn't want to die. Still, he was willing to, if that's what was necessary. Some things were worth dying for. Because of the man relaxing inside, a four-year-old boy was now an orphan.

Jon silently ran toward the side of the house, sidling up to a ground floor window, He reached into the pocket of his dark cargo pants, retrieving a lockpick set. It was identical to the one Carrie had used at the Colosseum. In recent weeks, Jon made it his business to learn the skill, in part as homage to his dead partner. And, in preparation for tonight.

The windowsill met up with Jon's waist. It took him six minutes to unlock it. Compared to Carrie's abilities, it was not an impressive achievement, but he was in no rush. He put the picks back in his pocket, carefully opened the window, and quietly climbed inside.

CHAPTER 76

Casa de Las Naranjas, Andorra

Gun in hand, Jon slowly walked through the dark home, passing a large dining table, silver candelabras visible on its shiny wood surface. Further ahead was a large room, French-inspired, lit by a fire roaring in the hearth. The walls were lined with neatly-packed leatherbound books, various trinkets scattered among the shelves. Boris was not there.

He was about to move on when he heard a low hum from the other side of the room. Jon approached the knee-high rectangular freezer. It was locked. With his free hand, he reached into his pocket for the lockpick kit.

"Well, well. Agent Jon Steadman."

Jon spun around to find Boris Tierney, hands in his pockets, looking relaxed. Jon kept his gun on him. *Why isn't he armed?*

"I must say this is an unwelcome surprise. How did you find my home?"

"Let's just say you got sloppy." He asked, "How is it you've come by such luxury? Skimming off the don's investment wouldn't pay for all this."

"I like to think it was my great-granduncle's generosity. Though studying him as I have, it was more likely an advance on services rendered."

"Resurrecting him."

"Yes."

"With Germain gone, you've failed."

Boris smirked. "Not quite."

"Open the freezer."

Boris didn't budge.

Jon backed away, gesturing with his gun. "Now."

"Do you know what's inside?"

"The Mussolini embryos."

"You know a lot about my work. I suppose Dr. Lavi is one of yours."

"Dr. Lavi? Never heard of him."

Boris smiled. "I'm not quite sure I believe you. I would have killed her myself, but after our meeting at the don's house, I was short on time. I had a choice to make. Her or the embryos." He looked at the freezer. "Despite Spenser's death, I have no regrets."

Jon was losing patience. "Take them out."

Boris shook his head. "I have spent too much of my life on this project for an ignorant thief such as yourself to walk away with them. I am an old man. My life's work is the Lenins and these clones. If you want them, you'll have to kill me first."

A thought suddenly occurred to Jon. *He's stalling.*

"What are you up to, Tierney?"

As the words escaped his lips, two men entered the room, guns drawn. He recognized one from the embassy's underground prison. Without thinking, Jon came up behind Boris, shoving the gun into the fat folds of his back, allowing the older man's bulk to shield him. He probably could get off a shot at one of the bodyguards, but if he could walk away without killing anyone, he'd try.

"Drop your weapons! If I shoot him, you'll both be out of a job real fast."

The two men were spreading out, each seeking a vantage point, guns held steady, pointing in his direction. Jon had one hand on his gun, the other on Boris' arm, leading him toward the doorway on the other end of the room. He would need to remain aligned with the walls until he got there, essentially switching places with the thugs. His back to the hearth, he felt the heat of the fire, making sure to steer clear of it.

Boris spoke in his irritatingly calm voice. "You'll never leave this house alive." Quick as a viper, he struck his head backward, slamming into Jon's nose. Jon heard the crack, cried out, loosening his grip on Boris, blood blocking one eye's vision. A shot rang out and Jon dropped to his knees, rolling behind a nearby club chair. Using his sleeve, he awkwardly swiped at his face. With his gun still in hand, he aimed at the blur in front of him. And fired. The sound was near-deafening in the enclosed space, but the heavy thud that shook the floor told him one man was down.

Boris shouted, "Shoot him!" His voice was now filled with rage.

Crouching low behind the chair, Jon didn't wait for another bullet. He fired three more times, spacing them out as best he could. Another thud. He knew he still had thirteen rounds remaining in his Glock. And only one more adversary.

His ears ringing, Jon couldn't hear who else remained. Sensing the swelling in his face, he knew his vision would soon become further impaired. He ventured a quick look, and saw Boris crawling toward one of the dead guard's guns, grabbing it.

Jon shouted, "Stop where you are!"

Despite his bulk and age, Boris moved fast, got off a shot. The bullet ricocheted off Jon's Glock, propelling the firearm from his grip, spinning out of reach.

Jon was disarmed.

Boris stood. "You've played your last hand, Steadman. You are as big a fool as the others. What do you think the point was of making several clones? Felix Salko has slipped right into Spenser's shoes. No one will ever know the difference."

Jon scurried to the other side of the chair, keeping it between him and Boris, who rounded the dead bodies and lifted his weapon. Jon leapt toward the hearth, a bullet barely missing him. He grasped the black iron poker, twisted his body, and with all his might, he lunged upward. The poker met its intended target. Boris emitted an otherworldly moan, the gun dropping from his hand. The poker had impaled him through the solar plexus, cutting off his nervous system. His eyes shrouded over and like a toppling domino, he fell backward.

Surrounded by three dead men, Jon reached into Boris's pocket, pulling out a set of keys, finding the one he needed. He walked to the freezer and unlocked it. A cloud of icy air escaped as he pulled open the door. Inside was a tray, four test tubes standing up inside it, each clearly labeled, *Benito Mussolini.*

Jon took out the tray and turned around, facing the hearth. And without so much as a moment's thought, he tossed it into the fire.

EPILOGUE

CHAPTER 77

Haifa, Israel

J on walked beside Terry along Technion's main campus
road. They had visited the genetics department where
Terry introduced him to Dr. Perlman. Several people
stopped to greet her, pleased she was back on campus.

Jon enjoyed watching his friend in her natural habitat. A
cool breeze blew through the eucalyptus trees, shearing off
their gentle scent.

Terry slipped an arm through his. "What did you think of
my new lab?"

"It's incredible. You have top-of-the-line equipment. Did
you receive an endowment recently?"

Terry said, "Something like that."

Jon sensed there was more, but her tone left little room
for questions. He let it be. "I also enjoyed the tour of Dr. Perlman's lab. He's quite impressive, even if his staff were somewhat unfriendly."

She nodded. "Geniuses can be that way, I've learned.

They've made fast progress in the few weeks I've been gone."

"Too fast?" he said.

Terry looked at him knowingly. "I hope not. It's what I wanted to speak with you about. Let's find a quiet spot."

The sun was high in the sky, the kind of day that offered promise. Terry asked, "How was the memorial service?"

"Devastating. Beautiful. Carrie would have loved it."

"I'm so sorry I couldn't be there. How was her son?"

"I didn't see him there. I guess Carrie's parents decided he shouldn't attend."

Terry led him to a secluded, shaded bench. "How are you holding up?"

"It's been tough. The work probation didn't help."

"Sounds to me like Matthews let you off easy."

Jon nodded. "If not for him, I would have been suspended for insubordination when I went after Tierney. Matthews still feels guilty for abandoning me and Carrie at the Russian embassy."

"I know your intentions were pure when you tracked Tierney down. Carrie would've been proud."

Jon looked down at his lap. "I didn't intend for things to end up like they did. So much death." An image of an impaled Boris surrounded by two dead guards flashed in Jon's mind. He shook it away.

"You rid the world of a resurrected Mussolini. Surely the American government is grateful for that."

"Probably why I still have my job. And the mandatory therapy. When my shrink suggested I come see you, I didn't think I could do it. Getting out of bed was a struggle. The thought of traveling across the globe again was daunting. She insisted I need a change of scenery."

"I'm glad you came."

"Me too." Then, "How about you?" Jon asked.

Terry shrugged. "Same." She brought her voice down. "I killed a man. I won't ever get over that."

"You saved a life."

"I know. But still—"

Jon put an arm around her. "We're in the same boat. We'll power through this together, okay?"

Terry gave a melancholic smile, nodded. "Yes, okay."

Jon asked, "Did you see the news this morning?"

"Not yet."

"Carrie's boss took credit for rounding up the SAU and Committee leaders. Both groups have been disbanded."

"How does Matthews feel about that?"

"He's livid, but knowing him, he already has something up his sleeve. He'll find a way to set things straight."

"And the nomination?"

"The original archived cloning file was leaked, presumably by the President's coercion. Salko has been outed. The party nomination went instead to the real estate developer. It's so close to the election, he doesn't have a prayer. Looks like the incumbent president will get another four years in the Oval Office. So, what did you want to talk to me about?"

Terry pulled up her sleeve. On her wrist was Carrie's bracelet. "When you and Carrie were brought to the hospital, I was tasked with releasing her remains. They gave me her personal effects to pass along to her family."

Jon said nothing. He'd assumed the bracelet had either been lost in the shuffle, still lying on the stony floor of the Colosseum's underground tunnel, or resting on Carrie's mother's dresser. He hadn't been in any condition to track it down.

"We need to do something about what you and Carrie found."

"What are you suggesting, exactly?"

"We make it disappear." Terry said this without hesitation.

Jon was incredulous. "You want to destroy the formula?"

"No one knows it exists anymore. Not our governments, not even Claudio."

Jon was shaking his head vehemently. "If we get caught, we'll both end up in prison. Besides, all we'd accomplish is kicking the can down the road."

"I've given this a great deal of thought. It's the only moral thing to do. Clearly you and Carrie had your own reservations or it wouldn't be here." She waved her wrist in emphasis. "Carrie died for this. Not to mention Dr. Sousa and Alexander Bilka. If we don't get rid of it, others are sure to meet a similar fate. My hope is in the next few months we will have an ethical symposium comprised of members of both our countries. Eventually, we can welcome other governments to discuss ramifications of human cloning and agree on responsible regulation."

"There will always be people who will subvert the law, gain access to the science for their own needs, try again to clone the next despot."

Eyes downcast, Terry said, "You are right. But you and I have no control over that. All we can do for now is slow the process long enough to establish ethical standards."

Jon became silent, indecision on his face.

"I know it's a difficult choice. Think it over. We'll discuss it again soon."

Jon stood, needing to lighten the mood. His stomach grumbled. "I'm starving. Is there somewhere to get a bite?"

"Follow me."

They walked for several minutes, arriving at a café. After placing their order, they carried their food trays to an outdoor table overlooking the campus garden. Jon looked around. "Terry?"

She took a bite of her falafel. "Hmm?"

"Is that...?"

Terry followed Jon's gaze to a ponytailed man sitting alone, his back to them.

Terry grabbed a napkin and wiped the tehina from her mouth. She seemed to be holding back a grin.

Jon was stunned. "You didn't!"

Terry looked around, put a finger to her lips.

"How on Earth did you bring him here without Matthews

or the CIA knowing?"

"They do know. Only a bit later than they would have liked."

Before Jon could ask any more questions, Terry stood, approaching the other table.

The man turned, a relaxed smile slowly creeping across his face. "Shalom, Doctor Lavi. Ah, Agent Steadman, bienvenido. I see you've been confided in."

Momentarily speechless, Jon quickly recovered. "You're looking well."

Claudio held out his left leg. "Other than this of course. After the Colosseum, the burn became infected. The grafting I had done here in Israel was of the highest quality. Thanks to Dr. Lavi's connections."

They chatted for a short while, careful to avoid sensitive topics. As they said their goodbyes, Claudio asked Jon, "Will you be staying in Israel a while?"

"I head back tomorrow."

"Then I'll wish you arrivederci."

Terry escorted Jon to his rental car.

"Agent Steadman."

They both turned. Terry looked genuinely surprised. She addressed the woman in Hebrew.

Jon looked at the dark-haired, highly-fit woman. "Your face is very familiar. Have we met?"

Shira nodded. "It was a few weeks ago in Rome. In a sewing factory in the middle of the night. You were in questionable shape."

It took a moment for the realization to dawn on him. "Oh!" He approached her, opened his arms. "May I?"

Shira extended a hand. "I'm not a hugger."

Terry laughed as Jon instead grasped Shira's offered hand in both of his. "Thanks for saving my life."

"As I told you then, you have Dr. Lavi to thank."

Jon nodded, turning to Terry. "Agreed, and I know just how to do that."

Terry looked at him, a question in her eyes. When he didn't offer an explanation, she asked Shira. "What brings you to the Technion?"

"I have a proposition. A car is waiting to take us to Jerusalem." As if on cue, a black Mercedes sedan with darkened windows slowed to a stop in front of them.

Terry frowned. "I can't go with you now. I have too much work to catch up on."

The agent shook her head, said something in Hebrew.

Terry raised a brow. Both women faced Jon, who looked from one to the other. "What?"

"The proposal is not for Dr. Lavi. Agent Steadman, I came here for you."

***

Jon excused himself and walked a distance away. He dialed Matthews.

"Sir?"

"Seems you're finally getting used to calling me that."

Jon laughed. "Shall I revert?"

"Watch it now."

Jon heard the smile in his boss's voice. "A Mossad agent wants to give me a ride to Jerusalem."

"I've been waiting for your call."

"What is this about?"

"After Claudio Giovanni vanished, the CIA got wind of him surfacing in Israel. The incident could easily have undermined U.S.–Israeli relations. I reamed Kahn for derailing that part of our mission."

Jon knew full well that given the chance American interests would have done the same.

"I know what you're thinking. And you're not wrong. Which is why I encouraged him and his CIA counterpart to work out a more equitable solution. Since I have you on the ground, you will be my eyes and ears. Listen to what Kahn has to say, but also read between the lines. There's more at play than what he'll share with you. You have my consent to participate in a preliminary meeting with Kahn. Your job is to listen, not offer any information. Understood?"

"Yessir."

"I expect a full debriefing when you're done."

Terry signaled she needed to leave.

"I'll be in touch." Jon hung up. To Terry, he said, "Do *you* accept hugs?"

Terry walked to where he stood and embraced him. "Don't be a stranger."

"You'll be hearing from me soon enough."

"That have anything to do with paying me back?"

"Something like that."

Terry smiled. "Ok, I can handle a bit of mystery. Good luck at the meeting."

Jon walked toward the Mercedes, giving the Mossad agent a sidelong glance. "Thanks, something tells me I'll need it."

CHAPTER 78

Haifa, Israel

J on strolled through the Bahai Gardens. Anemones carpeted the hills in a spectacular sea of red. He mulled over
his meeting with Yosef Kahn. The groundwork was being
laid for the installment of an FBI–Mossad liaison. Jon was
being considered for the job. It had kept him in Israel longer
than expected. He turned his thoughts to his most recent
meeting. This one only minutes ago.

It was early morning in Dallas, a good time to reach his
friend before he would begin his workday. He hoped Gabe
would take what he had to say well enough.

Jon made the call. "Hey, Gabe." He knew his voice
sounded tentative, but he couldn't help feeling uneasy.

"Wow, the elusive Jon Steadman. Haven't heard from
you in a while. How've you been, buddy?"

"Working like crazy."

"How's that case you told me about?"

Jon dodged a stream of boisterous schoolgirls rushing
past, their teacher seemingly unperturbed. "Got dicey there
for a while."

"I can barely hear you. Where are you?"

Jon found a quieter spot. "So, here's the thing—I'm in
Israel."

A pause. Then, "Huh?"

"Now that the case is over I've been given clearance to
tell you. I really didn't want to keep you in the dark, but I had

no choice."

"Keep me in the dark about what?"

"I've been working with Terry."

Gabe was silent.

Jon feared his friend had hung up. "You still there?"

"How is she?" His voice was soft.

"Sad, like you."

"Can you tell her I'm thinking of her?"

Jon hoped his next words would be helpful. "Why don't you tell her yourself?"

"You know I can't do that."

"Maybe now you can."

"What do you mean?" Gabe asked.

"I just met with Hannah Lavi."

"Terry's mother?"

"Yeah. She heard I was in town and asked to meet me. She has a letter for you. Asked me to pass it along."

"A letter?"

"Listen, I know this sounds crazy, but Hannah said you should come here and get it," Jon said.

"Can you read it to me?"

"She asked me not to. Was insistent you be the first to read it. I already told her you can't just pick up and leave your job to fly across the world to read a letter. I guess I can mail it to you."

"I'll come," Gabe said.

"You serious?"

"I work for my uncle, Jon. I can get away if I need to. Obviously, there's something up. And if I can even steal a glance at Terry, the trip will be worth it."

"You're nuts."

Gabe let out sigh. "Tell me something I don't already know."

CHAPTER 79

Zichron Yaakov, Israel

G abe was relieved to finally get out of the taxi. The driver must have once been a competitor in the Indy 500. He'd shaved off twenty minutes from the GPS's estimated time from the airport. The address Jon had given him turned out to be a boutique winery outside Haifa in the quaint, historic village of Zichron Yaakov. He paid the fare, retrieved his bag from the trunk. Inside, a young sommelier standing behind the bar was pouring a white wine for an elderly couple whispering in French. He looked up as Gabe entered. "You the American?" he asked with a heavy accent.

"Uh, yeah, that's me."

"You can leave your bag with me. Your friend is in the back."

Gabe did as he was told and walked to an alcove at the far end of the room. There, sitting at a small round table laden with two wine glasses and an open bottle of Chardonnay was Terry.

"Hi," she said.

Gabe desperately yearned to go to her, take her in his arms, but he stayed frozen at the door.

"I'm sorry to throw you off-guard like this but my mother insisted. She wanted me to meet you personally. I have no idea what's in the letter. I'm sure it feels like a trap—Jon telling you he would be here and finding me instead."

Gabe found his voice, walked slowly to the table, and sat. "It's the best honey trap ever."

She bit on her bottom lip. "Honey trap? I don't think I know that one."

"Would you like me to explain?"

She offered a smile. "Maybe some other time. I believe you came all this way for this." Terry took a large envelope from her bag, handing it to him. It was sealed, Hebrew writing printed on the front.

"What's this all about?"

"Open it."

He did, pulling out a printed report typed in English. At the top of the page was a colorful pie chart. "It's my DNA results. I'd forgotten all about them." Gabe perused the chart highlighting the countries from where his ancestors had originated. 81% from Spain, 15% Portugal, and the remainder, Italy. He knew his biological mother had Italian lineage but never knew about the rest. Having grown up in Texas with his fair-skinned sister, Ashleigh, they often fielded comments about how they looked nothing alike. She was blond, he with dark curls and olive complected. Back then he just shrugged. It was easier than explaining he'd been adopted as an infant.

Gabe flipped through the pages, perusing his mother's elaborate family tree. As he read, confusion began setting in. He looked up at Terry, noting the question in her eyes.

The last page was a letter from Hannah.

Gabe,

I hope this letter finds you well. My occupation is a challenging and rewarding one. Every now and then we come across exceptional results that change the very course of people's lives. Yours are those kind. It's not every day we find a member of the tribe who never even knew he was one.

Yes, that's right, Gabe, you are a Jew. Not half Jewish. There is no such thing. According to Jewish law and tradition, if a mother is a Jew, then her offspring is as well. We worked backward through your birth mother's lineage to fifteenth-century Spain, historically a very precarious era for the Jewish people. Forced to choose between conversion or death, some chose to observe their traditions in secret. You are a direct descendant of these hidden Jews, known as Conversos. This is no small thing. It is a sign of strong heritage, people who sacrificed a great deal and put their lives at risk to observe their faith.

However, this was not all we found. If you look at the family tree, you will see the name Rabbi Gavriel Fermi, one of the most revered leaders of the Spanish-Portuguese Jewish community. You were named for your great-great-grandfather. If you were to visit the New York synagogue on West 70th Street, you will see his portrait at the entrance to the main sanctuary. I know this is a lot to absorb, but I suspect you will want to share the remarkable news with Terry yourself. If you choose to learn more about your heritage, please let me know.

Wishing you much enlightenment on your future journey.
Hannah

Gabe read the letter twice before placing it on the table, looking up at Terry.

"Are you okay?" Terry asked. "You look pale."

"I need a drink."

"Luckily, you're in the right place." She poured them each a glass and he drank it in one gulp. She said, "Please tell me what all the mystery is about."

Gabe handed her the last page, her mother's letter. He watched her eyes widen as she read. "Oh my! Oh my!" She let the letter drop from her fingers onto the table, put her face in her hands, and sobbed.

He couldn't hold back any longer, stood and rounded the table, bringing Terry to her feet. "Don't cry, my love." He wiped the tears from her face.

"But—"

"The rabbi told me small miracles happen every day."

She sniffled. "What rabbi?"

"Now *that* story can surely wait."

His heart leapt as she folded into his embrace. After a few

moments, he stood back, pulled something from his pocket, and got down on one knee. "I've kept this with me since that day in the park."

Terry began to cry anew.

"Dr. Theresa Lavi, you are the most headstrong, brilliant woman I've ever met." He opened a small velvet box, its contents gleaming. "Will you marry me?"

Without hesitation, Terry kneeled down before her beloved, locking her damp eyes on his. "Yes, Gabriel. In a heartbeat."

CHAPTER 80

New York

J on stared at his reflection in the bathroom mirror, rubbing the stubble on his face. Actually, it was more of a beard now. Seeing a few gray hairs, he reached for his shaver, then reconsidered.

The doorbell rang. His only visitors since returning from Israel were Matthews and his co-worker, Craig. He wasn't expecting either. Especially not at 8:00 a.m. on a Sunday morning. He looked through the peephole. No one there. His heart skipped as he opened the door and looked down. "Randy."

Jon saw a woman standing at the end of the hallway. She offered him a sad smile. "He's been asking for you. I hope you don't mind. It's been a long time since he spoke."

Jon kneeled down to Randy's level. "Hey there."

The boy looked up at him, his large brown eyes filled with uncertainty. His voice was soft and tentative. "Wanna make an octopus?"

Jon swallowed back the lump in his throat. "That sounds like a really good idea." He swiped at his eyes. "But I think I forgot how."

Randy put his small hand on Jon's shoulder. "Don't worry. I'll show you."

Jon stood, shut the door behind him, and holding Randy's hand in his, he ventured back out into the world.

The End

JON STEADMAN INTERNATIONAL ADVENTURE SERIES

If you enjoyed Resurrection, you won't want to miss Spree. Find out what readers are raving about!

Spree (Jon Steadman Thriller Series Book 1)

When a survivor's search for answers unearths a lethal conspiracy, he must race against time to save America from a devastating attack.

Desperate for closure after the love of his life dies in a devastating massacre at Boston Technological Institute, Jon Steadman learns of eerily similar attacks perpetrated by students with no motive or history of violence. Supported by his best friend, a beautiful geneticist, and his new love interest, Jon searches for who is behind the attacks, and why.

Their quest unravels a shockingly sinister plot, leading them through America's heartland, the exotic Middle East, the wilds of Southwestern Utah, and the streets of New York City. Powerful people are standing in Jon's way, ready to protect their secrets at any cost.

Can the killers be stopped in time from executing a deadly event of catastrophic proportions?

ACKNOWLEDGEMENT

As I write this, the world remains in the midst of a pandemic, the likes of which have not been seen for over a century. My thoughts are with all who are grieving as a result of the awful illness.

One of the silver linings of being homebound for an extended period is having my manuscript beckon me from my work desk each time I walk by it. As a result, I've spent many 17-hour days lost in this story. The inevitable mental and social strain is relieved in large part by those precious members of my pod, the small group of people with whom my husband and I safely interact. For several months, I've been distanced from my family and friends in other parts of the world. The pod helped fill that void. I'd like to offer genuine gratitude to Leah and Ken Germain, happily married for over fifty years. Their friendship has been a delight, their devotion to one another an inspiration. Extra kudos for allowing me to steal your name, and to Ken, my go-to guy for all things legal.

Many thanks to my powerhouse alpha and beta readers: Susan Morris, Betty Atlas-Rumelt, Karen Sheff, Ken Germain, Marcia Schwartz, and Tamar Hazout. You are all indispensable. Your insights and attention to detail remain off the charts. And of course, todah raba to my husband Glenn who listens to every gripe, frustration and elation that come with this beloved occupation. Once again, I could not do this without you.

Thanks to Yechezkel. You are a rock star at brainstorming with me. I'm always proud of you. Thanks to my mom, Jeanette Neeman who among her many kindnesses, has taken on a quasi-agent role, telling everyone about my work.

Thanks to Kimberly Broderick, top-notch editor whose patience and timeliness kept me on track. I'm lucky to have found you. And of course, mega thanks to my wonderful readers. It's all for you!

ABOUT THE AUTHOR

Nellie Neeman

 Nellie Neeman is the author of the Jon Steadman Thriller series. A native New Yorker, she now resides in Cincinnati and Jerusalem. Resurrection is her second novel.

PRAISE FOR AUTHOR

"Neeman's debut thriller jumps off the pages and had me reading late into the night . . . Readers will find her plot terrifying, her characters captivating, and they will undoubtedly close the book anticipating her next Jon Steadman thriller."

- -JAY LEFKOWITZ, FORMER WHITE HOUSE ADVISOR AND WALL STREET JOURNAL BOOK REVIEWER

"In an era when fictional detective protagonists often fight villains with guns and fists, in Jon Steadman Nellie Neeman has given us a Holmesian hero who battles modern-day Moriarty's with science and wit. Neeman takes the reader on an international journey with a profound sense of place while conveying a feeling of actually traveling with the characters and being involved in their quest. Spree leaves the reader hungry for the next adventure with Steadman and his ensemble of sleuths."

- HOWARD BRESSLER, AUTHOR OF THE LAYMAN'S GUIDE TO SURVIVING CANCER